TIMED
BOMB

TIMED BOMB

A NOVEL

STEPHEN H. SCHWARTZ

New Harbor
Entertainment, LLC

For Melanie

"Whatever can go wrong, will go wrong."

—MURPHY, *The Law*

BOOK ONE

"When good men die,
their goodness does not perish,
but lives though they are gone.
As for the bad, all that was theirs dies
and is buried with them."

—EURIPIDES, *Termenidae*

April 27, 1942

2:46 a.m.

"Jesus, I am really hot!"

"So, take your jacket off."

"No can do... I'm in uniform."

"Then don't complain." NYPD Detective Douglas Grover was just as overheated. Detective Tim Murphy didn't want to upset his partner, so he kept his mouth shut and his necktie knotted.

Sunday's surprise springtime scorcher had come up suddenly and was a rude shock to everyone's system. By mid-day it had reached a very humid 86 degrees in Central Park.

From their vantage point the cops could easily hear a concert of whirring electric fans playing from a thousand darkened apartment windows. Sufferers in those apartments hoped for a flash of lightning and a sudden downpour to cool things down.

"Ya think anyone's sleeping up there?" Murphy glanced up from his crossword puzzle at the surrounding walls of brick and concrete.

"Nah, who can sleep in this?" Grover slumped back in the radio car's passenger seat. "The lucky ones are probably unconscious and everybody else is slowly sweating to death."

In addition to the unseasonable temperature there was something else in the air. New Yorkers had felt it for months now and accepted the cause. The country was at war and bad things were happening everywhere.

At 2:47 a.m. a thunder-like growl built up force as it rapidly approached the corner at Third Avenue between 84th and 85th. The rapid rise in the noise level announced to the neighborhood the overhead passage of the southbound IRT train moving along the El from distant parts of the Bronx. As it opened its doors at the 84th Street stop the clanking and rumbling was enough to jar the two men out of their developing stupor. NYPD Detectives Douglas Grover and Tim Murphy, overheated and low on sleep, sat on a stakeout.

This was the midnight to 8:00 shift and their third night on a so-far fruitless surveillance. Three nights shot to hell owing to a tip from a busted pickpocket, a tip that triggered a front-page story in *The Mirror*. It was politics and a community in uproar that put Grover and Murphy on the trail of the man the paper had nicknamed, "Yorkville's Katzenjammer Burglar," the moniker of an uncaught bandit whose MO was robbing older German couples in their East Side homes.

Grover's eyes stayed fixed on a doorway leading to a second-floor apartment. Murphy, the senior and more relaxed member of the team, had his eyes locked back onto his newspaper crossword puzzle. "Mmmm, what's a six-letter word for "paperhanger … the third letter is a T?"

"Hitler."

"Huh?

"The son of a bitch used to be a paperhanger."

"Oh yeah … great, it fits!"

The pickpocket's information was their first lead in two weeks bringing them to this dead-of-night parking spot under the El. From here all they saw was one lit apartment window and a moving shadow inside. Grover had already read the name on the buzzer in the vestibule. That shadow might belong to the Katzenjammer Burglar, someone listed as Eugen Haupt.

"Haupt! The SOB is a German, right?"

"Who knows what he is?" Murphy kept staring at his crossword, "I really gotta pee!"

"How dumb is this? We're protecting Germans from another German!" Grover wiped his brow. "We should let them kill each other."

"Maybe I can ask him if I could use his bathroom?"

Grover pretended to give his partner a sarcastic stare, but all he could muster was an uncontrolled grin. "You gotta pee? That's all you talk about lately. I'm glad I'm not your wife."

"It's a bodily function you jerk. You should try it sometime."

Grover kept poking, "And, how long can you keep doing that crossword crap?"

"I work on the puzzle until I finish it. And it's not crap, it's a puzzle. 'Keeps my mind fresh. Boy-o, a fresh mind is something a detective like you needs. You should try it sometime. Anyway, right now it's not my mind I'm thinkin' about, it's my bladder." Grover and Murphy made up the entire 19th Precinct burglary squad. While they behaved like fighting siblings, they were a solid team.

Seconds after the train pulled away from the station, the heat from Murphy's unrelieved abdominal pressure finally set him off, "Katzenjammer my ass!"

"Yeah! Crap!" Grover's boredom immediately bubbled to Murphy's level, "If it wasn't for that prick city reporter from the goddamn *Mirror* writing all that shit about this 'dangerous criminal' I'd be home in bed now." Thus began the routine cycle of stake-out frustration, and it didn't take long for them to lapse into the deeply scatological and crude aspects of bored-cop banter often dealing with the ergonomically impossible and the physically indescribable. They blamed *The Mirror*, the bosses and most-of-all the "dickwad-shithead" burglar.

Once his tirade was done Murphy calmed down, "So, this guy Haupt... pretty sure that's a kraut name, huh?"

"Yeah. So?"

"So, what was "Grover" in the old country?"

Grover kept his gaze on the apartment window while he answered. "My grandpa was Grubinsky, from Lithuania. It got changed at Ellis Island. I dunno for sure what the name means. What was Murphy?"

"I think it's Gaelic for pig thief." Murphy laughed to himself. It almost made him pee in his pants.

Grover and Murphy fit neatly into the classic NYPD mold as much as they fit as partners. Grover, the younger and more hot-headed of the pair, and Murphy, the older and wiser sage, both spoke and behaved with the same inner-city swagger. Each grew up on the streets in the city and was a local tough guy. Each might have easily gone on to pursue a lifetime career as a criminal. It had been just a year since their captain paired them as partners, and since then they had built a close friendship. But a week ago, though neither man would bring it up, their relationship was put in jeopardy. Grover, over a decade younger than his married-with-kids partner, was of prime draft age and there was a war going on. He received an official letter advising him that he was going to get a call for a physical at the Whitehall Street induction center. Now, on a stakeout in the awful heat, neither discussed it. They were on the hunt.

"Is this sonofabitch ever gonna come out?" Murphy was getting more restless by the minute. Then it happened. The lights in the apartment suddenly flicked off. "Hey look! He's either going to sleep or he's moving."

Three nights of stakeout might finally pay off. They waited and it only took a few seconds for a very large blond-haired man in dark shirtsleeves to emerge. He was obviously a muscle builder. As the vestibule door closed behind him the man's eyes scanned the street scene more by habit than to actually see any potential threat. He just stood there, looked up and down the block a few times and then bent over to tie his shoes.

"Jeeze, look at the size of him! That is one big German," Murphy mumbled to no one in particular.

"And they're off!" Grover did his best whispering impression of race track announcer Fred Capossela.

"This guy ain't no race horse, he's a Clydesdale." Murphy forgot about his bladder as they stared at their suspect, the man who might be the notorious Katzenjammer burglar of Yorkville.

"Maybe we should talk to him now," Grover mused.

"Nah, not yet." Murphy reminded his anxious partner about their overall mission. Burglary detail was premised on the idea of catching the bad guy in flagrante delicto, and that meant many stakeouts and a lot of patience.

This was a very important case to get right. The detectives knew that Katzenjammer's late-night sprees had no limits. As their politically sensitive precinct captain reminded them, "This guy is a goddamn blot on my chances for a promotion." "This guy," as he was referred to at the 19th, was a personal insult to those who were trying to catch him. Katzenjammer broke into apartments with people asleep in their beds, as well as into shuttered shops to steal money and goods. *The Mirror* headline had called him "a man for all break-ins!" The sad fact was that Katzenjammer had become seemingly unstoppable. The cops in the 19th wanted him bad.

"Ya know, my gut tells me that this guy looks too big to be a burglar. Guys that size just can't climb up fire escapes and fit through windows."

Murphy just stared at the figure in the darkness.

"A guy this big would have to have been seen somewhere... he would have left some tracks."

"I wouldn't be so sure. This Haupt guy's got no priors... he might be the guy. But also, maybe he isn't our guy. Ya know, we got nothing on him other than that damn snitch's I.D., no one's ever seen him face to face. Let's just see what he does."

The wanted burglar was very good at surprise, and even after numerous encounters not one of his victims could describe him at all. Katzenjammer would silently enter apartments while his victims slept. But when a few of his subjects awoke to find him in their bedrooms, they were still unable to see his face or his physical size in the darkness. His modus operandi included tying up his victims with available materials. Long johns were excellent for binding hands and feet and undershirts made useful gags. He hogtied them with their skivvies and left with their valuables. One sad soul was truly embarrassed when cops found him naked, tied to a chair with his wife's bra binding his hands, two pairs of her silk underpants stuffed in his mouth and a corset around his head covering his eyes.

"Yeah, I s'pose we do gotta bust him in the act." Yet, as the partners watched Eugen Haupt from inside their car, each man's cop street-sense kicked in. The oafish looking blond giant across the avenue from them gave off the aura of a man who was up to no good. Grover and Murphy were certain that the subject they were staring at was in fact the Katzenjammer Burglar.

While he was very large, the bigger surprise was that he was also physically graceful. As Haupt began walking northward he lit a cigarette, did a couple of three-sixty turn-arounds to make sure he wasn't being followed, and appeared to glide along the sidewalk. At over six feet tall and clearly a body builder, he managed to nimbly keep his torso moving in a level straight line while his feet absorbed the directional changes and the imperfections of the cracked concrete sidewalk below him.

"Jesus! This is like watching Fred Astaire," Grover supposed that some movie-musical inspired dance center in Haupt's brain had taken total control of his body.

Murphy laughed, "Nah, the guy looks like one of those dancing hippos I just saw with my kids in Fantasia!"

"The SOB is a dancer!" Grover added. "As I always say, if you're gonna be a cat burglar, ya gotta move like a cat."

"Funny, I never heard you say that before, ever," Murphy deadpanned.

"I'll follow him on foot, you bring the car around."

Haupt turned left on the corner of 86th and ambled toward Lexington with Grover following nonchalantly staggering and wobbling and making himself look like a late-night drunk on his way home. In the middle of the block Haupt unexpectedly ducked into the dark storefront doorway of a small German bakery. Grover almost missed seeing him turn in. There's nothing to steal in a bakery? What the hell are you up to? The detective sped up his pace and stood a few steps to the side of the bakery door waiting for his partner. From where he stood Grover could see that Haupt had made quick work of the front door and was somewhere inside and out of sight. What the hell do you want in a bakery?

Murphy made a U-turn and stopped close to the door. Quietly exiting their unmarked Plymouth, he sidled up to Grover and drew his service revolver. "Where'd he go?," he whispered

"He went into this bakery."

Murphy looked up at the painted sign above the window and read Pfeiffer German Bakery, "What's he gonna steal in a German bakery, a Kaiser roll? Jesus, I really gotta pee!"

Grover slowly and silently pushed the front door open. The light from the street lamps was enough for them to see the shadowy hulk of the alleged "Katzenjammer Burglar" rifling through a small carton of papers.

The burglar heard the creak of the door and before Grover could say, freeze police! or either of the detectives could react, the suspect's looming bearlike shadow morphed into that of a gazelle and he bounded toward the back door. Grover was fast, but by the time the young cop got to the rear door the man was gone. No trail, no noise, no nothing. In the darkness Grover couldn't see him at all. The dejected detective walked back into the bakery where his partner had turned on the lights and was looking through the box of papers now strewn all over the floor. "Well, at least we saw his face a little. It is Haupt, but this isn't the Katzenjammer M.O. Maybe he's not who we're looking for?"

"Oh, he's our guy, you can bet on that. Who the fuck breaks into a bakery in the middle of the night and looks through a box of papers?" Murphy's mood was noticeably better. He had discovered the bakery's bathroom.

"I think he's headed back to his crib. I don't think he saw us follow him here, so he thinks we're some cops on patrol and we caught him entering the store." Grover approached Murphy and the papers. "What is this stuff?"

"This is all in German, I can't read it, but these are lists of names."

"Look at these letterheads… *Freie Gesellschaft von Teutonia*, Friends of New Germany on this one, The Yorkville German-American Bund. These are membership lists from the old bunds. Remember back in December, right after Pearl Harbor was attacked, these Bunds were outlawed. Clearly, this guy was a bund member himself and held on to the membership lists.

" 'Must be the list of the elite Manhattan Aryan society, huh?" Murphy smiled. "Okay two questions: One, why are these papers in a box in a bakery, and two; Why the hell does a guy who normally steals jewelry break into that bakery and try to steal papers from that box?"

"So, if our boy Eugen was looking for this stuff, how did he know it was here, and what's so special about lists of names?"

"Hey, maybe he just wanted to see who was on the lists? Maybe himself?" The two cops scanned the hundreds of names listed in neat columns. "Here's a Rudolph Haupt, a John Haupt and a Karl listed on the Free Society of Teutonia list."

"Yeah, same guys and there's a Eugen Haupt on this one. It's a list of summer camp counsellors at one of those bund camps," Grover read.

Murphy picked up the other list from The Yorkville German American Bund, "Yeah he's on this one too. This is one loyal German-American, huh?"

"Ya know, I think Eugen might be home from work by now. Let's drop by and say hi." Grover started to neaten up the mess. "I think we should make this place look like no-one was here. There's more to this, I dunno."

The cops put the box back under the register and clicked off the lights. The baker might wonder if he had locked the place up the night before, but he wouldn't be sure.

"So, this is what we're gonna do Boy-o. I'll knock on his door and you wait for him outside on the fire escape in case he tries to dance off again." Grover nodded.

They parked directly in front and got out of the car. Murphy boosted Grover up to the first rung of the fire-escape ladder as a subway train going by on the El muffled the noise of his ascent. In position to outside Haupt's living room window Grover gave his partner a thumbs-up sign and waited. Murphy entered the building and about 30 seconds later Grover heard Murphy's knock. An instant passed and Haupt dived out his window onto the fire escape only to look up and face the waiting detective Grover. The next two seconds seemed to last minutes. Haupt had the upper hand, and as Grover seemed to have plenty of time to analyze in detail the angry glare of this charging bull, the rest quickly became a blur. Haupt grabbed the detective in a bear hug, lifted him up in the air and threw him over the side of the fire escape. Grover landed hard on his left leg, heard a loud crack and passed out immediately from the pain.

By now Murphy had already broken down the door and just as Haupt was ready to descend on the fire escape ladder he faced a .38 caliber chamber pointed at his forehead. "Police! Freeze, you kraut fuck!"

April 28,1942

7:15 p.m.

Grover's eyes, or rather his one open-able left eye caught a blurred view of a hanging single-bulb light fixture. His mouth felt really dry and he felt as if he had been drugged. There was a mushy wad of something inside his right cheek catching the output of a surgical drain that drew off oozing liquid from a large hole he had bit into the inside of his own face. Detective Grover was rapidly descending the altitude from the effects of morphine, and as he returned to Earth he recognized that he was in some kind of a room, in a bed and that any movement he attempted was difficult if not impossible. He tilted his head slightly and scanned the room for clues as to why he might be lying there. Right away he saw that his left leg was embedded in a thick white tube and elevated using some kind of a rope and pulley device. But he was able to move his hands and instinctively raised them up to his head. It too was wrapped up in some kind of a soft cloth that covered up his right eye. Searching for nothing in particular, his right hand came upon a push button attached to a wire. He pushed it and within a few seconds a woman in a crisp white uniform dress appeared at his bedside. Right behind her was Tim Murphy.

His nurse said cheerfully, "Oh good! You're awake. I hope you had a good sleep."

"Boyo, I thought you'd never wake up. I' been sitting out there for almost two days."

Grover stared at both of his visitors with a clueless look. "What the ...? Uh... Thorry meth. Whea the hell am I?"

"Do you remember anything? Haupt on the fire escape?"

"I wath out on what Fire ethcay? Hoopt?"

"Let me see if I can remove that wad of gauze from your mouth," the nurse's hand stroked Grover's jaw and he opened up. "There it is!" She deftly removed a bloody wad of wet gauze and tossed it. "I think that bleeding stopped yesterday. Just be careful how you move your tongue."

Grover's tongue gently examined the inside of his mouth. Indeed, something had been going on in there, but the morphine removed any curiosity.

"That kraut bastard... oh, uh sorry ma'am." Murphy did his best embarrassed grin for the young nurse. "Do you remember that Haupt guy threw you over the side of that fire escape two floors up? Lucky you landed on your leg first, not the other end."

Grover's one uncovered eyebrow furrowed. "Yeah, I was … I was waiting outside a window for someone from somewhere or other? Yeah, a big blond guy…what happened?"

"Okay, do you remember we were on a burglary stakeout? We followed a guy from a bakery back to his house and he threw you off a fire escape."

"Oh shit, yeah!" It was as if someone had thrown the light switch. "Now I remember! Well at least part of it. He rushed me, but what happened after that?"

"You went flying over the side and I got him when he was trying to run. They took you in a bus and I went with you. A patrol guy took him straight to lockup."

"Geez"

"But… hey buddy, we got the Katzenjammer burglar. You're a hero. McClusky loves you."

"So, the SOB broke my damn leg? How long have I been here?"

"Brother, you've been out cold for almost two days." Murphy tried to look cheery, but it was hard to keep up.

Meanwhile, as they spoke, the nurse, very businesslike, checked Grover's pulse and poked around at the bandage on his head. "The doctor says this can come off. You've stopped bleeding. Just, don't touch the stitches in your eyebrow."

"I only have one small bit of bad news for ya though, aside from your broken leg of course."

"What's that?" Grover winced slightly as the nurse lifted the stuck gauze from his ripped eyebrow. The eye underneath seemed to be working fine. "So, they didn't write it up in the Mirror?"

"No. No mention at all in the papers. Uh, the fact is they released the sonofabitch … oh, sorry ma,am… yesterday."

"Wha?"

Murphy paused for a second. "Excuse me ma'am, but could you leave us alone for a coupla minutes? My partner and I have some police business we need to talk about." The nurse nodded and walked out. Murphy stared at her rear as she left the room. "Has she given you a sponge bath yet? Hmmm? Uh … so, they let him go."

"Let him go? He tried to kill me, he tried to kill a cop. Who the hell let him go?"

"I dunno, but the order came from way high up. McClusky opened the cage door himself."

"What the …?"

Murphy pulled a chair close to Grover's bedside. "I think we gotta bite the bullet on this one. I'm trying to find out if someone likes him for some other crap or something, but …"

"So, you're telling me that this shithead we've been after for a month, we watch him break into a store. What more do ya need?"

"I hear ya partner. 'Just, this Haupt guy seems to have friends somewhere. His story is that he thought we were trying to break into his house. Get this, he was worried about this Katzenjammer burglar he's been reading about."

"Bullsh …!"

"And, he says he knows nothing about a bakery."

"What the hell? We saw him go into there. He's the guy. He's the damn Katzenjammer burglar!" He tried to use his left arm for emphasis, but the pain made him wince. "That is total bullshit!"

"Yeah, yeah, … can't say I disagree with you, but not much we can do about it. This is from way high-up."

"Ask me if I give a flying fart about way high-up. The cocksucker tried to kill me." Grover fumed.

"Boyo…ya need to turn down the volume. The NYPD moves in mysterious ways." Listen to me, I've been on this job for at least ten years more than you. I know for a fact that when something comes down from on high, it's best to accept the word of the gods. You need to calm down before you bust outa your stitches."

Grover calmed a bit. "Just between you and me Murph, I'm not gonna let this go so easy."

"Oh my god … is he awake?" The voice from the doorway was familiar, but it took the half-dazed patient a full two seconds to connect it.

"Hey Elly … hey, yeah I'm awake."

"I've been sitting around here for hours. I just went downstairs to get some coffee. I didn't know that Tim came to see you … I … oh… how … do you feel?" Ellen Kramer, Grover's girlfriend struggled for words. "I was worried that you'd never wake up."

"Yeah, well, I did." Grover's anger level immediately subsided. Ellen had that power over him. "Hey, I'm okay."

"Yeah he's back to himself, new and improved with additional plaster and bandages, and an extra level of Tabasco sauce."

"Doug, are you behaving yourself?"

Murphy was really glad that Grover met Ellen, a schoolteacher who knew exactly how to handle teenaged boys. "Yeah, his leg is in a sling, and he's goin' for revenge."

"You need to get better first and then you can talk about getting even." Ellen spoke soothingly but firmly. "I am not going to let you talk crazy. Tim told me the whole thing, and I think that if you make waves you're going to screw up your entire police career."

"Yeah buddy, they will screw you over totally as a troublemaker." Murphy remembered himself at Grover's age. Back then, his young wife Patricia had taken the same tack as Ellen was doing now.

"Yeah, uh, well, I get it."

"Boyo, workin' with you reminds me of me." In his youth Tim Murphy was also a hothead, but these days it was rare to see him explode on the job. Patricia Murphy allowed him to be a benign tyrant around the house, but she quickly shut him down if things got too aggressive. Truth be told, Murphy was always more bluster than bully. Once the pressure was released, he was a lamb.

"Douglas, I was so worried about you." Ellen timidly touched his bandaged head and then touched his cheek. "I was scared."

"I dunno why you worry so much. I'll be outta here in no time. I need to finish up this arrest."

"Partner, maybe not so fast. You been outta town for the last couple days, your leg is — what's that army word, FUBAR? — in two places and you could be on your ass for weeks. I think if I was you, I would let this thing lie."

Grover let out a deep breath. "This is not over. You can quote me on that."

The night nurse entered the room with syringe on a white tray. "Okay, time for some more of that happy juice! I think it's time for company to go home." Before any one of them could protest she lifted the sheets and professionally found the right place to put a syringe loaded with some very potent happy serum. Grover sighed and within a minute was sleeping again.

May 31, 1942

3:36 a.m., the North Atlantic

The cold damp pre-dawn air was being pushed into the harbor by a moderate westerly breeze. Still hours until sunrise, the captain and crew of U-202 readied the boat for sea duty. This was not going to be the usual trip hunting convoys in the North Atlantic, in fact, their orders forbade them from engaging the enemy at all. Their mission was to be a secret in every aspect. To emphasize those orders the submarine was stripped of any excess weight, such as torpedoes and shells. Instead she was fitted with extra CO_2 scrubbers so that they could travel beneath the waves for longer periods of time, undetected until they reached their target.

To the sleeping city of Lorient on the coast of France, the presence of this submarine, and the presence of the entire submarine base, was an insult to every French citizen except the collaborators. But like it or not, Lorient, a natural harbor on the Bay of Biscay, was a perfect place for the German navy's Atlantic wolf pack to maintain their U-boats and send them out to do their deeds.

Leaning on the inside wall atop the submarine's sail and gripping a hot mug of coffee, Kapitanleutnant Hans-Heinz Linder, in the faint pre-dawn light, checked his wristwatch. They are late! It would be light soon and the importance of leaving the harbor and submerging before daybreak was a strong safety issue for his boat and his men. His passengers had not yet arrived for their trip and Linder was getting angry.

It was a bit before 4:00 a.m. and the docks around the electric boat were quiet. Then, from somewhere in the distance his ears picked up the faint whirr of an engine. As it got louder in the darkness Linder was able to make out the shape of a truck moving without headlights. Ah, they are here. Finally!

It came to a stop at the entrance to the floating dock and four men got off the back. Each carried a rucksack and wore the uniform of a German infantryman. With little fanfare they approached the submarine, boarded, feigned a small heil-Hitler salute to a waiting submariner on the foredeck and were ushered aboard through the forward hatch. When the last of them was below, a crewman on the deck waved to Linder and he nodded in response. The captain lifted the comm phone from its watertight box and spoke softly but firmly, "Prepare the boat for departure."

In less than thirty minutes, U-202 was headed out to sea and within another twenty minutes she was underwater, a good hour left to go before the dawn.

8:35 a.m., Berlin

The first thing that went through the aristocratic Admiral Wilhelm Canaris' mind was that Oberleutnant Walter Kappe seemed not to have a neck. His pudgy head rested squarely atop his uniformed shoulders roughly at the same level as his epaulets. This is not the elegant body of a sailor, he thought to himself, this is a creature of the army. "Have a seat Kappe. May I offer you some coffee?"

"No thank you Admiral." Kappe lowered his uncomfortable body into the comfortable leather chair facing the desk of the notorious spy master.

"I'm pleased to hear the mission is underway. Oberleutnant, this work with which you've been entrusted is a very important task." Canaris, the head of the Abwehr, spoke clearly invoking a patrician tenor and the authority of his rank. Kappe, who arose from much humbler origins, totally understood the gravity of this meeting between him and the head of Germany's entire espionage operations. The Admiral was notorious as the manipulator, the trickster and the sly fox whose agents had infiltrated the Dutch underground and was rumored to have fifth column infiltrators planted in every American wartime factory, daily feeding him the plans of every tank, ship or airplane currently under construction. Canaris made Oberleutnant Walter Kappe feel very nervous.

"Yes sir."

"Please do not respond and simply listen. Germany is at a critical point; the Americans continue to supply their troops and allies with war materiel and while fairly effective our Atlantic hunters have been unable to cut them off completely. Our U-boats have their hands full in sinking the convoys... it's a huge task. As you probably know I personally have had some success with more seminal attacks on the sources of war materiel here in Europe using teams of unnamed heroes who, at great risk to themselves, have blown up a great deal of our enemy's ability to make and move goods to use against us. Of course, I have similar eyes and ears in place in America as well, but they lack the training and physical resources bestowed on your teams."

"Yes sir," Kappe blurted out, forgetting the order to keep quiet.

Canaris scowled for a fraction of a second. "Your next effort will take what those eyes and ears tell us, and you will act on their information. Your "Operation Pastorius" teams will sabotage factories and railroads thus slowing and stopping the movement of guns, tanks and supplies." Canaris stopped talking, an invitation for Kappe to finally speak.

"Yes Admiral. Of course, my teams will be successful in their missions. Their training has been beyond thorough." Canaris said nothing, and just stared at the officer. "Uh, I have been meaning to ask someone, what is the significance of the name?"

"The name?" Canaris repeated.

"Yes sir. What is Pastorius?"

"A good question Kappe. Francis Daniel Pastorius was the leader of the first organized settlement of Germans in America. You might say he was the first German to gain a foothold. Operation Pastorius will be a leader of another first of its kind. Appropriate enough, no?" Canaris did not wait for the lieutenant's answer. "Your team's efforts will take this war to the Americans' doorstep."

"They will do just that." Without wasting another moment on niceties, Kappe rose from the leather chair and unveiled a chart. "The two groups of four men each who are already at sea will blend in nicely once they arrive in the U.S. All of them are Germans who have lived in the U.S. and have returned home to help their fatherland in its hour of need." Kappe went on to describe how two U-boats would deposit the two teams along the eastern seaboard of America, one in Long Island and one near Jacksonville, Florida. "They will arrive in darkness and bury their explosives and equipment in the beach sand to be retrieved as needed to sabotage their targets. They should all be arriving in America within a few days."

"Good! God speed their journey in this important, and dangerous work. I wish them good hunting, Heil Hitler!" With a slight wisp of a salute Canaris moved Kappe toward the door. With his back to Kappe, Canaris flicked an intercom lever to summon his adjutant.

"I will keep you informed of progress Herr Admiral," Kappe's arm shot up in a salute. Then in a blur, the flummoxed junior officer found himself alone in the outer corridor. He noticed that he had sweated through the armpits of his uniform.

Passing by the exiting red-faced army officer was the entering Kapitänleutnant Horst Wenzl. Wenzl, a young blond-haired naval academy graduate with perfect Aryan features, realized it was now his turn. Wenzl was not a sweater; there was a coolness to him that was augmented by the three-inch long scar on his cheek, a leftover from his fencing days at the academy. His boyish look, with that added suggestion of violence was an asset in this job. Wenzl stuck his head into the doorway to the boss's office. "You wish to see me Herr Admiral?"

"Yes Horst, please come in."

Though it seemed as if Canaris often treated his adjutant as he would a son or a mentee, Wenzl never dropped his own sense of military propriety as he entered and approached his enigmatic boss. "Heil Hitler…"

"Yes of course," Canaris uninterestedly saluted back, "heil." Wenzel sat down awaiting further instructions. "I am concerned about Pastorius and its progress. Horst, you're a reliable devil's advocate, please tell me what could go wrong?"

"Admiral, aside from the obvious issues of submarine travel across the Atlantic the chance of the men being caught is small. This is a sound plan. They are very brave and very well trained. They will succeed."

"Yes, but I must tell you in strictest confidence that I fear their mission may fail radically. Yes, if they are able to get through with it, so much the better, but let us say that a failure, in this rare instance, is an option. Failure could open another door to something far more effective for our efforts."

"How so sir?"

"Are you a chess player Horst?"

"Yes, but I'm not that good at it."

"But you understand that the goal of the game is to capture the King?"

"Of course, sir."

"You lose men along the way to attain that goal."

"Yes."

"Without strategically calculated losses and your opponent's confusion of your method you will never capture your opponent's king."

"I understand that."

"Real life and chess work in the same way. What if something happens and one or both of the teams are caught?"

"Apprehended?"

"Yes, captured before their mission is accomplished? Do you suppose that the Americans will feel more or less confident in their ability to stop us? They'll be actively looking for more U-boats."

"Sir, I suppose they will feel more confident, but..."

"Confidence breeds complacency. An exposed area for a different attack."

"Yes, Herr Admiral?"

"Then, what if we threatened them in some other way. My instinct is that they would never see it coming."

"Yes sir, they would never see it coming," the adjutant repeated without really understanding what was being discussed. Wenzl knew that this was Canaris's method of organizing in his mind the details of an operation. The Admiral's ruminations were not about the two U-boat teams but about an as yet unspoken-of second part of the operation; a grander scheme up the uniformed Admiral's sleeve. "Herr Admiral, I will re-examine all the preparations and I assume, if there is another plan in the works you will share it with me when you feel I have a need to know the details."

"Uh, of course, yes. Yes Horst. I will share it then. I always find it helpful to talk these things through out loud with someone. It helps me to reason them out. In any case Horst, that will be all. Thank you." With that Wenzl rose from the chair, gave a small but crisp salute and marched out of the office.

As the door closed Canaris took a small leather-bound notebook out of his top center desk drawer and made an entry, a memory documenting the progress of this ambitious piece of audacious espionage. In his highly practiced penmanship, the meticulous, sly fox of the Abwehr wrote down the details and the progress of his plan.

June 8, 1942

7:46 a.m.

It was Douglas Grover's twenty-fourth birthday and he celebrated the event in the best way he knew by returning to work. Back at his desk for the first time in nearly two months he was happy. The cast on his left leg with his left tibia healing inside was elevated onto an adjoining desk chair, and he savored the momentary quiet of an unusually empty early morning 19th Precinct squad room. Grimy puke green walls, stark lighting, and the latent smell of years of congealed cigarette and cigar smoke on all the surfaces made this into a special place for a seasoned cop and it even felt magical. He had really missed it all.

The doctors told him that his cast probably would come off in a week or two and when the healing was all done his left leg would probably be "a bit" shorter than the other. Then his orthopedist dropped the bomb: "By the way, I don't know how you're gonna feel about this, but you're probably officially going to be 4F. The army doesn't want off balance soldiers, ha ha." Grover wasn't sure how he felt about that, but New York City still needed a police force. The idea of marching in an army was replaced by the idea of simply walking like a cop.

"Hey, you're back!" A booming voice drew him out of his dream state. "How's that leg healing up?" The 19th Precinct Captain Eamon McClusky seemed to appear out of nowhere. He pulled up a chair and sat down facing Grover eye to eye.

"Hey cap'. It's all fine. 'Cast's comin' off probably next week. Everything'll be almost as good as new." Grover swung around in the old wooden swivel chair and his plaster cast leg knocked over a wastebasket.

McCluskey smiled as he righted the trash can, "great thing that you're movin' again. Are you officially back to work?"

"I'm back, full steam Cap'." Grover aimed to exude enthusiasm, but as he stared at his captain, he sensed that there was something that made McClusky's affable greeting something more than just a simple welcome back to work.

Some more small talk came out, " ... and how's that leg healin' up?"

"It's looking good I suppose. At least I won't get drafted."

"Yeah, well I'm glad you're gonna stay here. 'You gonna have a limp?"

"Yeah ... 's lookin' like I'm gonna end up with one leg shorter than the other." Grover sighed, "I'll make it work though. I'm gonna have a swagger like a sheriff in those John Wayne movies."

"Your dad and uncles should be proud of you." McCluskey was referring to the NYPD's famous Grover brothers. "I worked with Sam … er … your dad, when I was coming up."

"Yeah, he told me that when I got assigned here." Grover's NYPD roots were almost legendary. His father, Officer Sam Grover (previously known as Shmuel Grubinsky), and his brothers Yitzhak (Izzy) and Baruch (Barry) had joined the NYPD shortly after getting off the boat on Ellis Island in 1918.

"I worked with your dad and your uncles too. Three great Jewish guys! Where'd they come from, Poland or something like that?"

"Lithuania."

"Yeah, I remember, from some dirt road village in the middle of nowhere."

"I guess they did good."

"Oh yeah, very good. They came to New York and tried to displace my cop ancestors out of their way! Ha ha! Maybe I'm a little jealous of them all." It had taken McCluskey almost his whole career to become a captain. The Grubinskys became detectives on a fast track.

"Cap, there's no way that three Jewish guys are gonna push the Irish out of the NYPD, not any way that will ever happen in this lifetime." Grover smiled at the mildly anti-Semitic tone from his boss. "My dad and his brothers moved up because the department needed cops who could speak something other than Gaelic."

"Yeah, speaking Yiddish helped them a lot. Good thing for that 'cause their English was awful."

"I think they did pretty good for three guys who learned a language on the way over here on a boat. 'Fact is, even then they knew that they wanted to be cops."

"I was in the same Academy class as your dad. He did … well, they all did very well."

"Dad used to tell me that he was the first Yiddish speaker in the department. They assigned him to the 5th on the lower East Side and he never left."

"Those brothers loved the job and set you up for great things here. They had a lot of faith in you becoming a cop."

"I couldn't not become a cop. I was the only boy in the family. All my cousins were girls and it was all on my back. But, I gotta admit I did get some help. I could have been walking a beat in Brooklyn somewhere, but dad pulled some strings and got me into the 13th. I was there for three years, then I came to the one-nine. Dad said the one-nine was a sweet job." The precinct house on East 67th between Third and Lexington sat close to the southern border of the 19th's territory, an area that took in the whole of the upper East side, from Fifth Avenue to the East River and from 60th Street to 96th. The 19th was a microcosm of the city.

"Your dad's right. From riches to rags here, on one end we got the Park and Fifth Avenue snoots, the Silk Stocking District, and on the other end we got a load of Czechs, Germans, Hungarians, Irish, Jews, Lebanese, Polish, Slovaks and all the others who can't afford to live on Fifth."

"Before I came here my Uncle Izzy also told me that the house was spiritually convenient."

"Huh?"

"We're right next door to a synagogue, get it?"

"Ha, we are indeed. Do you ever go in there to pray?"

"Actually, no. Never been inside the place. I'm really not religious, but as I was falling off that fire escape, I think I was praying on the way down."

"Cops do dangerous work."

"I suppose bad guys are bad guys everywhere, just who would have thought that the 19th could have ever been so dangerous a place?"

McCluskey sighed, "well, it isn't normally so dangerous. Most cases here, nobody runs into a giant perp like you did."

"Yeah, he was big alright."

"Speaking of that guy," McClusky found the moment to shift gears from the nostalgia talk. "Look, I'm not going to dance around this. I've heard about a few things you've said about this Haupt."

"Oh? What have you heard?"

"Things like, maybe you plan to get even."

"I... uh...."

"In any case, the boys downtown are wondering if you're gonna try and make something more out of it? Even your partner thinks you can't let it go."

"Cap, I got tossed off ...."

"And, the department has made it official policy not to make a big deal about this asshole's release."

Grover understood exactly where this conversation was going so he lied. "Oh, no Cap, I'm okay. I'm on to the next thing."

"No hard feelings?"

"Nah, this one is done. If he's not the Katzenjammer burglar it was my mistake."

"Well then, that's good to hear." McClusky kept talking as he stood up and started to move away. "That's good to hear. It'll make everyone feel better. You're makin' your family proud. You're makin' the department proud."

"Right, Cap."

"I mean... this Haupt guy... I mean... everyone knows that he's a scumbag, if you know what I mean?"

"Yeah, I understand Cap'. Murphy filled me in on all of it."

The Captain was hemming and hawing. "Look, truth is, he convinced a judge that he was innocent and that he thought you were the Katzenjammer burglar trying to rob him. That's why he fought with you on the fire escape. I don't believe a word of it, but we gotta leave him alone now."

"Cap, I am good with it," Grover bit his tongue as this was, in his mind, by no means over, or any kind of a done-deal.

"I gotta tell ya though, that if you had been hurt worse or killed I wouldn't have gone for it at all."

"I understand Cap." By now Grover was amused by his captain's babbling attempt to apologize for his orders. "I'm over it."

"Could it be this creep has friends in high places? I dunno?"

Grover bit his tongue again. "Cap, really, no hard feelings. When my cast comes off all I wanna do is get back to the job full time."

"Good. Let's leave it at that." McClusky walked away.

June 12, 1942

11:30 a.m.

Cinching tight the belt on his flannel robe, a visibly frail Karl Haupt opened the door to the apartment and greeted his son with a bear hug, or at least as much of a bear hug as he could muster. "Ach mein Bärchen!" a father's term of endearment for his overgrown "little bear."

Eugen hadn't visited in over two weeks. *Jesus, he looks worse than ever!* The younger Haupt stared at the one-time powerful soldier in the Kaiser's Army who now stood before him. Emphysema seemed to be calling muster on the old man, and he had not been out of his fourth-floor walk-up apartment in weeks. "Hello Poppa. You should have let Mutti open the door for me. You shouldn't exert yourself."

"Eugen, don't be such a stupid boy," he attempted a smile. Anyvay, your moser is out vit her sister und dere is notting wrong vit me. It is springtime and I haff some allergies to zeh flowers. Do you vant anysing to eat?"

"No thanks. I'm here ... uh ... you called me on the phone, remember?" Eugen laid down on the couch opposite his father and stared at the ceiling.

"Ummm? Yes, I did. So, how haff you been doing? Haff ze police bozered you anymore?"

Eugen smirked, "no poppa ... they've left me alone. I have friends."

"Ya, dat's gut... alvays gut to haff friends. Ya ..." The old man glanced around the sparsely furnished room as if looking for someone who might be eavesdropping and lowered his voice to a raspy whisper. "A "friend" needs your assistance."

Eugen sighed to himself. *The old man isn't himself any more. Where is he getting this stuff?* Eugen would have liked to believe that the friends were imaginary and part of Karl Haupt's way of staying vital, decrepit memories from his once colorful life on the periphery of underworld darkness. Yet, on the past three or four occasions that Karl had ordered him to help, the friends were not imaginary. They were old men just like his father and Eugen had set them up in apartments, given them money and helped them move around New York. He wasn't sure who they were, where they came from or what they were up to, but it appeared that there was still someone somewhere who relied on the sickly Karl Haupt for help. *Shit, another sad old man who thinks he's important!* "Yes Poppa, and what "friend" would that be, hmmm?" He instantaneously wished he hadn't said that.

Karl caught the sarcasm in his son's voice, "Don't you speak zat vay vit me."

"Geeze Poppa, don't get upset. I've done everything you've asked me to do. I find places to live for your friends, I go shopping for them, I get them food, I even order their wine for them. I go all over the place to do this stuff. I'm not being disrespectful, but you never tell me why I'm doing any of this."

"Vat if I told you Vilhelm Canaris himself asked my help?"

"Vilhelm Canaris who?" Eugen stopped himself. It was easier to go along with the old man than to fight. "Okay Poppa, what do you need me to do?"

"It's not for me, it's for our friends. Ve may be haffing anozer house-guest in a few veeks. Dere iss no room for him here but he vill need a place to stay and be private."

"I understand. Do you want for him to stay with me?"

"No. Find him a comfortable apartment somevere in ze neighborhood for ze duration of his visit."

"I can do that." Eugen had been through these drills before. Usually, as it was with this one, it began with a whispered cryptic request for some kind of quiet help for the fatherland, then a flurry of activity always followed by nothing. The rants of deluded old men who think they have some impact on the world. Eugen had unofficially declared himself to be non-political. While he did not at all share his father's fervor for the Reich he decided to use the connection for his own gain. The younger Haupt couldn't care less about how the war turned out; if the Americans were the victors his life would go on, and if the Germans won he would have established his bona fides in that realm as well. Karl Haupt's dramatically whispered request would likely be another of those useless endeavors to support der Führer, but Eugen was unable to refuse it. Unfortunately, as before, the request usually came with a price tag and Eugen was tired of shelling out his personal cash for what his father called "friends in need."

"What is his price range? I can't afford to pay for another one of these guys."

The old man had a hair-trigger rage and it exploded like a pistol shot, "Dammit, you are just like a Jew. You vill get ze damn money. It's alvays about money vit you. Just listen to me. Ven he arrifes here he vill need to be picked up in a car and he vill need a place to stay."

"I have to pick him up too?" There was annoyance in Eugen's voice and once-again he regretted it the moment it came out of his mouth.

Karl fumed, "… and ze place you get for him needs to be kviet, very kviet. Can you just take care of zat?"

"Okay Poppa." Eugen flinched, "It's not a problem, just calm down and I'll take care of it."

Karl Haupt's volcanic explosion ended as abruptly as it began. "Good.

You vill let me know ven you locate a place for him?"

"Not a problem." Eugen stared at his father and waited for him to bring up the subject that was foremost in his mind.

It took a moment, but then the old man spoke up. "Ah yes, and I have zose names for you. Some very un-American ideas vit dese two." Karl reached into the pocket in his robe and pulled out a folded piece of paper. Eugen didn't open it to read it, he simply stuck it into his pants pocket, he was only a messenger. Karl just prattled on, "It's a shame zat zere patriotism vill be kvestioned during zees troubled times. Ach, such a shame!"

"The shame is on them father. Enemies of the state! I'm sure that the authorities will want to speak with them at length."

"Yes, zey vill."

Eugen stood up and patted his pocket. "I'll pass this on to those who need to see it."

"Gute. Now go."

Eugen hugged his frail father and left. He had been on missions like this one before, but for the first time in his life he wondered exactly who was running Karl Haupt? The names he would pass on to his handler? Those were obviously Karl's enemies, but Wilhem Canaris? Really? Where was the "guest" coming from and why was it so important? It was more than he wanted to think about at this moment in time and so he forgot about his questions and left to begin his assigned task.

11:56 p.m., the Atlantic Ocean off Montauk

"Gruber, alert the crew for silent running. No one is to make a sound!"

"Jawohl Herr Kapitan!"

U-202 sat mere inches off the sandy sea floor and Kapitanleutnant Hans-Heinz Linder squinted as he scanned the surroundings through a slightly raised periscope. "I cannot see shit in this fog. Good!" The mist at sea level obscured any visual reference to the shore, but Linder, an expert navigator, was pretty sure that he knew exactly where he was. Star sightings and dead-reckoning had put the unterboot at the end of its journey to periscope depth within a mile of the beach. After fifteen days at sea with absolutely no contact with any other vessel, he had guided his submarine precisely to a spot about 17 miles west of Montauk Point.

"Our timing is perfect! There is no moon and the mist is above periscope height. We have brought the war to the enemy. Now we must deliver it."

U-202 sat silently in 20 meters of American water and the crew's mood was expectedly tense. In the wash of the red night lighting every unlit corner inside the sub's con led into deeper and darker shadows and the smell of fear wafted through the CO2 scrubbers. The crew members of U-202 were living in a real-life horror movie, and Linder tensely hoped his passengers would depart quickly.

Then all of a sudden it got worse. The horror manifested itself in a sickening crunching sound from underneath and a sudden halt to the boat's motion. "Shit! We are aground! If this fog clears before the tide lifts us we are all dead!"

June 13, 1942

2:00 a.m., Amagansett, Long Island

Coast Guard Corpsman John Cullen really hated this tour, but it was still better than sitting indoors. Yes, this was wartime, but it was also late spring with the clean night ocean air and no one bothering you for hours on end. From time to time it could also be entertaining — the summer people never expected anyone to be walking through the dunes in the dark. Over the past few months Cullen had become lord and master of about three miles of Long Island's shoreline, and ever since the blackout went into effect on the East Coast he guessed that he had marched up and down this beach at least a thousand times, in good weather and bad.

Earlier in the spring there had been a lot of debate about blacking out the Atlantic shoreline. Mayors and city councils in resort towns were against it as bad for business. *What are the Germans going to do, come across the ocean and attack Coney Island?* But that all changed on the night of April 13th when a U.S. Navy ship, USS Roper on coastal patrol off the Outer Banks of North Carolina near the Bodie Island light, came upon Nazi submarine U-85. The Destroyer chased the sub and after dodging a rear-fired torpedo she laid down 11 depth charges and sank her in a matter of minutes. The incident was a wakeup call and a nightly blackout was ordered by the U.S. government just a day or two later.

Now a player in the big picture, Corpsman Cullen, for the past two months did his duty one sandy footstep after another, marching to nowhere and back in the dark. His thoughts often drifted from his job to his comfort and to his stomach. *No Germans tonight... At least it isn't raining . . . I'm hungry. . .* This night's tour promised to be not much different, moonless and nearly pitch black, with a gentle warm sea breeze massaging his face. Cullen marched through the mist that hovered above the black ocean as small wavelets broke on the beach. His one visual aid on a dark night like this was the chemoluminescence of algae that glowed in the breaking surf at water's edge. The glow at the waterline was his only spatial reference. It pointed him eastward on a parallel line and then back again toward his barracks and dawn. There was a lot of beach out there and Cullen guessed that allowing for all the inlets and curves and tucks on the East Coast there must be hundreds of other guys just like him patrolling from the tip of Maine all the way down to Key West. Tonight seemed like all the others and he had no idea, how in just a few moments, all that would change.

June 22, 1942

1:30 p.m.

"Look at me Murph, no crutches!" Grover was experiencing a forgotten sense of lightness. That morning his cast came off and X-rays revealed that his twice-fractured tibia had healed nicely. He had spent the previous weeks at his desk fielding phone calls from the public and reading files. He was now able to get around with the help of just a cane. His smiling doctor told him to take it easy, "no running, no football and no kicking suspects until the bones mend completely."

Murphy looked up from his crossword in his normal deadpan, "Yeah, just don't break it again. I can't take your complaining."

Grover parked himself back into his chair and pretended to sulk. "Sorry I've been such a burden to you."

Murphy's burden was that he had to spend the previous two months working with substitute partners, none of whom provided the chemistry he had with Grover. In the past few weeks while Grover healed, Murphy did farewell tours with thirty-five-year NYPD veteran Des Richards, an overweight, gray-haired relic on the verge of putting in his papers. To Murphy's relief, Richards finally retired on Friday, allowing him to reunite this morning with the newly-ambulatory Grover.

"Yeah, it ain't been easy for me either since you landed on the concrete. I've suffered too."

"I feel bad for ya, but now we can get back to the matter at hand."

"That being?" Murphy put the unfinished puzzle on the desk and stared at Grover.

"Y'know I've been doin' some reading on Haupt."

"Oh, here we go again! Did McCluskey have a conversation with you yet? He had one with me. What part of leave the sonofabitch alone didn't you understand?"

"I'm not doing anything to the guy, I'm just reading a lot. I've had a lot of time on my hands lately, ya know."

"I know, but you're gonna get both of us screwed if you keep it up."

"Yeah, yeah. But, while you and your zoot suit, hep-cat partner have been out around the town, I've become an expert on all the Haupts. Did you read any of these files?"

"Where'd you get those files? I couldn't read anything. 'Captain took all my stuff about the guy the week after you hit the pavement. I never saw them again. Where'd you get 'em?"

Grover smirked. "From one of my uncle's pals in the DA's office. You really should learn to cultivate relationships like that. They could help you in your police career,"

"Hey, no one likes a smart ass."

"Look, I know someone downtown wants us to leave this alone, but this guy is so wrong we gotta take him off the street before he kills somebody."

"Yeah, yeah," Murphy let out a sigh. He agreed with Grover but at the same time he worried about his pension. "Y'know if your DA office pals gave you this stuff while knowing you, they are not your friends. They're not looking out for your welfare." Murphy tried to scowl but it didn't work. "So... you gonna tell me what you read?"

"Sure, it's a pretty good story and it's not just about our boy Eugen, it's about his old man too. He gets it honestly from Daddy."

"They investigated the father? When?"

"A while ago. This family is an American success story. 'Wanna hear it or are you just gonna sit there and tell me my career is over?"

What could it hurt to hear about it? Murphy pulled his chair next to Grover's, "...his old man, huh?"

"Yeah, this is a DA's investigation of Karl Haupt. This guy is a doozy!"

"Not his kid?"

"Other than with you and me, Eugen's never had a run-in with the law, but he shows up a lot in his old man's stuff."

"Nothing at all?"

"Crazy huh?"

"Well we didn't know about him either until now."

"He wasn't a good boy though. He had a lot of juvie trouble that kept his old man hiring lawyers, but after a bad childhood there was nothing. He went straight. His juvie files were sealed, so Eugen is clean, a solid citizen!

"Hmm!" Murphy was intrigued.

"Yeah, he is one highly under-paper-worked asshole who comes from one really bad family. He was born in Alsace, France. The family moved to Yorkville when Eugen was eight, just after the big war ended."

"He's French?"

"Technically yeah, but that place is just on the border with Germany. They're almost all krauts in that town."

"Okay, so he's German and lives in Yorkville. Surprise, surprise!"

"True, but most of the other Germans aren't knee-crackers. Old Karl has his name linked with all kinds of bad guys."

"Was he ever in the joint?

"Nope, never, but he should have been." Grover stared down at the papers on his desk. "Says here that Karl Haupt is linked with known crime bosses, goons and goddamn Nazi lovers all over Yorkville."

"You don't say!"

"In fact, I do say, and yet his son, exposed to all of this criminality during his youth, seems to have come out of it all with a clean record."

"Maybe he didn't want to be a part of daddy's business."

"Murph, the apple doesn't fall far from the tree. There's no reasonable way that Eugen Haupt, at least on paper, has never experienced even a fleeting connection with officers of the law, not once!"

"And you think that someone up high is protecting him? Does that report say that too?" Murphy already knew the answer in his gut. "Does the DA think that someone cleaned out the Eugen Haupt file?"

"Ya gotta read between the lines here. This is a file about Karl, not his boy. This old guy was a real piece of work." Grover leafed through the stack of papers. "Okay, he was born in France, but his family has German ancestry. Even though he was technically French, Karl volunteered to fight for the Kaiser, left his wife and kid in France and didn't see them for three years until the war ended. In the German army he worked as a horse wagon teamster pulling cannons to the front. By the time the war was over his kid was almost five. Karl's heart was in Germany, so he moved them to the other side of the Rhine to Baden-Baden."

"So, let me understand this, Karl is really French, but he went to fight for Germany?"

"Yeah, but the people in that part of France always thought they should be part of Germany, it's always been a movable border."

"One year your house is in Germany, the next it's in France. No more of those tough German winters, huh?"

"Murph, Karl must have been somebody big because in 1930 the New York DA's office sent someone to France and Germany to check him out."

"The old man? Why?"

"The DA talked to people who knew the family in Alsace. They told stories about how after the war, Karl Haupt came home and was mad at the world. He beat his wife and kid. He got into a bar fight with a total stranger and accused the guy of diddling his wife while he was at the front. The poor schmuck, just having a beer, lost an eye because of Karl. The family quickly left France because the gendarmes were after him for it."

"Not a great role model for his kid, huh?"

"Then, about a year later, he moved the family to New York. He told the immigration officer at Ellis Island that he left Germany because of his 'personal embarrassment' over Germany's 'humiliating' surrender in that French railroad car."

"And they still let him in the country?"

"Yeah, go figure. So, this discharged German soldier with nothing else to show for his loyalty, no money, no future, no nothing, moved here. Things didn't change here either. In August of 1926, a neighbor in Yorkville called the cops on him, she was sure that Karl was beating the crap out of his hausfrau and the kid, too."

"Some people never change."

" 'Same neighbor also told the D.A.'s guy that she thought he had a couple of loose screws in his head. She said that she saw Karl marching up and down the hallway a couple of times wearing his old German army uniform."

"So what? No crime there. He's a proud veteran of the big war. I'm proud to be Irish."

"Yeah, but the Irish never invaded Belgium. Karl was really serious about this shit. He sent Eugen to one of those German summer camps every year."

"Yeah, that one in Yaphank. I read that it was an indoctrination center. And that's where Eugen learned to be an asshole?"

"Nah, he was born an asshole. But this isn't about Eugen, this is about daddy. There are records in this file about Karl and his wife being called to the principal's office in Eugen's school. The kid was making anti-Semitic wisecracks in social studies."

"Like father, like son, I suppose," Murphy smirked.

"Yeah, in the meeting with the principal, Karl defends his kid. He tells Principal Morris Cohen, 'the German nation's humiliation at the hands of the English, the French and of course their masters, the Jews, was too much for any German to bear.'"

"That one must have gone over really well with the Principal. But, come on, don't be so sensitive. Everyone blames you people for all their problems. By the way, if you're really Jewish how come you ain't rich?"

"Fuck you and go eat a potato," Grover shot back with a smile.

"Buy me one."

Grover kept reading, "Listen to this, 'After the family's arrival in Yorkville, Karl Haupt tried his hand at one occupation and then another, but nothing seemed to fit. He quit or was fired from almost all of the jobs he tried, save for one. After a period of six months, the family was on the edge of being evicted from their one-room apartment, but they got some unexpected relief. In June of 1920, Karl met some men who saw him as someone in need, who also had a strong back. Karl got a job at a Bronx trucking company.'"

"Trucking what?"

"Prohibition beer. They needed strong guys to load and unload sacks of grain and then load barrels of suds from and to waiting trucks. Karl found his spot and he never complained about the work."

"Who told them all of this stuff?"

"There are no names, just lists of initials. Someone named J.M. says that he saw an incident at the Harlem brewery. Karl saw one of his buddies taking cash from another guy's coat pocket. He grabs the guy by the collar and tells him that he saw him do it. He tells the man to put the money back, "or else." The guy laughs in his face and denies taking anything. Karl doesn't ask a second time. He grabs the guy's right hand and crushes it against a wall. Then Haupt stomps on the guy's left hand and crushes it just as bad." J. M. says he heard Haupt say, 'now it will be harder for you to steal anyone's money again, and it will also be even harder for you to wipe your ass!'"

"The guy does have a sense of justice, you can give him that … something rare among goons."

"And because of that incident, Karl got the boss's attention. Guess who that was?"

"I dunno, who?"

"Someone they called Dutch Schultz!"

"That Dutch Schultz?"

"Yeah, none other than… but, Karl had no idea who that was, he couldn't read and so he never saw a newspaper. All he says that he knew about his boss was that his nickname was Dutch. Someone explained to him that the name really meant Deutsche so if Dutch Schultz was a German. Karl was happy to be in the company of another German."

"But, if I remember correctly, Dutch wasn't German, was he?"

"I dunno. It was a nickname, and really, who gives a shit? Now, Dutch takes a close personal interest in his new employee and Karl is flattered by the attention."

"Employee of the month!"

"Schultz, on the other hand, saw beyond the right and wrong of the situation. He elevated Karl to an executive level in the organization and Haupt became Schultz's shadow and personal enforcer."

"Schultz seems like he was a good judge of raw talent."

"Anyway, it was all good until late in 1935. J.M. says, 'Gangland turf wars and disagreements put Schultz at odds with his buddies and when Dutch started acting even crazier than his reputation.' Seems like the other gangsters took it in a bad way. Dutch made a decision that he wanted to kill Tom Dewey. All the other bosses immediately saw only the negative potential in what Dutch was proposing."

"Smart thinking, if you're running an illegal brewery in the Bronx it's not a good thing to kill the Attorney General of New York State."

"Yeah, they were sure that every cop in the world would come down

hard on all of them if that happened. They told Dutch in no uncertain language, don't even try it! "J.M. says here that Dutch came back with a 'kiss
my hiney.'"

" 'Charming guy."

"So, you might remember this story, rather than risk a huge crackdown
on all of their businesses, the other bad guys decided to kill Dutch instead."

"Oh yeah!"

"On October 23rd at 10:15 p.m., Dutch gets shot while urinating in the
men's room at the Palace Chophouse at Newark. He's mortally wounded
and dies a few hours later."

"I do remember all that," Murphy just made Sergeant a year earlier. "It
happened in Jersey, but the whole New York department was in an uproar.
And, if I remember correctly, passing-on, along with Dutch are two of his
bodyguards and his accountant, right? All of them got shot in the pisser."

"Yup, I was still in High School when it happened, but I heard my dad
talking about it. But you didn't know this: that by sheer luck Karl Haupt,
Dutch's number-one bodyguard, wasn't there at the time! What does that
tell you?"

"He was in a parent-teacher conference at his kid's school?"

"More like he was in a conference with the rest of the New York mob.
Karl wasn't going down with the ship. Just like he did back in Alsace, he
switched sides and gave up his boss to the other guys."

"Well, honestly it doesn't sound like the dumbest thing he could have
done, but why did he do it?"

"The DA thought that Karl got pissed off after he found out that his
mentor Deutsch Schultz was neither Dutch nor German. He was Jewish
and that set him off."

"There they go again with that anti-Semitic stuff."

"And, after Dutch was gone Karl continued his career working for the
competition. In 1936 he brought his son along during a few of his 'collection calls.' "

"A father bringing his son into the family business … how American of
him!"

Grover paused as he read down a page, "and, other than school problems,
by the way, is the first mention of Eugen in any of this."

"Funny how the old man got so much attention and his burglar kid gets
away with almost killing you without any paperwork at all."

"Yeah. So, this is the DA's physical description of Eugen in here from 15
years ago." Grover read, "K.H.'s teenaged son is over six-foot-tall and weighs
over 200 pounds. Eugen was a wrestler at Julia Richman High School.
Instructors said that in spite of his size he was very graceful."

"Yeah, remember what he looked like when we first saw him on the street that night, right out of Fantasia?" From that late-night moment back in April all the memories Murphy had of Eugen Haupt included a vision of a hippo in a tutu.

"Following Shultz's murder, Karl and son became a team. Karl made sure that Eugen shared his political views as well. In the late '30's the Haupts became more and more involved in German-American support of The Fatherland. They sent money, marched in parades and got swept up in all the goose-stepping malarkey. Eugen became a counselor at his old Bund summer camp on Long Island, a 'Camp Siegfried' in Yaphank, and Karl joined the major group's leadership council." The DA's dossier ended there.

"So, we're chasing maybe a burglar, maybe a street hoodlum, and pretty surely a Nazi, but in this most recent dust-up between him and the law, we lost the round."

Grover reluctantly nodded in agreement. "Fact is, Eugen is clean. We've got nothin' on him other than some lame snitch's say-so, catching him breaking into a bakery where there was nothing to steal and throwing me off a fire escape. Actually, and I'm talking like his lawyer here, we've got no reason to believe that he is the real Katzenjammer at all. He's got no priors, no arrests not even a jay-walking ticket. So, what do we do now?"

Murphy's eyes lit up. "What we do now is to keep it up and keep the screws on this SOB until we catch him fucking up in person."

Grover was thrilled to hear that Murphy had just agreed to work around the Captains orders to leave Haupt alone. "Now that's a plan!"

June 24, 1942

11:26 a.m.

Eugen Haupt was out and about in the daytime. While at night he was the man alleged to be the so-called Katzenjammer burglar, now, under the bright sunlight of an early summer day, he was just another Yorkville shopper. As he strolled along East 86th Street he was living a charmed life. His civil crimes were obviously explainable by his unseen benefactors as benign misunderstandings between an honest citizen and over-zealous policemen. His life, he thought, was that of a neighborhood prince.

His neighbors of German heritage, none of whom knew him personally, had heard his story by word of mouth and turned him into an anti-establishment folk hero. "They (the police) are harassing a poor innocent boy because he is German!" The story of his arrest and release after tossing a police officer from a fire escape became an immediate neighborhood legend. Haupt had come to believe that his late-night encounter with Grover and Murphy brought him the respect of every low-life as well as every up-right German-American citizen who didn't know him by sight, but had heard his name. Eugen Haupt proved to be as much a social acrobat as a physical one.

As he walked by the little German bakery on 86th, a pastry in the window caught his eye. He hadn't been back in the bakery since that night in April, but he craved some of his childhood favorite roasted marzipan cake, baked the old-fashioned way, with wax paper still stuck to the caramelized sugar on the bottom… and… of course, a mandelhörnchen or two, horn-shaped chewy, almond cookies dipped in chocolate and sprinkled with sliced almonds.

"Hello sir, what can I get for you?"

"Hello to you too. Could I have a slice of that almond cake and a pound of the mandelhörnchen, the almond horn cookies?"

"Of course!" The baker immediately assembled a carboard pastry box and began to stuff it, "You know, I'm fortunate to have been able to buy a decent amount of sugar to make this stuff. You're lucky, this is the first time I've had mandelhörnchen in two weeks!" Rationing had begun in May and sugar was now on the hard-to-get list.

"I am lucky then. I love your mandelhörnchen." Eugen made a note to himself to look into the profit possibilities of creating black market sources for rationed goods. He was sure that someone else was doing that already, but what the heck? He slapped a dollar bill onto the counter.

"Here you are." The baker blankly handed his customer the box of baked goods, totally unaware that this same man had, only a few months earlier, made a late-night break-in looking for papers, papers that might get him in trouble. "That's seventy-five cents, and here's your change. Thank you. Please come again."

Eugen stepped outside into the sunlight, pulled a Mandelhörnchen from the string-tied box and began eating it as he walked back toward his apartment. Staring at him from a parked car a few feet away from the bakery door, and against specific instructions from their boss, were detectives Murphy and Grover. "Look at this sonofabitch, not a care in the world!" Murphy wiped a line of sweat off his brow.

"I just wanna see where he goes in the daytime." Grover mumbled. "Let's just follow him slowly."

"I had the same thought." Murphy let out the clutch and the car inched Eastward on 86th.

Haupt, with no idea that he was being followed, window-shopped and munched as he made his way back home.

Grover's eyes were locked on Haupt, "you gotta believe that this shithead is up to no good. He's unemployed but he's got money. Doesn't that qualify him as a suspicious character?"

"Yeah, but remember what you told McCluskey?"

"I think we need to have a talk with him. Whadaya say?"

"I say that I know someone who isn't gonna like it one bit," Murphy exhaled with a sigh of resignation that the situation was beyond his control, "but, what the hell."

The unmarked police car drove past its slower moving quarry and rounded the corner ahead of him. By the time Haupt got to his building Murphy was inside and Grover stood outside the street-level vestibule. As he entered the front door he saw Murphy standing with the same expression he had seen back in April. He turned to back away, but this time Grover was expecting the move and stood there like a rock. Haupt immediately broke into a pleasant smile. Grover herded the man into the vestibule.

"Hello officers. How does it go?" While Haupt's speech contained only the wisp of an accent left over from speaking only German for the first eight years of his life his syntax didn't sound like that of a native New Yorker.

"It's going a lot better now, no thanks to you." Grover responded.

"Does your captain know that you are visiting me?" Haupt knew the remark would serve to goad the cops. Somehow he knew that Grover had been told to leave him alone.

Murphy didn't bite on the tease, "Nah, we wanted it to be a surprise." Murphy frisked Haupt and came up with a set of brass knuckles. "Hmm," he said with mock seriousness, "You know, I believe it's illegal for some citizens to carry these kinds of weapons in New York City. Of course, that rule doesn't apply to you does it? You must have friends in high places."

Haupt stayed cool. "I was just out buying pastries. I am very fond of German almond cake and especially Mandelhörnchen. I just bought some of both. Do you like mandelhörnchen? I have more in the bag."

"Nah, we'll pass for now." Murphy slipped the brass knuckles into his own pocket. "I'll keep these so no one gets injured. Public safety, ya know."

Grover was more direct. "Listen, I just want you to know that I'm back, and I'm going to be watching you. 'Truth-be-told, I don't like you at all." He stared steely into Haupt's blue eyes. "You screw up just once and I will make sure that you can kiss your sweet mandelhörnchen goodbye. I will bust your heinie so fast you won't know if it's in the cell with the rest of your ass."

"Officers, you misjudge me. I'm a truck driver, that's all I am," he smiled with obvious insincerity. "It is unfortunate that we had that earlier encounter. I am very, very sorry for your injury but, it was the middle of the night and I feared that you two were burglars attempting to harm me. Perhaps you were that Katzenjammer burglar that the newspapers have been talking about. That's the only reason you fell off my fire escape."

Murphy smiled back with a sinister edge, "Hey, no hard feelings Eugen. We do apologize for scaring you."

Grover put his face within six inches of Haupt's, "but let me personally scare the shit out of you for real right now, your burglary business is now officially shut down. The next time we see you out late at night unless you got a dinner date with Veronica Lake it won't be me ending up in the hospital. Catch my drift?"

"Oh yeah, I just saw her in that movie Sullivan's Travels... she's a real doll!" Murphy stared at Haupt with a menacing look, "Hey Eugen, are you dating Veronica Lake."

Haupt raised his eyebrows in mock fear. "Are you threatening me?"

"Nah, my partner is just movie-star-struck," Grover smiled.

"Well then, thank you for the advice officers. I will definitely keep it in mind." He paused for a second and smirked, "Are you sure you don't want to try one of these wonderful Schnekens, that bakery has a secret recipe for them somewhere. I wish I knew where I could find it written down."

Unamused Grover shot back, "keep it up smart-ass. You don't wanna go where this is heading."

Not breaking his smile, Haupt turned and headed up the stairs to his apartment.

Outside on Third Avenue Murphy looked at his limping partner, "Doug?"

"Yeah?"

"Let's go buy some mandelhörnchen."

June 26, 1942

10:00 a.m., Washington, D.C.

With a slight smile of satisfaction on his face J. Edgar Hoover spoke in a quiet voice. "Mr. President, I can say that this turned out well because first, we were lucky, and then second, we did some powerful police work."

'Wild Bill' Donovan, the head of the brand new O.S.S., hero of the first great war and now President Roosevelt's choice to head up the brand-new Office of Strategic Services recognized the politics of his own situation and sat there quietly saying nothing as the FBI chief bragged to the President.

"What I find immensely troubling is that they got this close." President Roosevelt was not smiling.

"Yes, they did get close, but the system worked." Hoover's eyes met the President's. "This 21-year-old young man, his name is Cullen, John Cullen, doing his job patrolling the beach, comes up in the dark on four men who look odd. He senses that something isn't right. He calls it in, and we follow up. That soldier needs to get a medal."

"I read the précis of the incident, but it was missing the details. What happened exactly?" The President lit a cigarette at the end of a long amber holder.

Hoover leaned back in his chair and began to tell a story, much as he would to a child going to bed. As this was no fairy tale, he omitted *Once upon a time.* "About two weeks ago Coast Guardsman Cullen, on routine patrol, was covering a four-mile-long section of the beach in Amagansett on Long Island. He had been on that same tour for a few months before that date and had not reported anything unusual in that time. Somewhere after midnight, he came across a group of men on the beach. They were dressed like fishermen and Cullen had no reason to believe that they weren't. Cullen, who was armed with only a rifle struck up a conversation to see what they were doing out there so late. The leader of the group said they were fishermen out of Montauk and their boat ran aground somewhere off the beach in the fog and they waded ashore to wait for the incoming tide to re-float her.

"Didn't the Coast Guardsman find that at all odd? Why if they were waiting for the tide would they have left their boat at all? And, if they had waded ashore wouldn't their boat have been visible from the beach," the President queried?

"Yes, and yes, and that made Cullen immediately suspicious, but it was very dark with no moon, so he played dumb. There were also four of them and only one of him."

"I see," FDR inhaled a long puff through the cigarette holder.

"Then, Cullen is talking to the leader of the group and he overhears a couple of the others a few feet away speaking in a whisper, that clearly sounded to him like it was German. He is now very suspicious, but he's outnumbered, so he offers to lead them back to his barracks to wait for morning light when he and his men can come and help re-float their boat. The stranger, of course, says "no thank you." Meanwhile, Cullen notices that there's been some digging going on in the dunes. He immediately deduces that these "fishermen" buried something in the sand. After a few minutes he tells them that he needs to get back on patrol, but he will come back to help them in the morning. The fisherman says, "no, not necessary, we can get it done by ourselves." Then comes a veiled threat from the leader of the group which Cullen pretends not to understand, then the man offers the guardsman some money to thank him for his help and maybe compromise him about reporting the incident. Cullen plays dumb, takes the money and goes back to his barracks to get the cavalry. But, by the time Coast Guard Patrol gets to the spot there's nothing visible but footprints. Cullen tells them to dig in the dune where the other fisherman were standing. They dig and quickly find a buried rubber boat, German uniforms and a lot of explosives. The "fishermen" are long gone."

"Did we get all of their explosives?"

"Unsure at this point, sir. They could have taken stuff with them with the idea of coming back to the spot to get the rest." William Donovan, silent so far in the conversation, spoke.

"And where did they all go?"

"Bureau agents, who were on the site by daybreak a couple of hours later believe the foursome simply walked off the beach and got on the Long Island Railroad heading into New York City."

Roosevelt listened carefully, "...so how did you catch them?"

"Solid police work, the Bureau's eyes and ears everywhere. Since the start of this thing in Europe, and even before our situation today, we've set up reliable sources to give us first-hand information into everything going on in German communities all over the nation. As we learned about this landing we also learned about a second landing off Jacksonville in Florida..."

Donovan asked, "Yes... that other landing. Don't you think it's the sign of something much more sinister if our enemy lands two groups of saboteurs on our shores at the same time?"

"Sinister? Yes of course, but," Hoover never took his eyes off Roosevelt while responding to Donovan's question, "Mr. President, let me say that from the first moment these men stepped onto American soil we knew they were here, and we shortly rounded them all up."

Roosevelt wasn't buying Hoover's simplification of the details. "Two submarines land a total of eight Nazi spies here within two days? That effort alone needs to be analyzed. What were they planning? What are they planning? Are there others that we missed? It all sends a chill down my spine."

An intra-agency spat was brewing. Donovan, not at all a big fan of the FBI chief kept his own counsel and thought to himself, "what a devious blowhard!" He knew, and what the self-promoting Hoover failed to mention, was that by the time the Special Agents of the FBI arrived on the beach at Amagansett the Coast Guard had begun an investigation of its own. That evidence had already been moved to Coast Guard headquarters in New York City where special agents from the FBI New York office, in a ham-handed attempt to muscle their Coast Guard allies, managed to alienate every member of the Coast Guard team at the location. The rivalry set the search back by days, and the FBI, while conducting the greatest manhunt in the history of their organization, was totally clueless about who they were looking for or where to look.

But the bigger unmentioned secret known to Donovan was that without George Dasch, one of the Jacksonville team of arriving Germans, the two groups would have been out there sabotaging their targets without Hoover having any idea of how to stop them. Donovan knew for a fact that what was being billed as savvy police work was really just a lot of luck and of Hoover's able manipulation of the facts when reporting up the food chain.

Just a day or two after his arrival in Florida, Dasch, who had lived in the States before returning home to fight for the fatherland, had for whatever reason a change of heart and decided to turn himself in and confess before anything happened. In fact, when he first contacted the FBI to confess they thought he was a crackpot and almost turned him away. But after some convincing that he possessed a large amount of cash for no apparent reason they finally believed him and Dasch revealed the whereabouts of all eight Nazis and their explosives. While he was a Judas, his confession would later help him to avoid his own execution.

"That's the way it's supposed to work but, frankly, we were very lucky too." Colonel William Donovan was leery of Hoover's hold on domestic security. He wanted the President to know that this was not simply another bit of FBI genius, but that the capture of the would-be saboteurs was also based on a great deal of chance. The OSS, created to complement the FBI's domestic security effort by keeping tabs on the international intrigues was only a week old and already Donovan was feeling Hoover's big foot on his back. It was a cold relationship and it seemed at the moment that the territorial rivalry between the two agencies would overshadow any chance of a compatible alliance ever, but Roosevelt insisted they work in harmony.

"To be honest, the capture wasn't that hard once we knew they'd arrived." Donovan found it difficult to add any praise to his remarks. "We were lucky. Every one of these guys lived here before and spoke perfect English. They could have gotten away with it too."

Hoover ignored Donovan's faint praise, "capturing them was also good on another level. Once we had them they all sang like Caruso. They gave us the names of their local contacts and we are having a look at the explosives they had in the crates, some kind of new concoction we've never seen before. We've confiscated everything they had with them including a couple of those Telefunken spy radios."

"Now it's up to the military courts." Donovan chimed in.

"So, let me understand this. Two submarines, sight unseen, come within three hundred yards of a beach in Long Island and another in Florida. They land two teams of saboteurs along with explosives on the beach in each place and then they slip away into the night. What if no one was there to see them when they landed? How am I supposed to feel comfortable about that?"

Hoover remained unflappable. "The good thing is that the Coast Guardsman was there on duty and did what he was supposed to do and the Bureau caught all of them."

Donovan turned his head toward the wall and rolled his eyes. "If I may Mr. President," Donovan stood up and uncovered a large chart. "We now know that they had a big plan to blow up factories, railroads and bridges from the mid-west to the ports in New York, Baltimore and points south."

Roosevelt interrupted. "We've got a great deal on our plates right now. Sometime soon we will have many men on the ground in Europe. We have to maintain our ability to keep supplies moving. As I keep saying, we are the arsenal of democracy. Any disruption at all could doom us, and I fear, our British allies as well."

Donovan became professorial, "Well, Mr. Hoover's men did get 'em! And yes, the U-boat that dropped them off in Amagansett did come very close. It was a lot of luck, but it was also the product of vigilance. The Coast Guard on the beach actually saw the mother sub leaving with the tide in the dawn light. They were stuck on a sand bar maybe five hundred feet off the beach."

"What? Why didn't we blow them out of the water?"

"By the time the Navy arrived they were long gone, submerged and making tracks to the open ocean."

"Too bad!" Roosevelt sighed.

"And sir, this bit of ironic coincidence... they surfaced within sight of one of our big submarine listening antennas, the one's that we've built up and down the coast to triangulate on the wolf packs, but these fellows were under radio silence. Had they transmitted a single message we would have sunk them before they ever got here."

"In sight of a monitoring station, really!" Roosevelt was aghast and leaned back in his chair, "and why do you think they picked those two locations?"

"Our analysts think they chose Amagansett because, from that beach point getting on a train to New York City is easy."

Hoover interjected, "They all got on an early morning Long Island Rail Road train to Manhattan."

"In Florida we weren't as lucky." Donovan continued, "No one saw them at all, they just buried their stuff and disappeared. But it worked all out in our favor and Mr. Hoover's men got 'em all, the ones from Long Island and the ones from Florida."

The President stared at Hoover, "We got them all?"

"Yes sir."

"What if there are others already here or still to come?"

"We'll get them too."

Roosevelt stared at the wall map of the East coast facing them. "I hope so, this is an awfully long coastline, don't you think?"

June 27, 1942

2:30 p.m., New York City

"I may stay here on occasion, but this isn't going to be my home. I'm an inventor." The customer eyed the filthy pipes that ran nearly everywhere across the ceiling.

"Oh, you're an inventor! Very exciting in these times." Julius Scharfman's lame praise for a potential renter was obsequious and obvious, but he did what he could to sell this one. It was hard to attract anyone to even take a look at it even in good times. Now the war had made it worse. While in a reasonably convenient location, between First and Second Avenues on 81st Street, the apartment looked more like a dungeon than a place to live. Mold and mildew stains were visible on a number of the painted surfaces and might have been the result of rain, some leaky pipes, or just plain sewage oozing through the walls. No normal person was going to rent it as a home. Building inspectors had cited the unit as having "hydrostatic issues," but Scharfman was always ready with a few twenty-dollar bills so that those issues never became a part of any inspection reports.

"I'll be storing some cases here. I may be down here to build my projects from time to time, either me or one of my associates. Really, I'm just looking for a quiet out of the way place."

"This one is really quiet," he assured. No one will ever bother you here. 'Fact is, the first-floor apartment above you is occupied by an eighty-year old woman who is almost totally deaf and can barely see. You can make all the noise you want down here. If you want privacy you got it here. And, as an added benefit, which I'm not charging for, it's furnished. If you do need to stay here you got a bed over there, and there's chairs and a nice kitchen with a table."

The customer eyed the room. There were just a couple of small windows near the ceiling, opening into an airshaft. Ambient sunlight only crept in at noon when the sun was highest in the sky. He played down the benefits. "Don't crap me, it's dark and also smells bad, and that bed looks like it's infested with bugs."

The landlord sighed, "If you take it I'll throw in a new mattress. How about that?" The obvious negatives of the place made Scharfman anxious to please any possible tenant. Now he seemed to have a live one, so he changed the subject a bit, "Will you be living, er... working here alone?"

The customer avoided the question, "How much are you asking for a month?"

"Well, a prime space like this would normally rent in this neighborhood for at least twenty-five dollars a month, but I like you. I'll rent it to you for twenty."

The customer became a bit irritated, "Don't bullshit me. I can afford eighteen, maybe, but I would need a concession of a month's rent to be able to do it." Eugen Haupt had found the perfect apartment to house his father's "friend."

The landlord made a face, but in his head he was excited. Finally, I make some money on this shit hole! "Very well. Eighteen a month. I'll give you back your first month's rent if you stay till the end of a year."

"Deal!"

"I will be moving some things in here in the coming week or two I hope that the rats don't eat them," he said with a smile. "I'll pay the first month's rent on July first."

"That will be fine." Then, the landlord magically produced a lease form from his jacket pocket, "and what is your name?"

"Uh, my name is…" he hesitated for a fraction of a second and smiled, "…Canaris, Willy Canaris." He had to control himself to keep from laughing out loud. This fat Jew should only know to whom he's rented his filthy basement!

"Thank you Mr. Canaris. Please sign here, and here are your keys. You will enjoy your privacy."

"Thank you, Mr. Scharfman. I know I will."

June 29, 1942

6:15 p.m.

Paddy McGlade's Tavern & Grill was one of those little neighborhood restaurant-bars that embraced old-country Ireland in the New World. McGlade's was a popular local spot paneled in dark wood that always smelled like spilled beer and stale cigarette smoke. What gave McGlade's a special boost was its location, just under the El on the corner of on East 68th Street and Third Avenue, just about equidistant from the 19th Precinct and the Manhattan headquarters of the FBI. It was *the* neighborhood law enforcement gin mill, a quirk of urban arrangement that meant both off-duty cops and the occasional off-duty FBI special agents could be found there co-existing. The cops knew who the agents were and vice-versa, they just never socialized. The bar was long enough to accommodate separate clusters of both groups without their having to interact at all, but this evening even McGlade's long bar was not going to be big enough to keep them apart.

It had been a warm day and that made for a lot of thirsty people. The front door to the pub was wedged wide open to let in any cool air and by 6:00 p.m., McGlade's was very busy.

Himself was at the door greeting the arriving crowd made up of locals who had assumed their usual positions at the twenty-or-so bar stools leaving nothing but standing room. All that was fine with one group of diners who were in reasonably good spirits. FBI Special Agents James O'Rourke, Burton Chase, Phil Burke and Edmund Witcover. They avoided the crowd and sat down for a meal in a booth across from the cash register. As usual they were talking shop.

At about a quarter past six, Detectives Douglas Grover and Tim Murphy entered McGlade's and seeing the large crowd at the bar also found their way to a booth, albeit unknowingly the one directly adjacent to the four dining FBI agents. Murphy slid in and Grover cushioned his sore leg as he sat on the other side.

" 'Place is jumpin' tonight." Murphy looked around the room.

"Yeah. It's hot and there's a lotta thirsty people." Grover picked up a menu. Murphy did the same. As they pored over Paddy's carte-du-jour neither cop could help overhearing the conversation going on in the next booth. It was both odd and yet oh-so familiar. It was cop banter, but it was clearly the Feds doing the bantering.

"I don't think it all would have gone down the way it did last week without him. I have to tell you, I think this guy is the greatest snitch we have," said the voice that belonged to Special Agent Burke.

"Yeah. Yeah. Two more names, two more arrests. I think he's totally broken what's left of the bunds, heh, heh," snickered Special Agent Witcover.

Special Agent Chase added, "Yeah. He's a giant alright, but I hope he doesn't fuck up again. It was a tough one getting him off the hook back in April."

But Special Agent O'Rourke demurred in his praise, "I wouldn't be too in love with this asshole. He threw a cop off a fire escape and nearly killed the guy."

"Those cops should have been more careful," Agent Chase added with a snicker in his voice.

In unison Murphy and Grover lifted their eyes off the list of daily specials and stared at each other. Could it possibly be that seated directly alongside them in the very next booth was a group of FBI agents discussing someone who sounded an awful lot like Eugen Haupt?

Grover's voice went into a deep whisper, "Are you hearing this?"

"Yeah." Murphy nodded and rolled his eyes, but his personal meter of impending doom suddenly went off scale. He saw that the volcano seated across the table from him was on the verge of eruption.

"Yeah, but he didn't kill the cop and he's still our boy." Witcover smirked. "Besides, let's face it, he's far more important to the war effort than one cop."

"Too bad what happened to him, but that cop should have been more careful," Phil Burke opined.

"Holy shit! Fucking Haupt is an FBI snitch! That's how he got sprung!" The whisper in Grover's voice became huskier with his rising rage at the new information he was processing.

Murphy stared as his partner and watched him turn beet red. Before the older detective could do a thing about it Grover was on his feet and glaring down at the four Special Agents at the next table.

"Can it be that you gentlemen are discussing a scumbag burglar named Eugen Haupt?" By now Murphy was also on his feet with a hand on his partner's shoulder.

"Who the fuck are you?," sneered Special Agent Burton Chase?

"Just the unimportant cop who got thrown off a fire escape, dickhead." Grover was breathing hard. "I assume that you guys are the assholes who got him sprung."

The four FBI men were momentarily stunned and stared at each other in amazement. Witcover spoke first and stammered a bit, "Geez. You're the…? Holy crap. Look, I, I get it that you're pissed off, b' but, but, this is Bureau business and, and we can't talk about it."

"Well, allow me then. He's a burglar, a bullshit artist and a knee-cracker. He tried to kill me, and you sprung him. Worst of it all is that he's playing all of you."

"Calm down, Detective!" Witcover stood and faced Grover eye to eye, "First of all, we're all sorry about what happened to you, but this is national security business and unfortunately you take a second chair to that."

"So, meanwhile this creep can walk into anyone's bedroom in the middle of the night, tie people up in their underwear and steal everything they own because you bastards have him on a really loose leash." By now Grover had developed drops of spittle that were flying out of his enraged mouth.

Murphy tried to get his body between Grover and Witcover. "What, are you guys too fucking lazy to keep a tail on him?"

"Hey, calm down, Detective or I'll arrest you for obstructing a federal officer," Witcover chided.

"Arrest me? Fuck you and your Brooks Brothers suit!"

Agent Chase chimed in, "You need to drop this, Detective. I can't confirm who our man is, but I can tell you that you'd better stay away from him."

"Or, what?" Grover questioned.

"Or, you will find yourself and your job in deep shit, that's what."

At this point, Murphy could no longer contain his partner. Grover grabbed the tablecloth on the FBI table and yanked it hard. Unlike the magician's parlor trick where the table items remain in place when the cloth is yanked away, food and dinnerware flew up in the air and landed on the three seated special agents. In an ill-timed reaction, Witcover wildly threw a punch at Grover. Grover ducked and Witcover's fist caught Murphy on the right cheek. Murphy, a nearly twenty-year veteran and experience at subduing violent street heavies, quickly had Special Agent Witcover's arm in a tight hammerlock and was pressing the agent's face into the coat rack pole built onto the end of the booth. "Okay shithead, that's it! You slugged a police officer and you're under arrest."

"Fuck you!" yelled Special Agent Chase.

"No, fuck you," said Murphy! "You're all under arrest." He drew his service revolver and pointed it at the FBI men.

It was Special Agent O'Rourke who, with some of his wits still intact, interjected a tiny spark of sanity. "Guys, guys, what is this all about? Let's all calm down. Detective, put your weapon away before this gets out of hand."

"He slugged me," Murphy responded.

"And your partner here dumped food on all of us. Can we let this pass without getting into paperwork?" A valid threat it was, as nothing is more fearsome than the threat of paperwork, and this encounter could turn into the worst kind of paperwork of all. "How about letting go of Agent Witcover's arm?"

There was a long pause as the stunned regulars seated around the bar had all stopped drinking to watch the action. It was like the Giants playing the Dodgers at the Polo Grounds. Two home teams battling it out. The two cops' eyes scanned the spectators, as did the eyes of the FBI men. None of this would look good to either side's bosses. Murphy released Witcover's arm and Grover stepped back from the edge of the table. "Okay, you're not under arrest."

"Thanks." Witcover rubbed his bent bicep hoping for a quick return of his circulation and now had a sheepish look on his face. He turned to Grover apologetically, "look, we heard about your leg, sorry about that. We'll try to control our informant better."

Grover said nothing, but the red color in his face faded a bit now, down to a warm pink. Murphy replaced the hand on his partner's shoulder. "Let's go somewhere else to eat."

"Yeah, okay." Grover and Murphy withdrew through the open door and the amazed barflies, one by one, turned back to their drinks. The FBI men just stood next to the booth wiping food off their clothing, stunned.

June 30, 1942

8:11 a.m.

The early Wednesday morning was drizzly and damp and Eugen Haupt's shirt was soaking wet and he was feeling a chill. The large wood box wedged under his right arm was heavy and he had carried it for many extra blocks to lose anyone possibly tailing him to the basement apartment.

The box was branded with the words, Chateau Pinchon Lalande, Longueville, an oenologists catchphrase for a pricey thick red Bordeaux currently out of supply in a war-weary wine drought. The box was a special order that Haupt had picked up from Rudy Schroder's Wines on Lexington Avenue. Schroder's was a mecca for New Yorkers who craved French vintages no matter what the cost and Herr Schroder had the connections to obtain any wine at any time from anywhere. The Pinchon Lalande came unopened and directly from occupied France via Mexico. Even a war in Europe could not stop Schroder.

At his father's request three weeks earlier Haupt had placed a special request for the robust '32 Bordeaux. The order was very specific and, Haupt even specified the name of a man at the chateau who would be packaging it. Now that it had arrived Herr Schroder called Haupt notifying him. "Please come early tomorrow before we open. We don't want anyone jealously coveting your wine, do we?" Haupt was there before 8:00 a.m.

At the basement apartment on 81st Street, his right hand fumbled with the outside door key while he balanced the wine box with his other arm. Once inside the apartment he turned on the bare light bulb above the kitchen table, placed the crate on the counter and stared at it. Taking a large screwdriver out of his tool box he lifted the top off the crate. Just under a layer of straw packing material, there were three bottles of the '32 Pinchon Lalande, but below the wine bottles was the more important contents of the box. Haupt lifted out a small fiberboard suitcase, one that might go unnoticed as someone's overnight bag. He unsnapped the locks, took a look inside, then quickly closed it up and hid it in a small cabinet above the stove.

Haupt's next step was to befriend the deaf lady upstairs. Perhaps an offer of fine wine would do the trick. Then he had to do a bit of shopping. From the front door vestibule, he rang the buzzer to apartment 1A and he was surprised how quickly the buzzer rang back unlocking the door. A small gray-haired head peered outside her apartment door and caught

Eugen Haupt's smile. "Hello Mrs. Krauskoph. I am Willy Canaris your new downstairs neighbor. I've brought you a gift. May I come in to introduce myself better?"

10:16 p.m.

The 10:00 a.m. situation meeting wasn't going to start on time. Special Agent Harwick accidentally dumped an entire cup of hot coffee on himself in the hallway and Special Agents Flynn and Wentworth accompanied him to the men's room in case he had burns or needed help. The absence of the coffee trio left Special Agents O'Rourke, Chase, Burke and Witcover seated around a dark brown conference table shuffling their report papers and looking at notes. No one spoke. These were the men who, along with the trio in the bathroom, made up the FBI's Nazi squad in New York. Seven young FBI men, all lawyers, all experts with firearms, all very book-smart but not a one of them with any level of hands-on street-wise law enforcement experience. Fresh out of law school, each man had been recruited by a Bureau anxious to get the best and the brightest out there in the battle against fascism.

The FBI's New York office was just a stone's throw from the NYPD's 19th precinct house yet it might have been located on another planet. The occupants of the FBI building studied crimes that were written about in books. The NYPD wrote those books. The conference room faced south on East 69th street and sunlight poured in, quickly heating up the room. It may have been hot in there, but in this formal world, not one man removed a suit jacket nor loosened a necktie. Agents were expected to be in control of their wardrobe, their actions and their emotions at all times.

"Congratulations. The press has been calling the Director's office non-stop about the arrest of the saboteurs. That should make all of you happy today!" FBI New York office Deputy Chief Mike Foreman walked in and sat at the head of the table. "By my watch it's five after. Where is everybody?"

"Sir, Agent Harwick spilled some hot coffee on himself," offered Agent Witcover, "and Flynn and Wentworth went with him to the men's room."

"What is this, a goddamn girl's school? Is it impossible for Agent Harwick to clean himself up by himself?"

"I'll go get them," offered Agent Chase, another Princeton graduate. He got up and moved toward the door.

"Chase, just sit down and we'll wait for the prom king and his court to return." Foreman didn't suffer fools easily. He was also the only man in the room who actually had some real-life law enforcement experience. Foreman joined the Bureau when Director Hoover took over and was on the team that caught Public Enemy Number One, John Dillinger.

As if on cue the errant trio arrived back at the room entrance and immediately saw the displeasure in the boss's glare. "Sorry 'bout that sir," mumbled Agent Harwick, the most uncomfortable of the three of them. Harwick was not only apologetic but was indeed burned by the coffee and was now wet and stained as well.

"Okay let's begin," Foreman took his glare off Harwick. "Naval intel has been reading the mail over the last few days on submarine radio traffic in the Atlantic. They've picked up messages probably from Berlin to the sub commanders. What bothers the intel guys is that they were able to decode all the messages pretty easily. They and OSS think these messages have been designed to be easily decoded."

"What did they say sir," asked Harwick?

"All of them were short, very short. After the address information there were only two words, "Pastorius leben." I think that roughly translated means Pastorius lives. "Are you all aware that Pastorius is the code name of the operation that we broke up last week? Anyway, Navy intel feels that if the sub commanders are getting a message that the operation is still going on then they don't think we're done with this yet."

"Or maybe they just want us to think it isn't over yet," added Agent Witcover.

"That's possible too, and so are about a hundred other possibilities." Foreman grumbled as this was the kind of information that bosses got every day.

"Well, what if they sent this message to the sub commanders because they know we're listening and want us to think that more saboteurs are coming by sub," Witcover asked? "What if they want us to worry about subs? What if we do?"

Foreman looked around the table at his team. "Honestly, this information is as useless as it is useful. We don't know if there are more coming by submarine, and if there are we have no idea what their mission is. All we can do is try to find out more and that means we need to rely on your informants and your legwork. Just keep looking under every rock and somewhere you will find a saboteur." He paused, "Also, of course, we've got eight prisoners in custody and our team in D.C. is working them over, as we speak."

"Just speculating here sir, but it makes you kinda' wonder why the two teams, the Florida guys and the Long Island guys, knew about each other." O'Rourke opined, "I mean, need-to-know and all that?"

Foreman looked over at O'Rourke and smiled. "Good point. I don't know the answer to that one. So, to that end, and to also look into O'Rourke's question, I want you all to press your contacts on the street for any details or rumors of anything, no matter how trivial it might seem. Got that?" All in the room nodded. "Okay, now let's begin. Who's up first?"

Harwick overcame his burned thigh and wet pants to speak and all of the agents became serious. "Sir, biggest thing to report today is that the cop, Grover had his cast removed last week and is back on the job."

"Good for him."

"Yes, sir, but troubling for the Bureau sir. He and his partner, Murphy, cornered our prime informant recently in front of his home threatening him with harm and exposure if they caught him in the act of any crime."

O'Rourke, Chase, Burke and Witcover looked across the table at each other in surprise at the subject under discussion as they had all recently met both Grover and Murphy and were enlightened by the experience.

"Yes? So what? The S.O.B. shouldn't be committing any crime while he's under our eye. We know he's is a lying piece of crap, but he's our lying piece of crap and we gotta keep an eye on him. He's still a resource. Is it a problem?"

"Yes sir, no problem at all. He's an amazing source for us." Harwick was unaware of his fellow agents' barroom encounter of the previous week.

"It really strikes me as hard to believe that we're taking the side of a thief over a cop," Foreman sighed.

"Sir," Harwick, the team leader of the group handling Eugen Haupt, defended his informant, "I would recommend that you call the police commissioner and request that Detective Grover be officially told from the highest rank to leave the man alone. He's been solid. He has the confidence of a lot of former bund members, and he's given us lists of people to keep an eye on. We all know he's a petty criminal, but we're at war and his burglary skills are an asset. To my knowledge no one has been physically harmed during any of the so-called Katzenjammer burglaries, and we are not even sure that Haupt is that guy. He knows where to look for information and he knows how to get it."

"I kind of think that we do know he's the burglar, but we have to live with that. It's also pure luck that no one's been physically harmed except an officer of the NYPD," Special Agent Burke interjected.

"Yes, but according to Mr. Haupt, that was self-defense." Harwick sounded like Haupt's lawyer. "He says that he didn't know that Detective Grover was a cop."

O'Rourke stepped in… "Mr. Haupt? Please! That is a load of horse crap and we all know it." O'Rourke's eyes searched the faces of his colleagues. "Of course Haupt knew that it was the cops knocking on his door. Yes, no one has been harmed during one of his burglaries…YET! He's our responsibility. We need to stake this guy out better before he really does kill someone."

"He's not gonna kill anyone," Harwick was getting annoyed at the criticism of his team's snitch management. "Agent Witcover is on point and has him under direct control. He knows that if he…"

Witcover, unwilling to admit any problem with his snitch, just kept his eyes on the papers in front of him.

"Sir," Chase interrupted, "we have information that Detective Grover is still pretty intent in his pursuit of our informant. He may not follow orders to a degree that we would like."

"He's a loose cannon on the deck," sighed Burke, "but I gotta say, he isn't wrong to be that way."

Foreman felt outnumbered and agreed, "okay, I'll see what I can do to keep this Grover guy in line, but the man does have a legitimate beef and axe to grind. Haupt did throw him out of a window."

"Sir, it was not out of a window," Harwick corrected his boss, "Haupt threw the man off a fire escape."

Foreman glared an exasperated stare. "Thank you for that clarification Agent Harwick. I'll make sure that I emphasize the distinction when I deal with the issue with Commissioner Valentine."

July 1, 1942

8:45 a.m.

Detective Douglas Grover arrived at his desk and realized that he was about to have a bad day at work. All of the physical clues pointed to that. A bunch of case file folders littered the desktop, all but the one he was looking for. "Murph, did I give you my Katzenjammer file?"

"The one you were reading, with the Karl Haupt story?"

"That one... yeah."

"No. You had it on your desk last time I saw it." Murphy had his feet up on his desk. He was reading the Daily News.

"Well, it's not here anymore." Grover shuffled through the pile one more time. "It's gone. Someone took it."

"You sure about that?"

"Well, for one thing my desk looks like a team of monkeys was looking for something, and second the folder's gone."

"Who would take it?"

"I dunno, but it's not here and it's everything I had on Haupt. All that stuff I read to you and my surveillance notes, everything about him. What the hell happened to it?"

"You left it on your desk?"

"No. I had it in this drawer." Grover shoved some file folder aside in the biggest bottom drawer. "Gone!"

Murphy attempted to play down Grover's anger, but he could hardly mask his own. "Geez... Those sons of bit.... Someone really wants to kill this case."

"I can't replace the file... but it's not gonna stop anything."

"It's a warning to us... drop this thing... we know where you live." Murphy was as pissed off as his partner. "This is a goddamn police station for Christ's sake. You'd think that this is a place where things are not supposed to get stolen."

"Well, I don't wanna point any fingers..." his voice got loud enough for everyone in the room to hear him clearly, "...but someone in one of these offices is a thief and that dancing German nightcrawler seems to have a lot of friends in high places, dammit!"

"Hey, take it down a level!" Murphy, though angry, was worried that their boss was in earshot of the tirade. "Don't be a schmuck, you do not want to piss off the captain."

Grover lowered his voice but kept ranting. "You and me are officially off the case and he's still out there, loose."

"Yeah, and I don't think our boy is staying out of trouble either." Murphy thumbed through a pile of crime report forms on his desk. "I was waiting to tell you this, but there was another Katzenjammer style burglary last night in Yorkville with an old couple tied up in their kitchen."

"Shit! For real?"

" Yeah, yeah, for real."

"What about Cooper and Brody? Aren't they on Katzenjammer now?"

"They were told to stay away from Haupt. They weren't watching him."

"No one is watching him? Not even the FBI! This is bullshit ya know!"

"Yeah it is, and the husband had a heart attack after it was over."

"And of course, thanks to the Feds there's nobody paying any attention, right?"

"Uh huh, 'seems like he can do whatever the hell he wants."

"Did the guy die?"

"Nah, he survived. He's at Lenox Hill."

"And, of course, the feds don't have him under control at all, so now he nearly kills somebody and we can't touch him."

"As you speak it!"

"And then, to make sure his record stays clean someone in this place lifts my files."

"Here's the thing, and I am with you 100%, but if you push that line you're gonna get your ass in some hot water, and mine with it. You can't accuse the boss of any shit. He's being told what to do."

"So, now we have nothing to go on."

"Dougie, they lifted my file on Haupt two months ago while you were laid up. As far as I "officially" know Haupt is a solid citizen. We are not gonna win this one."

"I can't believe how this bullshit artist has everyone wrapped around his finger."

"Well he does, and that is that. Case closed. Leave it alone. Move on."

"Yeah, I suppose." Grover faced reality. There was no way that the NYPD was going to put the screws to Eugen Haupt. The fix was in.

Murphy lifted up his newspaper to change the subject as Grover began to reorganize the mess on his desk. There was an uncomfortable silence between them. After a minute Murphy attempted to change the subject. "Hey, did you catch this story about the saboteurs?"

"The Long Island guys?"

"Yeah. 'Reads like another amazing piece of FBI police work. I don't know how they do it day after day." Murphy read out loud the entire newspaper FBI account of the event, all about the Coast Guardsman, the saboteurs, the subs, the beaches and the explosives. "Yeah, it's some really amazing police work by our partners in law enforcement." Murphy's words oozed with scorn.

"What kind of police work? You met those guys. They couldn't find Santa in the Thanksgiving parade."

"Don't shoot the messenger. I'm just reading the paper to you."

"They obviously had some kind of a lead or they never could have shut it down so fast. They must have a snitch!"

"That is pretty obvious."

"What if... what if our boy Haupt is their snitch?"

"Jesus Doug, give it up! He's making you a little crazy? I get it. You're pissed at the FBI, you're pissed at the department and there's really not a lot you can do about it. All that's gonna happen is that if you keep it up you're gonna piss off the bosses."

"So we just sit here and let this guy go on tying people up in the middle of the night and stealing their stuff... maybe even murdering someone?"

"Yeah, until we actually catch him in person doing it."

"Yeah... but! I guess that the rules are kind of in his favor at the moment, don'tcha think?"

"My mother always thought I was the dimmest of her five kids. I guess she was right. Who said anything about us following the rules?"

Grover smiled. "Detective Murphy, let me be the first one to never be the one to doubt your resolve."

4:30 p.m., Berlin

The newspaper clippings from the American papers were three days old. The accounts left him momentarily sad and a bit weary of the entire process. "Eight Saboteurs Arrested In Daring U-boat Attempt." Canaris pored over the clippings at least three times before letting out a deep sigh. Operation Pastorius had been compromised and all eight of the saboteurs had been apprehended by the Americans. Execution as spies would become most likely their fate. "Those poor brave men. I must personally contact their families to give them the sorry news."

Yet, the pang of regret was momentary and his wave of angst swiftly passed. The truth was that Canaris had expected exactly this to happen. It was less of a surprise than an understood inevitability and really part of his overall plan. Yes, it was a sad moment as these men would surely die as convicted spies, but it was a necessary moment as well. Yes, it would have been a good thing if the teams had succeeded, but the most important part of their mission was totally unknown to them. Not one of them had questioned the rationale of why two teams of saboteurs landing from different submarines in different areas of the U.S. would have a need to have any knowledge of each other's existence. Surely they could have carried out their missions independently of one-another, and if one was caught the other would still be out there able to cause havoc. Canaris reasoned that had either or both teams remained at-large they might have made the second phase of the Operation more difficult, but with the capture of the eight saboteurs he rationalized that the path was clear for the next and more deadly wave to go into effect.

He read the headlines over one more time and tossed them into a wastebasket. Then he took out a small leather bound notebook from the locked center drawer of his desk. He made a diary entry about the progress of the mission and then put it back in the drawer. He reached his hand across his desk and pushed the talk button on his office intercom. "Fraulein Grof, would you please come in here?" With that summons the door swung open and the pert and efficient Hilda Grof entered with a pencil and a notepad.

"Yes, Herr Admiral?"

"We have received some sad news about the status of a secret mission. I will need to speak with members of these families." He handed her a list of names. "Please also see that each family gets a gift from me as well, a box of chocolates."

"Yes sir."

Fraulein Grof exited the office and Canaris began to gaze at his wall map. "Yes," he thought to himself, "everything is going exactly as planned!"

July 2, 1942

6:30 p.m., New York City

It was still early and uncrowded at Paddy McGlade's. Grover positioned himself at the back end of the lengthy oak and cherry wood bar, a no-man's land out of the way of the waitresses and foot traffic to the bathrooms.

He had been sitting in the same spot staring into an untouched shot glass full of some amber liquid he had ordered about half-an-hour earlier. Grover never drank alone, in fact he wasn't much of a drinker at all. The truth was that Grover rarely drank anything more than an occasional beer. Drinking to forget stuff was morose, but then, at this moment, Grover was morose.

In the past when he wasn't working a late shift he would have dinner with Ellen, but this evening she was spending it with her sister in Hoboken and Grover was alone, in a bar, and all by himself. His leg was killing him and though the contents of the glass might work well as an anesthetic he hadn't sipped it once, but he really didn't need to get drunk, he needed the pain. The sting in his leg reminded him of Eugen Haupt and a yearning for revenge.

Before he left the hospital Grover's doctors had explained that because of the nature of the fracture it would heal quickly, but that he would probably experience a lot of pain during that process. They gave him morphine. Since the morphine ran out he had been taking aspirin. Tonight, without Ellen around he decided to try hard liquor as a painkiller.

Grover's blank stare focused on the faces of customers entering the bar's front door. He's only been at the bar for around ten minutes when he noticed a familiar face come in. It was that FBI agent who kept him from beating the shit out of the other agent during their face-off. Their eyes met and the agent, also alone, joined Grover at the back of the bar.

"Greetings. Remember me?" The FBI guy stuck out his right hand, "Jim O'Rourke."

"Yeah, I'm Grover, Doug Grover, good to see you again. Have a seat."

"Thanks." O'Rourke sat and ordered a whiskey, but there was no small talk. This may have been a chance meeting but he got right to what was on his mind. "Doug, can I call you Doug? You know, aside from what you think, we're all embarrassed about what happened to you and what we've been able to do about it."

"Oh?" Grover did remember that O'Rourke was the rational one at the table that day. Yeah, O'Rourke was probably okay, he thought. "Thanks for that."

"Y'know I understand where you're coming from. My dad was on the job in Boston, and two of my uncles too. All livin' that Boston Irish cop life."

"Oh? I come from a cop family too, part of that great Jewish crime-fighting tradition. There was no place left for me to go after I got out of high school."

"My dad was a cop, but my mom taught math at B.U. She made sure I went to get a degree. I decided to be a lawyer then Mr. Hoover recruited me." O'Rourke sipped his drink. "So, how've ya been? Bygones?"

"Yeah. Bygones. Everyone got a little too steamed too fast... I guess me in particular."

"Yeah. Lookit, we're all on the same team. We're all after the bad guys, huh?" O'Rourke motioned to the bartender pointing at his empty shot glass.

"But the one bad guy that I care about at this moment has got you guys wrapped around his little finger."

"Nothing I can do about that. There's a war going on and somehow he knows all kinds of stuff that we need to know."

"I dunno what kind of shit he's feeding you, but I'll bet you he's making it up. You know what he does at night?"

O'Rourke sighed in anticipation of a rant. He attempted a short-circuit, "yeah, he's a cat burglar."

The rant came anyway. "Here's what he does. He leaves his place at around three in the morning, puts on a mask and breaks into peoples' houses while they're sleeping. If they wake up while he's there he ties them up in their underwear and steals everything they own. After all these months we had him one night and he threw me off a fire escape."

"Doug, I'm gonna tell you one tale out of school. If you tell anyone what tell you I will deny it and call you a liar to your face."

"Yeah?"

"If you had busted him that night for breaking into the bakery we would have got him out because he was working for us. There was information in that bakery that we needed to see, but because you guys chased him out of the store, we never got those papers. You guys became an unforeseen complication. There's a war going on. Do you understand?"

Grover was speechless and just stammered a response, "So, uh, are you saying he's not the Katzenjammer... and you're admitting that he's an FBI informant?"

"Could be, but I can't say anything more."

"Well, let me tell you, he's also a fucking liar and a con artist. He's set up the perfect business for himself. He makes stuff up, tells it to you guys, and then he's free to terrorize the neighborhood."

"You may not like it, but he knows stuff that we need to know."

"Where's he getting his information from?"

"He has sources, I dunno. Here's another secret you can't tell anyone. He was the guy who dropped a nickel on where the Nazis who landed in Long Island were hiding out. Bureau got 'em all."

"So, have you thought about this, how does Haupt know about Nazis? He never leaves his apartment except to climb in peoples' windows at night." The skeptical wheels in Grover's skull were beginning to spin at a rapid pace. There was obviously a side of Haupt's persona that escaped the surveillance efforts of Grover and Murphy.

"Everything he's told us has been on the money. We don't know who his sources are, but… Lookit, these were bad guys who were gonna blow up trains and factories. They were gonna kill people and Haupt was the guy who led us to them."

"Is he on your payroll?"

"I can't talk about that."

"Well, if he is I think he's stealing from you too." Grover couldn't let it go.

"He's not."

"What if he's playing both sides? What if he's a Nazi spy and they're feeding you a ton of shit through him and you only think he's important?"

"Look Doug…"

"Yes?" This was turning into a relationship.

"I'm not going to say any more just, this is an important guy for us. I get it that you think he's a scumbag and all that, but he gets the goods. He's in with what's left of the bunds. He gets information to where the bodies are buried… he has sources." Grover's new friend O'Rourke stared directly into his eyes. His voice was pleasant enough, but there was also a tough edge to it.

A similar toughness came across Grover's face. "Then put a leash on him because the next time I catch him, if I catch him out there, I will bust his ass and tell the Mirror that we finally caught the Katzenjammer Burglar. Once it's in the papers his usefulness to the FBI will be bullshit because I'm sure he'll sing about his contacts with you guys. Hey I gotta go. Let's do this again real soon." With that Grover rose up from his bar stool and swaggered out the door on his bad leg. O'Rourke looked down at the bar, shrugged, reached over and finished Grover's untouched whiskey.

10:42 p.m., Berlin

"Is this the building, Herr Admiral?" Horst Wenzl pulled Canaris's car close to the curb at an unmarked door to a non-descript building somewhere on the outskirts of Berlin.

"Yes Horst, this is the place." It was dark and the Admiral did not want to be seen by anyone. He remained in the back seat of the Mercedes until his adjutant gave him an all clear that the street was empty.

"I will wait for you here sir."

"Good."

"Herr Admiral, welcome." A tall man in a lab coat greeted him at the door and immediately led Canaris down a long corridor. Two machine-gun armed soldiers wearing the insignia of the Waffen SS shadowed their passage to a locked steel door. The man in the lab coat opened the door and he and Canaris entered a large room leaving their SS escorts on the other side. The Abwehr leader scanned the concrete walls and very high ceiling, perhaps at least ten to fifteen meters high, he guessed.

"Admiral, what I am about to show you is the product of two years' research." No more pleasantries, the guide got down to business. "We have been experimenting with compact explosives for some time here."

"I am interested to see what you've come up with, Doktor."

"What I will show you first is a comparison."

"I am here to be amazed."

Canaris followed the man into a thickly walled space with baffled mirrored observation ports. "Admiral, for our safety please, we will watch from here." Through the mirrored window Canaris stared at the reflection of the experiment in front of him. "First I will detonate 10 grams of our current most potent explosive."

"This is the same material you recently provided?"

"Yes Admiral." The chemist had no idea how or where his explosives were being used. "I hope that it is helpful to the Führer's war efforts?"

"Yes, very helpful." Canaris made no mention that his Pastorius teams had been arrested and those explosives were now probably in the hands of American munitions experts.

"All clear," came a voice seemingly out of nowhere. Canaris's eyes moved to the observation window. Three loud beeps sounded followed by a loud bang. Canaris saw a cinder block wall placed roughly one meter from the explosion showing significant damage from perhaps a tablespoon of explosive material.

"Sir, the test you just saw used what is currently the most powerful explosive in the German army's arsenal, at least ten times more potent than

Trinitrotoluene. Now I will show you our newer version. Its added benefits include much more stability and much, much more power."

Technicians re-set the demonstration. They wheeled in another unbroken cinder block wall and set it the same distance from the test stand.

"Admiral," said the scientist, "the only difference in this second experiment is that we will use only five grams of the explosive to make our point."

The technicians exited the room. "All clear!" Three loud beeps sounded again then came a blast that shook the thickly walled protective bunker. Once the fans blew the smoke out of the room Canaris was amazed by what he saw. The cinder block wall had been turned into rubble, not one block remained in any original shape.

"And that was half the amount of the other one?" Canaris's face was expressionless.

"Yes sir. Half."

"How much of this do we have? "

"Admiral, we can give you at least fifty kilos within a month, but that fifty kilos will have the blasting power of nearly one thousand kilos of our other most powerful explosive."

"Only, we need it now, not years from now."

The scientist nodded. "Yes Herr Admiral."

Canaris had questions, "and what are the handling difficulties?"

"Difficulties? Really none at all. It is very stable. It will not detonate unless it is exposed to a flame or an electrical charge. You can smash it with a hammer and unless the hammer makes a spark nothing will happen, however, just a small… a very small spark or electrical charge will set it off.

"Amazing!"

"Would you like to hold a piece of it in your hand?" The scientist lifted a small glass canister from his desk and removed a small chunk of what looked like a caramel candy.

"Hmmm… it feels soft and malleable. You could make this into shapes…"

"Yes that is possible. It is very easy to work with and poses little danger to the soldier unless it is properly detonated. Another benefit of this new material is its chemical stability. It is much safer to transport and has a practically unlimited useful life. I believe it could retain its potency for perhaps even decades."

"Ha! It smells… it smells exactly like fresh pastry, maybe marzipan… doesn't it?" Canaris smiled.

"Ha! Yes sir, but with a much, much longer freshness. It can be easily transported safely and stored for years as long as it's kept away from fire or sparks."

"I am both pleased and amazed. We will need those fifty kilos sooner than a month."

"Absolutely sir! We will have it ready for you."

"Oh, Herr Doktor, one more thing."

"Yes?"

"This work you have been doing must remain secret."

"Of course, it is secret."

"I mean that it must remain in the control of the Abwehr. No one else must know about it unless I am the one to tell them. Do you understand?"

"Our research was done under your orders. It will remain that way."

"Good," and with that, Canaris thanked the chemist and left the building.

July 3, 1942

10:30 a.m., New York City

This Friday morning at the 19th was very quiet. The start of a holiday weekend with no calls coming in, had Grover and Murphy relishing the unusual quiet time back in the house.

Grover, still obsessed with Eugen Haupt, had his nose in a folder that the file thief had missed. "Y'know, we're still missing a big piece of this asshole's M.O. here. Somehow he's got an ear on the German spy shit."

"Can't we talk about something else," Murphy sighed? "Sports? Betty Grable? Anything?"

"He's a bad guy. He is wrong and we are the good guys, and…"

"Yeah, yeah, yeah, I know, I know. And, we are the ones who have to protect the citizens from this evil bastard." All that Murphy could do at this moment was to look for a doorway to get out of the room.

"Yeah, but, I…"

"Look, if you really wanna get into this, but seriously, there's one thing we have not looked at."

"Yeah?"

"If he is the Katzenjammer burglar what's he doing with stuff that he steals? Where does it go?"

"He's either fencing it right away or he has a stash place that we still gotta find. If we follow him we will…"

"Do I gotta remind you one more time? We've been forbidden by that man in that glass walled room over there from following him. I seem to remember that there was some kind of career threat in his voice."

"Murph, you're not gonna let something as stupid as that get in the way of solid police work, are you?" Feigning sanity, Grover put on a smile to suggest he was joking around.

As if on cue, at that moment Captain McCluskey appeared at the doorway to the detective's room. He looked over at Grover and Murphy and summoned them to his office with the beckon of a flexed index finger.

"I'm getting a little tired of hearing about you from the people downtown." McCluskey sounded frustrated but, oddly, not angry.

"Boss, we have followed orders and stayed away from the guy," Murphy protested.

"Well then, why am I getting calls from the commissioner's office saying that you're still chasing Haupt?"

Grover knew exactly why but denied it, "I dunno?"

"The commissioner says that the FBI called him and complained that detective Grover is obsessed with Haupt and he threatened to tell the newspapers."

Grover just stood there, blank-faced, and Murphy stared down at his shoes.

"Hear me now and hear me well. Stay away from Haupt and don't even speak his name anywhere near another law enforcement officer. If you do, the consequences will be extreme, I promise you that."

Like two schoolboys caught peeking into the girls' bathroom window, they sheepishly nodded in agreement and in unison said, "yes sir."

"Good," McCluskey just stared at Grover. He paused and then in the calmest voice imaginable said, "Detective Grover, I think you understand my point of view. Now get out of my office. Oh, and thank you for your time."

July 4, 1942

9:42 a.m., Berlin

What do they want me to do now, he wondered? Why is it so damn cold in here? He was uneasy but unsure of exactly why. He had been summoned by someone, he did not know who, to this sub-basement warren of officious rooms in the Berlin Wehrmacht headquarters. His superior officer told him, "They will be waiting there for you." *Where exactly was "there?"* Having made his way through long hallways to the leather chair in which he was now seated, he was somewhere under Berlin. Adding to his confusion, he was an army officer and this was the Seekriegsleitung, the directorate of the German naval war effort. *What do they want with me?*

No doubt, someone would soon tell him of the special task that only he could accomplish. They would play up the honor it would be for him to complete this mission for the Führer and the Reich. He'd heard that nonsense many times before and disregarded it. He was just a loyal German soldier whose unusual skills were the reason for him being here. He had never joined the Nazi party. They must know that, but they don't care.

It was down here, deep beneath street level, where the war planners made their chess moves. The place made him nervous but he was good at masking his emotions. His training and instincts taught him to leave nothing behind for anyone to remember. He was short in stature but muscular. His vision was perfect yet he wore eyeglasses made with plain lenses, an easy way to change one's appearance in a hurry. His complexion was average as was his unstylish average man's haircut. His round face was friendly but easily forgettable. He was dressed in an inelegantly tailored gray wool suit that no one would ever give a second glance. In his line of work he needed to be a ghost and he was perfectly suited for that.

The only person in this anteroom with him was a young secretary with blond hair tied into a tight bun. She was slim and her crisp white naval uniform blouse fit snugly revealing an ample bosom and a tight waist. He couldn't see her legs beneath the desk but he could see her sleeve emblazoned with a Kriegsmarine arm patch. What caught his eye even more than this Aryan beauty were the large double oak doors just to the right of her desk. On another day he might have tried his charm with her but this wasn't the time. Suddenly one of the huge doors swung open and an elegant man in an admiral's uniform approached to greet him.

"Hello Wolfgang, may I call you by your first name, or is that not your first name at all?"

At the first sight of the uniform he became flummoxed. This man is one of the big ones! Reflexively his right arm swung up at a 45-degree angle Nazi salute. "Uh, no it isn't, yes, sir, of course. Thank you, er… Heil Hitler," he muttered

"Yes, Heil Hitler," the man in the admiral's uniform returned the salute in a half-hearted way and smiled at Wolfgang's apparent discomfort with his rank. "You know you have the same name — or is it a code name? — as my most favorite composer."

"He was my father's favorite as well. Sir, I am trained to tell no one my actual name, but I am pleased that my code name reflects his musical tastes." The face in the admiral's uniform was familiar, but he couldn't immediately place it.

"Well, it is good you could make it today Wolfgang. We have much to discuss. Come in please. Oh yes, I supposed I am allowed to share my name with you," the Admiral smiled, "I am Wilhelm Canaris," he said. His right arm, the one just used for the obligatory heil salute, made a sweeping motion beckoning Wolfgang inside.

Now Wolfgang knew exactly with whom he was dealing. Wolfgang had heard of Canaris but they had never met. So far in his professional "career" he had done work only for the army and the Luftwaffe. In the course of the war so far he had been of great use to Himmler and Goering. He was now being summoned by the sly fox himself to complete a mission that he was certain would jeopardize his life.

Wolfgang heard stories that Canaris was a master chess player who also had Himmler's confidence and Hitler's ear. Whatever the chatter, this man was all-powerful with total responsibility for Germany's military intelligence effort. Yet, he seemed amiable and oddly without the coldness of most men of his rank.

"Please have a seat." Wolfgang parked himself in the center of a leather sofa and as his eyes scanned the room he saw that he and Canaris were not alone. Four other men were already seated in the grand office's conference area. One by one they nodded a greeting as Wolfgang's eyes met theirs. Two of the four were in uniform; a rather frightening looking young naval officer of some unknown rank with a large scar on his face and a tanned, blond, ruddy-faced man who wore the rank of Leutnant zur See. The other two men were dressed in expensive civilian clothes. Gestapo?

Canaris folded his lanky figure into a comfortable high backed chair. "As we are all stressed for time these days, allow me to get to the point," He gestured to the blond officer at his right, "Wolfgang, this is Kapitan Heinrich Garbers. He, like yourself has been summoned here today because of special skills. Skills, that if applied properly, will shorten the war and ensure Germany's supremacy."

Wolfgang nodded attentively.

Garbers stood and offered a hand to the new arrival. "Pleased to meet you."

Wolfgang shook his hand and wondered why the other men in the room didn't offer the same social greeting. "Pleased to meet you as well.

Canaris immediately got down to business, "Herr Wolfgang, let me ask you, would you use a sledgehammer to swat a moth? Would you use a fire hose to extinguish a match?" Perhaps not. That would be overdoing it, and you might injure yourself." He smiled. "The German Navy is without a doubt the strongest sea power in the history of the world, yet there are some missions that require something more discreet than a battle group to accomplish."

One of the men in plainclothes spoke without looking at Canaris. "We've been reading about your work." He quickly thumbed through pages of an official looking report. "Most impressive. You're a man who can improvise with apparently spectacular results."

Canaris continued, "Now, allow me tell you about Kapitan Garbers' skills and then we will discuss yours in more detail after that. A year ago I gave Herr Garbers orders to go to Brest in France to find an innocent looking ship to safely transport our agents to Africa and South America. He immediately grasped the challenge and quickly came to the conclusion that any ship crossing the Atlantic, no matter how innocent looking would become the subject of enemy naval scrutiny. Kapitan Garbers thought of a better way to accomplish his mission."

"You give me too much credit Herr Admiral. It was a simple observation that you yourself noted before my first mission." Garbers demurred.

Canaris accepted the acknowledgement, "yes but Kapitan Garbers also knew that enemy spies in Brest would take note of any large vessel leaving port for parts unknown but would pay little attention to a pleasure craft. So, as a lifelong yachtsman and former competitive sailor who had raced vessels while a cadet at the Marineschule Mürwik, he surmised that a private yacht would draw very little attention, especially if it was flying the flag of a neutral nation. Instead of a presenting himself as a German officer commandeering a large vessel for the German navy he posed as a foppish wealthy Swiss yachtsman looking to buy a vessel for cash. He was very convincing."

"I told the yacht broker I simply wanted to escape this silly war in Europe. The French are a greedy race and it wasn't hard to do at all. No one checked out my background after they saw the wad of Swiss Francs in my pocket." Garbers smiled.

"Yes, and within a day a yacht broker introduced Herr Garbers to a 55-foot luxurious sailboat, now a clandestine vessel owned by the Kriegsmarine." Canaris enjoyed telling the tale.

"When I first saw her I was sure that she would be perfect for the task at hand. To make it more believable I haggled on the price a bit, and the broker said that the seller would be disappointed with my offer, but he would present it anyway. He said that the seller was a down-on-his-luck French landowner whose vineyards were decimated by those, pardon my language, fucking Germans!"

The two plain clothed men had not heard this part of the story before and looked at each other with cold smiles. No doubt someone will deal with the yacht broker's loyalties at another time.

"Herr Wolfgang, do you sail?," Garbers asked.

"No, I never have. I'm a creature of dry land."

Canaris rose from his chair and picked up a pile of glossy photos from his desk. They were of a beautiful sailing yacht. He handed them to Wolfgang. "On examining the boat before the purchase it was clear to Kapitan Garbers that it has been excellently maintained and well equipped over the years. The sale was so normal that even the British spies in Brest would be jealous rather than suspicious."

"Well, I am not a boatman, but it is a pretty vessel."

"Within a day of the purchase, four of my old academy friends, all now officers in the Navy, arrived in Brest to sail her, and through the Reich's help they all had papers as Swiss nationals. She's called Pessim, and since we bought her she's transported many of our agents across the ocean without any naval interference at all."

"Across the ocean?" Wolfgang was getting the idea that this mission would be on much grander scale than any he'd ever been on before.

"Yes, she's been to Africa, Brazil and Argentina. We have never been approached by any naval vessel, let alone being stopped."

Canaris stepped back into the conversation. "Wolfgang, for the sake of security no one, not even any of the men in this room despite their total loyalty to the Reich and their lofty security clearances, will know any of the specific details of your mission. Those will be only between you and I. They may guess at what you're up to but they have agreed that they would enjoy hearing the news of your success as a surprise." Canaris smiled. "We have read your dossier. You're a man with profound particular skills, so with that in mind let me ask these gentlemen to leave us alone and I will tell you about what you will do for the fatherland."

July 5, 1942

12:30 p.m.

"I guess you could call this a date?" Grover said sheepishly.

It was July 4th weekend, and even during wartime while the U.S. Army Air Corps and the RAF were laying down bombs on the German aerodromes in Holland, thousands of miles from the front lines of the fracas, Ellen Kramer had finally convinced Detective Douglas Grover to pause for relaxation. "I keep saying this but you need to learn how to ease up a little bit, you need to learn how to relax," she scolded. Grover, unfortunately, didn't have a clue.

They decided to take the subway and bus to spend the day on a blanket at Orchard Beach in the Bronx. It was a newly built sandy patch on the sheltered saltwater of Western Long Island Sound and much safer from attack than the open Atlantic ocean exposure of Coney Island. But, it was also much smaller than Coney Island and by late morning when they arrived the sand were already packed with sunbathers and wildly romping children.

"Here's a spot!" Grover found a vacant ten square feet and staked his claim to it. He sat down on the blanket and ogled at Ellen as she stripped to the bathing suit under her street clothes.

"Hey, pervert! Don't look at me, take your own clothes off!" She mocked him and dashed into the Sound.

Grover obliged and within a few seconds he was standing beside her in the water. It was really a perfect day, "El, thanks for making me come out here. It's nice."

"Glad you could make it. It's really hard to get you to let go even a little bit."

"I've got a lot going on." He looked down from her face to the long scar on his left leg where the compound fracture had broken through his skin.

"Well, why don't you let me make it a bit easier on you." She took his hand and started to move into the water. As they got in chest deep he pulled her close to him and kissed her hard on the lips. She was surprised for a second, as the usually non-sensual Grover had never done anything like that before. With that she wrapped her arms around his neck and kissed him back. The warmth of her body pressed against his in the cool water felt good and he didn't really want to let go, but the magical mood was suddenly shattered by loud "ooooohs" and "ahhhhs" coming from the crowded beach. "Oh dear!" Ellen's face turned beet red. Grover's embarrassment turned into something else. He poised himself to charge the beach and intimidate any-one who would have the gall to make fun of his brief romantic minute. "Doug... forget it. They're just having some fun. When do you stop being a cop?" Grover cooled down and despite his temper he was in a good mood.

For the next couple of hours they swam, they sunbathed and they talked. He bought her an ice cream sandwich from the vendor and then they swam, sunbathed and talked some more. He just never stopped being the cop, always a sentry in a dangerous world. It was during one of those moments that someone caught his eye. Less than a hundred feet away a large, very pale man was prone on a beach blanket and looked like he had spent too much time in the sun. Geeze, this guy is gonna really suffer later when he gets home. But in addition to his sympathetic feelings, there was also something familiar about the guy.

Ellen noticed a sudden pained look on Grover's face and it made her anxious. "Doug, is everything OK?

"Uh, yeah. I guess. Yeah everything is fine."

"What are you looking at?"

"Uh, there's a guy over there who looks familiar, that's all. I can't place him." It was a lie because Grover had already placed him. It was the same mug he had encountered that April night on the fire-escape.

"El, give me a second. I know that guy. I'm just gonna go over and say hello, okay?" He got up to approach the sunbathing Eugen Haupt, conve-niently forgetting that he was forbidden from doing so.

"Sure." Ellen saw no harm in her boyfriend going to say hello to a pal.

Grover slowly walked across the sand. Though the sunbather was now face down with his nose buried in a towel, Grover knew exactly who it was. "Pretty bad sunburn you got there pal."

Eugen Haupt looked up squinting and immediately recognized who was staring at him. "Detective, so good to see you again!" There was that mocking tone in the voice. "How odd that we're sharing the same resort spot, no?"

"Still tying up old people in their skivvies?"

"Detective, as I've told you before I know nothing about any of this." Haupt smirked and then noticed the long scar on Grover's leg. "My good-ness, that must have been painful!"

Grover ignored the taunt, "so, what are you doing here? Shouldn't you be out there ratting on your kraut buddies to the Feds?"

Grover's remark visibly irked Haupt, but he remained cool. "Detective, I have no idea what you're talking about, but what I do know is that you are supposed to leave me alone. I will sue the police department if this harass-ment continues."

"Okay, I will leave you alone. You might not see me, but just know that

I will be watching you, and the next time you do see me it will be when I bust your ass. Understand?"

"I do understand. I certainly do," Haupt's response was syrupy and poorly hid his building rage. "Now if you will allow me to take advantage of this beautiful sunshine I would like to be left alone. Perhaps you should go back to your girlfriend over there, Miss Kramer I believe it is, isn't it?"

Even in the broiling heat of the sun an icy shiver seized his gut and he felt as if he was about to breathe fire. He knows Ellen's name, he must also know where she works and lives. "Listen shithead, this is between just you and me. If I hear anything about you bothering, or even looking cross-eyed at anyone close to me I'm gonna come after you. I really don't give a shit what the FBI says. At that point it will be personal."

"Once again Detective, you've misunderstood me."

A grin came onto Grover's face and with it he got down on one knee and said, "Well anyway… hey, great to see you old friend!" Then he chummily whacked the palm of his right hand between the shoulder blades on Haupt's sun singed back. Haupt yelped in pain as Grover got up and walked back to his blanket and Ellen.

"Who was that you were talking with?"

"Just a guy I met on the job. He has a really bad sunburn. I think he's gonna be in a lot of pain tonight. Hey, I really don't wanna get a burn like that. How 'bout we wrap it up here? Maybe you wanna get some seafood on City Island? There's a great place for fried clams at the end of the Avenue there."

"Sure." She said happily. They quickly dressed, rolled up their blanket and headed for the bus.

July 7, 1942

6:03 a.m., Washington, D.C.

"Harriet, is there any coffee anywhere?" Wild Bill Donovan arrived at his desk unusually early.

"Yes sir, brewing now. It'll be ready in five minutes."

Yesterday's mound of papers was exactly where he left it the night before. His goal was to get through all of it by the time his team arrived for work. Then it dawned on him that his new assistant, on the job for only two days, was at her desk earlier than he was, and at least two hours before her scheduled in-time. "Say, you're in bright and early, aren't you?"

"Sir, as you told me when you interviewed me, there's a war going on." Harriet Winston, a recent Mount Holyoke grad with a rumored photographic memory could recite every word of that earlier conversation but chose not to show off.

"Yeah, that's a fact. Thanks for putting yourself out and getting here so early." In his new job Colonel William Donovan, a hero of the Great War, was in charge of the first ever U.S. agency dedicated to the gathering of intelligence world-wide. His fledgling OSS was growing bigger every day.

"Sir, can I ask a question?"

"Of course."

"I've been working here for two days, but no one has been able to tell me why this agency exists." Born roughly the same week as the German submarine incursions, the OSS was a wartime agency created from necessity.

"Hmmm?"

"We already have the FBI. How are we different?"

"Pretty simple. The rules say that the FBI deals with domestic stuff, Naval Intelligence deal with the Navy, Army Intelligence deals with the Army, and the Office of Strategic Services deals with the rest of the world."

"Are we spies?"

"Not specifically, but we're here to gather intelligence for the war effort." Donovan removed his jacket and hung it on the back of his office chair. "Even before last December 7th, President Roosevelt was concerned about America's deficient intelligence efforts. The Japanese attack made having an agency like this much more necessary."

"So who do we give the information to when we get it, the FBI?"

"Hmmm, you are asking some really political questions here. No, it's our choice. We share information with the affected services as well as the

President. When we think there's something that the FBI needs to know we tell them, but otherwise, no." Donovan sat down staring at the paper piles. Taking that as her cue to leave the boss alone, Miss Winston backed out of the office.

Donovan, who just a year earlier had been Roosevelt's special envoy to Belgrade and was the diplomat who had attempted in vain to talk those crazy Slavs out of joining the pact with Germany and Italy, was now the head of the brand-new Office of Strategic Services. In his previous job there was much less reading to do. Reaching into the first stack of papers, he realized that Miss Winston had separated the administrative material from the rest. There were memos, requisition forms, a few budgetary authorizations for men's' and ladies' room supplies, typewriter purchases and a special request for disappearing ink and flash paper.

The second pile was more interesting. There were intelligence analyses of German gasoline stores. Hmm they seem to have plenty of fuel! Luftwaffe manpower estimates, where are they training their pilots? And intercepts of secret ciphers from the U-boat fleet. One note was more ominous, a decoded and translated memo to the German submarine fleet. What made it interesting to Donovan was its source, an Abwehr Enigma machine enciphered this message.

The Enigma machine, an encoding/decoding device developed by the German military, resembled an extremely over complicated typewriter with rotating wheels and switches. In simple terms, the operator would adjust the machine's wheels to a setting, write a message and the machine would translate it into an unbreakable code, and vice-versa. Each day the settings would change and without the knowledge of the settings without a similarly set Enigma machine coded messages would come out as gibberish. Out of all that, the Germans remained totally confident about Enigma's enigma. But in July of 1941, the British were able to quietly capture a machine and under the direction of the brilliant mathematician Alan Turing, were able to figure out how it all worked. Using the secretly obtained Enigma machine, Turing and his team of puzzle solvers came up with a code breaking technique they called "Banburismus." All of a sudden the British knew how to decode the German communiqués and were very successful keeping that situation totally quiet, that is except for the British allies in Washington. Turing's team could even determine which branch of the German military was sending the messages. Turing and his team were able to break every new variation of the Enigma code without the Germans ever finding out.

Donovan's eyes focused on the message. It was short and unclear but none-the-less chilling. It read simply, "Pastorius progress good. Good hunting ahead." His brain wrestled with the words. "Pastorius," the OSS and

FBI had learned from the interrogation of the captured would-be saboteurs, was the code name for the operation. This note sent within the past 48 hours from an unknown source to a most likely need-to-know recipient, coded by an Abwehr Enigma machine claimed that progress was good. How could that be? We got them all, didn't we?

Miss Winston knocked on his door and entered with a large white mug filled with hot coffee. "Here you are sir."

"Thank you," he waited for his secretary to exit. When the door was shut he reached for the final item in the pile, a dark green envelope, the kind that conveyed the most secret of secret documents meant for Donovan's eyes only. Donovan sliced it open and read it carefully. Once he digested the message he crumbled the note into a ball and placed it in his desk ashtray. With the strike of a match the flash paper on which it was written vaporized and the secret message from inside the Nazi HQ in Berlin was vaporized. Then he called out, "Miss Winston, I need to speak with Mr. Hoover immediately."

7:00 a.m., New York City

"I became a cop partly because I got a D in High School English. It seemed like the perfect move at the time!" Murphy grumbled as his two fingers searched the typewriter keyboard for the proper letters to type on the arrest form. "I should be on the street, not writing a crime novel." Paperwork was the department's way of humbling even the most attentive officers.

"I know, I know, but this one was your turn."

Murphy glared in a friendly way, "My turn?"

"Yeah, I wrote the last one up, you do this one and I'll get the next one," Grover said with a laconic smirk.

"Stuff like this makes me sorry I went out for coffee." Yesterday, the Monday after the July 4th weekend, they were leaving a Third Avenue coffee shop when a running purse-snatcher crashed into Grover knocking the cup out of his hand. "I know this one was a GA, but damn...." Roughly translated a "GA" was a Gimme Arrest, but what it really meant was, Gotcha A-hole! By all standards it was a beautiful arrest. The running thief was very surprised as Grover, now with one hand freed up from his coffee cup, stuck out his arm and knocked him to the ground. Murphy got credit for the collar but now was suffering the consequences at the keyboard of the Underwood.

Then a voice from the corner of the squad-room. "Gentlemen, come and see me right now." Captain McCluskey stood in the doorway to his windowed office. He didn't sound too happy.

"What did you do now, Boyo?"

"Me? Nothing."

As they slowly made their way to McCluskey's den Grover and Murphy girded themselves for the boss's standard overblown outrage. "Close the door and sit down." They did.

"Boss, we…" Grover attempted to say something.

McCluskey shut him down, "I thought we understood each other?"

"About what?"

"Don't screw around with me Detective. Did we or did we not have a conversation about that guy Haupt?"

Murphy stared quizzically at Grover, unsure as if he had missed something. Grover hadn't mentioned anything to him about the encounter at Orchard Beach.

"Cap, can I say something and then I'll shut up?" Grover made an effort to control himself before saying something that would maybe come out stupid.

"Yeah what?"

"Cap, I was on the beach on Saturday with my girlfriend and that guy was on a blanket no more than fifty feet from me."

"Did I not say that you had best leave him alone?"

"I just went over to say hello. None of this has anything to do with me getting even with him."

Murphy took a step back. He was glad this didn't involve him.

"How nice of you. Glad to see you're letting bygones be bygones." McCluskey leaned back in his chair with his hands folded behind his head. His feigned smile rapidly became the icy stare of a parent dealing with an unruly child. Grover noted the huge armpit sweat stains on the boss's white uniform shirt. Clearly the Cap was hot and bothered and overall pissed off. "Haupt says that you hit him."

"What? I never!… why would I ever do?…. No sir, I did not hit him."

"Jesus Christ detective, you make my life a pain lately."

"Here's what happened. I thought it was him on a blanket near me and I went over to see if it was him. No intent of making any conversation." Grover searched his boss's expression. *Ah, he believes that one!*

"And why didn't you walk away?"

"Y'see, then he saw me and said something about the scar on my leg, I was actually surprised. He expressed some remorse about my pain and I gave him a pat on the back for being such a gentleman about it all. After the talk I just walked away. I didn't hit him."

McCluskey stared daggers at Grover. "I'm going to say this to you one more time, stay away from that guy. I don't need another phone call from J. Edgar Goddamn Hoover."

"J. Edgar Hoo…?" Grover's jaw dropped slightly as he spoke.

"Boss," Murphy cut off his partner before he could do more harm, "you know that there was another burglary last night that fits the Katzenjammer MO?"

McCluskey paused, "No, I haven't seen that report yet."

"Yeah, uniforms responded to a call from East 88th at 6:00 a.m., two Hungarian sisters were tied up overnight in their lingerie. They managed to get the gags out of their mouths and scream until neighbors heard them."

"Really?"

"Yeah boss, I know that you know in your heart that it's gotta be Haupt." Murphy paused and waited for another tirade.

There was none. McCluskey paused and rubbed his eyes. A 25-year veteran of the NYPD, McCluskey did have a sense of honor. Right, most of the time, prevailed over politics. He'd been forced to pull back on his sense of honor once, and despite the frustration he expressed seconds earlier, now he eagerly sought a place to draw the line. "Okay, listen to me. Let's just say that if this guy Haupt is out there, and you just happen by chance to be nearby, and if, and only if, you see him in the act of committing a crime, a real crime, not littering, only then can you arrest him. Otherwise, stay the hell away from him and work your other cases. I don't want to hear any more shit about this unless you catch him in the act. Got it?"

While not the license he was looking for, Grover accepted the rules of the game. "Thanks, Cap." Murphy gave his young partner a tap on the sleeve, nodded toward the door. The two detectives made a quick exit.

McCluskey thought for a second and added, "But, if you do watch him, he won't see you watching him, right?"

Grover smiled. "Yes sir, we're just shadows in the night."

11:30 a.m., Washington, D.C.

The green telephone phone rang on the FBI Director's desk. Hoover picked it up.

"Edgar, this is Bill Donovan."

"Hello Mr. Donovan," a formal voice filtered through the phone even after Donovan's casual entreaty to conversation. "What can I do for you."

Oh so it's going to be Mr. Donovan then? "Mr. Hoover I've received an intercept this morning."

"What is it?"

"It's a decoded message that I believe is aimed at a fifth columnist at work somewhere here in the States. It implies that Operation Pastorius is moving along as planned."

"Is that so? The Pastorius operation was stopped. Their leader told us the whole story and we got all of them."

"All of them that we know about."

"And by the way I think the way their legal defense is going we'll be executing the lot of them before the summer ends," Hoover said.

"Well, be that as it may, this message was sent using their most advanced encryption code. I don't think they had any worries at all that we might intercept it at all and I believe it is credible."

"Every one of these men who we arrested told us the same story during pretty intense interrogation. They told us that there were eight of them, and eight only."

"But there's something else that worries me, the intercept also meshes with some other intelligence that we're hearing from assets in Berlin that Abwehr is planning something very big that will really get our attention."

"And we have no idea what that big thing might be?"

"My analysts think that since both Pastorius and the information from our sources are coming from the Abwehr that they must be the same mission. There's something brewing."

Hoover paused before responding. Donovan could hear the director's heavy breath on the phone. "Mr. Donovan, are we talking about facts here or your personal intuition? Do we have any other information before we launch an all-out Chinese fire drill to find egg-foo-yung in a haystack?"

Donovan was irritated by his rival's attitude. "Mr. Hoover," he tried to keep the conversation on the same level of formality that Hoover had adopted, "I take these intercepts very seriously, as should you. This is what we have to go on at the moment and we are gathering more information all the time. OSS will share whatever we learn with the Bureau as we learn it. However, in the interim, I think we need to get off our duffs and start thinking about what that "big" Abwehr plan just might be. I do believe there is something specific in the works."

Hoover became icily placating on the phone, "Mr. Donovan, the Bureau appreciates your input in this process, but frankly, we have all domestic conditions under control. Our ears are in the German partisan community all over the country and we would have heard about something of this nature already."

"And what if you don't? What if there's another Pastorius saboteur loose? How will you locate him and stop him?"

Hoover wanted no more of the chat. "Thank you, Mr. Donovan. We will check into it and I'll keep you posted if, or when we learn anything. Goodbye." The phone clicked off before Donovan could respond.

"What an asshole," Donovan cursed out loud. The wild part of the Wild Bill nickname was coming to the surface.

"Do you need me, sir?" Miss Winston called to him through the open door.

"No Harriet, I was just remarking what a capable man Mr. Hoover is." Donovan eyed the clock. Time was wasting and he was sure the enemy was moving ahead with its plans.

July 8, 1942

9:00 p.m.

"The more things change the more they stay the same, huh?" Murphy leaned back in the drivers' seat as he stopped the unmarked Plymouth beneath the El.

"Yeah." Grover trained his eyes on the entrance door to Haupt's building. His memories of that night three months earlier made his leg ache.

"We're gonna be here a while, I think." The lights were on in Haupt's apartment and they could see glimpses of him moving past the open window. Murphy reasoned it was only a matter of time until the man decided to go to work.

"No one is talking about this guy any more. There hasn't been a thing in the papers about him in weeks."

"He's old news. Nobody gives a crap about him. It's all war news now."

"I think the Valentine has something to do with that." The most recent burglary of the Hungarian sisters didn't make the papers, most likely at the behest of the Police Commissioner, and for the moment, as far as the public was concerned it seemed like the Katzenjammer crime spree was over. The cops, however, knew otherwise. They had access to the crime reports and it was clear that someone with the same modus operandi was burglarizing a minimum of two apartments a week and often three or four.

"I just want to get this asshole off the street so your leg can heal properly." Murphy smiled at his partner, "or at least so you stop talking about him."

"I'll stop talking about him after we rip up his FBI get-out-of-jail-free card."

Shortly after ten the lights in the apartment flicked off and a moment later Haupt was standing on the street in front of the building looking left and right. He didn't see the cops in the darkened car.

"Crap he's going downtown!" Reflexively Murphy made a quick U-turn and stayed about a block behind.

Unaware of his tail, Haupt continued to move downtown on Third Avenue until he got to 81st Street. "Murph, he's turning West." The cops kept him in sight and closed their gap to a half block. "Where's he going," Grover wondered aloud?

"Somewhere no good, you can be sure of that, Boyo." At Lexington Avenue Haupt turned and walked downtown. It began to seem that Haupt was onto his tail and was trying to lose them.

"If he goes back Eastward on a Westbound side street, I'll betcha he's got us."

Haupt crossed 79th and walked to 77th. Just as Grover guessed the suspect turned East and they were unable to follow him against the opposite one-way traffic. Grover jumped out of the car and attempted to follow on foot. He was only a half-block behind his quarry, but the more agile Haupt was already at the corner and took a turn to the right and disappeared from sight.

Murphy arrived on Third Avenue and by the time he met his partner hobbling down 77th Street Haupt had disappeared into the night. Grover limped up to the car door and got in.

"Did you see him?"

"No, he's a ghost."

"I lost him!" Grover was mad at himself and cursed the pain in his leg. "Shit."

"Don't beat yourself up over it. Maybe he's not going out to steal tonight, maybe he's got a sweetie," joked Murphy. "We'll catch him sooner or later."

"That son of a bitch!"

"Seriously, maybe he made us outside his house and he's trying to piss us off. Let's call it a night." Murphy swerved the car back around the next corner and headed toward the precinct house on 67th.

As the cop car pulled away from the curb Eugen Haupt's head stuck out from a building vestibule doorway on Third Avenue and looked around carefully both ways before resuming his walk. He made his way to his secret basement apartment that no one could know about other than perhaps his nice old upstairs neighbor Mrs. Krauskoph. Certain that he wasn't being followed he chuckled to himself and continued his journey.

July 9, 1942

3:00 p.m., Berlin

Canaris didn't care for all of his part in the war effort and he cared even less for Himmler or Hitler's personal sycophant Bormann. He was leery of Goering and Goebbels, but he still had to exhibit total loyalty to the war effort. The admiral's aristocratic background in fact made him distrustful in general of the Nazi party leaders all of whom he regarded as unreformed street thugs. So he buried his feelings and seemed a Nazi enough to keep access to Hitler's ear and confidence. Today he would enlighten Hitler on the intricacies of Operation Pastorius.

It was a short trip from the Abwehr bunker to Hitler's office bunker and Canaris was prepared for the encounter. As he waited for the Führer he decided not to sit, but rather to meet Hitler standing tall and forceful. Five minutes after Canaris's arrival in the secret meeting room the door swung open and Hitler entered followed by a pair of faceless SS officers and then Bormann. *Shit, I hope this monkey keeps his mouth shut while I am here.* Canaris nodded politely to his nemesis and raised his hand in an officer's salute to a perceived equal. Bormann smiled at Canaris and returned the gesture. Neither man said a word to the other.

Hitler spoke first. He seemed to be in an upbeat mood. "Admiral, thank you for coming."

"My Führer, it is good to see you today. Shall we sit?" Canaris sealed his ownership of the meeting.

"Yes, sit." Hitler lowered himself into the room's biggest armchair and Canaris sat down opposite him. Bormann and the rest of the men in the room remained standing.

"My Führer, what I have to report to you today is highly secret and I wonder if I might speak with you alone. My request for privacy is not any issue with anyone's reliability, but since there are many brave lives at stake I believe that the fewer people who know about this the safer it is for all involved." Canaris wondered what Bormann would do about this obvious power play for the Führer's attention.

Hitler thought for a moment and agreed, "Yes, everyone leave us alone for a few minutes."

"Of course, my Führer." Martin Bormann motioned all to leave but not before shooting Canaris an icy stare. The Admiral was not a member of the Nazi Party and his request that Bormann, one of the highest ranking members of the Nazi Party, leave the room during a discussion involving secrets was a clear slight if not an actual insult. The spymaster sensed the threat but didn't care. It was clear to Canaris that he had indeed insulted Bormann and at some juncture the Nazi would try to get even. But it didn't matter. Canaris was in control of this mission, and total control without Bormann or any of the other Wehrmacht geniuses putting their thoughts into the plan was of utmost importance.

Once the room had cleared Hitler started with some small talk, "I am astounded that Churchill was victorious with his confidence vote in their parliament yesterday."

Canaris forced a smile, "Yes, I am not sure if he is bribing his opponents with large sums to keep them on his side, ha."

"Ha, that is probably the case." Hitler laughed for a short second and then said, "and what now is this big secret?"

Canaris drew a deep breath and told the Führer the story of Operation Pastorius and the teams that had been caught and arrested in America. He made the case that this was all according to plan, a plan that in the end would make a huge impact on the American enemy. Then he, in intricate detail, explained the plan step by step and its very strong chances of success.

On hearing the details Hitler became very excited. "Audacious! Yes Admiral, this will indeed change the course of the war. We will bring it right to their doorstep and they will have a new fear of us. Very good. Very, very good!" Hitler stood, and Canaris rose with him. "When will this all happen?"

"It is in the plans for the latter part of next month. By that time all of the parts of our puzzle will be in place for this watershed event."

"Magnificent. Please keep me apprised of your progress." Hitler shook Canaris' hand and left the Admiral alone in his room.

8:09 a.m., New York City

The detectives were scheduled for an 8 to 4 tour, in at 8:00 a.m. and without any paperwork or overtime, out at 4:00 p.m. Grover arrived first as he had the easiest commute, and Murphy clocked in at about 3 minutes after the hour. McCluskey was already at his desk and in a friendly way invited his burglary team in for a quick chat.

"Have you heard the good news?" McCluskey had a broad smile on his face.

"Uh, no sir, what news," asked Murphy?

"Sit down." They sat. "We caught Katzenjammer last night."

The detectives stared at each other. "See that," Grover looked at Murphy "he was on his way to do the dirty when we lost him!"

"A couple of uniforms on foot patrol on 77th Street heard some screaming from a second floor window," McCluskey continued.

"He must have gone and done it when we lost him on 3rd Avenue," Murphy surmised.

"Yeah, two beat cops ran up to the apartment there and the guy was running out the door with a bag full of silver and jewelry. The people inside were tied up in their underwear but spit out their gags and started screaming while the guy was still in the house." The Captain couldn't contain his pleasure at telling them the news.

"Hey boss, that's great news," Murphy said with a big smile.

"Yeah, and when we got him in here he confessed to a whole lot of other ones. He could describe them in detail."

"Great! We tried to keep an eye on him last night but he gave us the slip and, just like you told us we were good, he never saw us keeping an eye on him!" Grover smiled. It was safe now to make jokes about all this. "Can we say hello to him?"

"Yeah. Sure, but I haven't done that yet. In case the FBI tries to free him up again I want to keep my nose out of this."

Murphy nodded. "Understood."

"Wow, I can't believe it. That is great news. This putz is finally off the street." Grover was pleased to hear the tale. "Where is he now?"

"We have him in lockup downstairs. If you wanna see him you should go downstairs soon. He'll be on his way downtown for arraignment. Oh, by the way, I hope you guys aren't upset, but the uniforms who grabbed him get the credit for the collar."

"Cap, I think we're just glad that he's off the streets." Grover didn't care who got the collar.

"We're all good then. Now, I guess I gotta call the FBI and let them know too." All was warm and friendly again with the Captain. "I'm glad I could make you boys happy."

Grover and Murphy smiled and headed for the stairs down to the basement holding cells. At the outer door to the lockup, the sergeant who was in charge saw them at the gate and smiled, "Hey, we got your Katzenjammer kid in here."

"Good deal," Grover said. "We wanna visit with him."

The sergeant opened the gate. The first cell in the corridor held three hookers who had been picked up the night before trying to work the bar at the Hotel Carlyle. "Hey, Aunt Greta, what're ya doin' in there? Wait'll I tell Mom where I saw you." Murphy joked as they walked by and he made Grover smile. The women scowled at them.

Two cells down from the hookers Grover saw him first. The suspect was seated on a bench leaning over his lap with his face down in his arms. Grover immediately sensed that something was amiss. With a bit of trepidation mixed with hopeful euphoria he wanted the man to look up at him, "hey shithead, we finally caught you huh?" The hulk on the bench lifted his face.

"What the fu…?" Murphy was stunned.

"Who are…?" Grover was jolted. This wasn't the Katzenjammer burglar whom they came to know and loathe, this was someone else. "Who are you?"

"I'm the Katzenjammer burglar you idiot."

"No, you're not," retorted Murphy.

"I sure am. I did them all. I broke in and stole stuff all over Yorkville. I'm the guy. I'm Katzenjammer! Yes, I am!"

Grover eyed the man. *This guy is a loony.*

"Yeah, I broke into the Heinz place on 80th two weeks ago and I took their tea set. I got a lot for that silver stuff. I also tied up those old Hungarian sisters, and…."

"Yeah, yeah, and when did you start doing all this?" Grover queried.

"I been doing it for months, since May."

"Oh, so sorry, you've answered incorrectly and unfortunately all of your winnings are now lost. You go home with nothing. Oh, oops, so sorry again. Actually you can't go home, asshole. You were just arrested for burglary," Murphy teased.

"And I think we have you on an additional count of impersonating a known felon. There's gotta be a law about that. There is one, and only one, Katzenjammer burglar and pally, you ain't him." Grover was amused, but not very. At this moment Eugen Haupt was still on the streets.

With that the two cops turned to go upstairs to alert the Captain not to call the FBI or the press. They got a nutcase copycat burglar, yes, but the real guy was still out there.

"But, I am him!," the man sputtered. "I really am the Katzenjammer burglar."

"Yeah, I believe you," said Grover, turning on his heel, "And I'm the Lone Ranger, and this is Tonto."

"Shit, I thought I was gonna be the Lone Ranger this time." cursed Murphy. He and Grover turned to make their way out of the holding cell area. As they walked past the caged hookers Murphy added, "Hey, Aunt Greta, I'll let Mom know that I saw you today."

Grover looked at him. "She's not really your aunt is she?"

"What do you think?"

"And you're not Tonto either? Are you? I'm so disappointed in you."

The bars to the holding cell slammed behind them.

4:00 p.m., Washington, D.C.

The two men sitting with Wild Bill Donovan in his office were his closest advisers Col. Robert Solborg and Cpl. Arthur Schlesinger, Jr. a pair of the brightest intelligence analysts in the country. Both had read the latest intercepted message from Abwehr.

"So what does this mean?" Donovan at this moment, was open to any possible answer.

"Well," Solborg jumped in, "it seems obvious that Pastorius is moving ahead and that the men we arrested weren't essential to the bigger plot, or perhaps their arrests were anticipated." Solborg was an immigrant born in Poland who had served in the Tsar's cavalry before the Bolsheviks drove him out of Russia. While he lamented the demise of Nicholas's aristocratic family he was also a devout anti-fascist. "What that plot exactly is, remains the question."

"All the information we're getting is originating from the same place," Schlesinger added, "the offices of the Abwehr. I think it is a certainty that they are running Pastorius and the different elements of a bigger plot."

"Yup, a bigger plot. My thoughts, too." Donovan kept re-reading the translated message. "Think we're missing something because we're not reading this in the original German?"

"Maybe so, but even in its English translation, it's a pretty clear message; Pastorius is moving ahead, keep doing what you're doing and it will happen." Schlesinger was a recent OSS recruit. "Let me explain my thinking. What if the men we captured were the total extent of the Pastorius plot, then it's done and we have nothing to worry about. But then, why this secret message to some spy here in the States?"

"Maybe just to cause confusion?" Solbord opined.

"Maybe so, but we also know that Abwehr is unware that we've broken the Enigma code. They have no expectation at all that we can read this transmission. For that reason this message is unlikely to be a ruse. This needs to be taken seriously. Pastorius is still in play."

"You're correct Arthur," added Solborg, "But we may have been misled by those captured saboteurs about what Pastorius was aimed at achieving. Those men probably don't know all of it either."

Donovan had something else to share and this was probably, he thought, the best time to share it. "This is totally top secret and need to know only," he leaned forward to his office guests, "but we have developed a high placed source in Berlin, someone who is very close to this situation and the Abwehr leadership."

"Can this source give us more details about what we're talking about now?" Solborg asked. "Not sure yet." Donovan sunk into his chair. "I am not sure who this source is and his or her proximity to the leadership, but we have gotten a few actionable tidbits in the past couple of weeks. I'm hopeful that there will be more. It's just too dangerous for this source to send things on a regular basis."

Solborg's expression brightened. "Perhaps this is good news!"

"There are a number of odd things about this whole situation."

Donovan made a verbal list. "How did we come to find out about the two submarine teams? We only noticed one of them when they arrived. We never would have known about the Jacksonville arrivals without one of the saboteurs turning himself in to the FBI and ratting out the rest."

Schlesinger nodded, "Yes, that is odd."

"Then, another mystery coming from our friends across town. Didn't the Bureau also have a source in New York who knew about the saboteurs as well," Donovan asked. "How did their New York source come to know that? Was there an order from Berlin to their in-place spies in the U.S.?"

"Yes, if I were planning this operation neither team would have any knowledge of the other," Solborg thought out loud.

"Speaking as an intelligence officer myself," Donovan went on, "I would keep all the information of my teams compartmentalized. One team would not know about the other, nor would anyone else, except for maybe a single ground support individual who would only know the minimum. If one team got caught, then the other would still be around to do what they came to do. Why didn't they do that?"

"Since it was relatively easy to catch them, I think," Schlesinger surmised, "they set this up to make us keep looking for more submarine incursions along the coastline and to spend our resources there."

"So then, what is Pastorius really about? If you're correct, and I think you probably are, what are they planning?" Donovan leaned back in his chair.

"Obviously something a lot bigger. They have another plan. It's a bigger and more devious plot and its use of human pawns underlines its importance to the Abwehr." Schlesinger stared at the other two men.

Solborg rubbed his chin. "What could hurt us the most? I don't think that blowing up railroads and factories by eight operatives, while messy and irritating is the thing that is supposed to get our attention. There's already been unpublicized sabotage in a number of factories and that hasn't broken anyone's spirit. I would deduce from what we've seen and read, that their move will try to totally devastate us in some grander way and make us lose some of our resolve."

"I agree," said Schlesinger, "something to demoralize America. Something to slow us down."

"Yes, much like how the Bolsheviks took over Russia when they murdered Nicholas and his family."

"We need to figure this out before we get to read about it in the newspaper." Donovan folded the translated Abwehr intercept message and placed it in a file folder on his desk. "In the mean time we'll see what else comes in from our source in Berlin."

"Can we communicate with him or her, or them, to find out specific things?" Schlesinger asked?

"Sadly, no. We just get stuff, frequent stuff, but we have no idea how they're getting it out. There's a danger of sending a specific request because if intercepted, it could alert the other side of that person's presence in their midst." Donovan searched his desk for a snippet of paper. "By the way, this may be part of the same question, but I'm not sure. Can either of you do some research?"

Schlesinger nodded, "I can do it sir. What would you like to know?"

"I have an odd feeling about this Admiral Wilhelm Canaris fellow. From details I've been receiving from a few other sources he seems to be, shall we say, less than a team player among his buddies in the German high command."

"In what way?"

"Some things don't seem to add up."

"Hmm?" Schlesinger rubbed his ear.

"Like, we know that about four years ago he made a secret trip to Spain to meet with General Franco. We have intel that he was there trying to convince Franco to not allow his fellow Germans to use Spain as a launching post for an attack on Gibraltar. Not very helpful to the Reich's efforts, is that?"

"That is odd."

Donovan opened a file folder and took out a piece of paper. "Let me read you this, it's part of a profile I had compiled about Canaris... 'some time after Germany invaded Poland operative reports overheard conversation between Field Marshal Keitel and Admiral Canaris. Canaris is concerned about what the Nazis are doing. He tells Keitel, 'the world will one day hold Germany responsible for barbarism since these things are taking place under its nose. Keitel cautions Canaris to keep his mouth shut about that stuff,' hmm?"

"I'll look into it sir," Schlesinger volunteered, then he added, "Do you think Canaris himself is our source?"

"Ha! No, I don't think it's him, but it's someone around him for sure. Or, it could be part of the whole Pastorius plot." Donovan lowered his voice to almost a whisper. "Do the research quietly, they may even have spies in here."

"Yes sir."

July 13, 1942

11:30 a.m.

"Something is wrong, totally screwed up." With the arrest of the man who claimed to be the Katzenjammer Burglar the every-other-night rash of Upper East Side burglaries seemed to come to an abrupt halt. Since the self-confessed fruitcake, as Grover referred to him, was locked up there hadn't been a single burglary anywhere in the 19th for almost six days. The multiple weeknight break-ins in Yorkville suddenly stopped on a dime.

"We were wrong. Simple as that." Murphy shuffled some papers across his desk. "Haupt wasn't ever the Katzenjammer. Yeah, he's still the scumbag who threw you off a fire-escape, but he's not the guy."

"He says he didn't start doing burglaries until May. Katzenjammer started in late February or early March. How about that?"

"Boyo, obviously this guy is a fruitcake and not that reliable as a witness to his own time frame."

"I'm not so sure that this isn't an FBI setup. C'mon, he's too stupid to be a burglar. Maybe he did it for a while, a copycat who reads the papers. To do this stuff the way it's been done so far the burglar needs some brains. He's a piece of carbon paper."

"Whatever, but a guy who claims to be the guy we're after confesses. He knows about the details of some of the burglaries and miraculously they suddenly come to a stop after his arrest. 'Not too much more you can draw from that." Murphy attempted to reason with his fixated partner.

Grover was clearly not about to let it go. "What if it's Haupt's way of getting us to leave him alone? What if those FBI suits figured out a way to get someone else to take the rap? What if it's his way to keep us from following him? What if he's up to something else?"

"What if? What if? What if my Aunt Sophie had balls, would she be my Uncle Stu? Doug, get a grip! The uniforms caught a guy in the act of committing a burglary and he says that he's the burglar we've been looking for. What else do you need to know?"

"Because he's not our guy. Our guy is Haupt. The guy who says he's our guy only knows the burglary details that he read in the papers. He didn't cop to one single burglary that wasn't written up. He doesn't know about the big bunch of stuff that never made it into the papers. He might be a psycho but he's not the Katzenjammer Burglar. Also, he's a hoarder and never fenced anything he stole, so where's all the crap he stole before he got caught?"

Murphy drew a deep breath before he spoke again. "We could ask the same question about Eugen Haupt. If he's the burglar where is the stuff he stole? He hasn't fenced anything either."

That question threw Grover slightly, "Yeah, well."

"Look, I am with you in all of this, but we're up against a stone wall." All this negative attention from the bosses wasn't going to do Tim Murphy any good toward any kind of promotion before he retired. "Everybody's tellin' us to leave this Haupt guy alone, but you think different."

"We caught him once at that bakery!"

"Yeah, and about that bakery thing… Wasn't it an FBI agent who told you that Haupt broke in at the request of the Bureau? They told him to do it! They sent him in there to get them the lists of old bund members. Was there anything else missing when he left? The cash register wasn't touched… shit, the guy didn't even take a goddamn piece of pastry, not even a Schnecken!"

"If he had nothing to hide, why did he throw me off a fire escape?"

"Maybe what he said was true. Maybe he did think we were out to roll him? Did you ever think of that? He didn't see our faces in the bakery before he lammed out the back door. He didn't see us following him before the burglary. He had no idea that we knew where he lived. Then, you're out there on his fire escape. The rest of the story writes itself. He's a scumbag who, in his career as a scumbag, has surely pissed off a lot of other scumbags. Maybe he knew about a vendetta against him and was afraid of the worst."

Grover had to agree, at least in his mind, that maybe this Haupt guy wasn't who they were looking for, but something about Haupt was distressing, none-the-less. "I dunno. I just dunno," he sighed.

"Look at it this way, someone who thinks he's Katzenjammer is now in the slammer. How do I know this? I don't just know this because it's written in the newspaper, I have seen his face in person downstairs in a cell. The public knows this, as does the NYPD Brass. We move on to the next thing. Eugen Haupt is innocent by default. We can't pin anything on him, and, in fact, he may be the solid citizen who saved us from some deadly Nazi saboteurs, or whatever your FBI buddy told you." Murphy took a deep breath and girded himself for Grover's next volcanic salvo, but it didn't come.

Grover just stared back at him stone-faced. "Yeah. You're probably right." After weeks of feeling nothing but a desire for vengeance, he was beginning, reluctantly, to agree with his partner. "Maybe it is time to leave the sonofabitch alone."

But, Murphy knew in his heart that Grover really had no intention at all of leaving the "sonofabitch alone."

July 16, 1942

9:00 a.m.

It was Grover's day off and he wasn't going to be seeing Ellen until the evening. The day off afforded him some good midweek free time to unofficially scrutinize the source of his nightmares. Grover staked out Eugen Haupt's apartment in the daytime. He would never admit to Murphy that he was doing this because the more rational part of him knew that the surveillance of Eugen Haupt would officially be viewed as a vendetta and it would be toxic to both of their careers.

Grover, the accomplished stakeout master, planted himself across Third Avenue from Haupt's building at 8:00 in the morning and blended into the street scene. Just a relaxing day on, what he called, a Kraut watch. His wait took about three hours before it paid off.

A refreshed-looking Eugen Haupt left his apartment building at a few minutes past 11:00 and paid absolutely no attention to anything on the street around him. Without a care in the world he turned to walk toward 86th Street. Grover fell in behind him about a half block away, the perfect shadow. As the hulking goon neared the 86th Street corner, Grover briefly slinked into a shop doorway. The man turned East on 86th and slowly window-shopped his way down the block that was densely crowded with people. Grover used them as cover as he moved slowly forward, at no time ever losing sight of his quarry. Haupt came to a stop outside of a hardware store. Here his nonchalant demeanor underwent a quick transformation; he suspiciously glanced around in both directions. *Yeah... I knew it! He wants to make sure he's not being followed.* As Haupt entered the store, Grover, now solidly suspicious, inched his way toward the window to get a closer look.

The place was big with lots of aisles and shelves. The rows of shelves were visually impenetrable and Haupt ventured to the back end of the establishment and quickly disappeared. Haupt was in there for sure, and Grover debated whether to enter the store and see what his nemesis was doing, or simply wait outside and continue following the man as he exited. He decided to go in. Pretending to be a shopper himself, he finally spied Haupt looking at a shelf by the store's back wall that was full of electrical supplies, radio tubes and batteries. Grover inched his way down the adjacent aisle for a better view. Through a narrow opening in a shelf he watched as Haupt grabbed two 100-foot spools of number sixteen copper wire and a pair of Eveready 67 volt radio "B" batteries.

Haupt examined his selections and brought them to the cashier at the front of the store. Grover watched him pay for the batteries and wire and exit the store, continuing his eastward movement. Grover kept him in sight from a manageable distance. Haupt was walking much faster than before and Grover, who by now had been standing for hours on his recently-healed broken leg, was feeling a twinge of pain as he sped up his pursuit.

Haupt was in a hurry to get somewhere with the wire and batteries, but he wasn't headed home. *Where is he going?* Grover's fracture was not ready for this kind of a chase and his pain became more intense with every footfall and by the time Haupt reached 81st Street Grover's leg was on fire, rendering him unable to go on. Haupt took a quick turn onto 81st and Grover lost him. As the detective rested on the fender of a parked Chrysler, Haupt was gone into the ether, and Grover's suspicions reached an all-time high.

July 20, 1942

9:00 a.m., Washington, D.C.

Anyone else would have been awed by the group that walked past her desk and out the door of her office. There were two U.S. Navy admirals, one four-star general of the Army and a four-star general of the Marines. Missy LeHand was not impressed in the least, and in fact she had slightly intimidated all of them. Missy was used to the brass and as FDR's personal secretary she didn't even look up from her typewriter as they exited.

"Missy, would you please come in with my calendar?" The summons from the President required immediate response. He was the only one who did intimidate her.

"Yes, Mr. President." LeHand had been working for FDR for the past twenty-two years. For all practical purposes she was his gatekeeper and ran his life. She stepped into the Oval Office.

Franklin Delano Roosevelt, The President of the United States, sat facing the window and staring out, almost as if he had been daydreaming. As she approached his desk he spun around and thought out loud. "I'd like to plan out next month's activities in some broad strokes."

"Yes, sir."

"I don't know what the brain trust has planned for me, but I would like to spend the Labor Day weekend at the house in Hyde Park, if at all possible."

"We'll make it possible, sir." Missy knew that it was important for FDR to get away from time to time and that Hyde Park and Warm Springs were the two places where he reduced his stress load. She controlled his calendar and that meant that, barring a catastrophe, it would happen as he had requested.

"We can take the team up to New York a day or two before and work from there and then we will slide out to Hyde Park on the Friday night before Labor Day. How does that sound?"

"It sounds totally workable sir. I will block out that time."

"Good."

"I'll make arrangements with the Secret Service so that they have time to plan things out for the trip. Mr. Wilson is always grateful for an early heads-up so that he can get your railroad issues onto a fast track. They'll be grateful for the early notice sir. I would imagine the plans will be the same as the last time we did this?"

"Yes, tell Frank don't change anything. It's hard enough to get to the places where I know how hard it is to get to, ha ha."

"Mr. Wilson will be happy to hear that sir."

The President often traveled to New York City by train in his personal heavily-armored private railcar. The very wealthy often traveled in opulent private cars but this one was different. Save the fact that it had no windows, the coach was nondescript in exterior style. It could easily be mistaken for a U.S. postal mail car but unlike a postal car it had no exterior markings. Inside, it was different from any other piece of rolling stock anywhere. Roosevelt's railcar was a moveable fortress with ample room for his automobile and a slew of armed Secret Service men who could see out in all directions and fire on any assailants from multiple armored spots throughout.

Roosevelt paused and changed the subject, "Have we heard any more from Bill Donovan?"

"No sir, but I will check with his office immediately. Anything specific?"

"No, nothing specific, but I think he'll know what I'm asking about. Let him know that I'm not pressuring him I'm simply curious."

"Yes Mr. President. Will that be all?"

"I think so for now, Missy. Thank you."

She closed the door behind her and the President turned back toward the window for another minute or two of simply daydreaming. There were twenty-two minutes left before the pace would accelerate once again.

9:30 a.m., New York City

"Gentlemen let's start the situation meeting." Special Agent Mike Foreman looked around the table at the familiar faces staring blankly at him, his own personal brain trust. "Big Picture this morning...we have a special directive from the home office. Intel from our OSS brothers suggests that the saboteurs who we picked up last month with that German Operation Pastorius, that's the German code name for their op, were not the only ones involved. There may be more of these guys out there or still to come."

"Are any other agencies involved in this search, sir," asked Special Agent Witcover?

"No, but Coast Guard and Navy have stepped up sonar searches for Nazi U-boats along the coast. We also have a way of monitoring their activities at sea now, but that's more than you all need to know at this point. If there are more of them coming by sub I think that they will have that covered."

"Sir, have we any idea what they're up to?" Special Agent Hardwick asked.

"No, if we did we wouldn't be having this conversation, would we?"

Foreman stared at Hardwick with a mildly annoyed gaze, this guy went to Princeton? After a pause he continued his thought. "Here's the odd part about this case as I see it, we know from the men who we caught that they were here to blow up some rail lines, some factories and some aluminum plants. If you think about this hard enough these guys might have done some damage if we hadn't caught them, but unless they were going to plant some kind of a super bomb somewhere, they could do nowhere near enough damage to justify sending two teams over here in two U-boats. OSS is pretty sure that Pastorius is a bigger plot about something totally different than factory and rail demolition, only no one seems to have a grip on exactly what they're up to."

"Sir, we can lean on our informants and see what they know." Special Agent Witcover jumped in.

"I would expect that, but there's more to this. Because of that intel from OSS we need to follow every lead to its end. More so than usual."

Witcover jumped in again, "I think we can get the story from our informant Haupt. He's been very accurate so far."

"About Haupt, Sir," Special Agent O'Rourke interrupted, "I had a friendly run in with that cop, Grover. Remember the guy that got thrown off the fire escape?" All in the room nodded. "Grover thinks our informant shouldn't be trusted at all and that he's lit both ends of the fuse. I don't know if I agree, but my street sense says that Haupt is still a heavy and we need to watch him better. I mean, what if it's true? Have we figured out just how big any of the information he gave us really was?"

"His information's been right on the money so far. He's been giving us names for months now and he led us to all of the submarine arrivals. We caught them all in two days." Witcover was getting mildly defensive about his informant.

"That's exactly my point. We caught them in just two days. How did we catch them? We didn't get them through great police work. They all just fell into our lap. We caught them because one of them surrendered himself to the Director personally and told us all about his buddies, and then we rounded them all up because of info from our snitch. It just seems too easy to believe that there isn't more going on. If what the Chief here is saying is true, and that Pastorius isn't over, how come our snitch hasn't come to us with anything about that yet?" O'Rourke's question caused a pause in the conversation.

Haupt was Witcover's informant. He had recruited him and paid handsomely for the information that Haupt would provide through his ties to the underworld. Witcover's response to all of this was a cold stare directed at O'Rourke, an attempt at intimidation. Witcover was Haupt's only FBI

contact. Now the veracity of that informant's information was being challenged and for some cockeyed reason Witcover felt the need to defend his
pet hoodlum from the others in the room. O'Rourke stared right back unin-
timidated in the least.

Witcover spoke up, maybe only for the benefit of his own ego, "I think
this informant is totally on the up-and-up. There's no reason to expect he
has any pipeline to the German high command and of Pastorius or that
anyone else may be involved. That's probably the reason we haven't heard
anything else about this. Let's understand this man's position clearly. He
hears things from people who might know people who might know things."

"Or he's just playing you and us for suckers," O'Rourke responded.

Foreman saw a fistfight in the making and stepped in to break it up
before his boys bloodied each others' noses. "Witcover, let's continue to
cultivate this Haupt guy, but let's also keep a closer eye on him. I know all
about the burglary stuff..."

"We got him to stop that sir," Witcover interjected.

"Yes, I know that, but let's make sure that he's working on our side only
with this sabotage intelligence. Let's find out how *did* he get that info about
the subs? How *did* he get that inside line on the saboteurs? Who are his
sources? Is he at personal risk when the other side puts two-and-two together
and figures out that he's the guy who turned them all in, or is he a part of
something else? We can't let our guard down. This man is still a bad guy."

Hiding his eyes from what might be perceived by some others at the
table as anger, Witcover said, "Yes sir. I will keep a closer eye on the man."

"Good." Forman moved on.

The rest of the meeting dealt almost exclusively with the agents' vacation
schedules in the coming months. They talked for a half-hour about it and
unanimously decided to forego any time off for a while. There was a war
going on.

July 28, 1942

2:49 a.m.

The waiting burglar was sweating heavily in his long-sleeved black shirt. Tonight's target was a rear-facing apartment in the back of an East 90th Street rowhouse. As he identified his target, an open fourth floor window by the fire escape, he briefly considered forgetting about the whole endeavor but decided, *Oh, shit, I'm already here. 'Might as well.* The previous day had been a scorcher, and all over the city overheated apartment windows were wide open. This one would be simple and quiet, they're all asleep for sure. No reason to tie anyone up or be seen. The genuine Katzenjammer burglar, aka Eugen Haupt, had learned from his father that the couple who lived there, both in their seventies, had jewelry and a collection of pocket watches hidden in a bureau drawer. The elder Haupt gave his son information as to where the couple kept their baubles and timepieces and it would be a simple quiet in and out.

This was the piece of the puzzle that the cops never could figure out. If Haupt was indeed the Katzenjammer burglar, why then were none of any stolen goods ever seen again? Detectives never found any relationships with known fences, pawnshops or anyone else. Haupt was a loner and an apparent mama's boy. The only regular part of his life was visiting his elderly parents. He regularly brought them groceries. What no one ever suspected was that those brown paper sacks contained more than milk, eggs and bread. Nor would anyone have suspected that an old man with a breathing disorder could be involved. In fact, the elder Karl Haupt, aside from his ties with the master race was running the show as a mastermind as well as a master fence. It was a perfect situation. Karl had the names of personal enemies who were avowed Nazis. He fed those names to his son, who gave them to the FBI in return for protection from local police investigation. Still, Karl was a pro and knew when it was safe to resume business, so they waited. It had been some months since the incident with Detective Grover and Karl felt that it was now safe to resume the crime spree.

All the apartments are dark except for that one. He decided to wait until that final nightbird went to bed before he began his work. The burglar's greatest tool was patience. *The light is out, good!* Ten minutes later he moved. His first step would be an acrobatic leap to the fire escape ladder that was hanging just a bit above his reach. His target, the open window, would be the easiest part to handle. *The old shits will probably be dead asleep.*

Haupt's blue eyes centered themselves in two cut out holes in his knit cap. Someone might see him but no one would see his face. A small jump up and a quick grab of the lowest hanging rung got him on the ladder. A surplus of upper body strength allowed him to easily pull himself up and then, just as he had planned, it was a quick trip up to the third floor.

Ah, a loud fan! So much the easier! This apartment dweller's solution to the excessive oppressive summer heat and humidity became the burglar's best tool. In the dim glow from the street lights, Eugen scanned the room for the chest of drawers that his father told him about. It was up against the far wall opposite a small sofa. Taking a deep breath, he stealthily stepped inside without making the slightest noise. *So far so good!*

What wasn't good was the almost unbearable heat and the sweaty build-up under his wool mask. *It is so fucking hot and damp!* By the time he crossed the room he couldn't stand it any longer. Since the occupants of the house were in a deep sleep, he removed the mask and tucked it into his back pocket. The air movement from the oscillating electric fan blew a whisper of breeze across his dripping visage and it felt thrillingly good. *Still, no time to amuse yourself... get the jewelry and get out!*

His father had drawn him a diagram based on information provided by his friend Herman Gruber, the iceman. Gruber had also worked for Dutch Schultz and the mob veteran's own joke was that he'd "iced" a number of people before he himself started delivering the stuff. Gruber had access to hundreds of apartments, and his pen-and-ink sketch of this place detailed exactly where the old couple hid their treasures. Eugen quickly located the drawer from the diagram and gave it a tug, but it didn't budge. In the overwhelming humidity, the wood had swelled up. *Shit!* After two minutes of attempts he was able to pull it open just enough to slide his hand inside. Lulled by the rhythmic whirr and breeze of the swinging fan, he stood there in the darkness with his hand stuck in a drawer groping for gold and pearls. *Ah, that's something, I think! Ouch, dammit!* He stuck his finger on the open pin of a gold brooch. Startled, he tugged at his hand and in the process rattled the chest of drawers ever-so-slightly enough to knock over a tiny perfume bottle. It made the quietest of noises. He froze and looked around the room. Was there any movement from the adjacent bedroom? Again, relying on his patience, he froze and waited. Nothing. No movement. *Quiet. Good!* At worst, if they awoke to his noise, he would have to tie these people up in their skivvies as he had done many times before.

When he was certain that no one had stirred as a result of the fallen perfume atomizer, he went back to work. His first find was a string of pearls. As they came out of the drawer, the lustrous beads rolled over the edge of the drawer and made a light rattling sound. He was becoming more confident.

They are deaf as well as old. Then, piece by piece he removed three lovely gold pocket watches with shiny fobs, a diamond pendant, some rings and silver bracelets. *Yes, all this stuff is worth at least a few hundred dollars, a good night's work!* As he felt around the inside of the drawer he was pretty sure that he had it all, and with a silent sigh of relief he stood and turned to go back out the window.

"Schwein-hund!" A raspy old voice rang out above the whirr of the fan. Haupt turned toward it and was startled as he saw the old man of the apartment swinging a wooden bridge chair directly at his head. He made a move to duck but it was too late! One of the chair legs caught him hard on his right cheek and the center rung somehow got underneath his chin forcing him to shut his mouth very hard. He bit his tongue and heard a tooth crack as he fell to the floor.

While the attack caught him unprepared, Haupt's reaction was swift. He yanked the chair out of the old man's hand as the startled old German stared directly at his face. *Shit, he has seen me!* The rest was reflexive and happened very quickly. Haupt raised the chair up over his shoulder and swiftly brought it down hard on the septuagenarian's head. The old man crumbled to the floor unconscious with blood oozing from the top of his bald skull. He looked dead. Without a second thought Eugen Haupt was back out the window, down the fire escape and lost in the night.

11:30 a.m.

"So tell me again, what the hell happened in that apartment last night?" Captain Eamon McCluskey was steaming mad, yet he really couldn't blame his burglary detective team. He'd called them off the case. While no one knew for certain that last night's brutal home break in was the work of the Katzenjammer burglar, and also that no one knew for certain that Haupt was that so-named Katzenjammer burglar, the action that took place in apartment 3C last night seemed awfully familiar to all three men in that office.

Grover spoke quietly, "Cap', this is really a sad one."

"Yeah, that old guy is in really bad shape," Murphy kept the same tone.

The detectives glanced at each other. Both men felt like gloating with a big Itoldyaso but thought better of it. No need to pour gasoline on the captain's inflamed temper.

"Murph and me were all over the place for the last three hours. 'Seems like the burglar climbed up a fire escape, came in the living room window and took the family jewels. The wife says that her husband tried to hit the man with a chair, but I guess that didn't work out so well for him.'"

"Did she get a look at the guy?"

"Nah, didn't see anything, she never came out of the bedroom," Murphy added, "while it's not the usual Katzenjammer way of doing things, it was ninety-five percent within his M.O."

"The other five percent being?"

"He didn't tie anyone up in their skivvies."

"So, maybe it's a whole other burglar?," McCluskey asked "If he is Katzenjammer, why did he whack the old man? He never hurt anyone before."

"Who knows. Maybe it was so hot last night he couldn't find any long Johns," Grover smirked. The Captain was beginning to acknowledge that Haupt might be the bad guy.

McCluskey let the remark go by without a response. "By the by Detectives, how is the old guy doin'? Have you interviewed him yet?"

"No, not yet. He's in a coma at Bellevue. He lost a lot of blood. He's 77, and they're not sure if he's gonna make it." Murphy sighed.

Grover added, "And his wife had to be sedated."

"Anyone interview her yet? Did she see anything?"

Grover opened his notebook to refresh his memory on the details, "Uh, one of the uniforms on the scene this morning spoke to her after they carried her hubby out. She says she was asleep throughout the whole thing and only woke up when she realized her husband wasn't next to her in the bed. She went looking for him and tripped over his body in the living room."

Murphy summarized the events. "I figure that it was a hot night so these folks left all their windows wide open. Our guy finds the right moment and climbs up the fire escape. By the way, the ladder was not pulled down to the ground and there was nothing to stand on to reach the ladder. So that means that it was either someone from Ringling Brothers or maybe our bad boy had to shimmy up to the first floor without making a lot of noise to wake the neighbors."

"That does fit the Katzenjammer M.O. perfectly, and also Haupt," Grover added emphatically.

"So," Murphy continued, "he climbs up to the third floor and he seems to know exactly where the jewels are. Only one drawer was opened, nothing else was messed up."

"Again," Grover piped in, "just like Katzenjammer."

"So now he's done stealing the jewels and he's on the way out. He runs into the old guy and whacks him on the head with a chair."

"Y'see, this is the part that doesn't fit. Katzenjammer ties his victims up."

"Well Cap', as was my own experience, it appears that when cornered the guy gets violent. What if the old guy surprised him and he reacted?"

"What if the old guy surprised him and could identify him," Murphy added, "but now he can't?"

"Cap', I know that this is sensitive, but if we do like Haupt for this stuff we're perfectly within our rights to at least interview him about it. The FBI can't object to that. Can they?"

McCluskey had been won over. "Yeah… they did promise to keep Haupt on a leash. Yeah, do it. Go talk to the sonofabitch. And also, see if you can figure out what he's doing with the stuff he takes. Where's the stuff he took last night? It could still be in his crib."

"Thanks, Cap." They spoke in unison with a broad smile. "We're on it."

11:30 a.m.

"Let's settle down and get this meeting started. Gentlemen, we have more naval intercepts from the Bureau that something is happening and we still don't know what that might be." Foreman was in no mood for idle chit-chat today.

The faces around the conference table were blank. No news about anything in New York or elsewhere. The navy and the OSS were picking up coded messages indicating something was going on, but there was no physical manifestation of that anywhere that anyone could see. Agents across America in Chicago and Detroit were closely watching known Nazi sympathizers, but all seemed to be quiet. It was a perplexing time for the FBI.

"Witcover, what about your boy Haupt? Anything from him about any of this?"

"No sir, he's been quiet lately. I haven't heard from him in over a week. Usually he contacts me when he has something."

"Maybe you should pump him, hmm? We're paying him and we need to find stuff out now, not when the moment suits him."

O'Rourke bit his tongue to keep from speaking out, but it wasn't enough of a deterrent. "Sir, my source at the 19th Precinct says that another Katzenjammer burglary in Yorkville went down last night."

"What's this?" Foreman looked at O'Rourke.

"Yeah, Agent Witcover's snitch was robbing an apartment and he smashed a chair down on a 77-year-old man's head. The guy is in a coma at Bellevue."

Witcover snarled back, "there's no proof that it was Haupt. No one's identified him."

"Maybe that's because the guy who saw him face to face is now spending his time staring at the insides of his own eyelids. You're supposed to be watching that guy."

"It wasn't him." Witcover was defensive.

"Ya know, while we're protecting the United States of America from spies and saboteurs, shouldn't we also be protecting our citizens from run-of-the-mill criminals? Especially those who work for us?"

"Why don't you mind your own fucking business O'Rourke? I'll deal with my informant in my own way."

"Hmm? Your way? Well, I guess that means New York City is in for a major crime spree."

"All right that's enough," Foreman stepped between the combatants, "stop this crap. We're all on the same side. Agent Witcover, what do you know about this burglary?"

"Absolutely nothing sir."

"Exactly. When was the last time you spoke to your informant?"

"Exactly? Probably nine days ago. I met him at our normal drop-spot by the Battery."

"What was the meeting about?"

"He gave me a name of a guy who was handing stuff to couriers traveling to Mexico and then onto Berlin."

"What came of that?"

"We've got the man staked out and when he makes another move we'll arrest him, or we'll use him to send false information." Witcover was looking for a way out of this interrogation, but there was none.

Foreman continued to probe, "Did your snitch mention anything about any extension of Pastorius? Anything?"

"No sir. Nothing."

"Then why are we paying him? He's not giving us anything but small-fry spies and he says he knows nothing about a big plan to do something horrible."

O'Rourke was gratified to see that Foreman was busting Witcover's chops. He remained quiet and said nothing that might stir the pot.

Foreman wanted results. "Agent Witcover, you need to corral your informant and tell him that his game is up unless we learn something about Pastorius, and also he stops his night job completely. I don't wanna hear any more about this guy breaking and entering anywhere. Got it?"

"Yes, sir." Witcover looked in his boss's eyes and then quickly down at his hands folded on the table. He would have to watch Haupt much closer than he had been watching.

O'Rourke pretended to make some pencil notes on the pad in front of him, but really he was savoring the moment.

July 29, 1942

10:04 p.m.

"I think this is a waste of time." They were back in their old spot, sitting in the darkness under the Third Avenue El. Murphy just wanted it to be over. "He's gotta know that we're onto him."

"Hang on cowboy, the Indians are gonna attack at any minute. We just gotta make sure we're up at the walls of the fort."

"Inflagrante-delicto. I love those words." Murphy was totally sick of Katzenjammer. "I just want to see this asshole actually doing something that we can arrest him for. Otherwise I see dim prospects for my retirement years at a patrolman's pay grade."

"We will get lucky. Just be patient."

"I'm running out of it. How many nights out of my short life have I spent right here in this very spot looking up at that second-floor window? Maybe we should shoot this guy and do society a favor."

Grover smiled. He needed to re-kindle Murphy's enthusiasm. "I got an idea. You're right, he's probably laying low tonight. He knows that we're watching him, right?"

"So?"

"So, this might be the perfect time to pay him a social visit. You know, we walk up to his apartment and gently knock on the door and ask to speak with him."

"The last time we did that he ran, and I lost you for two months."

"We'll be more careful this time."

"Ah… I don' t know if that's such a good…."

"Yeah, I'll bet you that he's up there sitting on his sofa and reading a newspaper while he's listening to Burns and Allen. He's just a quiet guy with a very unfortunate set of friends who want to do him harm. I'm sure that he'd love to chat with us."

"Us?"

"Mmm, hmm, just the two of us in a nice way. If he's worried about people wanting to hurt him we can offer police protection. Anyway, the Captain said we could, so let's." With that logic Grover opened his door and got out of the car.

Reluctantly Murphy, mumbling his personal trepidation quietly to himself, followed his partner as they crossed Third Avenue. They took the flight of stairs to the second floor and at the top they took places to either side of Haupt's doorway lest he started firing bullets through the door. Grover knocked gently. Inside they heard a stirring and both cops reached under their jackets for their weapons, just in case.

"Yes? Who is it?"

Grover spoke, "Eugen, it's me, Detective Grover and my partner Detective Murphy. We would like talk to you."

The voice inside the door hesitated before answering. "I don't have to talk to you. I've done nothing wrong. What do you want?"

Murphy interjected figuring that Haupt might not trust Grover's motives, "we really just want to ask you a few questions. No rough stuff. No arrest, just a chat."

"I will not open this door. Go away."

"Eugen, you know that we're not going away until we talk to you so open the goddamn door and stop with this fucking Three Little Pigs routine," Grover huffed and puffed.

There was a long pause and a silence with it. Grover thought he could almost hear Haupt's brain at work analyzing the situation. Then, without a word the cops heard the lock tumblers turning and the door opened a crack. Haupt's face was half visible through the crack. "So, what do you want?"

Murphy glanced at his partner, and Grover nodded in agreement, they were going in. The cops used the small opening crack as a starting point and together pushed in the door knocking Haupt across the corridor by his apartment doorway. The burly tough guy groaned loudly as he fell back against the opposite wall. The detectives pinned Haupt against the wall and frisked him for weapons. "He's clean," Murphy shrugged. "No more of those brass knuck, huh?"

"I thought you had orders to stay away from me?"

"Orders? Those orders were made before you sent a 77-year-old man to the hospital in a coma." Grover looked Haupt directly in the eyes, but there was absolutely no recognizable reaction to his accusation.

While Grover was staring into Haupt's eyes Murphy was looking at the right side of the man's face. "Hey buddy, what the hell happened to you?"

"Nothing. I fell off a rings exercise at the YMCA gym. I landed on my face."

Grover joined his partner in looking at Haupt's wounds. Grover knew the gym story was a lie, and Murphy did too. "I suppose if I go speak to the YMCA gym guy he'll corroborate your story, huh?"

Murphy joined in. "Which Y is that? The one on West 63rd or the one on 23rd Street? Don't they have mats under the rings?"

Haupt remained silent, eyeing the cops with total contempt. He began to turn beet red but was able to hold his tongue while his brain crafted a benign response that feigned respect but concealed venom. "Officers. I have done nothing wrong. I know that you think otherwise. Please, why are you so intent to hurt me?"

"Eugen, when are you gonna get it through your thick skull that we are onto you, and since you nearly killed that old man we're gonna start putting the screws to you even if your FBI buddies send J-fucking-Edgar Hoover to save your ass." Murphy really enjoyed making cop threats.

"Here's a another goodie for you," Grover teased, "the old guy isn't dead, and his doctor thinks he may come out of this coma in a day or so. My guess is that he saw your face before you bashed in his head. When he wakes up he'll be able to tell us everything and then we'll have you on both burglary and attempted murder."

"I have no idea what you're talking about."

"Let me ask you something, how do you make a living, and how come you're not in the Army?" Murphy asked.

"I would like you to leave my home. You have no right to talk to me like this."

Murphy turned his back to Haupt at the doorway and walked into the front room, from the living room window he could see their regular parking spot across the avenue. He remembered that this was also the room he entered the night Grover got tossed off the fire escape. He looked around. It was sparsely furnished with nothing on the walls except for an awful green coat of paint and a calendar hanging on the wall over a big Philco radio console. The radio was a beauty with an AM and three short wave bands. "Hey Eugen, can you get the Führer on this thing?"

Grover jumped in, "Yeah, can you hear Germany on this?"

Haupt wasn't sure where the questioning was going, but he had some pride in the ornate cherry wood console, so he answered. "Yes, it's a very sensitive receiver. I can listen to the world on it, but most of the time I just listen to radio dramas."

"I got a little bit smaller set in my apartment, I can't hear shit on it. How does this one pick up Europe?" Grover asked.

"It has a built-in ferrite coil antenna, but some smaller radios need bigger outside antennas for the short-wave bands. You should string a long piece of bell wire out your window and attach it to the back of the set. Bell wire makes a great antenna. My radio doesn't need that."

"What are you some kind of a ham operator?" Grover chided.

"I have always been interested in radios. That's why I have a nice one, perhaps better than the set you have in your own home."

"Yeah pal, you do live really well here, don't you?" Grover's sarcasm aimed at perhaps inflaming Haupt's building anger wasn't working.

Murphy also realized that this interview was going nowhere. "Hey Eugen, we're gonna go now, but we're going to be watching you. You won't lose us on the street anymore."

"Yeah, one wrong step and your heinie is in the tombs." Grover headed down the stairs with Murphy close behind.

Haupt stared at the cops as they left him. From what he just heard he had a new concern, that the old man in Bellevue would awaken and cause him trouble. There are options in dealing with that possibility. He slammed his door for emphasis to make sure that the cops heard it before they left the building.

Murphy waited to speak until they were outside the building. "Okay… now let's leave this asshole alone. We put the bull on him and that's that."

"Leave him alone? Why?

"Because every time you get hot about him we get a call to see the captain. I got a wife and kids and I'm more than halfway through my twenty years. I want to get out of this job the best way I can."

"Why wouldn't that happen?"

"Because I think we're playing with fire with this guy. He has friends in high places."

"Don't worry so much. I'll take the blame for any trouble he causes us. Nothing's gonna screw up either of our careers, unless there's no room in your trophy case for the medals you're gonna get when we bust his ass."

"Yeah. I'll believe that when I see it… and what was all that shit about short wave radios and bell wire?"

"Murph, I gotta confess something to ya."

"What?"

"On my day off a couple of weeks ago I followed him when he went shopping."

"You followed him? Without me?"

"Sorry, I wasn't sure how you would feel about it."

Murphy was only mildly offended. "And? … What did you find out?"

"I followed him into a hardware store. He didn't see me. He bought a few hundred feet of bell wire. If he didn't buy it for his radio what did he need it for? Like he said, that Philco in there has a ferrite core antenna, it doesn't need any bell wire for an antenna."

"Good question. I guess you need something to keep you up all night, this one is as good as any."

"Hey, kiss my ass."

They got in their car and closed the doors. Murphy declined that invitation with an earthy reference to romantic bestiality and they drove back to the precinct house.

July 31, 1942

6:40 a.m., Berlin

"Herr Admiral," Horst Wenzl entered the fox's lair with trepidation. He found Canaris writing into his leather bound notebook.

"Yes, Horst what is it?"

"We have a message from Kapitan Garbers. He is concerned about the the date of his voyage."

"What is his rush to know?"

"Sir, the hurricane season in the Atlantic builds during August and for the sake of safety he wants to get under way."

"I see. Let him know that I am awaiting specific dated information that will dictate when Herr Wolfgang must be at his location. These are like the movements of a fine watch. Tell him to be patient. It will be soon."

"Yes sir." Wenzl was very curious and wanted to ask more about the mission, but he decided that he best not.

"I know that I have not shared with you very much of this," Canaris picked up on Wenzl's interest, "but it is of utmost importance that as few know about this as is necessary. Yet, I trust your instincts beyond a doubt so I will share a bit of it with you. You should also know that I have not told this to anyone but the Führer, not Goering not Himmler not Goebbels. In a way, you are the only person who is not directly connected with the mission to learn anything about it."

"Thank you Admiral. You have no reason at all to doubt my loyalty and my silence on this or any matter."

"That is good. Very simply we're on a mission to totally demoralize the enemy, to stun Americans in their own homeland. I expect that once we're done the Americans will lose their taste for fighting. This is why my reaction to the capture of the two teams we sent in May was outwardly minimal. The capture was planned. Now the Americans are looking for our U-boats off their shores, but they won't find any. There's no need to use them for our operation." There was a coldness to Canaris's dismissal of the two teams of Germans that would no-doubt be executed by the Americans.

"So, there is another mission in the works?"

"No, not another mission. It's the same one. Pastorius continues in its second phase."

Wenzl felt sorry for the men and their families, but his boss seemed to have bigger plans. "Admiral, I assume that whatever will happen will shorten the war?"

"It could end it very quickly."

"Yes sir."

"Yes, but now we have to begin the final push. Tell Kapitan Garbers to be patient. We will be with him shortly."

"Yes, Herr Admiral." With that Wenzl rose from his chair, saluted and left the room.

Canaris continued to write in his journal.

August 1, 1942

11:15 a.m., New York City

The bags of groceries were heavy but that wasn't his concern. Eugen Haupt didn't have a free hand to remove the keys from his pocket to open the door to his parents' apartment. "Shit." He mumbled to himself as he put the bags on the floor and fumbled with his keys. Just then the door opened wide.

"Eugen, vere haff you been?" Karl Haupt stared at his son. "I vas vorried about you." Then the old man lowered his voice so as not to be overheard by neighbors, "I read in ze paper that someone got robbed vas in ze hospital. Vat happened?"

The younger Haupt picked up the groceries from the hallway floor, kicked the door shut behind him. "It didn't go as easily as some of the others." He put the bags on the kitchen table.

"Vas Gruber's description of ze apartment wrong in some vay?"

"No, Gruber did fine." A morose Eugen Haupt sat down on a kitchen chair. "Just that the old fart who I thought was sleeping, got up and hit me with a chair. I'm lucky the old bastard didn't kill me."

"Let me see your face. Ach, zat vill leaf a scar, I sink." The elderly goon touched his only son's face with an uncharacteristic bit of tenderness, "You are okay?"

"Yes Poppa, I'm alright, but I don't think I can keep this up. The police paid me a visit , they're watching me, especially that cop." Eugen didn't have to mention Grover's name. The elder Haupt knew who his son was talking about.

"Perhaps zat one didn't land hard enough the last time he fell, ha? Maybe you need to teach him another lesson, one zat he may not recover from… so quickly." The old man smiled.

"Pop, I need to lay low for a while. If that old guy in the hospital wakes up, he saw my face. It's over then, for good."

"Don't worry about him. He probably won't recover. So, vere are ze things you found zere?"

Eugen reached into the bag of groceries and on the bottom was a smaller brown paper bag that jingled when he lifted it up. It was quite large and heavy.

"Aha, Gruber vas right!" Karl took the bag from his son and one by one removed four gold pocket watches, three strings of fine pearls, four diamond pins and numerous rings and bangles. "Ach, a fine haul! I vill reward old Gruber for zis."

As he watched his father ogling the jewelry, the swaggering Katzenjammer Burglar, The Terror of Yorkville, remained emotionless. He had been here before. "Yeah, Gruber's map was perfect. Just, there was this very loud fan in the room, and I didn't hear the old man creeping up on me."

"A sorry accident for both of you."

"And, he saw my face."

"Vonce again Eugen, you don't haff to worry about ze old man. I'm sure zat von't be leafing ze hospital on his feet." Karl spoke as matter-of-factly about the lone witness's immediate future as if he were talking about doing the laundry or boiling an egg. "Ja... he is old and he vill not survife."

Eugen said nothing. Karl still had connections in the underworld, and Eugen had seen this icy cold side of his father before.

"By ze way, Gruber has another map zat I vould like to follow up. It's supposedly an even bigger treasure."

"Poppa, I think I need to stop for a while. These cops are watching me. I think they watched me as I came over here with your groceries."

Karl stared at his son. He recognized a new, ever so slight, reticence in Eugen's tone. He had given marching orders, and his once dutiful son expressed reluctance to follow them. Karl's youthful meal ticket, his strong-armed acrobat of a boy was showing a bit of youthful rebellion. He couldn't allow that to continue. "You haff eluded zem for months now, zere's no reason you cannot continue. You simply vait and make sure zey're not looking and zen you go and do vat you haff to do."

Eugen continued to stare blankly at his father.

August 3, 1942

1:15 p.m., Brest, France

It was a very warm day and the doors to the Café Carnival were open wide to the Rue de Siam allowing whatever sea breeze was able to make its way in from the harbor just across the street into the restaurant. In calmer times Brest was a resort of sorts. While there was lots of commercial shipping and ship-building happening in this French port, it was also a haven for yachtsmen, a sort of northern version of Nice or maybe Marbella in Spain. It was not unusual to see among the grizzled faces of working seamen, the idle rich poking their way through the marine chandleries and then dropping in for a midday meal at one of the many restaurants and bistros adjacent to the docks. So, the German naval officer Heinrich Garbers drew little attention in his guise as the wealthy Swiss yacht owner Heinrich Garbers.

Despite the clean sea air and bright midday sun, the sea port of Brest was a snake pit of foreign agents and international spies keeping an eye on each other. This was of no concern to Garbers. He was confident that no one at all suspected that he was anyone other than who he said he was. Over time, he had established the perfect cover. Since he purchased the sailing vessel Pessim using cash, untraceable Swiss Francs provided by the German navy, the locals took him at his word that he was a wealthy visitor from Basel, caring neither for politics nor the war, and only interested in sailing. From time to time, Pessim would go out for lengthy cruises, often for weeks, manned by a group of the owner's friends. Even the unusually nosy dockmaster assumed that they were all Swiss nationals enjoying camaraderie at sea. He believed that Pessim was just a playboy's plaything.

"Bonjour, Garçon! May I take this table?" Garbers' preferred seat was inside the Café Carnivale's open doors, just steps inside from the boulevard.

"Why yes, monsieur, it is all set for you."

"Thank you," Garbers enjoyed watching the strollers who passed by while he was dining. From this vantage point he had a good view of the street scene without becoming a part of it. The street on this day, and every day since Germany occupied France, was full of his countrymen. He could see that the situation distressed the local wait staff at the restaurant, and he amused himself by pretending to be in a similar state of pique. If a waiter was in earshot he would provocatively grumble in perfect French, "Look at those bastards. They think they own the place!"

"Yes monsieur, I wish that they would go home," the waiter might carefully respond. Nothing seditious in that remark, though it was blatantly non-supportive of the cause. Garbers often thought that given a reversal of fortunes with the French occupying Berlin he might also grumble in a similar manner.

Canaris himself ordered Garbers to meet the spy named Wolfgang at this café at this time. He obliged and waited sipping his demitasse to keep occupied. Wolfgang was going to be the passenger on Pessim's next and maybe most important voyage so far. Garbers knew where he had to take his passenger, but had no idea of the nature of Wolfgang's mission.

Just across the street he noticed a bit of a fracas also brewing. Two German navy men were teasing a French news dealer for not carrying a local German newspaper from Koblenz. The news dealer at first attempted politeness in dealing with the issue, "Monsieur, that newspaper is unavailable here." But the Germans continued to needle him and mock-threatened to shut down his stall and have him arrested "We have already won the war and I want to read about it in my local newspaper." Garbers found the scene as offensive, an affirmation of the world's sense of German belligerence, but he could do nothing about it without blowing his own cover. The sailors kept on baiting the man, who became so frustrated that he talked back to his uniformed tormentors. This was exactly the reaction that the Germans were trying to elicit and exactly the wrong reaction for the news dealer to display. Garbers watched in growing disgust. He outranked the Navy men and in normal circumstances would have had them arrested, but today, his cover and this mission was too important to jeopardize. One of them, a brawny young-ish lieutenant, removed his pistol from its holster and beat the man to the ground with the gun butt. Then a woman, presumably the news dealer's wife, emerged from the building adjacent to his kiosk screaming and ran to her bleeding and moaning husband crumpled on the sidewalk. The two Germans then smiled at each other and nonchalantly left the scene. Walking away, one of them turned back and with a broad smirk on his face said to the fallen dealer, "Make sure you have the Koblenz newspaper the next time we come back."

The tragedy across the street was eased a bit as the news dealer was able to sit up and then walk back to his newsstand aided by his wife. A crowd of locals gathered around him to help and that brought the curtain down on the small drama.

"Excuse me," a voice from over his right shoulder made Garbers turn.

"Ah, hello again, good to see you in the sunlight." Garbers stood and shook Wolfgang's hand as if they were two old friends meeting for a friendly luncheon.

"Good to see you too." Wolfgang smiled as he sat down. "I just viewed that scene across the road. Quite ugly, don't you think?"

"Yes. Very unfortunate. Not at all a good way for the Germans to win the hearts and minds of the French," Garbers opined in his Swiss persona.

Wolfgang nodded in agreement. This time he was dressed in an expensive suit, a crisply ironed white shirt and a dark blue necktie. He still wore his glasses but his pale complexion was now darker and his features were almost Mediterranean. Garbers thought to himself, *What an unlikely physique and look for a member of the Reich.*

They were alone for the moment and out of anyone's hearing range. Wolfgang spoke quickly as the waiter had not yet approached the table. "I am waiting for my supplies to arrive in Brest. I expect that they will be here this week, before Friday."

"Do you need anything from me," Garbers asked?

"No, I will have everything in my supplies. I understand that you will acquire provisions and such for our trip?"

"Yes, the boat is stocked with everything that is needed. If you've never been on a sailboat before, I only caution you that the weather at this time of year is unpredictable. The Atlantic is prone to hurricanes and such. I hope you are not prone to mal-de-mer." Garbers smiled.

The waiter approached the table, "Monsieur, would you like to see a menu?"

Garbers answered, "No, thank you. My friend will have a demitasse and please bring another for me as well."

"Oui Monsieur," the waiter turned and went back to the kitchen.

"I've never been on a sailboat before but I have been on navy ships. I don't get seasick. I have an iron gut."

"Good." Garbers was amused by Wolfgang's bravado. *We'll see about that gut if the weather gets rough,* he thought to himself.

"And how long will it take to arrive at our destination?"

"I estimate between fifteen and twenty days at sea. It really depends on the weather." Garbers hated predicting arrivals. It was something that his superiors always wanted to nail down, but as a sailor who used the wind to move the boat he knew that a prediction like that was at best a rough guess. One day they could be speeding while the next five they could be becalmed and go nowhere. "So, you have your arrangements made for when we drop you off?"

"Yes. Once you radio the arrival confirmation from the boat my contact will be there."

"Good, because after we put you ashore we will immediately leave."

"No need for you to sit around. Everything is arranged. Let's say that I will be on board Thursday night. I think that will be ample time for my supplies to arrive here."

"Very well then, we will sail on the outgoing tide in the morning, if I correctly remember the tide information." Garbers was relieved that his plans were set.

The waiter approached with the two cups of coffee and placed them on the table. "Anything else I can bring you gentlemen?"

"Non, merci," said Wolfgang in perfect French.

"No. Non, merci, et l'addition sil vous plait." Garbers said.

"Oui monsieur," said the waiter.

The two men sipped their coffee without speaking another word. They stared at the commotion around the news dealer across the street as the man's wife dabbed the blood off her husband's face with a pink handkerchief.

August 7, 1942

8:30 a.m., Brest, France

It was sunny with a steady fifteen to twenty-knot south-easterly wind off their port side rear quarter. From Pessim's cutter-rigged fore-triangle to the dainty mizzen all of her sails were up and working. She was on a broad reach and flirting with nine knots of boat speed through the water and also helped along by an ebbing tide that added at least two knots to her overall velocity over the bottom. A small Swiss burgee flapped noisily in its rail mount above the transom. They would soon pass Pointe des Espagnols out of Brest on their way out to sea. British spies might report on its departure, but such a report would not be worth risking a clandestine radio transmission.

In peacetime, Brest was a perfect harbor for commerce and yachting. Sheltered from the Atlantic's direct power it was a deep-water port with lots of room for big ships and pleasure craft as well. The fury of many an Atlantic storm was easily broken by prominent headlands leaving the harbor areas generally placid while an outside tempest ensued. At the moment the tempest was centered inside the harbor.

The German fleet was using Brest's ample dry-dock and ship building space for maintaining its fleet of U-boats, battleships and heavy cruisers. This, by definition attracted frequent air raids by RAF bombers but few got through the German defenses to do much damage. Brest was far enough away that British planes often ran out of fuel before they could make a safe return over the southern English shoreline. The city was so strategic to the German naval war effort it became a center point of intrigue and spying. No ship arrival or departure went unnoticed. Pleasure craft, however, were another story. With her gleaming varnished teak and mahogany brightwork shining in the morning sun, Pessim appeared as an unmistakable thing of beauty that posed no risk of anything to anyone. Garbers felt secure that his boat's track to open water would be viewed by anyone who happened to be watching as purely benign. For the moment, Garbers was not at war, but the skipper of this magnificent yacht out for a pleasure cruise with friends.

Upon his arrival at the docks the night before, Wolfgang had carried two large suitcases. The bags were heavy, but he wouldn't allow anyone to help him. Garbers was impressed by the stocky man's cat-like movements as he lifted his luggage aboard the sailboat for the first time, never once losing his footing or balance. Garbers showed the man to the yacht's lone private cabin and that was the last anyone aboard Pessim saw of him for a while.

August 15, 1942

5:47 p.m., New York City

"Try this one..." The cosmetics saleswoman sprayed Ellen's wrist. "I think you'll like it."

She took a sniff, "Yes, I do!" It was Saturday afternoon at Macy's and Ellen was in a rush. "I'll take the small one."

"Very good. I'll get it wrapped up," the saleslady turned toward her cash register.

"Thank you." Ellen glanced down at her wristwatch. *Oh my God, it's already 6 o'clock?* She'd already decided that nothing would prevent her from being on time for this evening's date with her Detective Douglas Grover of the NYPD. *Pay and get out of here and you'll be okay.* On most of their previous dates Grover would be late, or something else would go awry. She was determined to make sure that if something did go wrong, it would not be her fault.

"Your perfume, Miss. That will be one dollar and fifteen cents."

Ellen dug into her purse and handed the saleswoman the exact change, "Here you are." She took the small bag with the perfume and dashed out to the street. With only a bit less than a half hour to get to their meeting spot at Grand Central, she decided to walk fast.

Ellen Kramer first met P.O. Douglas Grover on the job. She was sitting on a bench in Duane Park having a lunchtime sandwich. As Grover remembered their first meeting, "a creep named Patrick Dolan grabbed her purse off the bench and ran." Unfortunately for Dolan, patrolman Grover was standing directly across Duane Street and saw the theft happening. He arrested the thief, returned the purse, and got Ellen's phone number all at the same time. After one date they became inseparable.

If there had been any single good thing to come out of this war it was that new professional doors opened for women. Much of the male workforce was busy with the military allowing many women new chances at a life outside the family kitchen. Ellen graduated with a teaching degree from City College with the class of 1941. She got her first job at Western Union. The company at its big, downtown Manhattan headquarters ran its own school for its delivery boys. Many of them had dropped out of regular school driven by a need to make money to help support struggling parents at the latter end of the great depression. When they weren't out making telegram deliveries they were in her classroom at 60 Hudson Street.

Until she met Douglas Grover, Ellen's idea of a date had always involved some kind of group activity like dining, dancing, movie-going or even bowling with a date and her friends. With Grover, none of those activities were ever on the program. Finally, she came to understand that Douglas was extremely shy in social settings, and lately, since he broke his leg, it had gotten worse. He'd become self-conscious about his new limp. But she loved him, and Ellen Kramer knew that if she wanted to continue her relationship with Grover she needed to, at least temporarily, give in to his neuroses.

So, she was thrilled about his evening's plans—dinner and a movie. Grover suggested a small Italian place in mid-town on East 45th Street. They would meet by the information booth in Grand Central Terminal at 6:30 and go on from there. Ellen was confident that the ultra-punctual Doug would be there on the main concourse at exactly at 6:30, no earlier, no later. She hustled to their rendezvous spot.

Her speed-walking paid off and she arrived five minutes early. The terminal wasn't very crowded on this late summer Saturday afternoon and she expected to see Doug's face approaching her at any moment.

Grand Central Terminal was strikingly beautiful as sunlight poured through its western windows, but it too displayed the mark of wartime. Men and women in uniform outnumbered Grand Central's routine travelers, and the eastern side of the interior displayed a gigantic, wall-sized banner promoting the sale of war bonds.

Searching for Doug in the flowing crowd her eyes moved from one stranger's face to another. Ellen liked to play a self-created game she called, "Oh, I've met you before." She would look at a unfamiliar face and try to make a story about it. There was the beefy old woman sitting on her haunches near the entrance to Track 30. The woman appeared to be homeless with all of her worldly goods sitting next to her on a small wooden mover's dolly. *I'm sure I've seen her before near my office building. You were once a Russian princess before the reds killed your uncle, the Tsar. How sad!* There was a teenage couple laughing over a couple of popsicles as they walked by, oh those two again. *He's taking her home to meet his mother. How cute!* There was a soldier speaking with another man in a conductor's uniform, *Oh, one of my delivery boys from Western Union. I hope he stays safe.* And yet another man with a briefcase who was running to make a train, *Oh, that's the lawyer from the third-floor apartment in my building.* Then there was a husky blond man reading a newspaper over by the Eastern staircase. She caught a glimpse of his face for less than a second. He, too, looked familiar, but for some reason he was much more familiar than the others. She had no story about this man as she actually attempted to place him. *No matter, probably someone I met at work or something.* Seconds later the most familiar face of all came

into her view. Doug descended the stairs from the Vanderbilt Avenue terminal entrance and walked toward her.

"Hey... you look terrific!"

"Thanks," she was really glad to see him.

"Damn, I thought I was going to be late. The buses on Fifth aren't moving as often as I remembered."

"That's no problem at all. I've only been here for a few minutes. So,
where are we going?"

"I thought I would take you to this new place called Horn and Hardart's...
It's very exclusive with a big menu." Grover smiled broadly.

"If the Horn and Hardart doesn't employ an Italian waiter holding a
glass of Chianti I don't want to have anything to do with you anymore."
She smiled back.

"Well, okay then, I knew you might have a problem with that so I made
a safety reservation. I think they have an Italian waiter."

Ellen smiled, "Oh, that sounds so much better."

"But I'm afraid it may not have all the charm of the Automat."

"I'll live." She took Grover's hand and began to lead him toward the
doors on Lexington Avenue.

They took a few steps forward and then Ellen stopped as something
came into her head. "While I was waiting for you I saw a man who I think
I know, but I can't place the face. He's standing over there reading a paper.
'Recognize him at all?"

Doug looked. Over by the gate to Track 23, just ahead of the walkway
to Lexington Avenue, a man attempted to look inconspicuous by hiding his
face behind a large-font wartime headline. It took a fraction of a second for
Grover's cop instinct to kick in. This guy is wrong. Seconds later the man
turned away and headed through the track gate. *Some guy waiting for a train?*
Nope. There was no destination posting at the gate entrance, which meant
there was no train on the track inside. He let out a small sigh and silently
cursed himself, *Asshole you have a dinner date. Stop it!* Grover grabbed her
hand, "Ah, forget him. Let's go... our reservation is in fifteen minutes."

"Okay." Ellen pulled at his hand, continuing their move toward
Lexington. Then she had a mild revelation, "Hey, you know what... It just
came to me. I know where I saw him before. He's that friend you met at
Orchard Beach, you know, the guy with the really bad sunburn." For all of
her gifts of perception Ellen hadn't linked Doug's "friend" on the beach to a
man she had only known by name from Doug's rants.

Grover froze in his steps. "Wait here, I'll be right back." He turned on his
heel and with some pain, raced toward the gate that the man just entered.
The sliding door to the track gate was slightly ajar, just big enough for a man

to squeeze by. Grover pushed his way in and jogged down the short ramp to the train platform. There wasn't a soul there, yet he was sure that he had seen the man go through the gate. Grover leaned over the tracks and peered into the dark abyss at the end of the platform. *Where the hell did he go?* Then, in the darkness at the far end of the platform a flicker of movement registered on his retina. It could have been a sheet of newspaper caught in a draft, but instinct told him someone is down there in the tunnel for whatever reason. Grover was certain it was Eugen Haupt.

He quickly weighed his options. He was off duty and his date was waiting for him to go to dinner. He wasn't one-hundred per-cent sure that he actually did see anyone or anything on the northbound tracks, he only felt it. If indeed it was Haupt, which it might not be, what was he doing anyway? Did Haupt work for the railroad? Was this a crime that called for a detective's intervention? He decided to give it up.

Seconds later he was back at the sliding gate door and Ellen was standing there staring at him. She didn't look happy. "So, are we going to eat Italian food or are we going to have a fight right here?"

"Honey… I'm sorry, but you said it was my pal from the beach. I just…"

"I don't want to hear about it."

"My mistake, 'just wanted to say hey."

"I really do not want to hear about it now, or ever." Ellen wasn't thrilled with his apology. "Oh yeah, leave me standing alone again in the middle of Grand Central one more time and you'll really be sorry, you can be sure of that."

At this point the only thing that Detective Doug Grover was sure of was that he had seen Eugen Haupt dash into the darkness of the railroad tunnel, and now he was wondering why.

August 17, 1942

8:30 a.m.

"Hey, nice of you to come. Order anything you like, it's on me... just make sure it's not more than eggs, toast and coffee." Grover smiled and motioned for his guest to sit.

The Clarion Diner on Third Avenue was located in the law enforcement neutral-zone between the 19th precinct on 67th street and the FBI office on 69th. Because of its location it was also a place that the rival-camp soldiers could be seen together in public. Today's meeting was at Grover's invitation and Special Agent O'Rourke was happy to take advantage of the opportunity for a free breakfast. In the first few minutes sitting in the same booth neither said a word to the other until the waitress arrived with two grimy ketchup stained menus.

O'Rourke got the conversation going. " 'You pay attention to baseball?"

"Yeah, some..."

"I think all of us at the Bureau like the Yankees."

"That's a rich man's team. We're working stiffs at the 19th. We like da bums."

"I'm not rich. I still like the Yanks."

"Any team that can pay someone like DiMaggio over forty-grand a year is a rich man's team."

"Well. We'll have to disagree on favorite teams. How about we can agree on Rita Hayworth's legs, hmmm?"

"No problem there." Then some more light shop talk. "So how often do you guys get on the range?"

"Often, we have a shooting room right in the building. We can go down there when we want. Nothing that formal."

The waitress interrupted their brilliant repartee. "What can I get you gentlemen? Coffee, juice?"

As they ordered breakfast they were in awe of their server, a strikingly pretty blonde in her early twenties. Her presence made both Grover and O'Rourke tense up just to speak with her. As she turned away to get their coffee both men ogled her perfect legs with nylon stocking seams working their way up her calves into the netherworld under her waitress uniform.

"Forget Rita Hayworth!"

"She is something, you can say that again."

"I wonder if she'd be interested in dating a beefy yet crude federal law officer?"

"Give it up, I think she's engaged to a marine somewhere in the Pacific."

"How do you know? Did you ever ask her out?"

"Me? Nah, I'm spoken for. Ellen would kill me. They'd find my body on the steps of the precinct. This one here just talks to me about how much she misses her honey."

"That's one lucky marine."

The two men sneakily ogled the waitress as she made her way back to their table with a glass coffee pot. She poured two cups and smiled again. "I'll get your eggs out here in a minute."

"So, did you write to that man of yours recently?" Grover looked up at her, saying anything he could to keep her at their table.

"I write to him every day, but I haven't had a letter from him in more than two weeks. I guess where he is the mail isn't so regular." Her smile briefly disappeared.

"Well, tell him that we're all thinking about him," Grover offered.

"Thanks, I will." She turned and walked back behind the main counter.

O'Rourke raised the hot cup of coffee. "Okay, tell me now, what's on your mind?" He took a noisy sip.

Grover's led with his best shot. "Be honest with me, and by telling me this you're not giving away anything I shouldn't know about your informant, okay? Nobody's got an eye on him ever, right?"

"What do you mean? You think no one is watching him?"

"I mean at night when he goes out and does his professional work, there's no FBI gumshoe taggin' along, is there?"

O'Rourke had to weigh his answer. Should I tell Grover that Witcover screwed up and never kept tabs on his snitch? He'd already violated Bureau rules when he and Grover first shared a drink at McGlade's. In fact, even acknowledging that Haupt was an informant was a violation of the rules, but by this point that horse had long left the barn. Instead he decided to feint, "Listen, I'm pretty sure that you've been told to leave him alone?"

"Yeah… sure. I am doing that, but only to protect Tim's career."

O'Rourke easily read the smirk on Grover's face. "So, is your partner as crazy as you are?"

"Murph's okay, but he thinks I'm screwy… but he backs me up anyway. That could classify him as crazier than me."

"Okay," against the nagging inside voice telling him to keep his FBI mouth shut, O'Rourke relented. "Doug, this is strictly confidential. If you tell anyone at all I will deny it and then you'll be on my shit list, and you don't want to be on my shit list."

"I know, I know. We had this conversation before. Anyway, I'm currently on my girlfriend's and my captain's shit lists and two shits lists at a time are enough. So?"

"Are you wondering why I agreed to meet you?"

"Because I said that I was buying?"

" 'Part of it, but actually, the reason I did want to talk to you is that I... I mean the Bureau could use your help."

"Even after all we've been through together?" Grover kept up his deadpan. "Yeah, bygones."

"Great, bygones. What's the Bureau's problem?"

"Remember those Nazis that we rounded up in June?"

"The Long Island guys? Yeah... good catch, 'made all the papers."

"Thanks. Those guys, they're probably all headed for an electric chair somewhere, but we have reason to believe that they weren't the whole story."

"How do you mean?"

"I'm gonna tell you some stuff that isn't for public consumption, but for some dumb reason I trust you with it."

" 'Cause I'm paying?"

"Umm, yeah, let's call it that. These guys were all part of a high-up Nazi operation called 'Pastorius.' We busted them all within a week after they got here and hid out."

"I sorta know about this story. You got 'em all after one of them ratted out all his pals. I would call that okay, but really not great police work."

"Well, we did get all of them."

"All of them, yup. So?"

"At the start we only knew right away about the boat that landed in Long Island."

"But there was a second landing, right? In Florida?"

"And one of the guys from the Florida boat ratted out all the others, I get it."

"That's the public story."

"Public story?"

"We already knew about all of them. Our little birdie told us."

"Birdie?"

"Yeah, our pigeon. He told us everything even before the other guy ratted out his mates."

"Eugen? How the...?"

"His source knew about them."

"Before anyone?"

"Seems that way. He was really a huge help. He's got an ear to the ground in Yorkville."

"He's a total bullsh..."

O'Rourke cut off Grover's brewing tirade. "Sooooo, anyway, we think we have them all, eight guys from two submarines. Then, about a month ago the Navy's intel guys intercept a German transmission to U-boat command-ers in the North Atlantic and to whoever-the-hell-else they talk to saying Pastorius lives."

"What's that mean?"

"Good question. Then we get word from some deep source in Berlin that they're up to something very big over here. It suggests that they're still running this operation, but we still don't know what it is."

"Well, yeah, there is a war going on, no?"

"My bosses seem to think that the Germans wanted us to catch them, and the guys who got here by submarine were saps in a big setup."

"How?"

"Think about it, we knew about all of them even before we were sup-posed to know about all of them."

"Yeah, and why would a trained German spy rat out his pals, I mean, really? And after a trip across the ocean in a damn submarine?"

"That's exactly my point. And here's another thing to consider. If you're the Germans and you're sending guys over here to blow things up, and you sent them to land in the U.S. a thousand miles apart from each other, why would either team have to know anything at all about the other?"

"Good question. And, what's in it for the guy who rats out his pals? They're all gonna get the chair for this?"

The stoolie isn't gonna die. He'll get a reprieve 'cause he led us to the rest of them. The other guys, not so lucky."

"And you think that the arrest was a setup? Pretty cold blooded if you ask me."

"That's the Germans. We think they want us to think that there are more submarines coming with more saboteurs so we'll waste our time looking for them."

"Did these submarine guys have a specific mission?" Grover hadn't paid too much attention to the war since he was told that he wouldn't be drafted, but now he was interested.

"They told us they were here to blow up railroads and factories. They brought explosives with them to do some of that, but they didn't bring that much stuff to do much damage."

"Why are you telling me this?"

"Because I'm starting to agree with you that Eugen Haupt might not be all he pretends to be."

"But you just said that he helped you capture these guys?"

"I'm starting to question his loyalty."

"How did you hook up with him in the first place?"

"About two years ago we raided a Bund meeting in Yorkville. We had reason to believe that one or more of them were in the business of leaking Liberty Ship movement information. Somehow the U-boat packs seemed to know the routes we were using and were out there waiting for the convoys. Two of these scumbags worked on the docks in Brooklyn and we're pretty sure it was them."

"Did you stop them?"

"Yeah, we arrested 'em and it took a couple of days to break 'em but in the end they confessed. I think we may have saved a few ships from attack, but still the crap goes on. After we first rounded up the lot of them one of the guys opened up to us that he wasn't a Nazi. He said that he went to the meetings for business purposes only. He admitted that he was a thief who thought he could make some money out of the fanatics."

"Our boy Eugen?"

"Yeah. He said that his parents were German but he was still a loyal American citizen. He offered us his services to help us bust the Nazis in New York with only one request, that we protect him from his enemies; that would be you, the NYPD. We tried him out and came to know that his information was highly accurate."

"You knew he was a burglar?"

"Yeah, we knew that all along."

"And now you think he could be a saboteur?"

"I do, but no one on my team thinks like I do. Everyone at the office thinks he's a treasure chest."

"D'ya believe him?"

"When he tells us about Nazi sympathizers, his information is always on the money, but no one on the team has any idea where he gets the info. We used to watch him when this all started, but he was boring. He didn't do anything most of the time but visit his parents and hang out in his own apartment."

"So that's why you stopped tailing him?"

"There was too much else going on and the lead agent on the team who's running him said that if Haupt or anyone he was meeting with saw a tail it would screw his ability to gather information. I used to agree with that, but now I can see that with no one holding his leash, he's a junkyard dog without a fence."

"Here's the crazy thing from my side, I've been tailing him against orders since my cast came off and I haven't seen him do anything wrong since that burglary the night when he threw me off the fire escape."

"I'm glad he didn't kill you."

"Yeah, so maybe you owe me? At least can you tell me what he was looking for?"

"I can't answer that."

"Okay, then tell me this, if Haupt never goes anywhere, how is he getting all this information for you? Where did he get the info about the subs?"

"I honestly do not know."

"This is FUBAR. I can't arrest him because you guys'll spring him as soon as I do, but we both know he's a low-life and probably a Nazi spy at the same time!

"Yeah, but I'm not allowed to share information from any on-going investigation."

"Well, that may be a bit of water under the Brooklyn Bridge, hmmm?" Grover smiled. "But what you say makes some recent stuff I've watched him do start to make some sense."

"Like what?"

"A few weeks back I was off duty and decided to stake the SOB out on my own time. I followed him in the middle of the day. He goes into this big hardware store on East 86th and buys a couple'a hundred feet of bell wire and two 67-volt radio batteries. What does anybody need that for? He's not a ham operator or anything?"

"That is a little odd, but people do buy that stuff."

"But, he doesn't go home with it, instead he keeps walking East on 86th and down First Avenue where I lose him in the crowd. He's moving in the total opposite direction from his house."

"Maybe he has other errands? Maybe he has a radio at home?"

"Murph and me went to his house… he has one of those big four band shortwave consoles and he bragged that it had an internal antenna and it didn't need any other wires for him to listen to the world."

"Interesting."

"Then, this past weekend I meet my girl for a dinner date in the middle of Grand Central. I'm pretty sure I saw Haupt hiding behind a newspaper and then suspiciously disappearing into a train tunnel."

"And you're sure it was Haupt?"

"Well to be honest, I'm not one-hundred percent sure, but I think it was him."

"In Grand Central? That might fit."

"Fit what?"

"Well, if he is really a Nazi spy or something like that… the railroads… the Pastorius teams were planning to blow up railroads, you know, to stop the flow of war materials to the ports. Grand Central is a railroad hub."

"Yeah, but," Grover reminded, "those kinds of trains don't go there.

Grand Central is just a passenger train station."

"Terminal," O'Rourke corrected him. "Grand Central is a terminal... the end of the line. Trains go through a station, they end their trip at a terminal."

"I didn't know that."

"It's an amazing place. Did you know that all of Park Avenue up to 97th Street is basically a bridge? There's tracks all the way up."

"How'd you come to know that?" Grover was impressed.

"I've got relatives who work for the New York Central. And did you know that from about 44th Street up till about 50th, all those tracks fill up the space West to East under street level all the way from Madison Avenue to Lexington. They start to narrow after that down to four tracks as they go further uptown, but all of the buildings on either side of Park Avenue below about 48th Street are built over the railroad tracks and tunnels."

"Yeah? Hmmm! Okay, so what's he doing in the tunnel in the terminal?"

"That's the "Take It Or Leave It" question."

O'Rourke's reference to a radio game show was lost on Grover who really never listened to radio. "So the sonofabitch is a Nazi spy!"

" 'Can't say that yet. We need more information, but that's something we can do together without my boss's permission. You can be a source for the FBI, sort of an informant, just, I can't pay you." O'Rourke was opening a door that Grover was happy to enter.

"Why don't I get paid like other informants?"

"The way this works is that you get to buy me breakfast, and maybe the occasional drink."

" 'Sounds fair, but I want a piece of this guy."

"Okay. We work together, but nothing crazy from you,"

Grover smiled. "Do I tell my partner about any of this? Murph's entirely on the case with me."

"Yeah, I think that's a good idea. He seems to be the one who keeps the keys to your furnace room."

"He'll love it," Doug wasn't really sure about that, but he signed Murphy up anyway. "Jim, can I call you Jim?"

"Sure."

"What happens when your boss finds out I'm working as a snitch. How do I fit in?"

"Doug, may I call you Doug?"

"Okay."

"You need to stay away from this guy. We can track him together, but you as an individual need to keep your distance. I'll be the one who does the following. I'm admitting to you for a fact that the Bureau, well at least this member of the Bureau, knows this is a bad guy, and yeah, he's probably into things we don't want him to be into. But, we need him."

"And that's it?"

"That's it. Now we understand each other."

"You can follow him, but I'm going with you." Grover could be relentless, even annoying.

Then real life added the punctuation to their conversation. The waitress dropped a check onto the table. "Thanks boys, see you again soon."

9:30 a.m.

Grover was back in the squad room about fifteen minutes after his breakfast with O'Rourke.

Murphy was already at his desk. "By the looks of that smile you either won money or just got laid."

Grover was unaware of his telltale smile. "Neither, but I am happy." He removed his suit jacket, hung it on the back of his chair and sat down.

"And to what can we attribute this bout of unrestrained ... er ... euphoria? Euphoria was a word on my crossword puzzle this morning."

Grover spoke in a subdued tone. "I just was talking to that FBI guy O'Rourke. He agrees with me about Haupt."

"You found someone who agrees with you on something?"

"That's not so hard to understand."

"What does he agree with?"

"Well, maybe it's not actual agreement, but he does think that Haupt may be into something bad."

Murphy stared blankly at his partner before saying a word. He was satisfied to play the role of Sancho Panza to his good pal Don Quixote. But like his partner, Tim also had a hot-tempered side, and instinct told him to show it now, "What the fuck does an FBI stooge know about a cheap-shit burglar like Haupt? You shouldn't be talking to those guys about anything."

"Who stole your dog? O'Rourke agrees with us. He thinks that Haupt might not be just a burglar and a snitch."

"We know all about him. Why the hell do we need the FBI? Those suits want something from us."

"O'Rourke wants our help about something big. You might not believe this, but it's even bigger than the burglaries. It can't come down to us as official orders from Spring Street, and his boss would also be pissed off if he knew O'Rourke talked to me."

"Bigger than...?"

"O'Rourke says that the Bureau has information that there could be a Nazi saboteur running around. He's starting to think that our boy might be something more than just a slick burglar."

"Haupt? A saboteur? You can't seriously believe that? What a joke! He's not smart enough. That's just FBI bullshit. They're protecting the SOB."

"Whoa, take it easy. You're starting to sound like me." Grover stared directly into his partner's face and understood what was going on. Murphy was jealous! "Murph, both O'Rourke and me... we wouldn't do this without you."

"Oh, okay then." Murphy was easily mollified. "Well, why don't they share it with our bosses?"

"Dunno. Maybe the commissioner knows about it and maybe not. But, you and I know about it and we also know Yorkville and Haupt. O'Rourke was smart to share it all. We are feet on the ground."

"So what's the sabotage thing all about?"

"They don't know, but what they do have is a source somewhere in Germany who's been feeding them bits of stuff. This is serious."

"The war has come to the 19th!"

"I think it's been here for a while; we just haven't seen it. I really stopped thinking about the war after I realized I wouldn't be drafted."

"You know, I think it's time to ruffle Mr. Haupt's feathers again."

"Well, before we do that there was another robbery last night."

"Katzenjammer again, huh?"

"No, this time just a scumbag breaking into an apartment with no one at home and taking their silver. Pretty run of the mill."

"No spies or saboteurs?"

"Nope, just some random asshole. We gotta get statements from the occupants."

"Okay, let's." With that Grover neatly stacked the files on his desk and locked them into the biggest drawer, no need to lose any more papers to internal office misplacement. Within a minute the detective duo was on its way out of the squad room.

August 18, 1942

10:45 a.m.

"Poppa, it's all in place. I ran the wire from the roof like you wanted without anyone watching me. The apartment is ready."

Karl Haupt let out a big sigh of pride. This was his boy, capable, strong and eager to please his ailing father. "Eugen, he iss not just my guest, he is our guest." He sank back in his easy chair and closed his flannel robe tightly across his chest. It had to be 85 degrees in the apartment and yet the old man felt a chill.

"I understand Poppa. I'll put some food and ice in the icebox just before he arrives. I put that box of wine in there as well."

"I'm sure you haff made ze place comfortable."

"Yes, as far as a stinking basement hell hole can be comfortable, yes I did."

"Vat about ze tunnels?"

Eugen, not much of an artist in his youth, given to doodling stick figures for most of his adolescent daydreaming, had somehow become quite adept as a freehand cartographer. "I have pretty much mapped out the area you asked me about, and I left it in the apartment on top of the case of wine."

"Good, good." The old man was clearly excited. He began to cough.

Eugen blanched at the uncontrolled sound. Karl was unable to catch his breath and it was distressing to his boy. Perhaps his father's excitement would lessen a bit if he changed the subject of the conversation slightly. "Poppa, I don't suppose you can tell me what any of this is for?"

"No, perhaps it iss better zat you don't know too much more zan you already know. Ve don't want your FBI friends to catch on." The hacking ebbed.

"The only things I tell the FBI are those names you give me."

"Vat do zey giff you in return for ze names?"

"They give me money and they keep the police away from me." Eugen grabbed an apple from the fruit tray in the center of the dining table. "I'm their prize. The FBI told the New York police to stay away from me as their interference with my movements would certainly jeopardize national security. Pretty funny!"

"Yes, I zink so. And also it helps us veed out ze traitors in ze movement. I'm sure ze authorities are grateful for your information too."

"Yes Poppa." There was a mildly dismissive tone in Eugen's voice.

"Eugen, you need to understand zat we are at war and zat ze Führer hass great plans for us ven ze fighting is over." Karl took a moment to remind his son of their goal. "It vill be a near-perfect vorld vonce ze Reich hass taken over from ze Jew-lover Roosevelt and his communist allies."

"Poppa, the politics of it all really doesn't interest me. I will do well with whoever is in power."

The old man sighed. "Yes you vill." Karl picked up a folded calendar from small end table adjacent to his chair. He flipped a page and studied the dates. "Let me see... I belieff zat our guest should be arrifing in a very few days. I vill know more about ze exact time und place soon. He might not arrife at a regular port. You must be able to get a car and pick him up from verever he lands."

Eugen was a bit confused. This wasn't the first mission he had gone on for "the fatherland" but none of the others required so much of his personal time. "I think I can get my hands on a car for a short while."

"Good. I vill giff you all ze details tomorrow or the day after as soon as I learn about hiss travel plans." The old man became lost in thought.

"Poppa?"

"Hmmm? Yes?"

"I'm going to leave now. I have some business to attend to."

1:15 p.m.

FBI Special Agent Edmund Witcover waited patiently at their regular meeting spot, a park bench down the block from the Whitehall Street induction center. As was their practice Witcover brought a sandwich in a brown paper bag. At the top of the bag was a roast beef on rye with tomatoes and mayonnaise and at the bottom was a wad of twenty-dollar bills. It was a pleasant enough day and the patrician Princeton grad perfectly fit in with the local crowd. Witcover clutched the sandwich bag a bit tighter than most al fresco diners might, but his heavy grip got no one's attention. He glanced at his watch, his appointment was running about ten minutes behind schedule.

Eugen Haupt emerged from the Rector Street subway station and walked to the meeting from there. Always suspicious, he figured that if he was being tailed he would have a greater opportunity to see who was following him and to shake him off if he took a longer route. Haupt also had a sandwich bag, a bag similar to that of the one carried by the FBI agent Witcover. In Haupt's bag was another sandwich and under that, a folded white envelope. As he made his final approach to the park he saw Witcover. Haupt took a seat on the bench next to the FBI agent. They pretended not to notice one-another, but they spoke immediately.

Witcover, spoke first, "Lovely day isn't it?"

"Yes, absolutely lovely. I see you brought lunch."

"Yes I did. What are you having today?"

Haupt pointed at the bag in his lap and sheepishly smiled, "I have a sardine sandwich." Nonchalantly he raised it up slightly to show Witcover his lunch.

"I have roast beef today." Haupt's eyes lit up ever so slightly.

Both men scoured the faces of passers-by and other park lunch eaters until they were sure no one was looking and they switched lunch bags. It was a piece of inept theater concocted by the boy-scout-stiff lawman and his crude street-wise snitch. Of course, no one was watching them. No one ever watched them as they repeated this charade at least fifteen times before. No one cared.

Underlying the actual purpose of this meeting was Witcover's usual disappointment with Haupt's lunch selection. Witcover, in previous meetings, had always brought along something he thought was good. Haupt always went for boring or worse. When Witcover brought a turkey sandwich, Haupt brought two slices of Swiss cheese on white bread. When Witcover brought meat loaf, Haupt brought grape jelly on a stale Kaiser roll. Witcover never forgot the ultimate indignity of their relationship, in one meeting he brought a fresh lobster roll from a fish bar in the Fulton Market and Haupt brought a single slice of salami between two pieces of dry pumpernickel. Clearly, Haupt was not a gourmet and Witcover always came away gastronomically disappointed.

After downing his roast beef, Haupt crumpled the bag and stuffed it into his pants pocket. Witcover reached into his bag and removed a folded piece of white paper and stuffed it into his jacket. Both men now had what they had come for. "What's going on in your world?"

"Just the same thing. I think you will find those are names you may not have known about."

"Thanks. I've been meaning to ask you, where do you get these names?"

"I just have a close ear to my community." Haupt knew the benefits of being a man of mystery. As long as he produced he was the Bureau's golden boy. While Witcover kept asking, both men knew that Haupt would never reveal his sources. Witcover would take the names back to the office and the FBI would either arrest or begin following some more treasonous bundists.

"What else have you heard on the street lately? Anything big going on?"

Eugen paused for a moment before his answer. He needed to sound convincing. "No, nothing big that I know about."

"We hear that something is in the works. Something much bigger than those guys in the submarines."

"I haven't heard anything, but then I'll keep my ears open and let you know."

"You do that and there'll be something extra in your next lunch bag. I need more out of you than's been coming lately." Witcover looked directly into Haupt's eyes and made a weak attempt at intimidation.

"Yes, I understand." Haupt, a master at the art of intimidation himself, pretended to fall for it. Little did Witcover know that the offer of more money pushed Haupt into the eye of his own storm of personal opportunism. He wasn't about to be disloyal to his Nazi father, but he also loved the idea of extra money in his lunch bag. "I will see what I can find out from my sources."

"Good. Keep in touch." Special Agent Edmund Witcover got up from the bench, crumpled his brown paper bag and tossed it into the gutter. During these troubled times the misdemeanor of littering seemed really unimportant to anyone. "I'll be waiting. And, hey, do me a big favor and stay out of trouble."

Haupt said nothing as he watched the FBI agent amble across Broadway and disappear into a downtown canyon of gray buildings. He thought to himself, there is opportunity here, but how do I take it?" Haupt then stood up, removed the brown paper bag from his pocket, took out the ten crisp twenty's inside and added his crumpled bag to the other detritus at the curb. *How do I take it?*

August 24, 1942

6:00 a.m., the North Atlantic Ocean

Kapitan Heinrich Garbers had the watch. He had been at the helm for
the past three hours and that was unfortunate for him. He was very cold
and very wet. From his cockpit position he saw it coming and only had a
second or two to wince before the impact. In the faint light of the oncoming dawn a gray-green wall of water at least twenty feet high broke over the
bare bowsprit. The splash blew back with the speed of the wind, once again
soaked him and quickly flooded up across the teak deck almost as far as the
aft companionway doors. A rubberized rain suit offered little protection
from the gale. From his semi-sheltered position, cowering in the well by the
steering wheel, he surveyed for any damage at the bow of the boat. There
wasn't anything wrong that he could see from this far back and he was in no
way planning to stand up and move forward for a closer look. A tiny storm
jib was tightly set and kept the hove-to nose into the wind. Drogues tied
to the foredeck seemed to keep the bow into the waves and increased the
chances of the boat not being rolled over abeam or getting pooped. There
wasn't much else to do now other than to ride it out. That would probably
take a while. By the look of the sea around him he guessed that the winds
were Beaufort force eight or nine. He couldn't see very much else as the
wind tossed a wilted wet salad of seaweed, spume and froth into his eyes
every time he tried to look into the direction of the blow. "This isn't too
bad," he reasoned, but the shriek of the howling gale nearly drowned out
even his loudest thoughts.

The others sat below, tossed and bounced inside the belly of the yacht.
They were dry, but no one was comfortable. The vessel's motion was erratic.
Two slept, two tried to read, and the other two took turns sharing a vomit
bucket. Garbers swung the companionway open, and yelled down "Hey,
Otto, know the two stages of seasickness? The first is that you think you're
going to die. The second is that you are afraid that you won't." Otto looked
up at him from below with a pale face and a grim sneer. His face was a visual
dictionary of a thousand unpleasant words and thoughts. "Garbers, with
all due respect to your rank, you are an asshole." Then, without missing a
beat, he continued emptying his distraught stomach into the zinc pail. The
captain smiled at his crewman and thought, "mal de mer," the great leveler
of surly men.

In the hours before the storm descended on them, Garbers had been watching the barometer fall rapidly. It gave the voyagers time to shorten sail and prepare the boat for bad weather. Otto, before his embrasure of the zinc bucket, had fashioned elaborate drogues made out of ten canvas buckets and a couple of fifty-meter long hemp dock lines. The idea was well known to sailors. The buckets and line were extended off the bow and as the wind blew the sixty-five-foot hull backwards they would act as sea anchors. Wind pressure on the boat would keep enough tension on these bucket warp lines that the bow would remain pointed into the wind. As the waves were traveling with the blow, the boat would take incoming seas at the bow not broadside. A broad side wave could roll her over and that could end in disaster, especially for their cargo and the man entrusted with it. The drogues seemed to be working well so far.

One day out of Brest and out of the sight of land, Captain Garbers had quietly changed Pessim's name by mounting on her transom a new name and hailing port, engraved in elegant gold leaf, "Honeychile, Atlanta."

Honeychile, nee Pessim, was built at the best yard in Germany by the best craftsmen of the best materials. Even in this confused sea, Garbers had no worries about her strength. She was a slim beauty with classic lines. Painted a pale gray above a white waterline stripe, seventy-two feet from the tip of her sprit to the tuck of her transom and all powered by a schooner rig. The creature comforts below were magnificent by any standard and that was a big plus for her seasick crew who, despite the occasional retch into a bucket, were enjoying their journey. The condition of their passenger, on the other hand, was unknown. He remained locked in his cabin unseen by the others since they left Brest.

From the sextant sighting that Garbers was able to make before the weather deteriorated, he concluded that they were somewhere near Portland, Maine, but, that was three days ago. For all of Garbers's time on the water he had never experienced first-hand the full force of a well-formed nor' easter. He had sailed in hurricanes, but that air was warm. The nor'easter left him chilled and weaker, but experience told him that as with any storm, the wind would die down in a few hours and the seas would eventually calm. They might be close to the coast, or they might be miles further East or South. For now he simply prayed that some important part of the boat wouldn't break in the tempest. Most importantly, he needed to see clear skies again to get his position, and soon.

August 27, 1942

10:00 p.m., Shelter Island, New York

Danny Mancini felt that victory was at hand. This had been going on for his entire senior year and now two months past graduation he had finally sweet-talked Amy Pastore into a date. She expected a trip to the movies in Greenport and maybe an ice cream sundae before, perhaps, a roadside smooch and a goodnight kiss in her driveway. Danny had other ideas.

Amy's vision of the evening's events was problematic for her. Danny, as the captain of the Greenport High School football team, was voted among his peers as the most likely to score with Amy Pastore, Greenport High's number one draft choice among young bucks. But, while his friends saw a lustful romp in Danny's future, Amy had not yet signed on for the trip. She liked Danny okay, but a strict Catholic upbringing made her think twice before acting on any impulse. Danny was indeed desirable. At six-feet tall, he weighed close to 180 pounds, an imposing yet desirable hulk compared to Amy's thin but busty five-foot three-inch wisp of hormonal womanhood.

So far Danny's goal for this night was proving to be as elusive as ever. She was nice to him but wasn't responding at all to any of his double entendre remarks. She was a tough one, so tough in fact that it had taken till this summer night and the announcement that he was planning to enlist in the Marines that she would even get in a car with him alone. But, Danny reasoned that his story line for the evening might actually pay off. He decided to play to her emotions. Sympathy for him was the new goal and he had a sense that it might work. "Gosh, he's going off to war. He could get killed.... Well, maybe just this one time."

The theater was showing "Mrs. Miniver" with Greer Garson and Walter Pidgeon, the story about a middle class English family and their sacrifices at the start of the war. The film was only out for a couple of months since its premiere at the Radio City Music Hall. Danny watched the movie with an arm wrapped across his date's shoulder and thought that the emotional effect of the wartime struggle was sure to help him in his struggle to get into Amy's bloomers.

"Did you like the movie?," his voice almost cracked.

"Oh, it was so... uh... inspiring. I think war changes people for the best, if you know what I mean." She stared into his eyes.

"Yes, I do." Danny really didn't have a clue to what she was talking about, yet he nodded his head affirmatively anyway. That stare, he surmised, was encouragement for what his brain was thinking. Anyway, war wasn't going to change his plans for this evening, not if he could help it. "So what do you want to do now?"

"I don't know. Can we get some ice cream?" She smiled.

"Sure thing." *Ice cream could work to soften her up maybe?* They walked one block to the drug store soda fountain. It was late, but the place was still open and busy. At the big marble fountain a bunch of kids from the high school recognized the graduated football star and did the usual expected fawning. After a few smiles and a number of "Hey Dannys" he was sure that his local fame was becoming part of a positive picture in Amy's mind about him. Danny ordered a chocolate cone and Amy had strawberry. As they left the drugstore neither said too much as they finished the cones. Again she looked briefly into his eyes and he saw an opportunity to improvise, "Hey let's go over to Shelter Island on the ferry. We can look at the stars off Ram's Head beach." She nodded in agreement. Yes! The ice cream worked! It was only 10:30. He figured that they would be able to get the last ferry back to Greenport and be home at 1:30.

The entrance to Coecles Harbor on the Eastern side of Shelter Island is narrow and shallow at low tide. Most mariners with local knowledge avoid it, fearing going aground. Kapitan Heinrich Garbers was not encumbered by local knowledge, he had U.S. government charts showing eight feet of depth at low tide, and that, he guessed, was more than enough for Honeychile to safely navigate. He felt especially safe at the entrance because the tide was high and had just begun to ebb. He would have at least three or more hours to drop off his passenger and get out of there without having to worry about running aground.

It was a bit after midnight and the big sailboat took advantage of the whisper-like five-knot southerly breeze to simply glide into the harbor as silently as a fish swimming in deep water. Just as silently, the experienced crew dropped the mainsail and anchored almost silently in the near-total darkness. Then they waited. It was eerily quiet. The summer people in the few cottages that ringed the shoreline were fast asleep and the sound of crickets in the surrounding brush covered up any slight noise made on the boat. Now came the wait.

Garbers sat on deck trying to discern movement anywhere on shore. He heard none. Then quietly, but all of a sudden, the sound of a distant automobile engine broke the silence. It got slightly louder, but without headlights it was difficult to determine where the sound was coming from. Still it got louder. Garbers' keen sense of direction pinned it down to an onshore spot about fifty yards from his anchored yacht. The car's engine shut off and Garbers watched closely as a match was lit and extinguished, then another and then one more. "That is the signal!" From his position at the cabin door he whispered to his passenger, "Your limousine is here."

Wolfgang emerged from the cabin, took a deep breath of the warm night air and gazed at the shoreline. His arrival at this destination ignited some internal flame and whatever he was feeling seemed to change his physical shape. In the dim starlight Garbers saw the shadow of genuine menace and evil. For the first time since they met, the captain understood why this was no ordinary passenger. He would no doubt achieve his mission, whatever that might be, and the war would change course because of it. Garbers, even as a loyal German soldier, now feared the man, and was glad for their impending separation. They shook hands and Garbers wished him safe work.

Just as he had done when he first boarded the yacht in Brest, the quiet passenger gingerly lifted up his two heavy suitcases and brought them up onto the deck. By now Otto had climbed aboard the rowing dinghy and was waiting to ferry Wolfgang toward the shore. Without saying a single word of goodbye or thank you to anyone else on the crew, Wolfgang lowered himself and the suitcases into the rowboat. Silently Otto untied the painter and began rowing. Garbers watched the shadows in the darkness arrive on land. It took only a couple of minutes more and once Otto was back on board, they readied the yacht to set sail on the ebbing tide to make their way back to Germany. Garbers waited to hear the car's engine start up, but it didn't. Otto and two other crewmen raised the mainsail and then the anchor.

As Honeychile ghosted out toward the narrow harbor channel Garbers kept his focus toward the shoreline. Why was it taking so long for his passenger to be on his way? Then, just as the yacht was almost out of earshot, he heard some muffled grunts and groans, and finally, the sound of the car's engine, at first near, and then moving off into the night as silently as it came. Garbers guessed that the suitcases were heavy and it was hard getting them into the car from the beach. In any case, his part of the mission was accomplished and with any luck Honeychile would be well beyond Montauk Point by dawn.

11:30 p.m.

Danny's dad had loaned him a great car for this kind of thing. It was a 1939 Chevy with a huge back seat. As the big car approached the beach in the dark, the excitement in Danny's pants threatened to bust through his zipper. Even better for his plans, the place was totally deserted. Not another car, not another couple of lovebirds. Danny parked the car off the road in a thicket of small scrub brush in case anyone came up the beach and saw it. No one would be coming, he was pretty sure. The Great Depression and now the war had decimated the summer house population and there was really no one there to bother them. "Let's go in the back seat." She didn't say a single word but got out of the car and got in the back. By the time the door slammed his lips were on hers and his right hand was working its way under her skirt and up her thigh while his other was cupping her breasts. She gave in to the moment and began to undo his belt. Now even this big car was no longer roomy enough to contain their lust. "Hey, there's no one here. I have a beach blanket in the trunk. Let's go out on the beach." Again she followed him without a sound.

Danny carefully laid the blanket out on a sandy patch hidden between some tall reeds and by the time he turned around to see Amy he was stunned. Even in the dimness of the ambient sky light he could see that she was totally naked. She came at him, tore open his shirt, and yanked off his pants. They fell down together onto the blanket in a tangle of limbs, lovers totally lost in each other's bodies. Their passion totally consumed them for close to twenty minutes, when suddenly Danny heard a small splash and noticed the shadowy shape of a large sailboat dropping an anchor in the harbor off the beach, no more than fifty yards away from them. Oh, oh! Shit! This is really embarrassing. What if it's someone who knows my parents, or worse, hers!

Amy attempted to stand and get her clothes from a few feet away but Danny pulled her back down to the blanket. He whispered as quietly as he could, "They're probably anchoring for the night. Let's just wait till there's no one on deck before we move."

"But there's no way whoever is on that boat can see us. It's too dark," she responded.

"Amy," he whispered in her ear. "Just be very quiet and we can get out of here without them seeing us. Your dad will kill us, or at least he'll kill me." So, they crouched down behind the reeds, naked and scared and waited till the movement on the boat stopped. Then they waited a bit longer to be sure that their tryst on the beach wouldn't become the idle gossip in Greenport for the next month. "Don't you move a muscle. I'll crawl up and find your clothes and mine." Amy watched as the shadow of his athletic naked body quietly located one piece of clothing after another. Danny was about fifteen feet away from Amy when they both froze at the sound of a car coming up the beach road right toward them without headlights. He managed to crawl to her on his nude belly and then they both cowered in the dark, completely silent and still.

The car pulled up to the beach near them and the sound of the engine stopped. A large shadow of a man got out. He paused and they could see him looking out into the harbor. He seemed to recognize the sailboat immediately. He walked over to the shoreline and the lovers watched as he lit a match. But there's no cigarette in his mouth? He blew it out and then lit another, and then repeated the action one more time. Within seconds Danny's attention was drawn to the anchored sailboat. He could hear movement. Someone was lifting large packages into a rowing dinghy and getting ready to come ashore. It was now clear to Danny that someone was smuggling something. A crime was happening right in front of them, and they really couldn't tell anyone about it lest they become the object of every wagging tongue in town. Amy now began to tremble and Danny didn't know what to do except stay completely still.

Within minutes the rowboat quietly touched the beach with two men aboard. The smaller of the two lifted a couple of large suitcases out of the vessel and carried them to the car. Apparently he was staying on shore because immediately after depositing his passenger on the beach the rower headed back to the sailboat. The driver of the car and the shorter man began to place the two suitcases in the car's trunk and then they paused, watching the sailboat. The man in the rowboat was already back on board and Danny could hear someone on the boat pulling up the anchor line and raising the mainsail. It all happened very quickly. In less than five minutes the sailboat slowly began to drift toward the harbor entrance. In his quietest whisper Danny spoke right into her Amy's ear. "This is great! Once they're gone and that car is gone we can move."

Now the lovers simply waited for the car to leave. The men were standing near the driver's door and talking in very low voices. Danny could detect some kind of a foreign accent between them. Then the level rose as the new arrival from the boat said, "Let me pee and then we will be on our way." He took a few steps away from the driver, walked directly over to the lovers' hiding place unzipped his fly and in the darkness he began to urinate right onto Amy's leg. She squealed loudly.

"Grundgütiger!" The man quickly zipped his pants in embarrassment.

Danny and Amy got up to run off the isolated beach but it was useless. The peeing man, no longer subject to the surprise, was on top of them before they could go ten feet. He was very quick, very strong and with one solid kick at Danny's left knee the football hero was on the ground moaning in agony. Amy simply froze in her tracks in total shock. Eugen Haupt, the driver, walked over to the scene and stared in mild shock at brutality so quickly inflicted by the man he had just met. The man smiled at Haupt and then at the startled teens. "Ach, lovers on the beach!"

The teens were more embarrassed than scared. The two men with the car, even in the starlit darkness, ogled the naked girl as she vainly attempted to place her hands over her private parts.

Wolfgang had already decided on a solution. He looked at Eugen and said in German, "'Sad thing how they drowned in a late-night swim. Passion can be such a dangerous thing." It was good that neither of the teens spoke German because they had no idea what was about to befall them. Haupt understood it all and stood there speechless. That was the end of Danny and Amy's trip to lover's lane. The next tidal cycle would wash away the tire tracks and all record of the incident. Police would only discover the Chevy in the bushes and the two naked bodies in the shallow water and wonder why they both drowned. Perhaps the boy had broken his knee on a rock while jumping into the water and in the darkness, and his girlfriend drowned while attempting to save him? It was a mystery that the local cops would never solve.

August 28, 1942

2:15 a.m.

As they drove away from the murder scene Eugen was silent. He was stunned by the brutality of what he had just witnessed and the two men didn't speak until they arrived at the Greenport ferry. There, they joined three other cars and a couple of small trucks for the night's last run. Finally, on board and in the quiet of the car they spoke in German.

"What do I call you?"

"My friends call me Wolfgang, and you?"

"I'm Eugen."

"Have you lived here all your life?"

"Pretty much, my parents came here when I was small."

"Is it a long trip to where you're taking me?"

"This late in the night we should be there in less than two hours."

"Good."

County Road 25A to the city snaked across the North Fork through Suffolk County farmland and small towns. Mostly clear of all traffic save the occasional pair of oncoming headlights, it was the route of choice for anyone hoping to avoid contact with anyone else. Now, Eugen Haupt and his passenger were just that pair of travelers. Haupt had been making some good time being ever so careful to avoid any speed traps or other reasons for a chance meeting with any law enforcement officer. The tension of the night's events did not allow for much conversation, but as they moved slowly westward along the North Fork out of the area their comfort level with each other eased a bit.

"How much more do we have to travel?"

"We'll be there before daybreak," Eugen responded. "You were quick-thinking with those beach lovers."

"It has nothing to do with thinking. This is war and we're both soldiers."

"In any case your response to the situation was both quick and clever."

Though his pants and shoes were soaking wet from his brief but lethal seaside activity, Wolfgang leaned back in the passenger seat, sighed and changed the subject, "It's good to be on dry land again. There were parts of my ocean crossing that were harrowing, to say the least."

"Well, you are here safe now. We just need to get you to the city."

"Can you drive any faster?"

"Yes, but if I do there will certainly be a policeman to follow. These small towns all use this road as a source of revenue with the fines," Haupt said with disdain. "and… I… personally, I really don't need another run in with the law."

"I don't wish to belittle your reluctance for getting a traffic citation, but I don't care about that. It is a piece of paper that you will pay. I need to get on with my task."

Wolfgang's impatience was amplified by his subtle but forceful manner and even the burly Haupt felt a tinge of fear. Wolfgang was a man who most likely always got his way.

Haupt was quick to oblige, "Well then, I will speed up."

Their drive continued in more silence, no more headlights to be seen in either direction. Through one small town center to the next the road was clear ahead and behind. In Wading River, a small hamlet a couple of miles from the shoreline of Long Island Sound a traffic light turned red in front of them. The driver looked around the sleepy surroundings, saw nothing and decided not to wait for it to turn green. He drove on for about 1000 feet when they heard the low whine of a siren and one light in the car's rear-view mirror. Eugen's traffic infraction had attracted the law. "Pull over to the side of the road. We don't need a chase," Wolfgang ordered.

The motorcycle cop was alone on a big Indian Scout. He pulled up behind the car and illuminated by the single headlight he approached, in silhouette, the driver's door. The driver smiled at the cop, "Good morning officer."

"Sir, you ran a red light back there in the town center."

"Yes, I'm sorry. There was no one else out here on the road and I didn't see any danger of hitting anyone."

"Well, that's not your choice to make now, is it? A red light means 'stop'."

"Yes, sir."

"Can I see your license and registration," this was not a question. Eugen pulled his wallet out of his pocket and handed the requested papers to the cop. The cop took the documents back to his bike to read them in the Indian's one headlight.

The two men in the car were rapt at the reflection in their rearview mirror and grew impatient as the officer examined Eugen's driver license. Eugen had stolen the car but luckily the registration was in the glove box. The man in the passenger seat mumbled, "This is taking too long. He is suspicious of us."

Eugen, while equally impatient, suddenly felt a sense of impending doom as the cop turned back toward the car.

"Mr. Haupt, who is Arthur Weinberger?"

Eugen thought fast, *who is Arthur Weinberger? Oh, shit, yes… that's the name on the registration.* "He's my uncle. My mother's brother."

"Hmm." The cop stood by the driver's side door and continued to scour state issued paperwork in his hands. "Mr. Haupt, do you know that your license expired two weeks ago?"

"Oh my god, I forgot to renew it."

"Well, I should write you up for that all by itself. Technically, you shouldn't be driving this car at all without a valid license. Anyway, what are you gentlemen doing out here so late at night?"

"Late? No, officer this is early in the morning for us. I'm driving my brother back to the city from our mother's house in Greenport so he can be at work on time," Eugen quickly concocted a story.

"There's a war going on, ya know."

"I understand." Eugen decided not to raise any protest.

"Okay, give me another minute here. I don't want to give you a hard time. I'm only going to write you a summons for running that stop light but you need to get that license renewed right away if you want to drive any more. I'll be right back." The cop turned and walked back to the Indian.

Eugen gazed at his rearview mirror as the cop opened his ticket book and began to write. "This son of a bitch is actually going to give me a ticket!" he complained out loud, but there was no response from his passenger, in fact, as he turned to his right there was also no passenger. "

What the…?" He looked again into his rearview mirror and saw that a noiseless struggle had begun in front of the motorcycle. Wolfgang had silently departed the passenger seat of the car and crept up on the unwitting officer from behind. With one powerful arm around the cop's neck and the flat of his other hand covering his mouth and nose he held the struggling cop with total control. It took less than a minute of silent flailing until the cop's body went limp and Wolfgang dropped him to the ground. Grabbing the driver's license and registration out of the unconscious officer's hand he dragged the limp body over to a pond alongside the road. He tore out the half-written ticket and shoved it in his pocket and stuck the rest of the stack of blank summonses back into the cop's belt carrier. Then, with his left foot he held the cop's head underwater until he was certain that his victim would never breathe air again and then shoved the body out into the center of the pond. Casually he walked over to the motorcycle and wheeled it up to the side of the pool, laying it in alongside the drowned policeman. Eugen felt a chill as he watched the third brutal murder of the night.

The passenger got back into the car. "It will seem to those who discover his body tomorrow that he accidentally drove off the road in the darkness and drowned on his own."

"Why did you do that?," Eugen asked

"There's no sense leaving your name and address with the authorities, is there now?"

"I thought that you didn't care if I got a citation for speeding?"

"I changed my mind."

They reached Manhattan an hour before daybreak, perfectly on schedule. Wolfgang only vaguely recognized the city he had last visited a decade earlier. Crossing over the 59th Street Bridge the driver turned uptown on Third Avenue and within a few minutes had stopped in front of a non-descript brownstone building.

"You're inside that doorway beneath the front steps. I must leave this car somewhere now. It is a borrowed vehicle and no doubt its owner will be looking for it." Eugen handed him a key and a said a quick "good luck, I'll be in touch." Eugen Haupt smiled and drove off leaving Wolfgang and his heavy suitcases on the street in front of the small four-story brownstone building.

Wolfgang descended three steps and came to a doorway leading to the basement apartment. In the darkness he found the keyhole and opened the door to a pitch-black room. His right hand found a light switch that lit a single bare bulb over an oval wooden table in the kitchen of his new home. *Hmm, one door, one window and a cot. It will have to do. Now, did my host leave me anything to eat?* To his surprise the icebox was well stocked with a fresh block of ice, a bottle of milk, some cheese and a couple of dried sausages. On the counter under the dish pantry he discovered some apples, a fresh loaf of rye bread and even a pound of coffee. Wolfgang hadn't eaten in the past eighteen hours and quickly prepared himself a modest meal. *This is a far cry from the dried crap on that sailboat, and what a nice wine to go with it!*

After dinner, and with a new rush of energy, Wolfgang investigated the corners of his new small universe looking for the locally provided physical tools for his mission. He found three men's suits, three shirts, a couple of neckties and three pairs of shoes in his exact size. *Hah! Canaris is such a master of detail!* Then, above the kitchen stove in a small cabinet, he located the main component of his quest, a small fiberboard case with metal corners and a thick leather handle. He took it down, placed it on the kitchen table and opened it. The first word he read, Telefunken, confirmed that all was well. This was the Agent's Radio, the Abwehr's latest Agenten-funk, the AFu. It was the choice unit used by his colleagues worldwide. He moved the suitcase next to the window where Eugen told him that he had strung a longwire antenna to the roof. There were fresh batteries as well. *Bless that Eugen! He's thought of everything.* Wolfgang connected the wire to the antenna terminal and then attached a second wire with a spring clip onto the radiator pipe as a ground. It powered up immediately with the tubes warming to a dull red glow. Wolfgang knew that Berlin would be anxious to hear from him and with luck the gods of radio wave propagation would carry the signal from this basement to Abwehr headquarters in Berlin. That was the plan. He knew that the Americans were also monitoring the frequencies for odd transmissions and he had to keep his on-air presence short to avoid detection. He tapped out his message on a Morse key in a coded script that even when translated would be cryptic but accurate, "Wolfgang continues to write his symphony." He transmitted the message three times over a six-minute period and then turned the transmitter off and hid the radio back above the stove. Chances were pretty good that no one had heard him, and he was comfortable with the idea that he was safe.

Quickly, the long overnight hours and the Chateau Pinchon Lalande took their toll. He suddenly felt very tired. Pushing his big valises away from the door to the biggest closet available he collapsed onto the cot. He was exhausted as he struggled out of his jacket and winced at the intensity of his own body odor. The jacket oozed the smell of salt water and nervous sweat. He pulled a Luger pistol out of the jacket pocket and placed it alongside his pillow. The bed was lumpy but clean and within a few moments he was in a deep sleep. Both the war and a shower would have to wait until he awoke.

7:16 a.m., Block Island Sound

U.S. Coast Guardsman George Keyes held Mohawk's classic wooden wheel with a light touch. A light southerly breeze came over their port side as they were nearing Montauk. Not much to report on his next radio communication to fleet command. It had been a quiet and uneventful night.

Coast Guard Picket Patrol boat Mohawk was not the usual USCG issue. Mohawk was a 60-foot on deck sailing schooner with a 14-foot beam and an almost 9-foot draft. Like many humans in wartime, Mohawk got drafted, a personal yacht conscripted into the Coast Guard's picket fleet. The picket boats were a flotilla of privately owned yachts that patrolled the coastal waters in search of German submarines. Sailboats were of particular interest to the Navy because they made no engine sound, and so were undetecable by German submarines. Many were pulled in to service. Since the Germans were unable to hear Mohawk, if a chance meeting did occur, Mohawk would have an upper hand and a radio aboard to call the authorities. Though she was rigged as a twin masted schooner, Mohawk officially was dubbed a "Coast Guard Cutter." Wartime also added other amenities to her newfound status. She was outfitted with a metal doghouse, to protect the helmsman from weather and perhaps bullets, and also a .30-caliber Browning machine gun installed just to starboard behind the mainmast shrouds. This vessel, which in her prime had gracefully raced across oceans and between continents, was now a lethal adversary in any shooting fight. But, Mohawk's mission wasn't to look for a fight. Rather, she was to be a listening post and a rescue vessel for those who needed help.

The smell of coffee and what seemed to be freshly baked muffins was wafting up from the galley. Keyes' empty stomach grumbled. He had been on watch since 4:00 a.m. The cook did not get up until 5:00, so there was nothing available to eat to stoke George's personal fire until now.

A head popped up in the open companionway and asked, "Hungry?"

"Yes sir, I am." Keyes reached over to the man who handed over a large mug of coffee and two freshly baked corn muffins slathered in melting butter. "Thanks." A sip of coffee and a taste of those freshly baked goods was all he could think about at this moment. The sun was now starting to come up behind them and in the feeble light he could now see the rest of the men on his watch sitting and moving around the deck. This was their daily grind and the boredom of their patrol. Though the boat had a crew of ten, Keyes was alone at the helm. In the darkness, his job was to steer the yacht on a straight compass course in one direction, turn her around and sail back in the other.

Coastguardsman Bob Hinckley, also enjoying hot coffee and a muffin, approached the doghouse, "Yo, George, how far are we from Montauk?" Montauk was the place they were scheduled to turn and go back in the opposite direction.

"I think we're about 15 miles out."

"Pretty quiet night."

"Yeah, there was no wind at all. We were just flopping around out here just drifting."

"I know why we haven't seen any Germans, they're afraid of these corn muffins," Hinckley quipped. "If we run into a sub, we can sink it with these things."

"Ya know what, they're out there somewhere. I can feel it."

"Maybe, but I've been on this same patrol for the last two months and other than a whale breaching, I haven't seen anything at all."

"Hey, you never know. What about that corpsman on beach patrol in June? He ran right into a Kraut sabotage team."

"Dumb luck I guess."

"Not dumb luck at all. He was smart."

"Good for him. But for me, this is really pretty boring."

"So, go read a book… I'm watching the water."

"Did ya hear, those Germans got the electric chair as spies a couple weeks ago."

"Tough crap to that! This is war." Keyes grinned. "I'm glad to be here on this boat. I'd rather be cruising in the moonlight than that poor guy who had to walk up and down the beach all night with a rifle on his shoulder. What's better?"

"Yeah," Hinckley sighed, "I s'pose you're right, this ain't that bad."

Keyes looked up from his compass and stared at the horizon. A low mist hung on the horizon, but the sky was cloudless. In the breaking morning light about two miles from their position he noticed a quick flash of sun reflection on something shiny. "Bob, look out there about two o'clock off starboard."

Hinckley turned toward the western horizon. At first he saw nothing, but then it flashed again. "Yeah, there's someone out there! 'Looks like a sailboat."

"No one is supposed to be out there." Keyes quickly called an "all hands on deck." There was someone in a boat in waters where boats were not allowed in wartime. All hands came up onto the deck quickly wearing flack vests and carrying assorted weapons. One man positioned himself at the .30 caliber gun. "Coming up to two-nine-oh!" The breeze had come up a bit and Keyes steered Mohawk toward the flash of light.

The skipper, Captain Howard Glenn, was now awake and in charge. He quickly joined Keyes at the helm. "What have you got?"

"Cap, I got a visual on some kind of a sailing vessel about two miles away. She's still in the mist, but she's definitely out there." Keyes's steady hand steered a more upwind course as the deck crew trimmed the sails to suit. It only took about ten minutes to get close enough to see that this was another large sailboat, much like Mohawk. "Looks like another picket boat or some fool."

The captain raised his binoculars and scanned the unknown vessel. "She's not a picket boat, no numbers on her hull. But she is a beauty. Some rich guy from Sag Harbor maybe. Rules never seem to apply to those guys. Okay, let's put a shot across her bow, that's figuratively speaking of course."

Keyes steered straight toward the offender in the light breeze and within another twenty minutes she was just about alongside the errant sailboat. Mohawk crossed her to leeward, tacked around her stern and onto starboard tack upwind and on a parallel course. There seemed to be only one person on deck and he looked nervous. "Captain, she's called Honeychile and her hailing port is Atlanta. What's she doing out here?"

Captain Glenn reached for a megaphone and hailed Honeychile's helmsman. "Captain, we are the U.S. Coast Guard Cutter Mohawk. Please drop your sails and heave to." The helmsman yelled something below decks and a few men came up. The helmsman pointed at the Coast Guard boat and after looking across at the weaponry pointed at them they quickly dropped their sails to the deck. The Coast Guard boat also slowed herself. "Captain, you are sailing in restricted waters. What're you doing out here?"

Below decks aboard Honeychile Otto Bauer reached for a rifle, but then thought better of that. Through a cabin window he could see that the other boat appeared to outgun them considerably. Leaving his rifle stowed below he leaped up the companionway stairs to the deck. He knew that this would be his time to shine. Otto was born in North Carolina and grew up there until the age of 14. His father, a well-established immigrant butcher in Asheville, never felt comfortable speaking English and moved the family back to Germany sixteen years earlier. Otto became German and got accepted into the German Naval Academy and it was there that he met his sailing buddy Heinrich Garbers. At this moment Otto's childhood life experience would be the difference between life and death for all aboard Honeychile, he never lost his southern drawl. "Hey, Cap'n. 'Sorry, we didn't know about the restrictions."

"Captain, these waters and all the waters along the coast have been off limits to pleasure craft since May. What are you doing here?"

"Geez, 'really sorry about that. We didn't know. This boat's been in Bermuda for the past 10 months. We're entered in the Vineyard Race out of The Stamford Yacht Club over Labor Day and we're on our way there." Otto was absolutely perfect in his response.

Keyes looked at the Captain. "Yeah, I think he's right. Ya know, Mohawk raced in that one a bunch of times."

A twenty-year U.S. Coast Guard veteran, Howard Glenn, while an incredible seaman, was not a sailor at all. His posting on "this rag-masted wind whopper" was a come-down from his over-all career in the U.S.C.G.. He knew a lot about engines, propeller pitches and diesel fuel pumps, but he knew and cared very little about sailing yachts and the lunatics who raced them. You call that a race when the boats don't go faster than seven knots? To Captain Glenn, the idea that a boatload of southern boys would sail hundreds of miles from Bermuda to participate in a sailboat race was both confusing and unbelievable, yet he knew that it happened. "Okay Keyes, let's cut these clowns a little slack." He picked up his megaphone and yelled. "Vessel Honeychile, you are free to make your way to your race. But, you need to get out of Block Island Sound immediately. These waters are restricted and dangerous. There are enemy submarines out here. Your vessel could be in jeopardy if you remain."

Otto gave his best submissive smile across the fifty feet of water between them. "Sure thing, sir. We're very sorry. We didn't know about any restrictions. 'Really, really sorry! We're on our way right now." Then he turned to Garbers who was at the helm and whispered in German, "We need to sail away from here fast. They believed me about the sailboat race, but if they check us out, we are doomed." Then both Otto and Garbers smiled at Mohawk, gave a wave and the rest of the crew raised the sails. Almost immediately Honeychile began to move eastward on a close reach. As the sun moved higher in the sky the southerly breeze began to build and she was up to hull speed within minutes.

"If he's going to Stamford why is he sailing east," Keyes asked?

"Maybe he wants to get into Long Island Sound through The Race rather than Plum Gut. I don't know. He's got more than a week to get there. Who cares?" Glenn was irritated that his sleep had been cut short by the false alarm.

"Do we have to report this now Cap?" Keyes wanted to know.

"Yeah we gotta report it, but there's no rush. I'll write it into the log anyway. We can tell HQ on the next radio check-in at 10:00 hours. Someone else can follow up on their progress." Then he shrugged and blurted out a one-word epithet that sounded very much like a curse, "Sailors!"

Mohawk was still on its way toward Montauk. It would take her another couple of hours to get there and then to turn and get back to this spot. By then Honeychile would be long gone and over the horizon.

6:30 p.m., Berlin

Canaris was at his desk staring at the huge map of Europe and the North Atlantic on the opposite wall. His personal leather-bound diary lay open in front of him. The map was a display of the breadth of his command. He was the head of the Abwehr. He had powers other military men did not, and he totally looked the part. With every white hair neatly in place, he resembled a patrician character in a magazine advertisement for some rare single malt scotch or fine cigarettes. In calmer times he might have easily been mistaken for Teutonic royalty, though he wasn't. Canaris's essence was his genius.

Though not a Catholic, Canaris confessed regularly... to his diary. Its pages contained a hand-written record complete with details of any personal angst, thoughts, clandestine plans and even his personal uncertainty about Hitler and where Germany was headed. He wrote everything down. Once he wrote something down, it relieved a burden. The diary was the perfect psychoanalyst to a man living in a world of secrecy and distrust.

He seemed to be daydreaming, enrapt in a silent analysis of the Mercator projection of the world with tacks indicating the places of ongoing Abwehr missions. There were a lot of tacks on the map, but there was one important tack missing. The story behind the missing tack, for the moment, remained as his personal secret.

Canaris was not daydreaming. His pensive demeanor disguised a real worry. There had been no radio contact with Garbers, Wolfgang, or his man in New York for a number of days and, out on that vast ocean somewhere, was one vessel that, if successful in its mission, could shorten the war and save the lives of thousands of soldiers. "So far so good," he wrote into his journal.

The Admiral's reverie was interrupted by a staccato rap on the door. He closed his logbook and placed it in the side top drawer as his aide entered the room. "Ah, my Kapitänleutnant!"

"May I come in sir? I have some news." "Yes of course Horst. What is it?" Canaris had recruited Horst Wenzl in February as a favor to the young man's father. Joachim Wenzl was a loyal German soldier who befriended Canaris socially. The elder Wenzl's story was that Horst got the large scar on his face in a naval academy sword fight that could have become deadly. Horst was defending the honor of a young woman. Following the occasion of that youthful romantic exuberance, Joachim came to the conclusion that his son was a hothead and would surely get himself killed in a war zone. He asked Canaris for help. Canaris never regretted the hire and he never pried about the origin of the scar.

"Admiral, a dispatch from Herr Wolfgang has just arrived. It is being decoded now and will be on your desk momentarily. I thought you might want to know."

Finally some news! "Thank you for telling me. I've been waiting."

"I'll bring it immediately when it's been decoded."

"Thank you, Horst." The door thudded shut and with that Canaris snapped himself out of the trance and dared the beginnings of a smile. A message from Wolfgang and not Kapitan Garbers would certainly mean that the master saboteur had successfully landed without incident. *Wolfgang would get through and do the deed!* While he didn't want to get his hopes ahead of reality, Canaris was beginning to believe that his plan was on its way to success. He keyed his intercom and an officious female voice spoke up immediately.

"Admiral?"

"Yes Marta, would you please call Admiral Doenitz?" Grossadmiral Karl Doenitz was in command of Germany's U-boat fleet in the North Atlantic. "Tell him that I have interesting news. If possible could he come here?" Canaris' offer to go to Doenitz was perfunctory. He knew by instinct that Doenitz would come to him.

"Immediately sir!"

The head of Abwehr leaned back in his leather chair and exhaled. While he would need to mend some fences with Doenitz he was certain that the message from Wolfgang would be a report of success so far. *Ha, and they crossed the ocean in a damned sailboat!* As the radio transmission from Wolfgang was received on schedule there was every reason to believe that Kapitan Garbers had accomplished his part of the mission.

Within five minutes Wenzl returned with a sealed envelope. He handed it to Canaris who waited until the young officer left and closed the door behind him before slicing it open. As he read the news Canaris's smile grew wider, "Wolfgang continues to write his symphony." The admiral read the message twice and placed it into the same drawer as his journal. *Now we wait.*

Doenitz knocked at Canaris's office door and impatiently entered without waiting for a response. The men were equals in rank and Doenitz bore a certain amount of distaste for the entire spy thing. "Wilhelm, your secretary said you had something important to discuss?" Doenitz didn't like spies and he didn't really care for Canaris either. He thought the Abwehr chief, because of his natty look, was a fop. Canaris, more a student of psychology than his peer, internally laughed it all off. He saw Doenitz as a rigid martinet, a stickler for useless detail and pomp. Doenitz saw himself as a navy man from the classic mold and he felt that Canaris did not. Of course, there was no real basis for that attitude as Canaris had also risen through the same ranks. "So, what are we talking about?"

"Ah Karl," Canaris smiled and motioned his guest to be seated. "I have some interesting news to share."

"Do tell!" Doenitz sat on leather armchair opposite the desk. *Is this going to be another one of his self-aggrandizing lectures?* No matter, he had to listen. His duty to the Kriegsmarine forced him to pay attention to everything. Hitler relied on Doenitz and his wolfpacks to wreak havoc on the supply convoys crossing the Atlantic to England. His lethal undersea killers had caused the Americans, Canadians and most of all the British much serious death and damage over the previous year. Though Doenitz wasn't fond of his peer, Canaris had some information to keep the hunters at work and he had to pay attention.

"Let me get to the point as I know you are a very busy man," Canaris feigned courtesy. "I am sure you remember that within the past few months your submarine fleet was of immense help to Abwehr. You successfully landed two saboteur teams directly onto American soil. I say bravo to that!" Canaris paused a moment for any reaction from Doenitz. There was not even a raised eyebrow, so he just moved ahead. "We both know very well how the re-assignment of even one U-boat from its hunting duties made your work more difficult and dangerous, and that the departure of two boats from fleet work was, for a short time at least, a heavy burden for the entire

U-boat fleet."

Doenitz now glanced upward at Canaris from the armchair. He smiled, but his friendly expression did little to blunt his visceral irritation. "As you know I was against it from the beginning. I make no apologies about my attitude. We don't have enough boats to do the job as it is."

"Yes, I understand…"

"And, the loss of any one vessel from the wolf packs could mean that a ship carrying many tanks will break through and land in England. Every single ship that gets past our hunters will mean the certain death of many German soldiers and sailors."

"I agree. The Führer needs to support the navy much more."

"I agree, I have been fighting Goering for some time for more boats, but everyone is more concerned about the Luftwaffe. Simply, Goering has the Führer's ear and my boats are not coming. The Luftwaffe gets more planes, and we remain severely under supported."

"I totally understand your, er… frustration. But, you must understand that the only way we could have achieved our mission was to do it with the support of your brave U-boats." Canaris walked around from behind the desk and sat opposite his guest. "But, I have good news and I wanted to talk to you here in person to tell you that the mission is progressing nicely."

Doenitz was confused. Of course, he was supposed to know nothing of the mission's details, but his own sources told him that the two teams of saboteurs that landed in America, transported by two of his U-boats, had been quickly rounded up and arrested by American authorities within days of their arrival. *So, …what the Hell is he talking about?*

"I know that you probably have heard that our teams were arrested. What you may not know is that the event was, regretfully, anticipated by all of us. Had they been successful, so much the better, but their success was never expected." He folded his hands in his lap and waited for Doenitz to ask the obvious questions.

"So?"

The Abwehr chief let out just a hint of a sigh. "They were brave men and they had our full support. They were all valiant soldiers who understood the difficulty of their mission to destroy the main railroad links to the coastal ports. They knew the danger before they left. What happens to them now, I suppose, is up to the Americans."

"Then how can you say that the mission is a success?"

"Because, my friend, theirs was not the main mission. Their arrival in New York and Florida was, let us say, a distraction."

"How?"

"In my world one must create believable lies. Would we ever land two teams who knew about each other's existence? Would we? It defies the basic rule of intelligence work, the need-to-know." Canaris shared a bit of his spycraft. "Think about it. If we land two groups of saboteurs apart from one another, if one is caught they should know nothing about the existence of the other. Then they cannot, even under torture, let the authorities know about the entirety of the mission, correct?"

Doenitz nodded, "Yes, this is probably true."

"In this case each team knew about the other. The mission was designed in that manner. If either team was caught and broken during interrogation the other was in jeopardy."

"Do you mean to tell me that you expected the two teams to reveal each other if they got caught?"

"Yes. Though, I am not certain how their FBI got information about either's existence, but somehow they were found so quickly it gave Americans the false assurance that they had cracked a major sabotage effort and caught all the individuals involved. This also has tricked the Americans to intensify their coastal efforts in the search for more submarines."

"Why would that be helpful?"

"It would clear the way for a third group, unknown to the other two, to go about their business."

Doenitz's thin eyebrows raised. "A third group? There is now another group of saboteurs in the picture? You haven't asked me for additional submarine transportation for anyone. Is that what this is about? You want more of my boats, especially now that the Americans are looking for more subs?"

"No, no Karl, nothing of the sort. The operation is already under way. No more of your boats are necessary." Canaris smiled slyly. "I wanted to share this with you because Abwehr is forever grateful to your submarine captains and their crews for their risky close approach to the American coastline."

"I am not sure I understand what the mission is, and what is the third team?"

"This is a mission that will break the enemy's will to fight. It will create for them a massive loss and cut to the core of their inflated sense of internal security. It will bring the battle to their front door. But, this is something I will have to share with you at a later time. For now I can tell you this, I have just received a dispatch indicating that our third team is safely in place and is about to begin their work."

"So tell me Wilhelm, how did you get them there without my submarines?"

"Do you know of a Kapitan Heinrich Garbers?"

Doenitz prided himself on a thorough knowledge of Germany's entire navy. "Garbers? Garbers? Yes! I do know him. He's the yachtsman, correct?"

"He is a very good yachtsman."

"Isn't he the fellow who put your agents ashore in Argentina and Africa from a sailing yacht?" Doenitz appeared to know a lot more about Garbers than Canaris expected.

"Yes. It's interesting how pleasure craft, even during wartime attract so little attention at sea. Hmm?"

"I suppose that you cannot tell me what his mission is?"

"Perhaps I will be able to share more information with you very shortly. For now, I wanted to tell you what I told you because I am grateful for your help in this mission. Thank you and thank your crews from me."

"Thank you, Wilhelm, for sharing this with me." Doenitz's ruffled disposition was mollified, if only for the moment. "I will indeed personally thank the captains and their crews."

"Can I offer you a glass of a very rare old French brandy that recently came into my possession?"

"Absolutely. While I have no idea where any of this is going, I believe, it deserves some kind of a toast."

10:06 p.m., New York City

It was an easy thing to go unnoticed on the Yorkville side streets. Wolfgang took advantage of this built-in anonymity, and for even more security he waited until nightfall before he left the basement apartment. At Third Avenue and 84th Street he climbed the stairs to the elevated subway platform and boarded a downtown train. It was 10:15 when he got off at the 47th Street station and decided to make the remainder of his trip on foot. He was supposed to re-connect with Eugen Haupt at 11:00 at the main entrance to the Chrysler Building, but he'd built in enough time to take a longer route down Park Avenue to do some reconnaissance.

Ah… there it is! The imposing Waldorf Astoria Hotel loomed over the streets around it. Wolfgang stood in awe for a long moment taking the time to examine the building's grand structure. This is quite beautiful, but his structural analysis would have to move to a later time. He decided to walk back toward Lexington on 48th and it was there that he caught a glimpse of what he had come to see. Mid-block on 48th Street was a porte cochere entrance to the hotel, and directly adjacent to that automobile entrance to the Waldorf was a narrow brass door that now attracted his intense scrutiny. So as not to raise any suspicion from anyone, he sauntered over to it and to kill time he made an effort to smoke a cigarette. He placed the Lucky Strike between his lips and went into a pantomime effort of searching his pockets for a match. His everyman's struggle caught the eye of a Waldorf doorman who approached him.

"Need a light?"

"Oh yeah, tanks a lot." Ten years earlier Wolfgang had briefly lived in New York and through an amazing gift for language, inflection and idiom he had developed a pure unvarnished Brooklyn accent. For all intents he was a native speaker, no one who conversed with him would know that he wasn't a local.

"Here ya go, buddy." The doorman flicked open a Zippo lighter and Wolfgang took a long drag.

"Tanks again." He smiled at the doorman. "Say pal, this door here? What's it go into, the hotel?"

"Nah, that door just opens to an elevator shaft down to the train tracks."

"No kiddin'? How far down's it go?"

"Just one floor."

"Why do ya need an elevator to go one floor?"

"That's because when Mr. Roosevelt comes to New York, this is where his private train comes in."

"No shit? Really?" Wolfgang already knew that part.

"Yeah, really. All the big guests who got their own train cars come into the platform right under the street here. I saw General Pershing come in here once, too."

"So why's he need dis door?"

For whatever reason the doorman felt an immediate kinship with the Brooklyn accented man. "They drive Roosevelt's car right off the train into the elevator with him in it, and it comes out here, and right into the car entrance to the hotel. He doesn't want to be seen when he comes in. He's a cripple ya know."

"Yeah I know he's a cripple, but deez rich guys, dey own the world, don't dey? Me? I got no elevator and I gotta walk up four flights, heh, heh."

"Yeah, me too."

"Well, listen, I gotta go, but tanks for the light. Nice talkin' to yuz."

"You're welcome. Keep cool."

"Yeah, you too." Wolfgang smiled and continued walking down 48th Street while drawing on his Lucky Strike. While he already knew every bit of what the doorman had told him, hearing it and seeing it in person made his task seem that much more real. He smiled to himself as he next made a beeline toward the Chrysler building for his 11:00 p.m. meeting with his caretaker. The two men had planned to spend some time that evening to talk about railroads.

August 29, 1942

3:13 p.m.

On this sunny late summer weekend afternoon, Eugen Haupt sat alone in his apartment staring at the wall. The small dots on the cheap wallpaper became touch beads in a mental rosary. He'd been depressed ever since he watched Wolfgang brutally dispose of three innocent people in front of him, and though in the past, he himself had also caused injury to others, Eugen had never killed anyone. Now he was complicit in three murders and it greatly disturbed him. He'd been unable to sleep for the past three days. He began to question where his life was going.

Haupt appreciated that he was a very lucky man, a low-level burglar who'd hit the mother lode, actually getting protection from the FBI. He could rob all the people he wanted as long as he kept feeding names of disloyal Americans. But his father wanted more of him. Karl Haupt's reliance on his son to commit burglaries coupled with the old man's pro-Nazi sentiments put Eugen's fate into a whole other rule book, and he was reasonably sure that he couldn't get away with it for too much longer. *I am not a spy, and I really don't give a shit about any führer or Germany.* Now in his early thirties he was on the eve of his first youthful rebellion and for the first time in his life he was feeling remorse.

Talking to himself aloud he vented his anger, "Damn it, I live here. I'm going to get caught in this sooner or later." With that he got up and walked into his kitchen and found a half-full bottle of Jack Daniels. He grabbed a dirty glass from his sink and filled it. A quick bend of the elbow and it was gone. He poured himself another and just as he was about to get on the highway to being blotto for the weekend his phone rang.

"Hello?"

"Eugen, I need you to come and help me viss some tings."

Perhaps it was fate that the elder Haupt would reach out to his son at just this moment, but Eugen's wallpaper rosary incantation took the conversation to its next emotional level. "Hello, Poppa. I'm busy right now, I can't get there."

"Dis iss not a rekvest, Eugen. Get your ass ofer here now."

Eugen's response was passive-aggressively childish, but it set the tone for what would become a watershed in his emotional relationship with his father. "Yes Poppa, I'm coming. I'll be there as soon as I finish drinking."

"Vat?"

"When I finish drinking."

"Drinking?" Karl was confused, but sensed the rebellion in his son's voice. That was something he never could tolerate, and the years and his current infirmities did not soften his hair-trigger anger either. "Listen you little shit, ven I tell you to come ofer here you get here right avay."

With the parental rebuff Eugen's voice sank back into the childlike tone it often had when he had displeased his dad, but this time he was determined not to take it any longer. "I'll be over in a while Poppa." He hung up before the old man could say another word.

6:00 p.m., Point Judith, RI

The U.S. Coast Guard station at Point Judith, Rhode Island had been in place since 1876. At the start of the war, there were restrictions on pleasure boats, and weekends were the station's quietest days of the week. But the war's advent also made the base the active command center for the sailing vessels on coastal submarine patrol. While the rescue of boatmen in distress on the water was in a state of decline, the paperwork that mounted from the constant flow of written reports was near staggering. Saturday and Sunday were heavy workdays and Chief Warrant Officer Ed Bates had been at his desk for more than ten hours, since 08:00 and he was getting tired of the routine. Bates' job was to go through the reports and codify the eyewitness accounts from the picket cutters that patrolled Block Island Sound for errant U-boats. Since June, after the Nazis landed in Amagansett, they were ordered to do that with a doubled effort. The work was important, but tedious and boring, but someone had to do it, and that someone was Bates.

The routine was to read the reports and put them into two separate piles. The first pile was big. It had all the reports that basically reported nothing. The smaller pile was for suspicious sightings or reports needing some follow-up. This week's small pile contained a report of a suspected periscope sighting off Block Island and a fishing boat going aground on the beach at Watch Hill. That was pretty much it. The periscope sighting was most likely not a periscope sighting at all, but a half-submerged log with a branch still attached. Yet, the reports all needed follow-up and scrutiny. Bates was nearing the end of his day's endeavor, going through the final pieces of the picket boat reports when something caught his eye and immediately gave him an ill feeling. It was the report, now almost two days old, filed by Captain Howard Glenn aboard the Cutter Mohawk. He read it over twice:

"To CG Submarine Track Command Group, Point Judith. Date,

August 27, 1942. 0600 hours. While on routine patrol sailing west on a line approaching Montauk point, Cutter Mohawk came upon a large sailing yacht at near N41:06:00 W71:42:00 traveling eastward out of Block Island Sound in restricted waters. USCG Cutter Mohawk requested said yacht to heave-to and vessel complied immediately. Skipper of sailing vessel indicated that she was SV Honeychile out of Atlanta, Georgia. CMDR Mohawk advised captain of SV Honeychile that she was sailing in restricted waters. Skipper apologized and said that SV Honeychile had just arrived from Bermuda and was unaware of current restrictions. He said she was on her way to attend the Stamford Yacht Club's annual Vineyard Race over Labor Day weekend. Honeychile's skipper apologized for the infraction, acknowledged restrictions and sailed on northeastward, expected destination Stamford Yacht Club, Stamford, Ct. USCG Picket Cutter Mohawk continued on its patrol toward Montauk Point."

Hmmm? Bates dropped the report to his desk and quickly went through another pile of papers that had been accumulating for the past couple of months. He remembered something that he had read earlier in a press release that he had skimmed only once. After about two minutes of searching he found it. As he read intently now for the first time an alarm went off in his brain.

"ADDRESS TO THE STAMFORD YACHT CLUB ANNUAL MEETING BY FLEET CAPTAIN GEORGE F HUBBARD, MAY 13, 1942

Gentlemen, while these are not the greatest of times for yacht racing I still have hope that members of this club and elsewhere on Long Island Sound can still enjoy some invigorating times on the water. The events of the past few weeks have placed some increased restrictions on what we're able to do on the Sound, but we still can continue if we follow the rules. I received a mimeographed paper that lists the Coast Guard's wartime special rules for sailors. We have copies available if you want to grab one when you leave this meeting. The restrictions don't affect us too much here, but, the same as last September, it will impact our plans for the Vineyard Race this year. As you know the club's classic Vineyard Race course from SYC to the Buzzard's Bay Lightship and then around the southern tip of Block Island on the way back home cuts across the newly restricted area for pleasure yachts. So, with all regret I must report to you that this year's Vineyard Race, which for the past decade has been our Labor Day Weekend major yachting event will be postponed until further notice. While the race in previous years has attracted competing vessels from all over the east coast, as far away as Bermuda and Maine, we will now notify all clubs that this year's event is officially cancelled. In deference and respect to the coastal security of our nation at war we will not run our Vineyard race this year."

Bates dropped the paper to his desk and mulled over the oddity. *A boat makes a trip from Bermuda to be in a race that was officially cancelled almost four months earlier in May. How could they not know about that?* Something wasn't right and Bates immediately picked up his telephone and had the operator connect him directly with the Commodore of the Stamford Yacht Club. He would ask if a vessel called Honeychile had attempted to register for the annual race. He was pretty sure of the answer he would receive. Following that he would call a phone number in Manhattan. That phone number was pinned onto the cork bulletin board on the wall in front of him, a number that would ring on the desk if FBI Chief Mike Foreman in New York City. This was just the kind of thing that Foreman had called to ask about just a couple of weeks ago.

August 30, 1942

11:00 a.m., Washington, D.C.

OSS Director Bill Donovan had his feet up on a brightly painted Adirondack chair in his small back yard. After an exhausting week of fifteen-hour days, the spymaster decided that this weekend he'd work from the comfort of his Georgetown home. He'd been relaxing with Paul Elliot's new book, "The Last Time I Saw Paris," when the fatigue finally grabbed him. Donovan's right index finger was jammed into the volume between pages 53 and 54 while he napped lightly in the late morning sun. His escape from the war was short lived. Lizbeth, Donovan's housekeeper, woke him from his snooze.

"Mister Donovan. Mister Schlesinger is here to see you. I showed him in to your study sir."

"Thanks." Donovan shook himself out of his catnap and lumbered toward the study to his waiting guest.

Schlesinger was already seated with papers on his lap. "Sir!"

"Arthur, to what do I owe this impromptu call?"

"Mr. Director, 'apologies for bothering you, but something important just came in. I expect you'll want to see it now."

"Please sit, Arthur."

Schlesinger parked himself back in the side chair.

Donovan sat down behind his big antique partners desk. "So? What have you got?"

"It's a coded message from our man in Berlin." Schlesinger handed a folded paper to his boss. "It was sent on Thursday but seems to have taken a while to get here through many hands."

"That's to be expected." Donovan unfolded the paper and stared at it.

"There are parts of this one I still don't understand. He knows one of our codes, but since we don't really have any direct communication with him we also don't know how he got a hold of that code."

"Yet you think he's credible?"

"Yes sir. He's on the inside over there. His information so far has been flawless."

"How do we know he isn't one of them and they've broken our code?"

"Because it wasn't just our code. He didn't want anyone but us to read this. He modified the original code in a very funny way so that only we could break it. To break it, we had to know the original sending code. Really

complicated. We didn't have the exact key. 'Seems like our man is very creative and also very careful. In fact, if we didn't have the original sending code
it would have been impossible for anyone including us to break. He knew
that we'd be able to do it, but no one else could."

"How do we know he isn't a plant sending us false stuff? As a matter of
fact, how do we know he's even a "HE?""

"We don't know any of that sir, but, his stuff has checked out before and
we've been able to act on it with some success."

"Well, let's sleep with one eye open with this one."

"Yessir."

Donovan stared at the text for a long moment. He frowned. "Well, this
looks like we are facing a pretty direct threat. "Pastorius means death to
Roosevelt. Wolfgang says the orchestra will soon take their seats.""

"It's somehow connected with those operatives who landed in Florida
and Long Island back in June."

Donovan breathed deeply and exhaled, "...and who or what do you
think is Wolfgang and his orchestra?"

"We'll have to figure that out." Schlesinger shook his head and stared
at his boss across the desk. "Sir, the message is very direct and I have been
asking myself, if it is a fake why would they suggest they're going to kill the
President?"

"Good question." While the message was dire, Donovan was also mildly
encouraged by it. "There appears to be one good thing in this at least, we
might finally actually have a well-placed solid source in Berlin."

"Well placed, yes, but also a mystery man. Our underground contacts in
Berlin don't know who he is. These messages somehow are left at a mail drop
and no one's seen who's been leaving them."

"Yet, it all could be false."

"Hard to say, sir, but the other things that he's sent over the past couple
of months have been spot-on. His information corroborated intercepts of
ENIGMA messages that the Germans don't know we know how to break."

"What kind of information?"

"Very accurate information about wolfpack operations and where the
convoys could go to avoid them. My guess is that he's German Navy and
he's operating out of Kriegsmarine HQ. He knows where the subs are, and
he's been informing us about them regularly."

"I think that the simplest thing to do is increase security on the President."

"Should we notify Mr. Hoover about this?"

"Oh yeah, Hoover...," Donovan sighed. "Leave that up to me."

2:00 p.m., New York City

Wolfgang prepared to check out of his basement apartment for good. After three nights in that rat hole he was glad that he wouldn't have to return. Haupt would come back later for a clean-up, remove the antenna and take the AFU radio to dispose of somewhere.

For his official daytime entry into the real world of New York City, the saboteur dressed in one of the suits that had been left for him in the closet. His suitcases were heavy, but he carried them effortlessly toward the 86th Street station on the Lexington Avenue El where he boarded a downtown local. At 42nd Street, he left the subway, entered Grand Central from the Lexington Avenue entrance, and mixed into the Sunday afternoon crowd. Five minutes later he was out the main doors on 42nd Street looking for a taxi. He looked like a tourist who had just arrived in New York and was on his way to a hotel. That was precisely the way he wanted it to look. He needed to arrive at his hotel by taxi to add legitimacy to his entrance.

A cab pulled up to the curb directly beneath the Park Avenue overpass and Wolfgang opened the door. He gingerly lifted his two heavy suitcases into the back seat as if they were empty and then got in himself.

"Sir, I can put those in the trunk to get them out of your way?" The cabbie offered.

"No thanks, they're okay right here."

"Where to sir?," the cabbie asked.

"Please take me to the Waldorf Astoria on Park Avenue." Wolfgang leaned back in the cab's back seat.

"Sure thing." The cabbie threw on his meter and zoomed away from the curb. "So, where ya coming in from today?"

Wolfgang had a prepared response for this and any other questions. He had designed it to be evasive without sounding so. He had concocted a story based on train schedules and his brief knowledge of a relative he had once visited in New York state's capital city. "I'm from Albany."

"Not a bad trip down today, I guess. Just a hot train ride, huh?" The cabbie tried to keep up a conversation.

"Yes, it was hot, but all the windows were open and when the train was moving I was comfortable." Don't give away too much information, but don't sound evasive. Make this a totally unmemorable trip for this driver.

On this late Sunday afternoon the city streets were pretty empty and the taxi was able to make it quickly to Madison Avenue where a right turn led them to a red light on the corner of 43rd. "Yeah, pretty hot and quiet day for me, too, here. I'm goin' off duty after I drop you off at the Waldorf. Nice place, that Waldorf, huh?

"Yes. I hear it is a nice place."

"Pretty expensive, huh?"

Don't say anything to engage this man any more that you have to. Keep the trip un-memorable. "I suppose. I'm only here for one night."

The light turned green and the cabbie engaged the clutch lurching the car forward with a slight jolt. Then, all of a sudden, Wolfgang's desire for an unmemorable short trip to his hotel became the stuff of dreams. An elderly derelict without warning appeared directly in front of the moving cab and was knocked onto his back right in the intersection. The horrified cabbie slammed on his brakes and leaped out of the cab to aid his victim. The old man was alive, but was bleeding and screaming in pain. His right arm was twisted under his back in an odd way and it was most likely broken. From the back seat of the taxi Wolfgang just stared at the emerging drama as a beat cop was now running to the intersection to help and passers-by stood gawking at the accident. Should I just take my bags and disappear? No, it is too late.

Within minutes the scene was full of onlookers and more cops. The driver was upset that he had hit the man and kept saying "Honest, I never saw him. He just jumped in front of the cab." Wolfgang just sat there. He was sure that he would have to supply identification as a witness to the accident. This wasn't good at all. To make things worse was the fact that the contents of his two suitcases would certainly raise an eyebrow or two if they were discovered. He just needed to remain calm and act as horrified as the others in the crowd.

Within five minutes more police were on the scene and one of them was on the emergency phone on the southeast corner asking for an ambulance. As the cop spoke with the dispatcher, his eye caught sight of the passenger in the back of the taxi. Wolfgang knew what to expect next . The cop hung up the phone and walked directly over to the back door of the taxi.

"Sir, are you okay?" The cop asked.

"Yes, I'm fine, but that poor old man. So terrible." Wolfgang tried to keep to his plan of "do nothing and say nothing" that would be memorable to anyone.

"I don't want to keep you here sir, but I will have to take a statement from you as a witness to this accident."

"Eh, not a problem officer. I didn't really see what happened but I'm happy to help."

"Can I see some identification sir?"

Wolfgang felt a chill go up and down his spine on this hot summer day. His papers said that his name was Roger Wilson, and they listed his address as 340 West 86th Street. If anyone went deeper than the surface in their questioning it would be easy to find something amiss with Wolfgang's story. If he lived on 86th Street why was he going to stay at the Waldorf? Why had he told the driver that he was from Albany? And the biggest of all, why was there no Roger Wilson listed at the West 86th Street address on his New York drivers license? It would be easy to figure out that Roger Wilson did not exist at all. Still, Wolfgang kept his composure and immediately crafted a made up reason for the two suitcases, I'm meeting some relatives staying at the hotel and I'm bringing them some clothing to take home to the family. With any luck the driver remembered nothing of their earlier conversation about Albany, and if the cops needed Wolfgang as a witness later on, well, they would also need good luck in finding him. "Here you go officer, my drivers license."

The cop read the license. "Thanks Mr. Wilson. I'll be right back to take a statement about what you saw... or didn't see." He took Wolfgang's fake drivers' license and walked back to the crowd hovering around the victim.

Wolfgang calmed down. He would get through this easily, but how would he get these heavy suitcases to the Waldorf five blocks further uptown and one long block eastward? It took what seemed like an eternity for the officer to come back and return the fake license. "Thanks again, Mr. Wilson, I don't think we'll need anything from you right now. The driver pretty much explained what happened and you're free to go on your way. In any case, I have your address if we need to get in touch."

"Thank you. Please let me know if I can be of any help." He stuck his fake I.D. back into his Roger Wilson wallet.

"You bet. Uh, listen, this cab isn't going anywhere for a while. Let me help you get another." The cop stared down Madison looking for a cab. As he saw one approaching he raised his arm and hailed it over. Wolfgang was astounded by his luck. Within seconds he had moved his bags to the new cab and was on his way to the Waldorf and the next part of his deadly plans. He was pretty sure that the cabdriver's discourse with the cop would probably omit the details of their earlier conversation. *Keep the trip un-memorable,* he reminded himself.

3:48 p.m.

By the time Grover arrived at work that Sunday afternoon for the four to midnight tour, Tim Murphy had already been there for over an hour. Part of "The Mirror" was open on his desk. "Aha! I see you're into your department work."

"Yeah, 'done with the crossword and I'm onto the Jumble. I'm already worn out." Murphy's feet were up on his desk allowing his pant legs to catch a breeze roughly every twenty seconds from the oscillating fan sitting on his desk return. "I needed to come in early. The mother-in-law's been in the house since Friday. Not a good thing. I don't know what's worse, that, or the heat."

"Sorry to hear that, pal."

"Ready for your daily briefing?"

Grover nodded.

Murphy turned his face nonchalantly toward the open Mirror, cleared his throat to read aloud. "Here now the news…" Murphy's reading was less like H. V. Kaltenborn's precise diction and more like Walter Winchell's staccato verbal barrage. "Police in Greenport are stymied by the discovery of the bodies of two naked teenagers, a boy and a girl, found drowned on a beach on Shelter Island. The boy's knees were broken and both were floating face-down in the sea grass by the water's edge. Foul play is suspected."

"Smart cops… broken knees are always a sign of foul play." Grover smiled. "No other clues, eh?"

"Yeah, and here's another one. A local motorcycle cop in Wading River on an overnight patrol was found floating face down in a pond with his bike in the water with him."

"Ran off the road in the dark?"

"Not likely in my book… 'Says here that this cop had been on Wading River force for 18 years. He knew every twist and turn of the highway out there. The pond was a good 50 feet from the edge of the highway. The local cops think it's another case of foul play."

"Foul play again. That's how we can lower crime rates everywhere. You might remember that back in April, I too was the victim of foul play."

"Huh?"

"If we eliminate foul play we will put an end to lots of bad stuff that goes on. Okay, humor me tonight. It's been a couple of weeks now."

"What?"

"You know what I want."

"Let me guess," Murphy lowered his newspaper and heaved a forced huge sigh, "We haven't heard a peep from you-know-who lately and you want to follow him if he decides to go to work tonight?"

"That's why you made detective… a very smart guy, despite what the captain keeps saying."

"Your confidence in my ability is appreciated."

"Hey, our boy's been lying low since he nearly killed that old guy."

"Correction, it's not 'nearly' anymore. The guy died overnight at Bellevue."

"Damn? I thought he was improving?"

"He was, but he was weak. They were holding him for a few extra days to fatten him up before they sent him home. 'Hospital report said that he suffocated himself in his sleep with his pillow."

"How does that work?"

"I dunno, I think he rolled over onto his stomach on the bed and couldn't turn himself back over."

"Then Haupt is officially a murderer."

"No, not officially or un-officially. The old guy died by accident in the hospital, that's all."

Grover's face started to turn red, "Haupt as sure as hell killed that guy during the burglary!"

Murphy knew he needed to shut this down immediately. "And you know this how? We have about as much to tie him to that burglary as the disappearance of Judge goddamn Crater. He hasn't fenced anything and he hasn't got shit in that apartment of his. As far as we know he's a solid citizen who, in fact, is helping the war effort by giving the FBI good info on our enemies."

"Now I wanna visit him even more."

"Jesus, Doug… let's leave this fucking guy alone until he actually does something?"

"I wanna get him before that. He hasn't moved since that last job. It's been weeks. I know this guy. He can't sit still for too long. I'll bet you a buck, he will steal again and soon."

"And what does your FBI buddy think about this?"

"What he doesn't know won't bother him."

"Ya don't wanna clue him in before we get into deeper dog crap?" Vainly Murphy tried to short circuit what he perceived as an impending disaster.

"We just have to follow the S.O.B. and see where he goes tonight, and the next few. If he does a burglary, we'll have him. If he visits his parents we'll watch him, and if he does nothing we'll go home. Whatya say?"

"The smart part of me says, 'Tim you should leave the room now.'"

"That's my pal!" Grover smiled broadly. "You wanna drive?"

"Don't I always?"

Within twenty minutes their black Plymouth was parked in a space across the avenue from Haupt's apartment front door. From the passenger window Grover's eyes gravitated to the fire escape, an unpleasant reminder of his broken leg and two months of missed work.

"Looks like he's home." Murphy's gaze was fixed on the living room window. "Lights are all on." Now would come the wait, would Katzenjammer emerge for another night on the town?

"There goes that light." As the dusk set in, the lamp on Haupt's living room chest of drawers flicked off. "Betcha two bucks he hits the pavement in less than five."

Tim patted his wallet pocket, "You're on. It's way too early. Twilight, hardly the time for a self-respecting cat burglar to go to work."

Three minutes passed and the front door to the building opened. Haupt neglected his usual survey and started walking southbound at a brisk pace. "Better that we do this on foot, and you owe me two bucks."

Wary of the situation and based on past experience with this perp, they stayed far enough behind that Haupt didn't notice them at all. "He hasn't done anything in three weeks, I bet he doesn't think anyone's watching him."

They followed him to 81st Street, close to First Avenue, and watched as Haupt disappeared into the basement entrance of a brownstone row house. By the time they moved in closer he was gone. A small name label above the buzzer said simply 'Willy Canaris.'

"He's inside! That was really fast." Grover's brow knitted involuntarily. He was perplexed. "Did this Canaris guy let him in?"

"No, this lock was opened with a key. No break in, no pickin's. No scratches on the tumbler." Murphy looked at Grover, "'Two things wrong here… one, it's still daylight, and two, he has a key."

"Seems so," Grover agreed. "'Kind of unusual for him. Let's go wait across the street. If he comes out of there with stolen stuff we'll grab him here, once and for all."

"Sounds good to me." The cops moved back across the street and waited in the darkness under a staircase, never once removing their gaze from the front door to that basement apartment. It took a little bit longer than a half hour until finally they saw movement. Eugen Haupt emerged from the basement apartment carrying a large brown paper bag.

"Holy shit! We've got him now!" Murphy seemed to be relieved that their long chase to catch this guy red handed at a burglary site had finally come to a close.

"'Looks good!" Grover whispered.

But all was not as it seemed. As they watched from their hidden position they saw that Haupt was doing something odd for any burglar. He was locking the door to that basement with a key as he left. Then, he carried the brown paper bag and tossed it into a metal trash can by the curb. Haupt began walking away empty handed. The cops were stumped and they allowed him to disappear into the twilight.

Grover was the first one to reach the trash can. Throwing the lid onto the ground with a crash, his hands excitedly went through the contents of the brown paper sack. His search was ever so disappointing and a whole lot disgusting. No diamond jewelry or silver tea sets in here. There was a lot of crumpled brown wax paper, eggshells, coffee grounds and pieces of salami rind. In fact the entire bag contained nothing but food garbage, not a note a receipt nor anything that would indicate who generated the trash at all. "This is just food shit."

"Did he come here to do housecleaning on the side? This isn't his parents' place, is it?" Murphy was as confused as was his partner.

Grover thought hard for a moment. "What if this is his special place. What if this is what the FBI could never find out about him? What if this is his spy place."

"You think so?"

"Let's get to a phone. I'm gonna call O'Rourke."

9:30 p.m.

The doorbell rang and Karl Haupt, with great effort, gripped the arms of his ragged easy chair and forced himself to stand up straight. After a breath and a sigh he slowly he made his way to the door and looked out the small peephole. A small smile broke on his face revealing his awfully tobacco-stained teeth. His prodigal had arrived. He swung the door open trying to make it look as if the action didn't take effort, but his son knew that all wasn't good. There was a coldness in the old man's face, probably because of Eugen's earlier behavior and he looked pale, very pale.

"Poppa, you don't look so good."

"Everysing iss fine. Just fine." He dismissed the concern and turned to walk back to his chair. "Did you clean out ze apartment yet?"

"Yes, I found a few of his papers with writing on them, I didn't think that I should toss them into the trash. I have them for you."

"Smart boy!"

"There's only one thing left in there and I don't know what you want me to do with it."

"Vat?"

"It's that suitcase with the radio in it. I didn't know if you wanted it back or should I throw it in the river?"

"I do vant it. You must bring zat here to me. It iss valuable."

"Yeah, I will bring it." The younger Haupt was becoming weary of running his father's errands. "Poppa, who tells you to do all this stuff? One of your old bund buddies?"

There was a condescending edge to Eugen's question and Karl caught it immediately. He snapped back. "I am an important part of ze effort. I speak to zose at ze top who rely on me and my loyalty to ze cause."

Karl's emphasis on the word "cause" threw a switch in Eugen's brain. He had been thinking about this for days and suddenly the simple mention of the "cause" triggered an emotional explosion. From this point in his life, and from now on, Eugen would no longer be the always-dutiful son. "Poppa, I love you but, to hell with the fucking "cause." I'll get you the damn radio tonight, but about that "cause," Poppa, I don't want to be part of it any more. I'm done."

Karl's eyes widened. He was shocked. "Don't talk craziness Eugen. Vat ze hell do you mean? Vat iss ze matter mit you? You are a part of it. You are a German! Zis is a very important moment for ze Fatherland."

"Poppa, I am not a German. I live here. I did what you asked me to do over and over again, but now I am out. I brought that guy to the apartment and I cleaned up his shit after he left it. I don't know what he's up to, and I don't want to know. I do know that he has no soul. I watched him kill two kids on a beach and then a cop for no fucking reason."

"Vatch your mouth in front of me! I am still your father." Karl drew as deep a breath as his sick lungs would allow. He calmed himself before he spoke again. "Zis is a var. Zese tings happen in a var."

"Well, I don't want any more of it. I gave him my drawings of those tunnels and now I'm done. I don't want any part of this crap anymore."

"It means nothing to you? Zis is for Germany, not me alone. Vat iss important here iss his mission. He is here to help end zis stupid war and allow the German people to finally overcome zat national embarrassment. Hiss mission iss very important."

"How do you know about his mission? Who the hell is feeding you this crap?

"Zis is none of your business. I get ze information I need from people who know me and trust me. I am a soldier and so are you. You have your mission as does he. You need to do vat you are told."

The human volcano, Mt. Eugen, finally exploded. "Fuck his mission! Fuck my mission! I want no part of it. I'm an American."

Karl reeled and slumped into his chair. He no longer had the strength to physically discipline his son, he could only show contempt and hurt. He sighed deeply to emphasize his disappointment, "Eugen, Eugen. You sadden me greatly. You are misguided."

"No, I'm just sick of it all. I want out. I don't want to do your burglaries any more. I don't want to give names to the FBI. I am done with it. You can find someone else."

Karl knew right away that this was a new turn of events that couldn't easily be reversed so his brain calculated options. His son would forever be lost to him, but there was a strict time-table at stake for the current mission to be successful and nothing could get in its way. "Yes," he let out a deep guiltful sigh, "you are done. But zis one last time you just need to finish zis vun sing and zen you can go avay and not speak to me nor your mother ever again. You owe me at least zat. You need to bring me zat radio and get zis envelope to our friend. It's very important. He needs to see ze paper inside it by not later zan tomorrow afternoon. Do you understand? Can you do zat for your fahzer?"

Eugen reluctantly agreed to finish at least this part of what he had begun. "I understand." Eugen took the envelope from his father and stuck it into his pants pocket. "I'll go back and get you the radio, but that is the last time you'll see me."

Karl sat in shock as his only son turned and left the apartment. At least zis vill be done, he thought. Germany vill win after I do zis!

10:35 p.m.

The FBI arrived at the brownstone on East 81st in less than an hour. Grover and Murphy watched as two unmarked cars pulled up in front of the building and out of them emerged some familiar faces. The lead car carried O'Rourke and two other men. An older man who seemed to be in charge, was followed by a short, very pale and frightened fat man. Out of the second car came Special Agent Witcover, then all the other agents who were part of the McGlade's near intra-agency melee. The older man walked over to Grover with an extended hand.

"Detective Grover or Murphy?"

"I'm Grover. He's Murphy."

"I'm Special Agent in Charge Mike Foreman. Nice to finally meet you both in person."

"Nice to meet you, too." Grover shook Forman's hand and eyed the nervous looking heavy-set man standing next to him. This guy is definitely not on the job, he surmised.

"Detective Murphy? Nice to meet you, too." Foreman reached out to the other partner. "Agent O'Rourke tells me that your work found this place.

Thanks! Once we had the address we went into action and got some more details."

"No thanks necessary. I blame it all on my wild partner." Murphy smiled.

Foreman returned the smile and then got down to business, "And, this is Mr. Julius Scharfman, the owner of the building."

"You found Scharfman here from the address?" Murphy queried.

"Exactly. And he has keys and has agreed to let us in to that apartment. Mr. Scharfman, please tell the officers what you told me in the car."

Scharfman, roused by the FBI from a Sunday evening with his wife, was sweating heavily, he had never been this close to so many cops, nor had he ever wanted to be. "Uh… yes. Okay, I rented this basement out to a Mr. Canaris, he said his name was Willy Canaris. He promised to pay his rent on time by mail and I never saw him again in person since that day."

"Can you describe Mr. Canaris to these officers?"

Scharfman then, in specific detail, described Eugen Haupt. "He paid me in cash for the first two months and I haven't seen him since. I got no complaints, y'know, he paid his rent and I never saw him again." The nervous landlord repeated himself.

Agent Witcover opened a manila envelope and took out a glossy eight by ten photograph and shoved it in front of the quaking landlord. "Is this the man you rented to?"

"Yes… yes… that's him! Did I rent to a criminal? I had no idea. I really didn't." Scharfman's denials were almost comical. No one had accused him of anything. He was just stunned by the law enforcement show of strength outside his building.

"Well, thank you Mr. Scharfman, would you please open the door for us?" Foreman requested.

"Sure." The rotund building owner quickly took a large key ring from his pants pocket and began searching for the entry key to the basement apartment. Miraculously the first key he tried in the lock was the correct one.

Four FBI agents rushed by him in the doorway with guns drawn. The place was empty.

Grover and Murphy followed them in and they were, in turn, followed by O'Rourke and Foreman. Scharfman stayed outside, not wanting to have anything more to do with any of this.

"There's nothing here. So what the hell was Haupt doing?" Murphy asked no one in particular.

"No Tim, it wasn't Haupt it was Willy Canaris," Grover joked.

O'Rourke spoke up. "Willy… I mean Wilhelm… Canaris is the Nazi naval admiral who's in charge of the Abwehr. That's their secret spy operation. Canaris is the Germans' spy master."

"Yeah, it's Haupt's inside joke when he rented the place, I guess." Foreman grumbled as he stared around the empty apartment. "Pretty stupid spycraft if you ask me." As he scowled, the other four agents were methodically working their way through the room looking for any clues about Haupt, but there was almost nothing left inside at all that wasn't there before the renter had arrived.

Grover noted that the bed in the other end of the room had been slept in and not re-made, but the rumpled sheets and pillows explained nothing. "Ya gotta wonder why he slept here in this crap hole when he has a nice above ground place on Third Avenue?"

The only visible evidence of anyone's recent presence was a small waste basket in the corner that had not been emptied. It contained four or five crumpled balls of paper and nothing else.

"This place smells like something familiar." Murphy said.

"Yeah, but it's not an unpleasant smell… it kind of smells like…?" Grover searched for an olfactory memory. "It smells like those mandelhörnchen that Haupt got at the bakery."

"Yeah, he loved those things. They were made from…"

"Almonds." O'Rourke finished Murphy's thought. "This place smells like almonds."

"Hey, Tim, Haupt's getting out of the breaking and entering business. He's becoming a baker," Grover joked!

"The guy really loves his pastry," Murphy nodded.

"Pastry?," Foreman asked.

"The smell… When we talked to him a while ago Haupt had a bag full of these German pastries called mandelhörnchen. They were almond cookies or something that smelled like almonds, maybe marzipan… can't really tell." Murphy paced around the room and grabbed the waste basket. "This crumpled paper in the wastebasket, looks like wrapping paper from a bakery to me," he said. "Yeah, Haupt loves that almond stuff. The mandelhörnchens." Murphy unfolded a twelve inch square piece of wax paper.

"I don't see any crumbs of pastry anywhere," Witcover said.

"Hey, got something here!" Agent Chase called from the other side of the room. He had opened up a cabinet over the small kitchen stove and discovered a fiberboard case with a handle. Everyone noticed it right away. With that discovery the gravity of their problem had just increased one hundredfold.

"Don't touch it. It could be rigged." Foreman ordered everyone out of the room and once up at street level, summoned three men wearing gray coveralls who were still seated waiting in newly-arrived black car.

The men in the coveralls entered the apartment while everyone else waited tensely on the sidewalk. Five minutes passed when one of the men in coveralls emerged, "All clear. It's safe to go back in."

The entire group reentered the apartment greeted by one of the other FBI technicians, "here we go… got it." He had found one end of a piece of bell wire coiled inside the air shaft window.

The lead technician called Foreman over to the kitchen table. "Do you guys know what this is?"

Foreman read the label aloud, "Telefunken? What is this?"

"Sir, it's a German radio transmitter." The technician informed his boss. "'Goes with the bell wire antenna over there going out the window."

"Thanks." Foreman gazed at the apparatus inside the small case. Alongside the device were two, 67-volt Eveready "B" batteries and a coiled up spool of bell wire. Foreman might not have known what it was before, but he was certain of what it meant now. He turned to Witcover and snarled, "Witcover, bring in your informant, now!"

"Yes, sir." The normally uncompromising Witcover, perhaps Eugen Haupt's biggest supporter in the FBI's New York office, now had a sheepish look on his face. His informant had been using him from the start, or so it appeared. This was the evidence that Haupt was a genuine spy, or so it seemed. Witcover quickly left the room along with Agent Chase to round up the snitch.

"What kind of a radio is it?" Murphy asked?

"If I'm not mistaken, It's one of the German army's most advanced communications devices; it's called the AFU, their spy radio." Foreman answered.

"And those must be the batteries and the bell wire that I saw him buying a few weeks ago. He was coming down here and sending messages to Germany." Grover was feeling a mild level of satisfaction that at last his suspicions were vindicated. "Maybe that's why he was sleeping here? He had to wait until certain times of day to send his messages."

"So the son of a bitch would come down here and send messages to Der Führer while he fed his face on the Mandelhörnchens," Murphy said. "Now I know why I didn't like him."

"Well, he won't be using this radio any more." O'Rourke smiled.

"Ya know, I bet if we search this place we'll also find all the stuff he stole. He was a spy playing you guys, and a thief all at the same time. This must be why there was nothing in his apartment and we never caught him fencing anything he took."

Foreman looked over at Grover, "When you watched Haupt leave here, what did he do?"

"He turned west, we thought he might be headed home to his apartment."

"What was he doing here?"

"Don't know, we just saw him walk out and lock the place."

"Nothing else?" Foreman pushed.

"Oh, yeah, he tossed that bag of trash into the garbage can outside. Detective Murphy and I went through it. Nothing but coffee grounds and food crap."

"Is the bag still in our possession?" Foreman asked.

"Sort of, we tossed it back in the can outside. Nothing there though, just leftovers."

"We need to look at it."

Grover raised an eyebrow so only Murphy could see it. Murphy immediately knew where Grover's mind was taking him. This Dick Tracy stuff is just too much to believe! "Me and Murph already went through it Chief. What are you gonna find in a bag of garbage?"

"We'll know when we find it." Foreman nodded to one of the crime lab agents in the coveralls. In less than a minute the agent returned with the bag of trash. Foreman cleared the radio off the kitchen table and then dumped the contents of the bag out under the single dangling one-hundred-watt bulb. There it all was, salami skins, coffee grounds, cheese rinds, an empty wine bottle and many more crumpled sheets of brown wax paper. They all stared at the mess for long moment.

The lawmen were baffled and stood around the table in silence until Agent O'Rourke spoke. "The wax paper. There's an awful lot of it here. No one can eat so much almond pastry." O'Rourke picked it up and sniffed it. "Here sir, smell it, almonds… that's it. Holy crap!"

"What holy crap?" Foreman snapped back.

"We just learned about this, the explosives that they found on the beach in Long Island where those U-boat guys landed? The explosives smelled like almond paste." He brought one of the crumpled pieces of trash up to his nose. "This is it… it's wax wrapping paper."

Foreman sniffed the paper and grimly nodded at Agent O'Rourke. "Mmm hmm. You are probably right."

Grover and Murphy watched with great interest but couldn't understand what was going on. "Would someone please clue us in here, the NYPD?"

"Remember those Nazis we caught back in June?" Foreman said.

"Yeah?"

"They brought explosives with them wrapped in wax paper, this kind of wax paper."

"There are explosives in here?" Grover looked around the room.

"I would bet you that there *were* explosives in here," O'Rourke opined, "and by the strength of the smell, I would say a lot."

"Don't jump to conclusions." Foreman cautioned, "It could be just those snookums almond cakes."

"Well, bombs or marzipan, there's nothing here now. Looks like our pal Haupt here cleaned the place out."

Though he was cautioning his team not to jump to conclusions, Foreman immediately grasped the probable impact of their discovery. Now, the group of lawmen stood in silence in the middle of the badly-lit kitchen and stared at one another. "While we're testing that wax paper for whatever it was wrapped around, let's also check the fingerprints on this wine bottle. I'll bet you it has Eugen Haupt all over it."

"Yes sir," one of the crime lab technicians carefully took the bottle off the table with his gloved hands and put it into a bag.

Murphy wrinkled his face indicating a new kind of dread, "So let me sum this up. We have a bigger problem now. If we're not looking for an almond cake, where's Haupt, and more importantly, where are the explosives?"

11:15 p.m.

As he turned the corner to the 81st Street apartment, Eugen Haupt stopped in his tracks. There were dark figures moving in and out of the basement door. Something not good was going on. The first person he noticed was the landlord, Scharfman, and then someone was carrying a bag of trash from the curbside garbage can into the place. A moment later he was sure that he saw the shadowy figure of his FBI contact Agent Witcover getting into a car with another man. It sped away down the block. The next shadows were surely that of Grover and his partner, Murphy. Some other figure was carrying that small fiberboard suitcase he had hidden above the stove. All of a sudden Eugen Haupt realized that the world as he knew it had come to an end. Scharfman had surely identified him as the man who rented the place, and that radio was a dead giveaway to anyone who knew what it was, and he was sure that they all knew exactly what it was. Still, as his mind rifled through his mental card catalog of escape hatches, he was sure he could talk his way out of it all. There was no evidence of anything in the place other than that fucking radio. He had cleaned the place up immaculately from that slob Wolfgang's visit. There was nothing else in the place other than the radio. *How the hell did they come upon it?* In the back of Eugen's mind he had a nagging notion that it was his father who had called the FBI. He was unable to put that one to rest. No matter what his excuse, Eugen Haupt knew that he was now a wanted man, and not just by the two cops, but also by his pals at the FBI.

Obscured by the darkness outside the glow of a streetlamp, Eugen moved farther out of eyesight of the brownstone, only poking his head around the corner for a few seconds at a time to check the action. *How am I going to get out of this?* His situation was ironic. Without Karl Haupt wanting to get even with his personal enemies and encouraging his son to deliver former bundists to the FBI, Eugen was sure that his house burglaries would have gone totally unsolved by the NYPD. The only reason the cops caught him that night in April was that he broke into that bakery, and that was just for the sake of the goddamn FBI looking for a goddamn list! Without all that, no one would know who he was. Well, too late! He left the scene on First Avenue, his shadow melting into the hot summer night.

Despite the dramatic encounter with his old man, he would have to let Karl know what had happened. After walking many blocks and shying away from cruising police cars, he found himself at the Second Avenue on-ramp to the 59th Street bridge. Eugen searched for a telephone booth. At 56th Street, the bright light of an all-night pharmacy beckoned. Avoiding eye contact with any of the three customers inside, Haupt slipped into a phone booth and nervously shoved a nickel into the slot. He dialed the same number that he dialed when he was a teenager calling home. It was after midnight and the elder Haupt had been sleeping.

"Hallo?"

"It's me. I just thought you should know that we had some unexpected guests at the apartment tonight."

A long pause followed before Karl's response, "...and?"

"The guests took your suitcase. They took it with them."

"Ze... suitcase?"

"Yes."

"Scheisse." There was anger in Karl's voice and absolutely no compassion in his next question, "And vat about you?"

"I'm out for a long walk. It's too hot to go home."

Another lengthy pause was followed by a sigh. "Did you see our friend and giff him ze envelope I gave to you?"

"No. Not yet. I'm not sure that I..."

"Listen to me! You need to get him zat envelope. It is very important to him."

"And what about to me, Poppa? Is it important to me?"

"Goddamnit, it is important to ME!"

Eugen paused. More than ever now he really wanted out of this life, but he did promise his father that he would get it all done before leaving.

"And what about me Poppa," Eugen pressed one more time. "What's important to me?" Eugen waited for an answer of any kind, a grunt would have been sufficient. Silence. There was no response.

"Okay, I said that I would. I'll get it to him."

"Ven?"

"I will call him in the morning to arrange a meeting."

"Good."

Karl's monosyllabic responses hammered into Eugen's head, but the hammering no longer had any impact. Eugen had finally broken away. All that he could say was, "Goodbye, Poppa."

A long pause followed with halted breathing and then the shallow sound of a click. For the moment the newly liberated Eugen Haupt sat alone in a late-night drugstore phone booth and quietly sobbed.

August 31, 1942

7:00 a.m.

At 7:00 a.m. an incessant ringing roused him. He reached across the bed and picked up the telephone handset. Maybe it was finally that oaf, Haupt. "Yes?"

"Good morning Mr. Wilson, this is your seven a.m. wakeup call."

"Thank you." He hung up the phone and looked at his watch. Shit! Where is Haupt? Waking up was difficult this morning. For Wolfgang it was the first night of sound sleep since he left Brest weeks ago. He was never able to totally adjust his nocturnal clock to the pitching and rolling of that damn sailboat, nor was he at all comfortable sleeping in the dank basement apartment. The Waldorf Astoria was a different kind of place. His room was spotless, and the linens smelled like some kind of perfume. It was quiet and no one at all suspected that Roger Wilson, a cash paying hotel guest, was anyone other than who he said he was. Indeed, he was aware of only two people who knew his whereabouts. One was Eugen Haupt, an unfortunate necessity, and the other was Admiral Canaris in Berlin. Before Wolfgang left the apartment he'd notified the Fox by radio of his progress with assurances that all was well. But now, without the radio, Canaris would have to read about the results of his workmanship in the press.

The plan was to remain as inconspicuous as possible. *Raise no suspicion. Blend in with the crowd so that no one notices you at all. What would a regular person do at the Waldorf Astoria?* He would order breakfast from room service. So, that's what he did.

After his breakfast he showered, dressed in one of the finer suits left for him in the old apartment. The clothes smelled of almonds, not an unpleasant odor at all, he thought to himself. Mentally planning his day of subterranean reconnaissance he filled his Roger Wilson wallet with cash. Canaris had given him a large sum to take care of his expenses leading up to and following his mission.

Now, somehow, he needed to get down to the tracks beneath the hotel. He needed to find Track 61, the place where he knew Roosevelt's armored railcar would be coming in. From there Roosevelt would transfer to his private automobile on that platform. The car was also loaded into the railcar for the train trip from Washington. Only a narrow window of opportunity existed to accomplish the mission. It needed to happen once the President's car was off the train with him in it. The limousine would be on the platform for perhaps a minute or two before it entered the elevator to the street above. Wolfgang would have one quick shot and then the moment would be gone. He only needed to know when to expect the train. Gleaned from sympathetic American Germans working for The New York Central Railroad, Haupt had that information detailing the presidential train's approach-track, date and time.

The Waldorf Astoria is where Roosevelt always stayed. It was unique among all hotels in the city. Built at a time when the wealthy magnates of American industry owned and traveled in their own private railcars, it was the only hotel in the city with its own private rail platform. For President Roosevelt the Waldorf's underground entrance served a double purpose. First, it allowed FDR to come and go securely traveling below New York City's streets, and second, no one among the voting public at street level would see the paralyzed chief executive being pushed in a wheel chair. Canaris already had specific intelligence indicating that Roosevelt would be spending a few hours before the American Labor Day weekend at the Waldorf Astoria. He would stop briefly there for a meeting with political supporters and then his train would leave for the Hyde Park estate. Wolfgang knew all of this from his briefings in Berlin and for now he was confident that with one additional piece of information he would be able to achieve his mission simply. For that piece of information he was relying on just one more contact with Eugen Haupt.

The lobby elevator door opened and Wolfgang stepped out. He purchased a copy of the "The New York Times" from the newsstand and took a seat on a sofa. When he wasn't looking at his watch or the newspaper, he was scanning the lobby for some kind of an access door that might lead him to the tracks below. It didn't take long. A housemaid pushed a cart through a swinging door that seemed to lead into a gray painted hallway. *Ah, that could be something!* While no one was looking, he headed for the door. The hallway led to stairs up and down, a service elevator and a room full of trash-cans. Descending one flight of stairs he was stopped by a locked steel door. *Not a problem for me.* He made quick work of the lock, and within seconds was walking on a back rail platform adjacent to a long track that disappeared into the tunnel. Even in daytime it was black, but his eyes adapted quickly and he was at once comfortable in the darkness.

Wolfgang felt his way across the platform wary of unexpected track workers or anyone who might question his presence. He reached into his coat pocket and pulled out a piece of paper. *At least I have Haupt's map.*

10:00 a.m.

Grover and Murphy had never been inside the FBI's New York offices before. They were there on special assignment from their captain who had been personally called by FBI Director Hoover regarding the loan of his prime burglary team. Grover, for the first time in some months was feeling empowered. Everyone now seemed to be in agreement that Eugen Haupt was a bad guy. For the detective it was a sweet, although long awaited, victory of sorts.

The FBI building was a far cry from their aging 19th Precinct house. When the elevator door opened to a huge open space on the third floor they were immediately impressed by the surroundings. The place had a number of private offices with windows and everything, from the floorcovering to the evenly painted walls, looked much neater than the 19th. Multiple rows of women at typewriters tapped away as men in natty suits and solid colored neckties collected their work, moving the papers elsewhere in the building.

"Y'know Boy-o, this place makes me wanna clean up my desk." Murphy half whispered to his partner. His eyes scanned the huge room and noticed the familiar face of Special Agent O'Rourke. He was waving at them in a beckoning motion.

Inside the room and already seated at the conference table was the usual crowd. Nods and small waves from those around the table were the only official welcome. Foreman smiled at the cops and motioned to them to be seated and then dropped his smile. "Okay, let's not waste any time. Eugen Haupt is a potential saboteur. We believe he has powerful explosives and we have no idea where he is or what he's planning to do. Thoughts?"

Witcover spoke first, "We staked out his regular place and that apartment all night. Haupt never came home. Also Agents Chase and Burke staked out his parents' apartment too, but he didn't show up there either."

"Let's get a tap on the parents' phone right away too. He might call them."

"Already done sir. We did it this morning." Witcover was no longer protecting Haupt.

"Since he hasn't been home or at that place on 81st Street we can safely assume that he's laying low." Grover spoke. "He's smart enough to know that you guys found the landlord and the man, for sure, I.D.'d him. He knows we've been to that other apartment and he must also know that we found that radio."

"What else do we think he knows?" Foreman asked.

"I think he's waiting for this to blow over. I don't think he thinks we know anything about explosives. Maybe he thinks that he'll be able to explain his way out of the radio." Murphy surmised, "But I gotta tell ya, I think this sabotage stuff is way out of this guy's level of talent."

"Don't write him off. He could just be playing with us. He could be a trained spy," Witcover opined, "...the worst kind! With that radio he could have been taking orders directly from Berlin."

Murphy smirked, "I've been on this job for a long time. I go on instinct. That tells me that our master spy is just a dumb bastard who's got the NYPD and the Feds after him for just being the dumb bastard that he is. He's not really smart enough to be a saboteur."

"'Could be true," O'Rourke agreed. "Nothin's back from the lab yet and we really don't know for sure anything about the almond wrappers. Might be that this guy could have a huge black-market business in contraband marzipan going for him."

"I know this sounds odd coming from me of all people, but I don't think we can't take that chance." For the first time since he heard the name Eugen Haupt back in April, Grover began to doubt his own low-ball assessment of Haupt's intellect. Until someone tells me otherwise, my gut tells me we gotta think that Eugen is a fucking genius of a spy and that there are explosives." Grover immediately regretted using that expletive so common in his workplace. As he spoke it he sensed an instantaneous tightening in the room. *Ah, the FBI doesn't use that word!* "...er excuse my French, this individual is up to something no good."

Foreman smiled. "I agree. Knowing what we know about Haupt, we need to assume he's guilty and figure out what he might be targeting."

Agent Chase spoke up, "Those Germans we rounded up in June confessed to planning to blow up railroads."

"Yes, but we put a stop to that one, didn't we?"

"What if they're still at it," Chase fretted

"And, our Eugen is on that same mission? And why is his operation coming out of a basement on East 81st street," Burke chimed in.

"Simple. He knows the neighborhood. He's comfortable there," Murphy added.

Grover questioned, "Yeah, but Murph, think about it, wouldn't he want to be in a place near the railroads and near tracks that carry war supplies, not the IRT?"

"Honestly, I don't think the neighborhood has anything to do with this. He could be casing rail yards on the West Side, lotsa war stuff moves through there," Chase added. "Or, what about Penn Station or Grand Central?

Foreman was skeptical. "I don't think so. There's nothing but passenger traffic moving in and out of either of those. Other than making people late for work, I don't see how blowing up one train station could make any kind of a dent in the war effort. I think we need to keep eyes on all those rail yards on the West Side. What else could he blow up?"

"Whew, there's all kinds of targets in the city," Witcover's mind immediately went to the location of his most recent lunch meeting with his snitch. "Our regular place to meet up is a park bench near the Battery. What if he decided to take down the draft induction center building on Whitehall Street, he knows where that is for sure."

"Yes, that sounds like a possibility. Look into that one." Foreman made a note on a pad in front of him. "Any other thoughts?"

"What if he bombed the Empire State? That would be like Pearl Harbor all over again, but much closer to home, also bridges, tunnels." Agent Phil Burke had a look of dread in his eyes.

"Good thought, the signature structures are targets. I agree that if the enemy successfully blew up one of those it could be awful for morale." Foreman made another note on his pad. "But, damn, there's a whole load of that stuff in the city. There's no damn way to check them all. We need more information or a lot more troops."

Grover scanned the faces of his new-found colleagues. "What if Eugen's not planning to blow up a what, but rather a who?"

Foreman looked up from his yellow pad as his face became noticeably pale. About an hour earlier he had spoken on the phone with Director Hoover. Could the information from Hoover have something to do with Eugen Haupt? He kept the thought to himself for the moment, made another note on the paper and moved on. The agents' meeting continued for about a half-hour longer with speculation on various pieces of real estate that might be targeted. Plans were discussed without any resolution, but then, no one else in the room knew what Foreman knew. He wondered, *Haupt and Roosevelt?*

2:00 p.m.

Wolfgang's earlier trip into the tunnels was all he needed to plan the next step of his task. He had gone onto the tracks from beneath the hotel and then continued southward finally climbing up on the platform of Track 24 inside Grand Central Terminal itself. He was stealthy and no one had seen him as he appeared on the platform. He simply looked like any other commuter or traveler who was coming or going on a train. He now knew exactly what he needed to do to accomplish his mission.

Leisurely, he walked into the main concourse of the majestic building, admiring the architecture, and exited on Lexington Avenue. By the time he was back in his hotel room he was relaxed. This will be much easier than I could have ever imagined. Wolfgang sat down on his comfortable couch, took off his shoes, put his feet up, and once again unfolded Eugen Haupt's detailed under-street map of the Grand Central train tracks. On his reconnaissance mission he had made his own notations as well, and some small drawings along the side of the paper. All he needed from Haupt now was the timing details.

As had been described to him back in Berlin, a huge part of the footprint of the Waldorf Astoria was built over railroad tracks. Almost the entire western half of the majestic building had no real basement. According to German engineers who had searched through the construction plans, most of the entire giant building was supported by an untraditional foundation of concrete and steel pillars. If those braces were strategically removed it would undermine the entire structure causing the hotel with its limestone facade, and its 47-story towers, some 625 feet high above the street level, to come crashing down on itself and over the surrounding streets. But, most important to Wolfgang's mission, the falling building would also crush anything on the railroad tracks below. Within his suitcases Wolfgang carried the stuff he planned to use to remove those supports.

All that the saboteur now needed to know was the special railroad car's arrival timetable. Roosevelt's movements were always top secret, but as this secret involved train schedules on heavily used tracks, it was simple for that information to fall into nefarious hands. Thanks to an ex-bundist who worked in the station master's office at Grand Central, Karl Haupt had that timetable and had given it to his son. Wolfgang didn't much care about the origin of the information, he just needed to know when. The death of Roosevelt will be a huge coup for the fatherland! It will destroy American morale! It could end the war!" His intelligence information would be complete once he connected with Eugen Haupt.

In the next couple of days, Wolfgang would carefully place the explosives that he carried in his suitcases atop the pillars holding up the hotel. There was much work to do, but once it was done Wolfgang could calmly wait in his hotel room for the American President to show up at the private train platform beneath the building. Once he learned the exact time of the arrival from Karl Haupt's source, he would leisurely go downstairs and personally welcome President Roosevelt to New York. Tonight he would begin his preparatory work, but for now he would take a nap and wait for the specifics from Haupt. All was going well.

2:10 p.m.

From that day at McGlade's when they almost got into a fistfight, Grover didn't trust any FBI agents. Well, maybe he trusted O'Rourke just a bit. At the moment, none of what was going on was about trust. It was about style. The manhunt for Eugen Haupt was the FBI's case and the cops were just tagging along. Grover and Murphy waited by the car while FBI agents Witcover and Chase interviewed some of Haupt's neighbors. "Jesus, Murph, these guys wouldn't know how to ask information for a phone number." Grover was unimpressed by straight-laced politeness of FBI training at work in the real world of the city's streets.

"Politeness has its place... but definitely not on Third Avenue." Murphy looked at his watch. "We're wasting time. No one's gonna talk to them. Haupt could be planting a bomb someplace right now."

"Nothing here," Witcover sighed as the FBI guys returned to the car. It was obvious, not one neighbor would give them an answer beyond, "I don't know," or "I never saw the guy." New York cops would have had better results. Still, Grover was glad to be included in any effort to put Haupt behind bars.

"Next stop?," Grover asked.

"Let's pay a visit to Haupt's parents. They may not know what their boy is up to but they may know where he might be hiding," Agent Chase opined.

"Interesting." Murphy was driving and gave a knowing glance to his partner sitting next to him. He put the car into gear and started to drive north on First Avenue.

"Do you have an address for the Haupts?" Grover asked.

"Yeah, they're on 89th between Second and Third." Chase handed him a piece of paper with the house address.

"How'd you get that address?"

"I dunno, the Bureau has a file on these people."

"I suppose that you guys all know about the old man, right?" Grover pushed.

"Huh? What about him," Chase asked?

"I mean you know all about who he is and stuff, right?"

"No, not that much." Chase looked quizzical. "What about him?"

"Daddy Haupt was a part of the old Dutch Schultz mob, a real knee buster," Murphy said from behind the wheel.

Grover's eyes scanned the faces of the men in the back seat. It appeared that Chase knew nothing at all about the elder Haupt, but as his glance drifted over to Witcover he noticed that the man was clearly avoiding eye contact. Grover took a long pause before he spoke as he searched for the right words. Murphy knew where the conversation was headed and he grimaced, awaiting the eruption of Mt. Grover. "I mean, you guys have the whole file that was in my desk a month ago… you know, that district attorney file that I had all about the Haupts?"

"What file," Chase asked?

Grover was pretty sure that Chase was clueless so he focused his boiling ire at Witcover instead. Witcover immediately understood what was going on and did everything he could to avoid the conversation. He pretended to be reading a typewritten piece of paper, "Ya know, when people in the law enforcement field work with each other we have to trust each other, too."

Murphy couldn't stand the tension any longer. He slammed on the brakes, pulled the car to the curb and turned from the driver seat staring directly at Witcover. "Look at me! What my partner is going to say is that we once had in our possession a confidential New York district attorney's investigative file on one Karl Haupt. It was on his desk one day and gone the next."

"What happened to it?" Chase asked.

Murphy glared at intently at Witcover with a look of malice. "Good question. We'll never really know, I guess."

"Oh! And you think I took it? You're accusing me? I had nothing to do with that."

"How did you know about Karl and his address? The white pages?" Grover demanded.

Witcover became defensive and sarcastic, "How did we find the address? We're the FBI. That's what we do for a living."

"Oh, please excuse me then." Grover's voice matched the tone. "There were only two people who knew I had that file, my contact in the DA's office and Tim. Someone was in there after hours looking around my desk." Grover remained remarkably composed and in control. "No one other than the DA was onto Karl Haupt's past, not the NYPD and certainly not you guys."

"Don't be so sure, detective. The FBI was dealing with his kind when you were still in knee-pants. I'll say this one more time. We did not take your damned file."

"Well, okay then," Grover feigned belief. "Funny though, how that was in the only file that ever walked out of my desk drawer all by itself."

Chase had had enough of the bickering. "Detective, if someone took that file from you without asking, that was wrong. We have no idea how the Bureau got a hold of Karl's address, but we do have it now."

Witcover snapped, "Yeah, I was given this stuff by Bureau investigators so we could locate a dangerous and on-the-loose Nazi saboteur. A guy lost somewhere in New York City with God knows what kind of high explosives, and with what kind of a mission. If you have some objection to that you can take it up with J. Edgar Hoover. For now, let's just forget about your vendetta with this guy and find him before he kills a lot of people."

Detective Douglas Grover, perhaps for the first time in his career, had nothing to say. There was silence in the car. Grover's eyes looked over at his partner for any kind of support.

Murphy said nothing and slipped the car back into gear. Fortunately for all, within five minutes they were double parked in front of a gray-brick six-story apartment house on East 89th Street. As they got out of the car Murphy mumbled out of the FBI men's' earshot, "Ya know, it could have been McCluskey who took it. Ya know, trying to keep a leash on you?"

Grover didn't reply. There was nothing more to say.

The four officers crammed into the building's small elevator and the silence between them continued until the fifth floor. In seconds they found apartment 5A and Special Agent Witcover rang the doorbell. At first there was no sound, then they could detect a stirring on the other side, it was followed by a cough and a creaky voice, "who iss it?"

"Mr. Haupt we are FBI Special Agents Witcover and Chase, along with New York City Police detectives Grover and Murphy. We need to talk to you about your son, Eugen Haupt. Can you open the door please?"

Grover rolled his eyes on the word *please*.

The door creaked open slowly and a frail looking old man in a robe greeted them. "Yes, Eugen Haupt iss my son. Iss he okay?"

"May we come in sir?"

"Yes, yes, of course. Please come in. Is Eugen okay? My vife is out shopping for food. She should be home soon."

Grover and the others followed the decrepit old man into the apartment's shabby living room. The slow moving sixty-something-year-old lumbered across the floor to a big easy chair and Grover thought to himself, *this guy looks fifteen years older than he really is! He was once muscle for Dutch Schultz?* Grover mentally compared Karl with his own Uncle Moshe, about the same age. Uncle Mike, is still lifting weights! Karl, on the other hand, had trouble lifting his slippered feet as he shuffled across the floor to sit down.

"So officers, vat can I help you viss?" Haupt's raspy question was followed by a fifteen-second long hacking cough and some phlegm spit into a blue and white handkerchief.

"Mr. Haupt," Agent Witcover spoke up, "We're looking for your son."

"Yes? You are looking for him, vye?" The elder goon feigned ignorance.

"He's been a big help to us at the FBI over the past months but now we can't locate him. I'm concerned that something may have happened to him.

Karl just sat there and stared blankly at his four visitors.

Chase, spoke up. "Mr. Haupt, when was the last time you saw him?"

Karl pretended to consider the question and started to draw a breath to speak, but what came out was another concerto of hacking, coughing and sputum. The episode of coughing legitimately drained him of the power to speak. Karl became momentarily breathless. The hacking was disconcerting and disgusting at the same time, but none of it fazed Detective Douglas Grover.

"Mr. Haupt, can I call you Karl? Let's stop the bullshit." Grover stood up to his full height. "I'll put money down that you know exactly all the shit that boy of yours has been up to."

"Ach, please sir, your language!" Karl Haupt stared at Grover with contempt yet his verbal response was meek and old. "I am sorry, I really don't understand vat you're talking about?"

"I think you do, and I bet you know exactly who I am, don't you? Is my name familiar?"

"No, should it be?"

"You mean that your shithead of a son didn't tell you about me?" Grover goaded the old man toward a cliff and hoped he would tumble over the edge. The two FBI agents were aghast at the interrogation, but Murphy could see in his partner's eyes that something else was in the works.

"Detective Grover, may I speak with you for a moment?" Witcover made an attempt to save this seemingly helpless old man from the junkyard dog.

Grover didn't care what Witcover thought and went deeper. "I'm pretty sure that what I'm telling you is no surprise, but you surely know that your son is the creep who beat up an old man in his apartment while he lifted the wife's jewelry. You know, that old guy died in Bellevue from his beating. That makes your low-life son a murderer, doesn't it?"

"No, he did not murder anyvun. He's a good boy. I raised him as a good boy," the former enforcer for the Dutch Schultz mob protested.

"You must have been some role model!" Grover went for the throat. "Hey, like father like son, huh? Y'know, the way I heard it, you got Dutch killed, didn't you?"

"I… I… don't…"

"Yeah, as I heard the story, good old Dutch was taking a leak and before he could put his dick back into his pants you came into the men's room and shot him."

"Vat are you saying?" Haupt looked even more weak and glassy eyed, yet there was something about him that said, *yeah, so what and screw you.* "I know nussing about zis at all."

Grover turned to Murphy and smiled as he verbalized the crime that appeared as a vision in his brain. "Yeah, now I have it all clear, you were off that night. You weren't there as his bodyguard. Pretty convenient, huh? And that's the very night Dutch gets it. You show up in the bathroom and shoot him. You're really good aren't you, really loyal to your boss, huh? What made you do it?"

Karl began to glare at Grover with a new intensity. His lower lip began to quiver.

"Yeah Karl, I bet you iced the guy because he was screwing you over. He was treating you like shit and all that. You couldn't take that from a Jew could you?"

That last remark did what it was supposed to do, it pulled the old man's hair trigger temper, "Go fuck yourself Grover. Too bad Eugen did not zrow you onto your head. You havff no proof of anysing. Now get out of my house and leave my son alone."

Grover stopped smiling, leaned in close to the old man's rough face and softly spoke directly into his ear. "Now we have it don't we. Y'see, here's the thing Karl… is it okay with you if I call you Karl? Your boy just did something far worse than stealing or murder, maybe even a worse thing than throwing me off a fire escape. Your boy is working for der Fatherland, isn't he? Your boy is now being hunted by both me and his old pals at the FBI. You know why? I'll tell you why. He's a goddamn saboteur. He's a fucking Nazi spy. D'ya know what happens to Nazi spies, especially when we're at war?"

Karl became somber. Whatever allegiance he had to his family was really only second to the allegiance to Germany. Karl was suddenly becoming very worried that Eugen would be caught before he could deliver that envelope to Wolfgang. So far, he guessed, the FBI and the cops knew nothing at all about Wolfgang. It seemed that Eugen was the object of their mistaken attention. This was a good thing. He took a deep breath and wanted to speak but more hacking and phlegm came out instead. When it stopped he was only able to whisper. The lion no longer roared. "Vat do you vant from me?"

"We want to know where he is and what he's up to." Witcover, now impressed by Grover's technique, stepped into the conversation. He wasn't sure exactly how much Karl actually did know, but he had to know something. "Where is he now? When was the last time you spoke with him."

Karl's mind reeled itself back to Eugen's last visit. This was not good. He already knew that the FBI had somehow found the apartment, but what could they have found in there that they would think the boy was a spy? Eugen told him that the place was clean, except … *Oh shit, the radio!* "I haffen't seen him for a few days. He brings me and his mother groceries every so often."

"What a nice boy, every parent's dream kid," Murphy said with mock seriousness. "So where is he now?"

Karl could only answer honestly. "I haff no idea vere he is." He let out a genuine sigh, "Ve had an argument. I don't expect to see him again any time soon."

Grover next tried sincerity with one more appeal. "Karl, I'm not gonna lie to you. This is serious. This time it's more than just him tying people up in their skivvies. If we don't find him soon something really bad could happen. I'm telling you, what he's up to could be awful for everyone, and even worse for you. You gotta tell us where he is before he goes through with it."

Aha! It seems zey no nussing about my guest. Zey tink zat Eugen is the saboteur! Karl regained his composure and looked Grover straight in the eye. With that thought in mind would he try to help? It was something that not even Karl Haupt knew at the moment. He waited for his mouth to make the decision. "Detective Grover, I haff no idea vere my son iss and if I did know, you vould be ze last person in ze vorld I vould ever tell, so screw you."

"Now I know where your asshole son learned to be such a charmer."

Witcover had a better idea than talking. "Mr. Haupt, I'm placing you under arrest for complicity in a sabotage scheme against the United States of America." With that the FBI agents lifted up the old man in his bathrobe, slapped on a pair of handcuffs and walked him out of the apartment. For once Detectives Doug Grover and Tim Murphy were impressed by agents of the FBI.

September 1, 1942

4:20 p.m.

Over the past few days in New York, as per his orders from Admiral Canaris himself, Wolfgang made himself very familiar with the geography of his sabotage arena including the train tracks beneath the Waldorf Astoria. It did not take very long for him to explore the grimy, hot and rat-infested warren of tunnels and become almost as familiar with them as he was with the streets of his boyhood village in Bavaria. As a hunter and a master predator he was comfortable in the dark, and quickly discovered good places to hide from the track maintenance men, who from time-to-time walked by inspecting the railroad bed.

Since his arrival at the hotel yesterday, everything seemed to be going very smoothly. Once he discovered the service corridor in the lobby that led down to the tracks, Wolfgang worked out a system to pretty much come and go as he pleased. He would simply wait for a moment in the lobby reading a newspaper, and then, when no one was around, he would slip through the doorway to the tracks.

His ultimate deadly task was, however, made more difficult to accomplish without the information from Haupt. Wolfgang knew the target, the location and the method, but he didn't know the "when." Just how long do I have to place the bombs? When is Roosevelt's train supposed to arrive? Without those specifics he was forced to work more quickly than he would have, lest Roosevelt's train come in early. For the mission to succeed, all of the roughly two hundred bricks would be needed to be in place before the President's train pulls into the private platform. With each brick as powerful as ten sticks of dynamite, there would be enough blasting power in his two suitcases to more than do the job.

On his initial foray into the tunnel he had discovered a forgotten extension ladder stored behind a wall. It was most likely there for workmen to reach light bulbs in their sockets often as high as eighteen feet above the tracks. He decided to use it for advantage. Rather than placing his bombs at the feet of the pillars, which was much easier, but much more obvious to anyone doing track maintenance, he would put them atop the supports, hidden from anyone's view at the track level.

Wolfgang began working quickly, carefully concealing the quarter-kilo slabs of plastic explosive atop each and every pillar he was able to identify that carried the load of the giant hotel. Into each small brick of the plastic explosive he embedded a newly-designed, tiny concussion blasting cap, roughly the size of a .45 caliber bullet. The caps were created just for this job. Any significant explosion within ten meters proximity would trigger them. A sparked explosion set off by the saboteur hiding in his blind on the other side of the underground rail avenue would create a cascading chain reaction of the explosives at the top of the pillars holding up the hotel. Canaris had thought this one through completely. For redundancy, in case his first trigger failed for any reason, Wolfgang planned to attach detonator wires to three nearby additional bricks. One quick jolt to the electrical trigger and the entire Park Avenue end of the Waldorf would catastrophically subside about twenty feet down onto the tracks, causing the hotel to topple like undermining the wall of a medieval castle during a siege. The falling Waldorf would, of course, crush the President of the United States and his armored railcar under thousands of tons of rubble.

Berlin's information indicated that Roosevelt would pass through the city in a quick visit shortly before the start of the American Labor Day weekend, leaving a very short window of opportunity for the spectacular sabotage and assassination. Without the information from Eugen Haupt, Wolfgang realized he would be forced to stay in the tunnel and wait, keeping eyes-on the train platform for the train's arrival. *Yes,* he thought, *at worst I could just wait down here for a few days until the cripple arrives in his train, but if I didn't need to bivouac down here I could wait in my hotel room.* It would be nice to bathe and be fresh for the event. He had become used to the Waldorf's comforts, food, toilets and soft beds with sweet smelling linens. The more he thought about the whole situation the less friendly were his thoughts about his accomplice. *Where is that shithead Haupt?*

Annoyance or not, he had a mission. The found ladder easily reached the tops of the pillars and columns that held up the hotel, each a neat place to tuck in a small bar of soap-sized plastic explosive. Once in place and camouflaged by the darkness, they were hidden from view by anyone walking beneath them. As he placed more bombs on the pillars near the ones he had already armed, even he was unable to see them. It was tedious work but simple to execute. No wires were necessary except for the wires attached to the central bomb and the two back-ups. Any one of those would detonate all the others.

Working with speed and precision, Wolfgang managed to put a small brick of the explosive atop nearly every single support column under the hotel. With the addition of a couple of hidden ignition wires, he would be done. Even he, who knew exactly where he had put them, couldn't see a trace of anything from below. *Five more kilos to go today and then I will bathe and have a good dinner. I will finish this tomorrow. Maybe that oaf will finally get me the train timetable by then.*

4:35 p.m.

The Exchange Cigar Store on the Northeast corner of Beaver and New Streets was similar to many others around town. Two open doors, one on New and the other on Beaver, led into an urban general store that stocked everything from smokes and candy to novelty toys and paperback books. A row of dark olive-colored phone booths along one wall stood across the floor from a long, glass counter filled with cigar boxes displaying inexpensive Optimos, Dutch Masters and White Owls. On top of the counter were piled up cartons of Lucky Strikes, Pall Malls and Camels. There was a big selection of chewing gum and candy bars and packets of Sen Sen for bad- or liquor-infused breath. In the narrow space behind the counter stood two shopkeepers, the store's owners, brothers Alex and Sig, tobacconists by profession. Dressed in identical pale gray linen jackets, with white shirts and striped ties, they watched over their treasures. Behind them was a wall of cigarette packs and glass-enclosed humidors containing a selection of finer cigars to be sold to the Wall Street types who could afford them. They had moved their business from the vicinity of Ebbets Field in Brooklyn to what they hoped would be a more lucrative location near the stock exchange. Business was definitely better here. After two years in this location, they knew all the regulars by their brand of smoke. Neither Alex nor Sig recognized the large blond-haired man who walked in and made a beeline for a phone booth near the back corner of the store.

It was here, in a classic New York City cigar store, that Eugen Haupt chose to raise his head and re-establish contact with his handlers. He had been hiding in plain sight for the past day, on the subway, in the Automat and just walking on side streets. While he had no contact with anyone since the night when the cops found that basement apartment, Haupt was certain that he was being hunted. He knew for sure that both his mentors at the FBI and that goddamn Detective Grover were looking for him. For Haupt, it was an easy guess about what all of them were thinking at this moment. *They found that radio and they think I'm a spy. My friend, agent Witcover, probably got his ass reamed out by his supervisor and is mad as hell at me, too.* He surmised also that Grover now had some kind of proof that would allow them to arrest him, and there was little he could do or say to talk himself out of going to jail, this time not as a burglar, but as a spy. *I could fry for this!*

As he sat in the phone booth, his brain continued to search up a response to the dilemma. There wasn't an easy one. If he confessed to knowing about Wolfgang, he would have to give up his father. That wasn't acceptable. If he told the FBI about Wolfgang's presence he would need an airtight story about why he had any contact with the man at all. *That fucking radio! Why didn't he take it with him when he left the place? How the hell would he talk his way out of this mess?* It was at this moment that Eugen Haupt had a moment of clarity. He was already sick of it all. He was sick of being dumb muscle for his overbearing father. He was tired of running from the cops, and most of all he hated his life. Eugen Haupt wanted out and he ran with that feeling. The soon-to-be former thug reached into his pocket, pulled out a nickel and dropped it into the slot. From memory, he dialed the number. It rang three times before it was picked up.

"Hello, this is Special Agent Witcover."

Eugen paused before speaking, long enough for Witcover to speak again.

"Hello, this is Special Agent Witcover. Are you gonna talk to me or not?"

"Yes, it's me." Even though the door of the phone booth was shut and the small electric fan in the upper corner whirred loudly Haupt spoke in a quiet voice so as not to be overheard.

"Eugen?"

"Yes. I… I… I can explain everything." Haupt's mind raced as he spoke. Somewhere in the seconds it took to dial the phone he had decided to give up Wolfgang to the Feds. He'd explain that one of his Bund contacts had asked him to find a man an apartment and that was all he did. He only learned that the man was a spy after he was asked to clean the place up and then he found the radio. Now he was running from angry bund members who wanted to kill him because of that knowledge. He would tell the FBI that he knew where Wolfgang was and he would lead them to him.

"I'm listening." Witcover's voice sounded cold and cop-like. This was no longer a chatty exchange of sandwiches and notes on a sunny park bench, this was an interrogation.

"You found that case with the radio."

"Yes, we found it."

"I know what you're thinking. I want you to know that I will explain everything to you in person. I just want to be safe when I do it."

"What are you up to Eugen? I thought we had an understanding." Witcover's voice was strained. "I'm in some deep shit with my boss because I trusted you."

"We do have an understanding. I can explain the radio to you."

"Great. I wanna know about the radio, but what about the explosives?" Witcover sounded like a girlfriend scorned by a suitor's deceit.

"Explosives?" Haupt's voice took an incredulous tone and it cracked. "What explosives?" He knew nothing of any explosives and he was sure that the apartment was swept clean, no dirt, no nothing left there except for that radio.

"The FBI lab found traces of a high explosive in there. You wanna explain that to me?"

Explosives? Suddenly Eugen Haupt, son of a former mobster, a willing participant in many a small time burglary, and, of late, an eyewitness to a couple of brutal murders, came to the realization that the man he had ferried into Manhattan in the middle of the night was not just a spy and a talented killer, but was going to do something really awful with those two heavy suitcases of his. Haupt didn't know what the man was up to, but the Feds seemed to suspect something big and terrible. *This is very bad!* Yet, this new information about the explosives gave him an idea. Eugen had just found a wild card in this poker hand full of crap. *Perhaps,* he thought, *I can turn this all around.* He still had to meet with Wolfgang and pass over the envelope from his old man. He could set it up for later in the day. When he did that he would lead the FBI to Wolfgang and it would all be over. He would say that he had been planning to deliver the spy all along, and he could actually be a hero. Eugen decided to be discreet over the phone. "I'll tell you everything when I meet you in person. Believe me, I have some information for you that you will thank me for."

"Where are you?"

"I'm in a safe place. No one will see me here."

"Come up to the FBI office and ask for me."

"No, I have to stay off the street. I'm afraid that every New York City cop has a photo of me and they will shoot me on sight, or some bundist will do the same."

"That's crazy. No one is going to shoot you." Witcover shook his head as his snitch was becoming dramatic.

"Meet me at our normal spot. You come alone. I'll be watching to make sure that no one comes with you; you're not going to arrest me. I'll explain everything to you when I see you."

"When?"

"In an hour."

"Okay." Witcover grabbed his suit jacket from the back of his chair and began to put it on even before he hung up the phone, "See you there in one hour."

Haupt hung up the phone in the booth and let out a long breath full of relief. Then his mind started to race. *That goddamn Nazi Wolfgang... explosives in those suitcases! Shit!* Haupt wanted nothing more than to be done with it all, the Germans, the burglaries, the FBI and most of all, his father. He would lead the FBI to Wolfgang this very afternoon when he handed the man that envelope, and then it would all be over. *They might even thank him!* Eugen started to feel better. He liked the dual ideas of patriotism and heroism. He pulled the phone booth door open and felt relief. Though it was hot in the cigar store, it was worse in the phone booth.

He was just a short, three-block walk from his regular meeting spot with Witcover. It would take him less than five minutes to get there. He had time to kill, but he still had to stay off the street. Leisurely, he decided to inspect the paperback books along the wall. Alex, the taller of the two men behind the counter, eyed his customer with a touch of suspicion. Shoplifters were always a problem. Eugen continued to look at the books, then stepped over to the candy counter and considered a choice between a Hershey bar, a Snickers, and a Three Musketeers. *All was going to be okay*, he thought.

Trouble came in from the New Street entrance with a rush of motion. Haupt was reaching across for the Snickers bar when he looked up to see Sig, one of the two men behind the counter staring past him toward the door with a frightened look on his face. Eugen turned his head to the left and saw the ominous tableau of a curly haired man holding5 a .38 Smith and Wesson pistol aimed at Alex.

"The money... I want the money." The robber looked very nervous as Alex dutifully pushed his brother aside, opened the cash register and began gathering bills. "Faster, faster!"

Eugen Haupt was motionless staring at the nervous thief. His eyes surveyed the distance between them. There was something about this event that rubbed him the wrong way and could not be allowed to go on unchallenged. Strangely, he was feeling outrage. *Who is this fool robbing my store?* Perhaps because of his sudden relaxation after speaking with Special Agent Witcover, Eugen had developed an affinity for this little shop. Now, this jerk had invaded the place that Eugen had adopted to change his life and it didn't sit well. All at once Haupt made a mental plan to take care of this nervous robber with a quick movement and brute strength. He was certain that Agent Witcover would take this as a positive thing.

Alex, having cleaned out the store's cash register, nervously returned to the center of the counter and placed two fistfuls of fives and tens in front of the armed man. Once the money was in a big, loose pile in front of the robber, Alex pulled back toward the corner near the shop's storage space, pushing his brother Sig along with him. As the thief started to grab the bills shoving them in his pockets, Eugen decided to make his move. He was a man with acrobatic skills whose fluid dancelike motion would be no match for this nervous piece of street trash. Haupt tensed his arms and legs, waiting for the right moment, much like a cat about to pounce on an unsuspecting prey. As the thief continued to fill his pockets, he lowered thegun slightly toward the tile floor. In one smooth movement, Haupt lunged at him. Eugen's left hand lifted the man's gun hand toward the ceiling, and his right clenched into a giant fist, coiling for a strike directly into the center of the sweating robber's face. An extensive background in the art of forceful persuasion gave him the knowledge to know precisely how to make the most of a single impact. But the robber saw what was happening and in a moment of atavistic reflex, coiled his own arm with its fistful of bills in defense. As Haupt lifted the gunman's pistol arm to the ceiling, the man pushed back and brought his money-filled fist hard into the side of Haupt's face making a sickening crunching sound. The wild punch landed directly on Eugen's healing scar from the chair hit during his last burglary. It really hurt and was unexpected.

"You fucking idiot!," he yelled. The blow might have disabled a smaller foe, but it did nothing at all to Eugen Haupt except make him really angry. Once again, he coiled his right arm and in a quick reflex, crashed his giant fist into the robber's chest. The contact was accompanied by the sound of crunching bones as the wannabe thief's rib cage collapsed from the blow, no doubt pushing broken ribs into his lungs and elsewhere. The man gasped and fell backward, his head cracking loudly on the floor. On the way down his gun hand, in a spasm, constricted its index finger around the .38's trigger. There was a loud bang and while Haupt experienced the joy of breaking the thief's skull and more than likely killing him, he slowly realized that he too was injured. He stared down at his shirt and curiously watched as a growing red patch of blood gushed from just above his belt and down his pant leg. Eugen Haupt, the alleged Katzenjammer burglar, the terror of Yorkville, stood for a moment staring at his vanquished foe, and then collapsed on top of him, mortally wounded. His last worldly thought was that he would never make his meeting with Witcover. He would never be seen as a hero.

The two brothers counter stepped forward from behind the counter, stunned at the randomness of the carnage.

"Sig, call the cops!" Alex shouted. "I think these guys just killed each other."

5:00 p.m., Washington, D.C.

J. Edgar Hoover stood by his office window staring out at the late afternoon D.C. street scene. It looked hot out there, and humid as well. The fans in his office whirred and only managed to push the overheated damp air around the room with little effect on cooling anything. This summer is a week longer than it need be, he thought. Labor day was September 7th, and that was the day that the summer was supposed to end, a full week later than it could have ended if Labor Day had arrived on the first of the month. He wondered to himself if the weather actually paid attention to government holidays?

"Mr. Hoover, Mr. Donovan is on the telephone," his secretary poked her head into the office.

"Thank you." Hoover sat down at his desk chair and reached for the phone. "Hello Mr. Donovan." His voice contained an aloofness that defined him.

"Mr. Hoover," Donovan had learned not to call him Edgar or to exhibit any level of familiarity. "OSS has obtained information that will be of help to you."

"Oh?"

"Naval intelligence three days ago intercepted a transmission to Berlin originating somewhere in New York City. The duration of the transmission was unfortunately too short to triangulate, but we were finally able to decode it. Even in its decoded version it remains somewhat cryptic, but it clearly states that something is going to happen in New York City in the next week. They seem to have an operative, or operatives, in the city and he, or they, are informing them that a plan is well under way and his target will be destroyed as planned."

Hoover wasn't surprised. He had already been alerted to what was going on in New York City. His man Foreman personally briefed him on the search for Eugen Haupt, the arrest of the man's father and the possibility that Eugen Haupt possessed high explosives and was planning to do something awful with them. "Thank you for that information Mr. Donovan. The Bureau is already aware of something going on in New York and we have a prime suspect and a manhunt going on for him as we speak. The Bureau is on the case."

"Well, that's very good news." Despite the prevailing sense of bureaucratic jealousy, Donovan was glad to hear that the FBI already was in action. He waited for Hoover to divulge more information but then realized that the erstwhile turf war between the OSS and the FBI would prevent that. Still, Donovan tried, "Do you have an idea of what the target might be?"

Hoover had no idea, but would not even reveal that. "We have some thoughts on the matter, but we also expect to have the suspect in hand within the hour and we'll be able to close this case without incident."

"Excellent! I'll tell the President that you have it under control."

"This shouldn't concern the President, it's just a routine police matter." Hoover attempted to thwart any significant contact between Roosevelt and the man he now considered to be a rival.

"The President is planning to stop overnight in New York on his way to Hyde Park for the Labor Day weekend."

Hoover was silent for a moment as he considered this news. No one had alerted him about Roosevelt's travel plans. Some underling was in for a severe browbeating. His second thought was worry. *Did the Germans know about the President's travel plans? Most likely they didn't, they couldn't.* He bluffed his way with Donovan. "Mr. Donovan, thank you for this information. It corroborates information obtained by our special agents in Manhattan and I promise you that the President is totally safe to travel."

"Well, that's a relief. I'll let you know if we intercept anything else. In turn, would you please let me know when you finally catch this man?"

"You will be the first person I call." Hoover huffed. "Please give the President my regards and wish him a restful Labor Day holiday."

Donovan was certain he would never hear from Hoover about any of this again, but he was comforted to know that the FBI had its feelers out, looking out for the safety of the citizens on the home front. "Thank you Mr. Hoover."

"Good day Mr. Donovan." Hoover hung up the phone. He was clearly annoyed. *How does Donovan know about Roosevelt's personal schedule and I don't?* Special Agent in Charge Mike Foreman would need to know about the President's travel plans. Hoover decided that he would pass the information on later.

5:40 p.m., New York City

Agent Witcover arrived about ten minutes early for his meeting with Haupt so he took a seat on their favorite bench in Battery Park and opened up a newspaper. Ah, for once the sandwich exchange would not be an issue. As agreed, he arrived alone and hoped that he would be able to bring Haupt in by himself. Witcover's mind raced about what Haupt might tell him about the explosives. Haupt sounded sincerely relieved to speak with him on the phone.

Witcover waited, and then he waited some more. Glancing down at his wristwatch he saw that Haupt was now almost twenty minutes late. The agent rolled up his newspaper and stood up from the bench as if that would make Haupt arrive quicker. *A half hour and still no Haupt? What happened? He said he would meet me here.* He seemed so positive on the phone. He waited for nearly an hour. Witcover's concern for Haupt's safety gave way to anger. He gave up and began walking uptown toward the car he parked two blocks away.

Witcover's path took him up the East side of Broadway. As he crossed Beaver Street his eye caught what appeared to be an NYPD crime scene just a short block away. There were five police cars parked randomly in every direction around a cigar store on the next corner. The activity piqued his curiosity and he decided to get a closer look to see what was going on. As he approached the scene, he elbowed his way through a gathering crowd of gawkers and saw even more squad cars parked on New Street, as well as a panel van from the New York City Morgue.

At the curb directly outside the New Street entrance to the cigar store were two men having an animated conversation. One of them was writing notes on a yellow pad. Witcover's instincts identified them as detectives. He walked over and flashed his FBI badge and ID. "Hello gentlemen, I was just walking by. 'Curious, what happened here?"

"Hey, I'm Lou Spiotti, first precinct homicide. This is my partner, Tom O'Mara." Spiotti, the cop with the yellow pad examined Witcover's ID, was friendly and smiled. O'mara was mute except for a brief nod and a small grunt. "Nice to meet you, Agent Witcover, is it?" Spiotti asked affably.

"That's right, it's Witcover."

The three lawmen shook hands.

"Well, this was one of the craziest damn things I've ever seen." Spiotti seemed almost jolly.

"Really? What happened?"

"According to the guys behind the counter," Spiotti glanced down at his notes, "a Mr. Alex Schwartz and his brother Sig, some yoyo walks in with a .38 police special and says 'gimme all the money.' So, Mr. Schwartz knew just what to do, these two have been robbed at least once a month in the past year. He reaches into the register and gives the guy a big wad of bills and then steps back into the corner. Meanwhile, this customer is standing by the candy counter and for whatever reason decides to be a hero. He decks the guy, punches him really hard in the chest. The bad guy falls to the floor and cracks his head open in the process. He dies from the blow."

"So the customer did a good thing, hmm?"

"Yes and no. Yes, he stopped the guy, but maybe a little bit too hard, but the sonofabitch was shoving a gun around, so also, no. As the guy with the gun is falling to the floor, he squeezes the trigger and on the way down to smashing his skull open, he shoots the customer in the gut. The customer bleeds to death before anyone can do anything with him. What we have in there is two dead bodies on the floor and an awful lot of blood." The cop shook his head from side to side in continued disbelief.

"That's crazy," Witcover was fascinated by violent street crime even though his Bureau spy chasing work never took him there. "Can I take a look?"

"Yeah, just don't touch. They're still in a pile in the middle of the floor.

We're waiting for the crime scene photog to get here."

"Thanks." Witcover's interest came off as slightly ghoulish, but Spiotti didn't seem to mind.

"Sure, and I bet you'll never see one like this again." The cop made a sweeping motion with his right arm as if he was inviting a guest to a gala event.

Witcover entered the cigar store and looked around. Behind the counter were two men who looked totally ashen, blank-face-stunned by what had occurred in their shop. Everything else looked normal. Normal, except for the two dead bodies in a heap in the center of the white and black checkerboard ceramic tiled floor. The FBI man stared intently at the demised duo and the blood all around them. He correctly guessed that the robber was on the bottom of the pile. It was a pretty safe guess as the man was facing up toward the ceiling with his eyes wide open and his head ringed by a dark red pool of coagulated blood. The gun was still clenched in his right hand. The customer was lying on top of him with his face buried on his victim's stomach. Witcover studied the back of the would-be hero's head. He was a very large man with blond hair and big hands. Just above the top of the deceased Good Samaritan's head, Witcover noticed that the robber's chest cavity was pushed in, as if the man had no ribs. Jesus, this guy really packed a wallop! It was all so strange, such an odd scene. Yet, there was something oddly familiar about hero's corpse.

"Do you know who they are?" The FBI man asked.

"Nah, I tried to go through their pockets, but I didn't wanna disturb the bodies until the crime scene photog gets here. Trust me, in my work you don't want to disturb the scene until everyone gets to do what he has to do. It pisses people off, ya know?" Spiotti was very genial toward the brother lawman. He spoke freely and Witcover appreciated his tone. Unlike his experience with Detective Grover, this NYPD man was okay.

No sooner than seconds after Spiotti's mention of him, a thin man with a cigarette dangling out of his mouth appeared at the door. He was carrying a large 4x5 Speed Graphic camera with a nine-inch diameter flash attachment, a hand case full of loaded film backs and a pocketful of flashbulbs. Wire rim glasses and a porkpie hat rounded out a cultivated style as he pushed his way into the cigar store. In his cheap wrinkled black suit and loose necktie, he was an archetype for aspiring crime-scene photographers everywhere, yet he was also a New York City cop. Without speaking a word to anyone the photog nonchalantly went to work shooting the scene from ten different angles. One shot after another the fiery magnesium flashbulbs lit the room and brightly highlighted the grim nature of the two weird deaths. Each flash left a bizarre after image in the eyes of anyone who might have been looking.

Then, in another flash, the photo session was over. It all took no more than ten minutes, and most of those were spent removing and replacing film backs and gingerly taking out and replacing very hot flash bulbs. The man finished his work and announced. "I'm done. You can move the bodies." He walked out of the store at the same speed that he came in, and that was that.

Detective Spiotti nodded to Witcover and whispered, "I'm so glad we got his permission, without him we have no murder." Spiotti and his partner O'Mara knelt to the floor and together got their hands underneath the customer's body. Spiotti first removed the gun from the dead man's clenched hand. No need for another bizarre accidental death. That done, he considered the task at hand. It would be hard to turn the top guy over onto his back because he looked like he must weigh more than 225 pounds, all of it now totally dead weight. Spiotti was the boss, "Tom, you yank on his arm and I'll push him."

"Can I give you a hand?" Witcover asked.

"Hey, sure, that would be a big help." Spiotti was totally non-territorial, and so much friendlier than Grover. "Okay, on my count of three we turn him over onto the floor there. Got it?"

"Hmm," O'Mara was monosyllabic.

"One, two, and three!" The man's dead body was now lying beside the corpse of his victim facing the tin plate ceiling. "Okay, now we can go through his pockets and get his name." The two detectives stood up and Spiotti looked over at Witcover. Witcover had turned completely pale. Spiotti was genuinely concerned. "Hey, are you okay? It's a only a dead body... yer not gonna heave, are ya?"

Witcover was momentarily speechless as he stared at the dead man's face. "No need to look for his wallet," he mumbled. "I know this man."

5:50 p.m.

Wolfgang had become a master of his new domain. The warren of tunnels and the darkened railroad beds under the Waldorf Astoria Hotel had become as familiar as anything he had ever known in his life. Even in the darkness he had learned where to plant his feet to avoid electrocution from contact with a third rail and at the same time he had become aware of good places to hide from the track maintenance men who from time-to-time walked by inspecting the rails. To abet this stealthy subterranean expertise, he had also managed to make his way down to this underworld from his posh hotel room on a daily basis without being seen by anyone. Wolfgang made himself totally transparent, a shadow falling on darkened corners.

As he worked on planting the last of his bricks of plastic, he kept doing the math in his head… the multiplication for chaos, two hundred cakes multiplied by ten, the equivalent of two thousand sticks of dynamite. *More than enough to do the job!*

And then for the final touch, he remembered his plan to make sure that if the first bomb was a fizzle there would be three additional charges wired to his detonator wires. He dressed the wires through existing ductwork so that no one could see them. One quick jolt from the cigarette pack sized electrical trigger that he kept in his pocket and 20th century history would be made in this very spot. With the push of a button switch attached to a small battery and capacitor, the entire Park Avenue end of the Waldorf would collapse in an enormous pile of rubble, destroying everything beneath it, and, of course, crushing the main target, the President of the United States, Franklin Delano Roosevelt.

As he neared the end of his work, Wolfgang also began to realize that Haupt was not coming with any more information. To Wolfgang's disgust, he understood that he would have to remain in the tunnel to make sure that he didn't miss Roosevelt's arrival. His moment of luxury was over. He would have to camp out below ground for the coming days until zero hour. He found the situation to be unfortunate, but history was about to be made. He had no other choice.

6:00 p.m.

"Yeah, honey, I totally understand. Yes, I know you're upset with me. I'm sorry, but this is the job." Grover's feet were up resting on his desk's extended return, his heels wedged in between the Underwood and the wood under it. A telephone handset was loddged between his right ear and shoulder. His tie was loose, his shirt was no longer crisp, and he was slouched in his hard-backed chair in a futile attempt at resting. The past day had worn him out. From the moment that he and Murphy followed Haupt to the basement apartment, he hadn't stopped moving. The manhunt meant no sleep, and no rest at all until the threat posed by a potential saboteur armed with high explosives was ended. At the other end of the line was Ellen Kramer expressing her disapproval of the way he had been avoiding her. Murphy could only hear Grover's side of the conversation, but he could guess exactly what was being said on the other.

"…Yeah, but… but… honey, lookit… I am off for two days around Labor Day. Um humm… I have Sunday and Monday." Grover frowned and rubbed his eyebrows. "Yeah. We can do that. Sure thing, up to the mountains? Good."

Murphy stared across the desk at his partner, made a face then smiled. Grover's only real master. *Ah, young love,* he thought.

"Okay, but I might be a little late to meet you today. Yeah, uh huh… ha ha… right… just like normal." For Murphy's amusement Grover shook his head from side to side in a visual affirmation of his current brow-beating. "Um hmm. Look, I gotta go. Yeah, of course, I love you, too." He hung up and Murphy gave him a knowing look.

With the social part of his life stowed away for a while, Grover steered his brain back to the matter at hand. If they didn't figure this one out correctly, no one would be going anywhere anytime soon.

Murphy was silent and waited a moment for Grover to recover from the whiplash phone beating he'd just taken from Ellen. Then he spoke. "Ya know, those FBI guys got nothing out of the old man."

"Hmmm, what do you expect? Karl would never snitch on anyone, let alone his own son. I mean, after the life he led? C'mon. Ya know, this guy has an idiot son who now looks like he's become the mastermind of everything bad. A burglar, a thief, a Nazi spy. And, he tried to kill me once. But, the poor old guy is proud of his boy. He raised him in his own image and he's never going to tell anyone shit about the golden child."

Murphy had heard this tirade before, he simply responded with an agreeable "Yeah."

"Yeah, y'know, when we walked in there and I kinda felt sorry for the old, sick sad sack, but by the time we left he was back to his old self." Grover noted that the old man actually seemed to get stronger and more bellicose because the cops were paying attention to him again. Karl had been enjoying his time in the spotlight, and was milking it for all it was worth.

Murphy had struck a pose very similar to Grover's, only his feet were planted firmly on the floor with his knees wide apart. He was slumped deeply in his tilted wooden chair, an attempt at finding a comfortable position for his head and a way in which to nod out for even five minutes. Against the odds though, he did begin to drift off just as the phone on Grover's desk started ringing.

Grover wearily leaned forward and picked up the handset. "This is Grover." Murphy's eyes glanced over and locked onto his partner's face. Suddenly he was roused out of his ennui. "Yeah? Yeah? Jesus! Holy crap! You're joking. Holy crap! Yeah, we're on our way over. Yeah. See you in ten minutes. Thanks. HOLY CRAP!" Grover hung up the phone and silently stared at the blank green squad room wall.

By now Murphy was wide-awake with his knees drawn directly in front of him. "So? Do I have to ask you what that was all about? Who was that?"

Grover, visibly stunned, slowly turned toward his partner and for a moment remained speechless. He wanted to talk, but his mouth was frozen in disbelief from what he had just heard. "That was Witcover. They want us to come over to the FBI office."

"That's what all the holy crap stuff was about?"

"No. Not all. Haupt... Haupt is dead."

"What the f....?"

"He was shot to death in a robbery."

"Robbery? I thought he was a saboteur now?"

"No, he wasn't the robber, he was shot trying to stop a robbery."

"Haupt? Trying to stop a robbery? Jesus! Where... what?"

Grover just shrugged. His brain was slowly digesting what he just heard on the phone. "Witcover says that Haupt was coming in from the cold and he never made it."

"Holy shit!"

"Witcover accidentally came on the scene and found him. It was good that he did that because he says he found something in Eugen's pockets that we need take a look at, right away."

"And he wants us to come and look at something?"

"That's the real 'holy crap,' that the FBI would like our help."

"This is too much for me at one time. I didn't hear you straight." Murphy cracked. "Haupt was shot to death trying to stop a robbery AND Witcover wants our help?" Murphy was already standing and reaching for his suit jacket. "Okay, so let's go. Who knows what other wonders may greet us!" The two cops raced out the door and trotted uptown on Third Avenue.

6:56 p.m.

Special Agent Witcover was sweating heavily. His normally crisp white shirt was nearly transparent from the moisture, and he wasn't the only heavy sweater in the room. The air in the Bureau office was hot and very sticky. Even with the whirring of the ubiquitous fans and wide-open windows it was just borderline tolerable. For once, despite the office dress protocol the FBI man had removed his jacket and draped it over the back of his wooden swivel chair. Witcover was hovering in that near-stupor zone when Grover and Murphy appeared alongside his desk.

"Hey, 'can't believe it!" Grover could barely muster an appropriate response to what had happened.

"So, our alleged saboteur is dead? So much for the threat, huh?" Murphy asked somewhat callously. "What happened?"

Witcover squinted his left eye and drew in his cheek in a look of uncertainty, then turned his head to stare at a paper on his desk. "I was supposed to meet him at our normal drop spot."

"The place where you gave him his payments?" Grover's words came out unfiltered with a slight hint of a sneer. Witcover didn't react and simply kept staring at the paper in front of him on the desk. Immediately after saying it, Grover regretted what he said. "Sorry."

"He called me on the phone and said that he could explain everything, and that he was not a spy or a saboteur." Witcover sighed, "He also said that he knew nothing about any explosives, but he really wanted to meet up with me. He said he had information that I would thank him for."

"What was the information?" Grover asked.

"He wouldn't tell me on the phone, he wanted to tell me in person."

"And?"

"So I went down there right away and I waited for him on the bench where I used to meet him. After a long while when he didn't show up, I thought that he was lying to me, playing for time so that he could do whatever with his explosives." Witcover stood up and started pacing behind his desk, looking at the floor as he told the cops what had happened and how he came upon the Haupt's corpse. "The son of a bitch died a hero, but we'll never know what he was up to."

"And that's it? You have no idea what he was going to tell you?"

"Not a clue. Just that he would clear everything up when we spoke in person and that I would be grateful to him. Nothing else."

"You said on the phone you had something we should see?" Murphy asked.

"Yeah. I went through his pockets. He had a drivers license, a few bucks, a draft card… would you believe that he was 4F! And, he had this paper in a sealed envelope." Witcover lifted up the lined sheet that he had found in Haupt's pants pocket. The blue line ruled single sheet had been neatly cut out of a marble cover black compositions notebook, probably with a razor blade.

"Can I have a look at that?" Grover asked.

"Sure." Witcover handed the paper over to the cop.

4-9-14-07- 721-762

Grover took the paper and stared at it intently. The otherwise empty sheet contained a single line of handwritten characters. It was some kind of a code. Under normal circumstances there would have been some innocent explanation for its being, but at this moment it became an inscrutable clue to something that might or might not be in the works, something that might or might not involve explosives and, at this moment, something that no longer involved Eugen Haupt. The trio of lawmen in the room stared at the scrawled characters on the notebook page, each of them waiting for the other to say what it all meant. No answer was immediately forthcoming.

The string of numbers and odd characters was written in the hand of someone who had been schooled in penmanship somewhere other than at a New York City public school. The cops knew that while it looked like nothing, it probably meant everything.

"I took it off his body." Unused to the outcome of street violence, Witcover's hands were trembling.

"There's no exchange name so I can tell you that it isn't a phone number, that's for sure," Grover opined.

"I've been looking at it for an hour." Witcover agreed. 'Means something, but it doesn't mean anything. It's a puzzle."

The word puzzle caught Murphy's ear. He repeated aloud his word-game solver's mantra, "If it's a really good puzzle you don't need to know all the answers to the clues to solve it. One right answer to part of it will lead you to the rest."

Witcover turned his head toward Murphy. "Hmm?"

Grover rolled his eyes toward the ceiling. He heard Murphy say it so many times before he jumped in before Murphy could speak. "A puzzle is something where parts of it reveal the rest. In a crossword puzzle if you get five across then you know the first letter of five down. One part of the clue helps you derive the rest."

"I do a lot of puzzles, not just crosswords. Lemme look at it again." Murphy reached across the table to examine the scrap. "This could be really simple. If this was in Haupt's pocket when he called you, I'll bet my pension that it was part of what he was going to tell you."

"And?"

"I don't know yet." Murphy plopped himself into the chair across from Witcover's desk. "But, if it's a puzzle it has a solution."

"We'd better do it fast," Grover chimed in, "I feel like a big wave of horse crap is gonna fill our stable really soon."

7:30 p.m., Berlin

It was the end of the day and Admiral Karl Doenitz was in a social mood. His stealth tactic of Rudel or Wolfpack submarine warfare in the past few hours had drawn blood on allied shipping, and he was feeling the afterglow of that lethal blow. An unlucky Canadian convoy somewhere in the North Atlantic off Greenland lost six ships and hundreds of men. The U-boats escaped, unscathed by the escort destroyers' depth-charges. He decided to share his good mood in a visit with Canaris.

Arriving at Canaris' office, and before Horst Wenzl could even speak, Doenitz strolled past the adjutant's desk and gingerly opened his peer's office door without a knock. He found the Abwehr head at his desk writing with a large fountain pen into a leather-bound notebook.

"Admiral I have come to share a toast. Do you still have some of that cognac?"

Canaris, a bit startled, looked up from his notes and hid his annoyance with a false smile. "Why, yes Karl, I save it for special occasions. Is this one?" He put down his pen and placed the notebook in his top drawer.

"Overnight we sunk a large part of a convoy off the coast of Greenland. The Rudel captains are cunning and hunt from different directions. That confuses the escorts and allows the pack to sink much tonnage. Goods are not getting to the enemy. I would say that from my point of view today, the war is going well."

"Good to hear!" Canaris poured two snifters of cognac and handed one to Doenitz while raising his own for a toast. "To the Rudel!" The feint allowed him some time to think about just how much he would reveal to this man who was heavily in Hitler's pocket. They were on the same side, but Doenitz was ambitious. Canaris was cautious but his instinct told him that it might be profitable to open up slightly. "Karl, the effort we spoke of earlier, if you remember, Operation Pastorius?

"Yes, Pastorius," Doenitz sipped.

"It is moving ahead nicely. We should know of its results within a day or two."

"Ah, that is also good to hear. Perhaps we'll be able to jointly give the Führer some good news?"

"Perhaps we will." Canaris approached Doenitz from behind his desk and the two Admirals clicked their drinks, "To success!"

"Yes, of course, to success!" Doenitz lowered himself into a big leather chair. After a moment's pause he pressed. "You know, you never told me the nature of this mission. What is it actually?"

Canaris felt cornered. He didn't enjoy the feeling. His immediate reaction to a subordinate putting him in a similar position would have come close to a beheading. A fellow naval officer of equal rank had asked a simple question and required an answer. Canaris chose his words carefully. "If you remember when Operation Pastorius deposited those unfortunate men on the American shores, I told you that they were part of a bigger plan. The plan is scheduled to come to a head tomorrow in New York. We have a highly experienced operative positioned in a place that, once his efforts are complete, will change the course of the war."

Doenitz was now extremely curious. Canaris was being coy and that didn't sit well with the master of the U-boat fleet. He wanted to know everything, but respect for his fellow officer stopped him from demanding a direct answer. Doenitz simply beat around the bush. "I suppose you will tell me what is going to happen before it does?"

"I would like to, but I think that you will be better pleased by it all when I can confirm that the deed is done. The surprise will be an early birthday present for you." Canaris smiled. "I believe that you'll be fifty-one in about two weeks, no?" Canaris prided himself in his mastery of the details. It was enough to put his comrade at ease.

Doenitz was both surprised and flattered at the same time, "Wilhelm, I am honored that you remember my birthday. If this is the case, I will await the news as a surprise."

"Good. I will tell you one thing to whet your anticipation, but you must not share this with anyone at all, not even the Führer. Can you promise me that?"

"Of course," Doenitz seemed a bit hurt by the question.

"Fine. Then I will tell you. If all goes well according to plan in New York, Roosevelt will be dead by Friday."

Doenitz was stunned and simply stared at Canaris. Nothing more was said as the men continued to sip their drinks. Nothing more needed to be said.

September 2, 1942

3:39 p.m., New York City

Wolfgang was beginning to feel like a rat. He was hot and he was dirty. By now his eyes had completely adjusted to the perpetual dimness as he scurried around hiding between the subterranean tracks. While his eyes adjusted to the surroundings, his body didn't. The end of summer heat made the tunnels nearly unbearable. *This is an oven, and I am a roasting chicken.*

Roger Wilson had officially checked out of his room at the Waldorf Astoria at ten in the morning. The saboteur had debated the idea of remaining in the room and continuing his daily venture down to the tracks during the day to be in place when Roosevelt might arrive, but it was too risky an option. If Roosevelt decided to arrive at night the entire venture would be a loss. He could not miss the opportunity so he checked out, not wanting to leave a trace of himself in the room in case someone came looking for him.

There was a touch of lament in his voice as he said a friendly goodbye to the desk clerk. *Ah, poor good fellow, such a shame that he will probably be dead by the end of the week…yet, if he has a day off perhaps he will live!* After paying his bill in cash Wolfgang lugged his mostly empty suitcases toward the Lexington Avenue hotel entrance. Down a short flight of stairs from the main lobby to street level he paused for a moment pretending to be studying a piece of paper. Once he was sure that he was alone and certain that no one was watching, he ducked into the service door behind the stairs and disappeared down to the tracks, suitcases and all. The tunnel, a sooty, hot and miserable place, would be his hotel until the mission was done. The vast warren of man-made burrows and alcoves was a perfect hiding place, a hiding place he was soon to turn into a killing field.

By now the saboteur no longer needed light. His eyes had become so sensitive to the darkness that at times he became momentarily blinded as the tunnel shadows filled with electric daylight caused by passing trains arcing on the lethal third rail. The arc light became a regular reminder of the existence of that lethal electrical pipe and he was ever wary of it.

Before he had even placed one of his bombs Wolfgang had taken a walking survey of his underground world. He was looking for places to hide and for a safe hunter's blind, a spot from where he could observe his target unobstructed from far enough away that the falling tunnel wouldn't collapse on him as well. There had been talk back in Berlin that Roosevelt's armored train car might be able to survive a blast and even the crushing effects of a falling sixty-story building. His superiors had concluded that it was best to do the deed while the target's car was exposed on the platform and in plain sight. He also needed to make sure that the arriving train was really the presidential railroad car and not some other train that had decided to park at the Waldorf's platform. He would have already had all these details if Eugen Haupt had done what he was supposed to do, but so be it. Resigning himself to the reality of the moment, Wolgang found a spot on the far side of the underground abyss, across the tracks from the hotel. *I'll know it when I see it.* Roosevelt's armored car won't look like any other railcar. From that spot he had a clear view of the designated destruction zone. He ran his wires to that spot and now all he had to do was wait.

But where would he sleep until the moment arrived? That question was answered early on in his exploration of the tunnels. He discovered an alcove that would perfectly suit his lodging needs, a tiny space totally hidden and already set up with a small folding cot. *So, this is where the track workers bring their dates, he smirked to himself.* While he couldn't see the presidential platform from within the alcove, he was only separated from his observation position by the width of two tracks, and he was sure it wouldn't be a problem to move into that spot once he saw the train pull in. Wolfgang shoved his suitcases in behind the cot. He had secreted some food and water into the emptied explosive carriers and was now settled in for the wait. He knew that Roosevelt was planning to be here before the weekend, but without the train schedule it could be in one day or in many days. It was irritating to think about the lack of information, and now he began to worry that something had happened to Eugen Haupt. He wasn't worried about Haupt's well-being, but that his lifeline guide had been caught and was spilling the information about everything to the authorities. *Maybe he was arrested for his idiotic burglaries, or perhaps he was just a coward?* The good thing was that the details of his mission were compartmentalized, so that Haupt, even if he was talking to the authorities, knew none of the details of Wolfgang's mission beyond the Grand Central map he'd drawn some weeks earlier. The saboteur knew that he was now on his own and would have to continue with his plan without the train schedule.

4:30 p.m.

"I made a photostat of the paper and sent the original to the FBI lab in Washington. Maybe they can make sense of the writing." special agent in charge Mike Foreman brought the meeting to order.

The late afternoon sun was streaming in through the big windows raising the room temperature to something just shy of unbearable. As sweat soaked every fold of every shirt, the cops had loosened their neckties and removed their jackets while the FBI men, other than the dazed Special Agent Witcover, stayed buttoned up and knotted. Yet, no one seemed to be paying any attention to the heat. By now they were all there standing around a conference table staring at the copy of the paper clue discovered in the late Eugen Haupt's pants pocket.

Detective Tim Murphy paced the floor in the FBI conference room. "I'm gonna make a guess about what's going on. Whatever it was that Haupt was going to tell Special Agent Witcover, it died with him, and that includes whatever Haupt may or may not have known about these numbers. I mean, what if there are no explosives, or he had a change of heart and dumped them in the river?"

"I would make you a bet that there are indeed explosives and they're a part of some big thing that Haupt was supposed to make happen in the city." Mike Foreman had always borne a sense of dread that something awful was in the works, "And, by the way, they're not all numbers. There are other characters as well. The more we talk about what we don't know, the more certain I am that there's a plot with some really bad stuff attached to it if they're able to pull it off."

"Who is *they*?" Murphy asked.

"The Germans. That's *they*. The Germans want to blow something up here in New York, and Eugen Haupt was either a bit or a big player in all of it."

"I say bit, not big." Grover sighed, "I know that you've heard this from me a lot, but Haupt was a lowlife and nothing else. You guys gotta know that he was playing you for immunity if he got busted for anything. He gave you guys the names of bundists that were on lists that he also stole and you gave him free time to do his burglaries, and…" he paused and took a deep breath, "…to throw me off a fire escape and get away with it."

Foreman stared at Grover and his face showed contrition, "I am very sorry about that, and you're probably totally right about him."

"Sir," Chase chimed in, "I agree with Detective Grover. We turned him, yeah, and okay, he gave us lots of names, but I really don't think he'd be capable of doing anything that involved deep thinking. I can't see him even knowing what a coded message was."

"That's another stumper. What does that message mean, and who wrote it? Is it part of this investigation or what? Is it a code or is it someone's suit size?"

The conversation brought Witcover out of his mournful stupor. "Here's another small piece to the puzzle. The lab team went through that apartment and couldn't find a single odd fingerprint anywhere other than a few of Haupt's on the front doorknob, the ice box door and near that window. That includes the wine bottle that was in the trash."

"So that means that Haupt was there alone, right?" Murphy asked.

"Yes and no. There were no other prints in the apartment, but there were other prints on the case and controls of that spy radio, and none of them were Haupt's."

Foreman looked beaten. "So then, what the hell is going on? We have Haupt's father in custody, who says he doesn't know anything about what his son is up to, but he obviously knows something. We know that was Haupt's apartment. We've got strong physical evidence that there were explosives in there. We got a spy radio, too, with someone else's prints on it. We have a sealed envelope with a piece of paper with numbers on it. Most likely this all means that either he was a spy or at least working with one. Haupt is dead, but it's possible that someone else has those explosives and wants to blow something up. Maybe Eugen wasn't intellectually up for the job of spy, but that means there's a smarter someone else out there going ahead with plans. Or, if we're not giving the dead man his due, and Eugen was smarter than us, he might have been that guy working alone and decided not to do it. Maybe the threat is over and we just have to find what he did with the explosives, or…."

Grover finished Foreman's sentence, "There's another bad guy out there with explosives."

"Yeah," Murphy waded in, "Eugen was never gonna be a panelist on 'Information Please.' He definitely was not the brains of anyone's spy business. The sealed envelope was in his pocket, and we don't know who gave it to him. He was going to pass it on to somebody. The real bomber."

"Ya know, the fact that the envelope was sealed means that either Haupt wrote it, or he actually never touched it," Grover surmised. "He was going to pass it on to someone…"

"We need to figure out the code on that paper. If Haupt was supposed to pass it along it never got there. That would mean that the guy with the explosives is still out there waiting to hear exactly what his target is." Everyone nodded at Foreman's analysis.

"Of course… that's it!" Witcover's eyes went wide… "He was going to tell me about it all to clear his name… he wanted to be a hero, he just didn't make it to that point."

"You're right sir, those numbers are in code for whatever the target is. The bomber doesn't have the details of what he's supposed to blow up?" Maybe we should interrogate Karl Haupt," Chase added.

"By the way he was yakking when we locked him up, he's not going to tell us beans. I suppose we can try but really, I don't think the old man knew what his boy was up to." Grover had no idea just how wrong he was about that.

"In any case, the crypto boys in Washington have a photostat of the numbers. They're working on it." Foreman was talking to no one in particular, and probably only to himself. "What in this city would attract a bomber? What would be the perfect target?"

"What wouldn't attract a bomber?" Witcover said in a small voice with an air of hopelessness, "there are a lot of perfect targets. This is a huge city. Any bomb going off is gonna kill a lot of people."

"The one thing in our favor may be that it's Labor Day weekend," Murphy offered, "war or no war I think it's always pretty quiet around Labor Day."

"I don't think the bomber is someone who's going out of town for the Labor Day weekend." Foreman's brow furrowed slightly. "Let's discuss every odd thing that's come up regarding Labor Day. I'll start. This is probably nothing, but about a week ago I got a call from a Coast Guardsman in Rhode Island who was suspicious about an encounter by one of their cutters off Montauk Point. They had stopped a big sailing yacht in restricted waters. The boat's captain told the cutter's captain that they were on their way to a sailboat race that was set to start in Connecticut off Stamford over Labor Day weekend."

"So? What does this have to do with Haupt?" Grover asked.

"Nothing, just that there is no sailboat race over the weekend. It was cancelled four months ago because of the restrictions on coastal waters. It's an odd story. I'm just making the point that we should be thinking about odd stuff. I want to hear about any odd stuff anyone heard from snitches or whatever." Foreman's query opened the door and for the next hour each man in the room brought up every odd snitch tale, citizen's report or newspaper story he had recently heard or read. Also, every item that was mailed or phoned in and every gut feeling about what might be the whereabouts of an unknown quantity of suspected explosives, possibly secreted somewhere by a dead man who left nothing behind except questions and a string of handwritten characters on a notebook page. It was not a lot to go on, but the overwhelming instinct among each and every one of the lawmen in that room was that something bad was in the works, and whatever they had to go through to solve it was the thing they had to try.

"So, after all that, what do we have?" Grover's remark punctuated the end of the round-table guessing session.

"We have a whole bunch of odd things around Labor Day weekend that don't have tidy answers," Foreman sighed. "So, let's focus on the one thing we do have. We need to try and decipher that paper."

Grover continued to gaze at the coded paper, "Y'know, let's put this code aside for a minute. 'Remember those guys you caught in June, that opera-tion Pastor something?"

"Pastorius. It was operation Pastorius," Witcover said.

"Right," added Special Agent Chase, "Pastorius... those guys confessed that they were sent here to blow up stuff, destroy war materials before they got to the ports."

Grover scanned the faces around the table and everyone blankly stared back. "Suppose that you only think you caught them all? What if all along Haupt was a part of it from the very start, and somehow you guys didn't find all the explosives that they came here with. Let's say Haupt had stashed all that stuff in that basement apartment and was going to carry on the work and blow up war supplies somewhere? That would also explain how that radio got in there, and didn't he lease the place in the same name as that big Nazi spy guy, Canary?"

"Canaris," Foreman corrected him. "We already know that Canaris has spies working in factories, we just haven't rooted them all out yet."

Murphy stood up and started pacing alongside the big table. "And our boy who knows who the Nazis are, he's been giving you bund guys' names for the last year right?"

Foreman nodded. "Yes?"

"Then Haupt was really a spy all the time!" Murphy weighed the impli-cations, "the burglary stuff was just a cover. We just thought he was a low-life thief but in working with you guys as a trusted snitch he was able to hide what he was really doing."

Grover theorized, "our Eugen was probably on his way to pass along the explosives and maybe the radio to the saboteurs in the factories and maybe he had a change of heart. He was gonna tell Witcover about all of it and clear his name and he'd be your hero again. It just got screwed up when he decided to be a hero in that cigar store."

"That still leaves the code," Foreman questioned. "What was he going to do with the numbers? He must have an accomplice."

"I don't know about that, Haupt was a loner." Grover made a confession. "Ya gotta know that even though we were told to leave him alone, me and Murphy never took the tail off the guy for very long. Fact is, we never saw him with anybody. He had no friends except for his father, no one else, no girlfriends and no boyfriends either."

"Kind of sad, this guy's life, but if we're right about this, there are a lot of other lives at stake. Let's see if we can find what the numbers mean."

Grover lifted the paper off the table and stared at it. " 'Reminds me of way my uncles used to write numbers. A lot of curly lines and stuff, 'stands to reason that it must have been written by someone who learned to write their letters and numbers somewhere in Europe, and with the current state of this case, I would bet they were written by a German."

"Which German?" Murphy looked at his partner. "We know what the numbers are, what are those other things, signs of the Zodiac?"

"Dunno. Does anyone here read European?" Grover joked.

"This is the FBI and we read every continent." As if on cue Special Agent James O'Rourke entered the room.

"Okay, what's that thing next to those last two numbers?" Grover handed him the photostat.

4-9-14-07-721-762

"Hmm? Let me see." O'Rourke cavalierly took the photocopy and stared at it for a moment. "My father is Irish, my mother is Austrian and if my memory serves me, I'd say that's the way momma writes her T's. That thing is the letter "T." The whole line reads 4-9-14-07-T21-T62."

"The letter T," Grover repeated for no one other than himself.

"Maybe it's a combination to a safe?" Murphy's puzzle instinct immediately kicked in.

O'Rourke conjectured, "The bigger question is why was Eugen Haupt carrying that paper in his pocket in a sealed envelope?"

September 3, 1942

3:24 a.m.

The radium dial on Wolfgang's watch glowed reassuringly in the pitch-black darkness. It was 3:24 a.m. In another two seconds that reassurance would disappear as Wolfgang abruptly woke up from the middle of a deep-sleep dream that was set in his boyhood village. While everything in the dream was familiar to him it just felt wrong. There he stood in the center of the town with an oversized hunting rifle cradled in his small arms. He had assumed this pose many times as a child standing alongside his father, yet this time he was alone. The village around him was the same, yet different as well. The dirt road main street was pockmarked with deep holes that had no visible bottoms, and huge piles of rubble and garbage surrounded them. He somehow knew that there were people in the houses having dinner yet he was hungry and totally alone. There were no people in the street, but he sensed a threat and it frightened him. As the saboteur slowly stirred from this reverie he was confused, I am waking up…what is making me wake up?

In a daze he thought, it might be that awful, filthy, reeking odor that now filled his nostrils, a concentrated smell of sewage and rotting waste. Whatever was causing the stench, it became an unwanted noxious alarm clock. He reflexively began to move his right arm in an attempt to push the stench away. It was then that his hand brushed against something soft, perhaps a child's teddy bear? What is this? Abruptly he snapped fully awake and his senses jolted to full alert. The teddy bear was moving. What is this? Rationally he knew that he was totally alone in his safe hideout spot, no other person was nearby, yet a primeval survival mechanism told him that he really wasn't alone at all. It took just another fraction of a second for the horror of what was causing that smell to overwhelm him in a visceral panic. The panic, then, was one-upped by a stabbing pain on his earlobe. All his training for how to remain silent in moments of stress fell away and he let out a primitive scream. His mind raced as well, "something is eating me alive!"

Wolfgang stood up and whatever was chewing on his ear fell to the floor with a thud. Then there were other thuds in the dark followed by sounds of scampering feet. "Rats! Agggggghhhh!" In the panic of his horrified reaction he stomped around in the pitch blackness, finally making contact with the soft flesh of one very large rat. Cursing wildly while his feet moved at a frenzied rate, he continued to kick and stomp the body long after it was clearly dead and the other furry denizens of the dark escaped his panicked rage into their holes in the railroad passageway. Another swift kick pushed the rat's body toward the dimly lit alcove doorway. Even the fearless saboteur was shocked by what he saw. The smashed lifeless corpse of his nocturnal aggressor, even in death, looked threatening. Wolfgang was now totally awake and studied the body. "Shit. It's as big as a cat!"

He was bleeding profusely from his chewed earlobe and he had to deal with that damage. First, he kicked the reeking bloody animal's body out the doorway across to the next track. In the mayhem Wolfgang's blood had mixed with the rat's and there was a wet shine spatter everywhere in the dim light.

He reached up to examine the damage to his bleeding ear. The contact from his hand sent a sharp pain through the side of his head. To his horror he discovered that his right earlobe wasn't just bleeding, it had been torn by the rat's teeth as the animal held on before being knocked to the ground. He needed to stop the bleeding and clean the wound. Stitches probably would have been in order, but there was no one around to sew them. He would have to make do with what he had. An infection could ruin his mission, or his escape afterward.

In the darkness he rummaged through his suitcases and found the small flask of brandy he had been carrying since he left France. Tearing the sleeves off one his freshly laundered shirts he made some washcloths and with some drinking water from a jug he had placed there days earlier he cleansed the wound and with the alcohol in the brandy he sanitized it. Then he made a bandage and soaked it with brandy. He tied it around his head, and while he looked like a soldier with a severe head injury he was somewhat comfortable with his field medical self-treatment.

Fully awake, and with his head wrapped, Wolfgang sat in in the darkness in fear of the tunnels. He would no longer be able to sleep comfortably down here. He cursed Eugen Haupt aloud. "If that lummox had given me the damn track information I could still be sleeping in a nice hotel room!" That option was now history.

In thinking about Haupt, Wolfgang worried what might happen if he were caught. *How much does Haupt know about me and the mission? Does he have any specific idea what I'm doing or where I am? If he was caught by the authorities, would he try to save his own filthy neck to give me up? No, he knows nothing of what I am doing. He knows nothing of where I am. He's just a messenger, a tool.* Wolfgang was also certain that even Haupt's father who was getting direct instructions from someone in Berlin knew nothing of the mission itself. He stopped his worrying, it was counter-productive. Wolfgang was certain that he would remain undetected and that he would deal with Haupt later, once the mission was completed. *Damn it all!* He was fine until the encounter with the rat, but the darkness, the horrible heat and the stench of the train tunnels were all taking their toll on him. He had been trained against it, yet he was beginning to feel paranoia and fear.

There was one thing he did know for sure, the final destination of the Roosevelt train car, the Track 62 platform under the Waldorf Astoria. He just needed to know when. If the explosion went off too early, Roosevelt's car might be a block or two away and survive. If Wolfgang missed the arrival and Roosevelt had already left his train car, the President might escape with his life as well. Those were the "ifs." The certainties were more definitive. As of yesterday, that small area just under one of the main streets in this American metropolis was peppered with enough high explosives to raze the giant hotel into an even bigger hole in the ground. All he really needed was a clear view of Roosevelt's arriving private railcar. He just couldn't allow his vision to be obscured by another passing train when the moment arrived. Wolfgang's biggest problem was that without the note from the Nazi operative working in the train-master's office, he wouldn't know the best place to stand. Haupt was supposed to bring that information. Haupt had failed in his mission.

Now he just needed to be patient. It was a difficult thing to do in the darkness and heat. He counseled himself as quietly as he could, *the rat bite was nothing at all, just a scratch, just an inconvenience. It would all be over soon. After all, he was an Übermensch, an Aryan master who could not be stopped.* Wolfgang bathed himself in the Nazi catechism, the hunt is not the important thing. The result of the hunt is what is important. There is no real reward without struggle.

It was early in the day. He would spend his time checking his explosives and concussion caps. It all needed to work perfectly. Roosevelt would be coming soon, perhaps today, perhaps tomorrow. *Rats be damned! I will be ready to do my duty.*

6:30 a.m.

Not one of the lawmen left the FBI's headquarters overnight. They took turns sleeping in chairs, couches and on the conference room floor. The shift-based sleeping arrangement only lasted halfway through the night. By 6:30 in the morning the only two souls remaining awake were the NYPD detectives. Yet the flurry of activity in the past hours led to some preventative progress and by now other teams of special agents were descending on the war manufacturing factories that shipped their products to Northeast seaports. At least if there was a bomber headed for a tank factory somewhere the Feds would be there too with a warm greeting. While everyone sensed that there was something in the air, that something was about to happen, not one of this group of trained investigators could figure out any of it.

Murphy had napped for a couple of hours past two a.m., but Grover hadn't slept at all. Nervous energy and lots of coffee fueled his engine while he sat up all night. Both men kept staring at the coded clue. Murphy stated the obvious, "We're missing a big something here. We only think we know more than we do know."

" 'You just figure that out?"

"We think that we know that he had something to do with spying, but we also do know some real stuff. We do know that a spy radio was in the place, and we do know that he was carrying a piece of paper with something written on it in some kind of code." Murphy leaned back in his chair and rubbed his weary face with his big hands, "And we do know that the son of a bitch is dead." The sun was already up and he needed more coffee. "So what are we missing?"

"We've got the how, and we're pretty sure of the why. What we're missing is the who, the where and the when." Grover sounded somewhat incoherent.

Murphy tilted his head and stared his partner in the eye with mock pity. "So, what you're telling me is that we don't know shit. You need to get some sleep."

"No, no, you don't get it. You're the puzzle guy. All we need to find out is one of those things to figure out the other two. Remember what you keep telling me? We think that we have five across. If we're right about that, we'll know the first letter of five down."

"Yeah. That's right."

"Okay, talkin' about letters, so we think that those characters are T's. What would they stand for? That's the key to this. What do the T's mean? Do they mean Time... is it a time? Do they mean Telephone? Is the whole thing a coded phone number? Is it his shoe size?"

"I don't think it's a code at all," Murphy said. "If it was in a code both parties would need to have a way of cracking that code. This thing is more like a regular note. It's in handwriting. That's all it is, a note."

"You two get any sleep at all?" Mike Foreman abruptly entered the conference room. He slept for four hours in his office and looked somewhat refreshed. "I just got a wake-up call from Washington. There's an added complication to the investigation."

"Complication?" Grover asked.

"While we're looking around town for a bomb we'll have another security issue to deal with. It looks like the President will be in town for about four hours tomorrow on his way to Hyde Park for Labor Day Weekend."

"Shit," Grover realized that when Roosevelt was in town the whole security situation became more intense. "Where in town will he be?"

Foreman frowned for a second at Grover's choice of language, it was something that just wasn't done at the FBI. "It won't be that bad. He isn't staying overnight. He's got a quick meeting with the governor of New York and then he's off."

Grover got the message and decided to weigh his words a little better, "Where 'they meeting?"

"Where he always goes, the Waldorf."

Murphy already knew the detail. He had been assigned to aid the Secret Service two times on earlier visits. "Not much to worry about. He's not going to get in trouble anywhere around the city. He's probably not going to go anywhere other than the hotel. He never sees the street. Roosevelt comes into town on his own private armored railcar, on his own special track and special platform and then leaves from there."

For a fraction of a second Grover just stood there silently staring at the photocopy of the coded characters and then the wheels of his own mental Enigma machine clicked into gear. "What, what did you just say?"

"He comes in on his own private armored railcar."

"Where did you say it goes?"

"Under the Waldorf. A private track." Murphy's eyes opened wide as he realized what he said. "Holy…! They were going to blow up Grand Central Station!"

"That's a terminal not station," Foreman instinctively corrected.

"That's it!" Grover's voice rose up. "Look at this! The letter "T"…I'll bet my ass that this is some kind of a railroad schedule. "T", it means TRACK or TERMINAL. Haupt was gonna bring down Grand Central with all the people under that huge roof. These numbers mean something too, but the T's relate to terminal numbers. Haupt was going to blow up a railroad terminal. We have five across! Now we can figure out five down."

"Told ya," Murphy smiled. "Those puzzles keep your brain in gear." He enjoyed the way this was falling together. "Why do you think Grand Central is the target?"

"Remember that day I told you that I was meeting Ellen and she saw Haupt skulking around in Grand Central? I tried to follow him, but lost him at the end of a platform… Look at this, T21…That's Track 21! That's the track platform where he disappeared. The Katzenjammer Boy was casing the terminal to blow it up!"

Foreman rubbed his tired eyes with both hands. "There's one small issue here. Haupt is dead. You said before that the guy was a loner with no associates. Let's say that we might have a little bit less to worry about. Unless you believe in a second coming, our guy is not going to be blowing up anything other than my Labor Day weekend plans."

Grover's brain was on overload. "Here's another part of the puzzle. When Witcover took the envelope out of Haupt's pocket it was sealed. Haupt learned penmanship in the New York City school system so we can be pretty sure that these numbers were not in his handwriting. Most likely he never laid eyes on this piece of paper; someone gave it to him, and since he didn't open the envelope it's safe to say that he was about to hand it over to someone else. So, ergo, he has an accomplice."

Murphy took the photocopy and began to study it again. Now that they suspected that they understood what the T's might represent, the rest of the numbers had to mean something as well. He read the numbers out loud, "4-9-14-07-T21-T62. Going with the idea that Grand Central is the target, could be those numbers be a locker combination like we thought before? Maybe there's a bomb hidden in a Grand Central locker somewhere between Track 21 and Track 62?"

"Are there any lockers between Track 21 and Track 62?" Grover queried

"We need to go and check," he turned his head out the door to the hallway. "Someone get me the floor plan to Grand Central Terminal, now, so we can…" Foreman caught himself mid-sentence, "Wait a minute. I ride the New Haven Railroad to my sister's house in Stamford almost every week. I know that place. There is no Track 62. On the main floor the track numbers go from 11 to 42, and downstairs they're in the hundreds."

"Well, then the T's have nothing to do with track numbers. What if it's a date instead?" Grover asked.

"Four-nine, April 9th?" Murphy said, "doesn't seem likely. But, wait a minute, Europeans write their dates with the day, month and year? If that's the case the first numbers are nine-four. September 4th. Tomorrow!"

The three lawmen stood around stunned. They suspected that, maybe they had most assuredly broken part of whatever code was on the paper, if indeed there was a code, and if indeed there was a threat. The fact was that all of this highly experienced police deduction was inconclusive. They had no actual proof of the existence of any mass quantity if explosives, and the numbers on the paper could mean something entirely different than they thought, yet it all seemed to fit together nicely. Grover kept staring at the message only to be interrupted by a thin blonde in a tight navy blue skirt and ruffled pink blouse who appeared at the doorway to the conference room.

"Sir, you asked for the floor plan for Grand Central Terminal?"

"Yes, I did. Thank you Miss Dewey." Foreman took a large roll of floor plans and opened them up on the conference room table. The three men silently stared at Miss Dewey's arrow-straight nylon stocking seams as she exited. It was a brief pause and then a turn back to the diagrams. "Not much to get from this, just tracks and lots of places to hide explosives. I would think, though, if he wanted to make the whole roof cave in he would be going for the 42nd Street wall. Hmmm?"

"How about this place?" Murphy pointed at an elevator shaft on the lower level of the terminal, "This one seems to go down only, where does it end up?"

"It goes to the dynamo room that's about ten floors below street level." Foreman had apparently gone over the Grand Central floor plans at another time. "That's the room where all the power comes for the tracks. But not a place anyone can get into very easily to do anything bad."

"How do you know that?" Grover queried.

"Since December7th, there are two MP sentries down there twenty-four hours a day at the elevator exit. They have orders to shoot and kill anyone who comes down there unexpected, with anything in their hands."

"Oh. I guess we can rule that out then." Grover's eyes drifted toward the rendering of the Track 21 platform, the track where he had last seen Eugen Haupt on that hot afternoon last month. Staring at the map his eyes drifted uptown along the Track 21 route until his eyes stopped and he drew a deep breath. "Chief, Chief, did Hoover... er, Mr. Hoover, tell you what time the President was scheduled to arrive?"

"Sometime around 2:00 p.m."

"Then I think we have a big problem."

"What?"

"You were wrong about one big thing before."

"What was that?"

"There is a Track 62. It's right over here." The three men stared at the track map and without saying a word. Each knew, though, that they had no evidence at all that President Roosevelt was Haupt's target. "The track is right under the Waldorf."

"Read that coded thing again." Murphy asked.

Grover picked up the photostat and read the characters aloud, "4-9-14-07-T21-T62."

Murphy reveled in stating the final solution to the puzzle, "Four Nine, that's September 4th, fourteen oh seven, that's seven minutes past two p.m., T21 to T62, that's Track 21 to Track 62. I'm not sure what that track stuff means, but isn't that the time the President's train is scheduled to pull in to Track 62 under the Waldorf?"

"Where did Haupt get this information? Who gave it to him?" Grover asked.

"More importantly, if he never saw the paper because it was sealed in an envelope, to whom was he going to pass it on?" Foreman replied and leapt into action barking orders left and right. "I need teams to go to Grand Central right now. We're going to get this guy… if there is a guy to get."

"Chief, Murphy and I have to tell our bosses about what's going on. Is that okay?"

"Sure," Foreman replied, "'couldn't hurt."

9:14 a.m.

The interior of Grand Central Terminal had become part of the homeland war hum; sights and sounds melting into a sensory tableau of a nation united against dangerous foes. Everything in this thirty-year-old, massive rail travel hub pressed the war's image into every traveler's eyes. There were the ever-present soldiers and sailors in uniform carrying duffels forming a fitting backdrop for the mood. The building itself wore its own sort of uniform. It had been dressed for the occasion. Immediately to the left of the baggage room on the east side of the vast interior stood a newly constructed USO service desk, a place for soldiers leaving or on leave to find a place to unwind. Above that hung a giant five-story tall mural as wide as the terminal itself, depicting soldiers, sailors battleships and tanks. It urged anyone who looked at it to buy defense bonds and stamps 'Now!'

Whether intended or not, the Grand Central experience was a necessary reminder that life at home was focused on bolstering the war effort and everyone had a part to play in that effort. Grand Central was always a place for the smiles of greeting arrivals and a place for the sadness around departures. The war made that ritual of travel more intense. It was a place where soldiers came and went, and a place where mothers, wives and girlfriends wept. It was a place that reminded travelers to steel themselves to the fact that there was new danger all over and possible spies, saboteurs and enemy eyes and ears hidden in every crowd. Grand Central became a place where the unaware became wary, and a notice to everyone who entered its resonant grandeur that there was a big task at hand.

For detectives Grover and Murphy and their FBI cohorts, this terminal was the closest thing to a battlefield that any of them would experience, but its significance to the war effort was no less pointed. The NYPD and FBI teams that just descended on Grand Central Terminal to look for whatever they thought might be there became a part of the wartime din, yet their efforts were subdued. On strict orders of the police commissioner, they were all ordered to keep a low profile in their search. "Don't panic the people just because of some loose, unfounded speculation." And that was the truth. No one, neither the FBI men nor their confidants in the NYPD, really could say for sure that there was any genuine danger from anyone blowing someone up. It was, without a doubt, just speculation.

Five teams of FBI and cops, under the direction of Mike Foreman, fanned out inside the giant transportation hub. Four teams were dispatched to check every corner of the huge terminal building for anything that looked suspicious. Two handlers and their dogs, dogs that had been trained to detect mines on the battlefield, accompanied those teams. The other team, without dogs, comprised of Grover, Murphy, Witcover and two track maintenance men as guides, entered the tunnels that led northward. Armed only with flashlights, the team without dogs began its search at the Track 11 gate nearest Lexington Avenue on the upper level. The plan was to scour every foot of rail roadbed for a possible bomb, or whatever. Not one man was really sure what they were looking for.

"Now before we go in there, I gotta tell ya some stuff. Ya need'ta be real careful down here," Artie Clark, one of the two track men advised his followers, "There's all kinds'a ways to get yerself killed down here." Artie was a rotund bald guy in bib overalls and a railroad engineer's cap, a walking and talking caricature of a railroad worker.

"Nice to know," Grover smirked at his cohorts. "How many ways are there?" His question was supposed to be sarcastic, and the other cops smiled as well.

Despite his looks, Artie was dead serious. "Well, the biggest thing you don't wanna do is to step on the rail over to the side of the two main tracks. That's the third rail... s'got about 700 volts goin' through it. Step on that baby and you'll be pretty much toast, if ya get what I mean."

The cops stopped smiling.

Artie began to lead his group down the ramp to the train platform. "Also, ya got t'watch yer footin'. Ya don't wanna trip on a rail tie and fall on that third rail. 'Pretty much the same thing would happen, only worse because on the way down you know that in a split second you're gonna be fried."

The cops slowed their pace as Artie continued.

"Then there's the trains. If yer walkin' along a track ya might hear them comin' and ya might not, but ya also don'know where they're comin' from. They sort'a come up on ya in the dark and ya gotta get outa the way fast cuz they don' stop fuh nobody. Ya gotta know where ta jump and let 'em go by. I seen a guy, one'a my buds down here, turned into raw meat. He didn' get outa the way quick enough." Artie's mood overtook the group.

"So, where do you go if there's a train coming?" Murphy asked.

"You move to a space between tracks, an' don't get yerself jammed up against a wall. 'Might be a tight fit when the train goes by. I move by feel. Ya see, if ya hear one comin' yer not gonna really be sure where it's comin' from.

Ya also hear it before ya see it, so ya gotta make sure that yer not gonna jump over to the track it's comin' on, know what I mean?... an' ya need ta make sure ya don't step on the third rail, too."

This was more than any of the lawmen wanted to know, but Artie matter-of-factly droned on.

"Ya also gotta watch out for da rats. Deese are da biggest rats you'll ever see anywhere. Dey won't botter ya if ya keep movin', but if ya stop and sit for a spell and they think yer dead, they'll try ta eat ya."

"Thanks." Special Agent Witcover had heard enough. "Big rats, electrocution, dismemberment, we get it."

"So, let's go. Maybe youse can find whatcher lookin' fer and I can go home to the missus by supper?"

Four hours later, by the early afternoon, in three teams they had covered over four miles in the darkness. No one had been electrocuted, nor was anyone hit by a train. Witcover had been briefly startled by a rat the size of a full-grown house cat, but it was more afraid of the FBI man than the FBI man was of it. There was nothing else to see, just dark tunnels and filthy tracks. No explosives, no unusual wires across the tracks. Nothing.

Wolfgang, however, heard them approaching before he saw them. The first thing he noticed were the beams from multiple flashlights moving along the Track 21 roadbed. He knew they were flashlights because a train's headlight gave off a straight and constant beam, but these lights were waving from side to side and up and down. At first he assumed that the lights were from a routine group of track maintenance workers inspecting the roadbed, but then he thought otherwise.

"I wish I knew what the hell we were looking for, because if I saw it I wouldn't know that I had found it." Grover was frustrated.

"Maybe we'll smell the almonds again?" Opined one of the FBI team in the dark as the group continued walking toward Wolfgang's hiding hole.

The saboteur could now hear the conversation very clearly. He could make out five distinct voices. These were not track workers. *Shit... Haupt got arrested and told them about everything. They are looking for me!* By now the Nazi killer knew his way around the posts and columns, third rails, tracks and the darkness, and he also knew that he needed to immediately hide. The group was getting closer and Wolfgang silently crept back into his sleeping alcove. The voices were getting louder.

"We're looking for brownish colored cakes that look like blocks of laundry soap. They wouldn't be much bigger than that." Witcover had seen some of these new plastic explosives at a training exercise a few months back. "They'd be wired together to some kind of a trigger. If we find something it will have wires dangling from it."

"The only brown stuff you'll find here is the rat crap." Murphy complained.

Without a sound, Wolfgang opened up his suitcase and removed his blackened Luger and quietly attached its camouflaged silencer. The weapon's metallic feel was comforting. He had a full load of eight rounds in the magazine and had another load in his pocket. If he were cornered he would kill them all and then run. Still, he thought, if I have to run the mission will be over and Roosevelt will escape. He decided to stay quiet and wait for them to go by. They were getting closer.

Walking by himself in the darkness, Grover examined every single railroad tie on Track 20. There was nothing to be found except for trash and roadbed gravel. If Haupt had been here earlier, he left no mark of his presence. Grover had no idea that he was only a few feet away from discovering Wolfgang's hiding place and most likely the surprise end of his own life. Holy crap... what is that smell! Grover noticed the dead body of an enormous black rat lying between the third rail and the track. Must've been hit by a train. Damn, that thing is huge!

Wolfgang was keenly aware of Grover's proximity. Moving himself into the darker shadowed area of his hiding place, he slowed his breathing, gripped the Luger tightly and prepared for the worst.

The flashlight's beam illuminated the portal to his hiding place and the footsteps were coming closer. The saboteur tensed himself. He would kill this one and then when the others came to look for their fallen comrade he would kill the rest. There were five of them and he had sixteen bullets. It had to be the only way. If he escaped he might be able to return to the spot after all the police work was done clearing the pile of five bodies away. He might still have a chance at killing Roosevelt.

Grover's footsteps became louder as he approached the saboteur's doorway. The flashlight beam started to bend inside the alcove just missing the hiding man. Suddenly, Wolfgang heard a voice yell out from somewhere nearby... "Hey detective, train's comin'! Get outa the way." The flashlight suddenly swung away from the portal and the footsteps moved quickly out of earshot. The killer hiding in the darkness let out a silent sigh while waiting for the voices to drift away. They did.

The rest of the day went quickly and the NYPD/FBI search proved futile. After spending close to ten hours walking the tracks of the upper level not one man noticed anything unusual. No wires, no blocks of soap, no nothing. An entire day of searching no one had noticed a speck of any of Wolfgang's handiwork. No one thought to look at the tops of the support pillars, but even if they did they wouldn't have seen a thing. The concussion blasting caps embedded into every block of the new super explosive eliminated the need for wires. The Canaris plan was perfect. If any single one of the three wired charges successfully blew up, the rest would follow. Roosevelt would be dead and Wolfgang would become a hero of the Third Reich.

By the end of the day the investigators regrouped. "I give up. We're looking for something that doesn't exist," Witcover said to the teams now massed in the terminal's waiting room. "I need a shower after all that."

"Yeah, but you said that Haupt had explosives. You had the wrappers. We found that radio?" Grover was equally tired, but there was still the obvious threat.

"Let's say there was a plan to blow something up. Logic says the target was GCT, but we're not sure about that. Let's also think the worst. Haupt was a Nazi spy and saboteur and he had explosives from one of his handlers, maybe even from Germany. I'm starting to think there's a good chance that he soured on the idea. He likes it here in America and he got rid of that stuff somewhere, probably the river."

"What makes you think that?"

"He wanted to come in. He knew about something big. He was excited to tell me stuff in person. He died trying to be a hero. If he was gonna plant a bomb anywhere why would he do any of that?"

"Yeah, I get it, but..." Grover was not reassured.

"You're right. He wasn't that smart and couldn't have planned any of this by himself. Someone was giving him orders, but he had a change of heart. I think Haupt was planning something and could have had explosives. I think he ditched the explosives somewhere, and that was that. I'm betting that if there is any bad stuff around it's now at the bottom of the East River somewhere off the coast of Yorkville."

"Do you really believe that?" Grover's memory of Eugen Haupt clouded the idea that there was anything upright in the dead man's way of life. "What about the code on the paper in his pocket?"

"Someone gave him an envelope. Haupt never opened it, and it could mean something entirely other than what we interpret it to be. Anyway, the envelope was sealed. He'd decided that he wasn't gonna do the deed. He never looked at it!" Witcover had convinced himself that the team was on a chase over a done or no-longer-existent threat. "Yeah, if he lived he was gonna 'fess up and wanted us to forget the whole thing."

"You really believe that?" Murphy asked.

"I do. I've been dealing with this guy for well over a year and I think I have a sense of who he is... uh, was. Look, we've walked down every single track coming out of that terminal and there are no bombs anywhere. There is no threat at Grand Central, and there's probably no threat anywhere else."

Grover looked Witcover in the eye. This was going to be the end of this one, "And, those explosives that were wrapped in the wax paper, they're in the river somewhere?"

"We may never know. But, if it will make everyone feel a little better we can put a couple of men on the train platform and when the President gets into town they can keep an extra eye out."

"I'm not convinced, but it all makes sense, but you better let the Secret Service in on it."

September 4, 1942

2:00 p.m.

Wolfgang had been up all night, worried that the rats would return look-ing for another meal. He had forced himself to stay awake. From his hidden vantage point he noticed two men sitting on the Track 62 platform all night and he could hear their voices complaining to one another about the heat. He would have to move with extra stealth to remain unseen. It was Friday and if Roosevelt's train was going to show up at all, he had a gut feeling that this would be the day. But the lack of sleep and a general malaise was catch-ing up with him and by noon he was having trouble not falling asleep. He had nodded off for ten-minute periods at least three times before noon. He needed to stay sharp, repeatedly patting his pocket making sure he still had quick access to his detonator pack. He rehearsed his actions in his head over and over reckoning that he would need less than twenty seconds to attach it to the wire ends at their hiding place, but now he was concerned that the action could take longer than that, and that he might be seen by those men on the platform.

Then things became more difficult. Wolfgang began to feel ill. This can-not be. He was so close to success and needed to stay awake and aware, but his energy level was low, his food supply had run out last night and his water supply was also almost gone. Whatever was supposed to happen needed to happen soon. The tension accelerated his heartbeat and he was now breath-ing fast. His sweat was most likely from something other than just the heat. A fever had overcome him and he guessed it might be from that rat bite. He had to keep awake, to move. In the security of the darkness in his alcove he stood up quickly and stretched. Unsteadiness struck him like a blow and he was shocked to experience dizziness. The fever was having its way with him. *I must drink some water or I will collapse.* Wolfgang guzzled his remaining water and felt himself ever so slightly better, but he was definitely ill.

Carefully he made his way unseen around the tracks deciding to check on his wired bombs just one more time. Everything had to work right. Wolfgang was confident he could pull off what would no doubt be called the greatest political assassination in the history of the world, it would rival that of Caesar. He would not only take down a world leader, but an iconic symbol of American wealth and might, as well. His work would drive a stake into the heart of American's most powerful city. This will be a huge victory for the Reich.

As he walked by the support posts holding up the Waldorf Astoria he had to steady himself. Yes, everything seems to be in order. He had done his work meticulously. None of the placed explosives were at all visible from the tunnel floor. He knew that he had done it all correctly and he knew that once he pushed the button in his pocket a million tons of hotel would crush into oblivion the spot where he was now standing. He looked at his watch. He had spent the past fifteen minutes checking on his nefarious handiwork. All was intact. It was three minutes past two in the afternoon. Some strains of sunlight was making it through the metal grating in the center of Park Avenue above. He wondered when Roosevelt's train would be pulling in. He prayed that it would be today. It had to be today!

Wolfgang's fever was rising and he was very uncomfortable. He wondered how he was going to make his way back to Germany after he did the deed. That was a point never discussed. Did they think that he wouldn't get back? Was he, too, to be sacrificed, like those poor idiots in the submarines? He didn't think so. He was Operation Pastorius. Wolfgang wondered if the Americans would be looking for him, or whether they had any knowledge of his existence at all. If Haupt was caught, Wolfgang was sure that the OSS or the FBI would know that he was here, but he had no idea where Haupt was. For the first time in the span of this entire endeavor, since his meeting with Canaris, he was slightly confused about what to do next. The exertion of the past fifteen minutes had left his feverish self somewhat breathless. He needed to stop the spinning in his head. Wolfgang found a hidden spot between two pillars next to the Track 62 platform and attempted to slow his breathing so that he might feel less light-headed through his fever.

His consciousness danced along the edge of a delirium. He needed something to give him strength. Suddenly, his eyes caught a glimmer of light appearing far down the tunnel from him. He felt a surge of adrenaline realizing that it was the headlight from a train shining on the tracks in front of it. He watched with building excitement as an unusual looking railroad passenger car, without any identifying markings, slowly moved towards him. *Holy mother of God... It is Roosevelt!* Wolfgang summoned whatever strength he had left. He needed to get across six sets of tracks to get to his safe spot and to detonate the explosives without being seen by the men on the platform. He was now possessed. It would take him minutes, minutes that he wasn't sure that he had. *Oh shit... after all of this I cannot miss this opportunity.*

He instinctively patted his pocket to make sure he still had the detonator and started moving. He was very dizzy and he had to be careful crossing twelve individual electrified rails without touching any of them. He ran as quickly as he was able. He had to be in precisely the right place at the right time to attach the battery switch and detonate his presidential death trap. He was confident it would all happen. He smiled to himself, three more tracks before Track 21 where he would access his hidden wires. Looking over his shoulder Roosevelt's car was just about to enter the final platform position under the hotel. *I still have time but they will move the cripple off the train the moment it stops at the platform. I need to move quicker.* Three track widths to go and Wolfgang was now confident that it would all work out. He looked over his shoulder one more time before crossing Track 20. Roosevelt's car had come to a stop. He could make it, there was only one more track to cross, but maybe he wouldn't have time to put plugs in his ears. *No matter, the deed would be done and Roosevelt will be dead.*

Wolfgang was so wrapped up in his sabotage plot and not paying attention to his own whereabouts. As his momentum propelled him across the final track between him and his wires, the New York Central *Laurentian* 2:05 train to Montreal was coming across the same subterranean thorough-fare. Leaving it's platform moments earlier, it had built up speed along Track 20 to 27 MPH. As he was running to his safe spot, Wolfgang saw it coming, but it was too late. He would not be able to stop his forward motion without planting a foot on the third rail on Track 19. The choice before him was daunting. Fling himself under the massive train, or touch the instant electrocution of the third rail. If he could dive in front of the train and lie down flat between the cars he would survive, and perhaps his mission would, too. All these thoughts came into his head in the last fraction of a second of his conscious life. As he dove toward the gully between the tracks, his left arm bumped one of the pillars holding up the tunnel. Wolfgang's body careened sideways across one of the two tracks and was severed into two pieces by the wheels. The following cars somehow attached themselves to the split halves of the saboteur's carcass and dragged the pieces northward in the tunnel toward Montreal. The *Laurentian's* driver, Russel Brant, one of the New York Central's best locomotive engineers didn't see anything but felt a slight bump as the engine and the ten cars behind it whizzed through the darkness on their journey upstate. He turned to his brakeman Clyde Tracy, "Hey Clyde…dijoo feel that?"

"Yeah probably just a bad track joint. Not a biggie. I'll write it up when we get back here."

September 5, 1942

9:45 a.m.

Ellen Kramer was thrilled that Detective Douglas Grover finally got a day off, and it was the Saturday before Labor Day to boot. She was aware that it had been a rough week for him and apparently whatever case he was so deeply involved in had been solved. To Ellen, Grover seemed to be oddly refreshed. But, shortly after arriving at her apartment for breakfast, he fell asleep in her living room chair.

"Hey, Detective, planning to wake up at all today?" It was getting close to 10:00 o'clock and she figured it was time.

"Huh? Oh yeah." Grover rubbed his face and for the first time, maybe since he got out of the hospital in May, he actually felt rested and without any pain in his leg.

"Just to remind you detective, today we both get a day off." Ellen walked out of the living room to the kitchen. "You promised me a trip out of town today." She was still dressed in a silk robe and the bleary eyed Grover sleepily eyed her slim body as she passed through the doorway.

"And I am one who keeps his promises." He stood up from the chair.

"I've got breakfast... coffee, toasted bagels with butter and your newspaper."

"What did I do to deserve all this?" Grover made his way to the kitchen.

"You had a rough week and Tim told me that the two of you spent a day walking in the train tunnels under Park Avenue."

"Yeah, we did have a tough week."

"What were you looking for?"

"You know, I really have no idea. Maybe we were looking for a saboteur, and maybe we were just chasing a false lead. I don't think we'll ever really figure it out."

"So, where are you going to take me today?"

"It's gonna be hot and we could go back to Orchard Beach?"

"Orchard Beach is not my idea of 'out-of-town'!"

"Okay, how about we don't go anywhere and spend the day in there?" Grover motioned toward Ellen's bedroom.

"Well, that would be nice, but you promised me the countryside." She smiled. "Here's your breakfast."

"Okay, okay. We'll have breakfast, go for a walk in the park and then we'll spend the rest of the day in there."

Ellen glared at him in an obviously mock expression of annoyance. "Here's your newspaper. I'll think about the rest of the day."

Grover smiled and reached for a bagel. The headline in the *Mirror* was about how the Russians were holding off the Nazis in Stalingrad, and how the allies were holding off the Nazis in North Africa. As he turned the pages a short, local story caught his eye. It reminded him immediately of what Artie the train track maintenance guy told them before they entered the Grand Central tunnels.

"Ellen, let me read you this. This could have been me."

Doug read from the paper:

"MANGLED BODY FOUND ON TRACKS, by Horace A. Webster. September fifth, New York. Early this morning city cops had to deal with a grisly scene on the Northbound New York Central tracks out of Grand Central. The corpse of an unidentified male was found at 97th Street and Park Avenue, where trains enter and exit the Park Avenue tunnel to and from Grand Central Station."

"Ha! 'Some reporter! He doesn't know crap. It's not a station, it's a terminal. A station is a stop on a railroad, a terminal is a final stop."

"Gee, you're so smart," Ellen teased.

"I guess I am." He kept reading:

"Rose Blumberger, a local resident walking her dog alongside the overpass on 97th Street and Park Avenue, said she saw — Whew, this is awful! — two badly-battered severed halves of a of a man's body laying alongside the Easternmost side of the tracks. Mrs. Blumberger screamed and ran looking for a police car."

"Good luck to her at 6:00 in the morning!," Ellen quipped.

"Because of the location of the two body halves, Police have not yet determined if the man was struck by a northbound or southbound train."

"So, why is this so interesting to you?" Ellen asked.

"I was actually walking through those tunnels yesterday. What was that guy doing there?"

"He's probably some poor man with no place to sleep."

"Or, he was someplace he shouldn't have been and didn't expect to get hit by a train. It's really dangerous down there. This is gonna be one of those that they'll never close. Hey, and look at that! Guess what?"

"What?"

"The reporter who wrote this story. Webster."

"Yes?

"Yeah, I know him."

"You know him? How?"

"He's the same guy that named Eugen Haupt the Katzenjammer Burglar. He's the guy who got the neighborhood all stoked about the burglar. Without him, I might never have had to meet Eugen Haupt, rest his ugly soul."

Grover closed the paper reached over, grabbed Ellen and undid her robe. They never got to the park that day.

September 6, 1942

8:10 a.m., Berlin

It was very early in the morning on Sunday and Admiral Wilhelm Canaris believed himself to be the only person at a desk. He was alone. Wenzl had not yet arrived and the quiet allowed the master of the Abwehr to make a journal entry. It took him less than two minutes to enter his final notes on Operation Pastorius, a vain operation that he had planned for months. "I am not certain what became of our operative in New York, but it is obvious to me that he will not be completing his mission as planned. Perhaps one day I will learn why he failed, or perhaps not. Now, what to tell Hitler?" Canaris closed his book, opened the top desk drawer and put it in its place and then stared blankly at his map of the world. *Such a big ocean,* he thought.

11:15 a.m., New York City

Artie Clark was called in to work on Labor Day weekend. Brakeman Clyde Tracy on the *Laurentian* had reported a possible track issue two days earlier after the train's recent trip out of Grand Central and Artie was the man to check it out. He was thrilled to be making double time-and-a-half pay for the day. The money was good, but shortly after the start of his shift he regretted agreeing to work. Searching for the loose or broken track joint, Artie became ashen-faced when he discovered a human hand and foot in the tunnel somewhere under 48th street. After vomiting out his breakfast, he was dealing with cops for the second time in less than a week, this time the New York Central railroad police, not the NYPD and FBI.

Artie led a small posse along the path of Track 21 from the platform in Grand Central Terminal to the location of the *Laurentian* brakeman's reported track bump, and now the center of attention because of the newly-found hand and foot. The train master had shut down Tracks 20, 21 and 22 to ease fears of electrocution, or a similar fate faced by the owner of the hand and foot.

"Dere's de hand," a white face Artie indicated with a trembling index finger, "and the foot is over dere."

Two railroad cops, the team leaders, moved away from their group and slowly approached the dismembered appendages. The taller man called over a man with a camera. Flashbulbs fired and their bright white light revealed not only the hand and foot, but a wash of blood and other small pieces of human being that seemed to litter the dark track bed northward.

"Yep, this has gotta be him. Whew! He really got slammed." Lead Inspector Bill Miller opined to his partner Stan Parks. "Same guy they found at 97th street."

" 'S gotta be the same guy for sure," Parks replied. "So, we can assume he was hit by the train here and dragged uptown, not the other way around."

"I guess that's the reason for your track bump, Mr. Clark. 'Nothing wrong with the track-bed here at all."

"Mr. Clark, did you move any of these body parts before you called us?"

"Hell no! I blew my cookies and den I ran t'get you guys."

"Okay, you did good." Parks stared into the darkness. "I think we're gonna need some light down here to pick up all the pieces. I bet there's smithereens of him all the way uptown to where the rest of him ended up."

"Yeah, and his clothes too. There's a pair of pants somewhere up there, unless he wasn't wearing any to start with."

"The SOB really got whacked, huh?"

"Yeah… We should do this quick. If we don't start pickin' up the extra pieces soon the rats'll do the job." Miller turned to Artie, "Hey, can you get us some lights so we can move up the track and see what we're doing?"

"Sure thing!" Artie, relieved to get away from the gruesome scene before anyone asked him to help clean it up, turned on a heel and gingerly trotted over the railroad ties back toward the train platform.

The railroad cops who had their own flashlights fanned out to search for anything related to the case at hand. It wasn't long until Miller heard a voice calling him from the west side of the tunnel. "Hey Bill, come and check this out."

Miller and Parks carefully crossed over the still electrified tracks and found their associate shining his lamp into a tiny, secluded alcove. In it was a cot, two leather suitcases, some blood stained pieces of a man's shirt and, lying in the open, on the cot, a Luger pistol with a silencer screwed on the front.

"So, what is this all about?" Parks exhaled.

"A gun? It don't look good," Miller responded. "Wasn't Roosevelt's train supposed to come through here yesterday?"

"Oh, yeah. Ya know, maybe this has something to do with that search party that went through here." Parks had been on duty when the FBI asked for the tunnel walk.

"Search party?"

"Yeah, it was all very much on the QT. You were off that day. About twenty FBI guys came to the main terminal. They said they were doing an emergency exercise. Just routine. And they didn't need me to tag along. It was just some kind of drill, but...."

"But, Roosevelt didn't come here this time. His train car came, but not with him in it. Eddie Markman, you know him right? He's the station sergeant with the Pennsylvania Railroad in Jersey."

"Yeah. I know him."

"He told me that it came here empty because the Feds got word of some plot to shoot Roosevelt. Roosevelt got off the train in Newark and they drove him to Hyde Park from there."

"Jesus Christ! I would put money on this one. This guy was gonna be the shooter."

"Maybe, maybe not. He could have also been just some homeless guy."

"With a loaded Luger with a silencer?"

"Who knows? He never got a chance to try."

"It's the one place where Roosevelt is exposed. He gets off his train and into his car on that platform. This is the best place to get a clear shot."

"So, who is this guy?"

"Dunno. His body was out of our jurisdiction. NYPD took over the investigation."

"Well, screw them. Now that we have a hand we can run our own fingerprints."

"What a stupid idea to kill somebody in a train tunnel."

"Yeah."

Later that day, the track crews found two shoes and the remnants of a pair of trousers at 87th Street, but they missed one small thing. Resting on the ground nearby was the cigarette-pack sized detonator wrapped in black friction tape. It had tumbled out of Wolfgang's pants pocket and into a crack on the side of the easternmost track, unnoticed.

The blood type found in the alcove matched that of the unattached hand and foot, but a fingerprint search for an identity came up negative. The suitcases contained some laundry and a man's suit, both with an odd almond smell. None of the railroad cops examined any of it very closely. The clothes, the luggage, and the Luger pistol went to the New York Central Railroad Police Property Clerk's evidence unit and eventually disappeared in the bureaucratic world of deep storage.

Despite the FBI warning about a possible plot against the President, the railroad police did not connect this incident with that warning. Two weeks later they closed the case of the dismembered body without a conclusive resolution. None of their information was shared with their brothers at the NYPD.

No one found a single one of the bar-soap-sized cakes atop the underground support pillars of the Waldorf Astoria.

BOOK|TWO

"The evil that men do lives after them."
WILLIAM SHAKESPEARE
JULIUS CAESAR, ACT III

June 8, 2001

9:10 a.m., Livingston Manor, New York

"Hey… 'morning Harry," a raspy chorus of voices met him at the door, a greeting from the seated group across the room. Harry Weinstein casually limped across the diner floor at a slow pace. His arrival and the acknowledgement of that moment was part of a routine, an appointment rarely missed by any of the older men already seated. The morning "business" meeting was their way of staying somewhat relevant in spite of the increasing irrelevance of their aging lives. Harry, probably the oldest of the whole group, arrived at the table and took his regular seat that was reserved for him on the banquette.

"Coffee, Harry?" asked Doris, the uniformed waitress. Her question was timed to coincide with the downward motion of Harry's body as he planted his butt onto the cushioned seat, a ritual and a question that need no answer. She already had his empty cup in place in anticipation.

"Yes. Thanks, Doris," Harry nodded.

Doris was the Star Diner's star waitress and for most of the past 35 years she served these guys pretty much on a daily basis. She had been waiting tables at this place, just off Route 17 near Livingston Manor, since Lyndon Johnson was President, when these old men at her table were young men. She was as much a regular at the place as they were. On days when she was on vacation or out sick, the breakfast group reacted badly. They would mercilessly harass the unlucky server who drew the short straw to be their waiter. They treated Doris differently. She was fun, full of banter and gave back as good she got. Maybe the male customers were even a little bit intimidated by her.

Doris had a name for this daily gathering. She called them "The Romeos," short for "Retired Old Men Eating Out," although she wasn't much younger than these customers. The core group met at the Star every day except on Sundays when three of the eight regulars attended church. On some days newcomers swelled their number to an even dozen, but the core group was there every weekday and most Saturdays. Some men at Harry's age found comfort in religion. Harry had found religion amid this group of comfortable old men.

"You want the regular?" She looked Harry in the eye feigning impatience.

"Yeah, just please try to keep your hair out my eggs this time, okay," he joked with a blank expression. Yet, Harry was not feeling particularly jocular today. His mood, the usual deadpan exchanges with Doris and his table-mates, this morning felt somehow different. He hadn't slept well for the past two nights and it made him odd, uneasy and fidgety. There was no apparent reason for the mood swing. With absolutely nothing new happening in his octogenarian existence than had happened any time before, he just linked his bad mood to what he thought might be the onset of a cold or virus. That seemed to work, but a part of his unease kept clawing his psyche, a sense of drowned-out old fears bubbling back to the surface to haunt him. Harry, for no reason, suddenly was feeling dread. Something stressful was in the wind and he had no idea what it might be.

"Okay, and by the way, go screw yourself Harry," Doris smiled back at him and turned away.

Almost every member of the Romeos was a local, born and raised no more than ten miles away from the diner. Each man's physical world had been circumscribed by his chosen career. Aside from tours in the army during World War II or Korea or Viet Nam for the youngest members of the group, not one of them had ventured much farther away than Elmira to the West and New York City to the East. Among them there were three mechanics, two farmers, one hardware store owner, one cop and Harry. Harry was not a local. He had a slight accent of some kind and that gave him away, but his pals treated him as one. In fact, not much was known about Harry's life prior to his arrival in town. He seemed to have just appeared in this southern edge of the Catskills village some time in the 1950's. No one ever asked him about his home or family. Within days of his arrival in the village, Harry got work at a local dairy farm as a driver and made his first visits to the Star in 1958 delivering milk. His English was poor, but he spoke enough to get him by. One morning he stopped in at the Star to grab some coffee and noticed that a couple of the mechanics who serviced his delivery truck were having breakfast. They invited him to join them and that started the ball rolling. Harry just seemed to appear one day and join into the flow of everyone else's life. People liked him and were charmed by his accent and his often exotic expressions of American syntax. Over time, others joined the breakfast informally, but with Doris's arrival in 1968 things got into a regular rhythm.

Harry was feisty by nature and enjoyed the banter. He was always up for an argument about any topic that anyone raised. Today's verbal face-off erupted when Bill, a retired diesel mechanic, stuck his nose into the New York Daily News. A mid-paper business story caught his eye and became the inciting incident that started the morning's breakfast table debate, a discussion that started hot and quickly became hotter. "This goddamn EPA crap about cutting down truck pollution is screwing with the whole industry."

"What?" Eddie, the farmer didn't hear that well and always started the debate with a "what?"

"Th' stinkin' EPA wants to cut down on truck pollution from diesels. Diesels don't add shit to pollution. Too much fuckin' government if ya ask me."

"What?" Eddie's second use of the word 'what' meant that the bell had rung and the gates were open. The race was on.

"I know diesels and those pollution controls make the trucks more expensive to buy, and more expensive to run." Bill took the lead.

"Yeah, but you don't know shit about science and the crap we're all breathing." Mike the cop stayed in character as a defender of the laws. "Goddamn trucks spit black smoke and who knows whatever other crap all over the place."

"I drove a truck for thirty years and I never thought about any of it at the time." Harry quietly contradicted the mechanic. "Those pollution controls didn't make a difference to the way my trucks ran. I don't think they made a difference to my mileage."

"Harry, you have no eff'en idea what those controls do to an engine," Bill the expert parried.

"I drove trucks with and without pollution controls for 30 years and I used the same amount of diesel to get there." Harry reasoned. "Other than paying more for the diesel over the years, the trucks ran just about the same."

Bill was quickly fired up, "I just mean, there's so much extra pollution control stuff on a modern truck that it adds to the cost of making one. That means everyone else who buys anything that moves by truck has to pay more." The source of this knowledge stymied Bill's klatch-mates, as all of them well knew that the last time Bill serviced a diesel engine was 15 years ago.

"Yeah, why don't you worry about that Bill, the next time you buy a semi. Damn, you can be a real asshole about stuff. Who gives a crap about the costs. We all breathe the same air," Mike needled.

"I just don't like it when the government tells me what I can do and what I can't do, government's getting too goddamn big," Bill grumbled.

"So you'd have your grandkids breathing that crap because it'd save the trucking business a few bucks?"

"I don't have grandkids, I just don't like to be dictated to."

"Dictated sounds a lot like the word dickwad and you can be a real dickwad sometimes. That's why there is a government in the first place. They make rules to protect me from schmucks like you." Mike shook his head in frustration.

Bill brushed off the insults. He had heard them all before. Bill was the breakfast group's resident reactionary voice and enjoyed making strident contrarian statements that set off debates among his friends. He fired off another one of his regulars. "The goddamn federal government is the problem. They're taking over my personal freedom. They tax me to pay for you and your pollution laws."

"Oh please... give it rest," Mike had listened many times to Bill's tirades about the government and was getting tired of the whole topic. Bill might be a harmless right-wing blowhard, but he was predictably annoying to the cop.

"Yeah, those Feds'r gettin' out of hand. They're gonna be goose stepping into everyone's life pretty soon. Every day it's another little bit of liberty be'in taken away. It's just like goddamn Nazi Germany here. Just like goddamn Nazi Germany."

"Jesus, Bill, you are dumber than a glass of sweat," Mike smirked, "the government is not Nazis. Just because they ask something of you as a citizen doesn't have anything to do with goddamn Nazis."

The rest of the group took that as a cue to jump in and abuse Bill till he gave up. As each member of rest of the group chimed in with their own opinion of Bill's political theories, Harry Weinstein remained oddly silent.

A good five minutes of solid abuse from his breakfast mates has put Bill into the punishment corner, but he tried one last parry. Sensing that Harry might be an ally in this heated conversation, Bill turned to him looking for agreement. "Harry agrees with me, don't you Harry? Goddamn Nazis, that's what they are. The Nazis are takin' away every part of this country."

"Nazis?" Harry, who had not said anything at all since that word first came up, twitched his brows as he spoke it. This was something Bill hadn't ever said before, comparing the U.S. government to the Nazis. "I... I... don't... know... Nazis?" Harry's voice cracked. The normally gregarious and argumentative truck driver suddenly lost his voice. Harry suddenly shut down and stared out the window. It wasn't just that he was unable to answer, he had lost the ability to speak. Usually, Harry would have been the peacekeeper of the group, saying something calming and reasonable, but when he tried to talk now, guttural sounds came out of his mouth. His skin seemed to lose color and he involuntarily shuddered. Something had triggered a spasm of aphasia and the others looked at him with concern.

"Harry? You okay?" Mike, as if he was reading Harry's mind about the possibility of a stroke, asked, "I got my car outside. Wanna go see a doctor?"

"Uuuh..." was all that Harry could say while he shook with a mild tremble.

Eddie, the least sensitive member of the group, asked in his own crude way, "Shit, Harry? You're not having a stroke, are ya?"

Harry's silence broke. "Uh... uh... no, I'm... uh... okay. I... don't...

think… it's… a… stroke." But Harry knew that in truth he wasn't okay at all. Bill's remarks made him feel something that had long ago been pushed out of his conscious life. He took a long look at Bill and quietly words came out. "It is not like Nazi Germany at all." He took a sip of his coffee and stood up. "I need to go to the bathroom."

Mike was still concerned about Harry's suspected diagnosis. He knew that Harry was on some blood pressure and cholesterol medications, "Want some company in there?"

"Nah, I'm fine." He made an excuse, "Bill just made me remember something unpleasant. That's all." He stood up and didn't look at all wobbly. They all were silent for a moment watching as Harry ambled to the men's room. It was a sobering moment for the members of the group. They were all at an age when thoughts of sudden debilitating illness often crept into their minds.

Bill stared at Mike, "What the eff is up with him? If it's not a stroke, what's with him?"

"Ya' know Bill, sometimes you say crap without thinking."

"Huh?"

"Did you ever ask yourself where Harry came from?"

"Well, no. I was just…"

"Yeah, you were just…"

"Jesus Mike, what the fuck did I say?"

"I checked him out years ago." The retired local cop spoke quietly so there was no chance Harry could hear him from inside the men's room. "He came here after the war. He's a Holocaust survivor and you're comparing diesel engines to shit that happened to him and his family in Nazi Germany. We still don't know who he is or who was in his family, but it seems like he has no one. He's alone. The actual Nazis must have killed them all."

"Crap, I never knew that." Bill grew quiet and felt embarrassed.

Carl, the other farmer sitting across the table added, "Yeah. My wife says that her friend Sally did house cleaning for him for a while. She says he lost his whole family in the war. He came here all alone and made a life for himself out of nothin'."

Bill was now humbled in spite of himself. "Shit, I really didn't mean to…. Oh crap, when he gets out of there I'm gonna apologize."

"Don't apologize, he already knows what kind of an asshole you can be. Just don't bring it up anymore. Leave it alone." Mike ordered.

"Okay. Okay. No more from me."

In the bathroom Harry Weinstein shocked his wrinkled face with two handfuls of icy tap water. The sudden cold managed to tighten some of the crags and bring back a little color. He stood close and leaned over the sink getting his face as close as he could to the mirror. The old fencing scar on his cheek was throbbing and the sight of it reminded him that after all the years that had passed he was still tip-toeing on the edge of a knife, hiding from it all. Harry stared at himself for a long moment and became frightened. Other old scars were throbbing in his soul and for the first time in a long while, he didn't see Harry Weinstein looking back from the bathroom mirror.

1:00 p.m., Riverdale, The Bronx, New York

Doug Grover ran his right hand over his scalp to smooth what remained of his silver gray hair. As the elevator door opened on the "assisted living" floor he stared down the quiet corridor ahead of him. It was designed to look like the hallway of a fine hotel, but to Grover its design was just a disguise. The place felt like a hospital. Every time he came to visit he vowed that he would never allow them, whomever them be, to put him in a place like this.

He walked toward the sunlit window at the end of the corridor and saw the standing figure of a man hunched over, holding on to both handles of a walker, staring south toward the George Washington Bridge and, in the distance beyond, the Manhattan skyline. The midday sun poured in around him and Grover easily recognized the silhouette. "Hey Murph! I'm here."

Ninety-three years old and long-ago-retired NYPD Detective Tim Murphy turned around to face the voice calling his name. "Boy-o! ... glad you could drop by and visit an old man."

"No problem, Gramps." Grover gave his old partner a hug. "Y'know, you're not really old, you're just a little bit moldy." Grover chided as he sat down motioning to his pal to do the same.

"Thanks for reminding me about the mold. I really gotta clean that up." Murphy let out a sigh, "I kinda forget everything these days." The deep wrinkles around Murphy's eyes and mouth meshed nicely with his normal deadpan delivery making him appear sad, but there was no sadness there at all. Murphy had always been a clown and despite his age the comedian's spirit was still doing just fine. "Well, in any case, here I am. I'll shower later."

"I appreciate that. So how are you?"

"Just about the same I guess. This place is okay, but what really gets to me is having to be around all these old people. Some of them come on a little strong, if you know what I mean," he smiled.

"No, not really... I don't know what you mean."

"So, yesterday there's a new old broad at my dinner table. She's been here now for two days. Her name is… I think… Ida, yeah, Ida Goldstein."

"How old is she?"

"Eighty, maybe eight-two? But that's not the problem. Ida invited me to come to her room and have some wine with her after dinner."

"You dog you! So, you like wine. Did you go?"

"Nah. By the time dinner was over I needed a nap. I went back to my room and the next thing I know it's morning. But she didn't stop. She was hitting on me at breakfast today." Murphy was never serious about anything, everything he said was a comic set-up leading to a punchline.

"This is what you get for living the life of a ladies man. I guess you'll just have to suffer." For Grover the frequent visits to see Murphy were always uplifting. The conversation with his nonagenarian former partner and life-long buddy was always good for a laugh.

Murphy lowered his voice to a conspiratorial whisper and stared seriously at Grover. "Ya know I'm feeling some mysterious forces in this place."

"How so?"

"Boy-o, I may be crazy but I think that your people wanna convert me." Murphy, the son of strictly religious Irish Catholics, was spending the last days of his life on earth at the Hebrew Home for the Aged in Riverdale. "I thought that you Jews didn't do that conversion stuff, only us Catholics. I know, we were pretty serious about it with the inquisition and all that, but this here is devious stuff. I mean, you know, planting the widow Ida at my dinner table. You Jews are really subtle about it all."

"You found us out. We are a subtle and crafty race," Grover went along with the flow. " 'Truth is Murph', I've been assigned by the high command to bring you over. Your kids are in on it too."

Murphy made a face. "So that's it! I couldn't understand why I didn't land in a more ethnically-friendly place."

"C'mon, I know you love my people."

"Yeah, I really do, but I was never meant to live through this Shabbos thing, and let me tell ya, in this place they really do Shabbos." Murphy began laughing which then aggravated his throat, ending in a short coughing fit.

"Hey, have a little drink and calm yourself." Grover handed his pal a glass of water from the nearby table. "You never were as funny as you thought you were."

Murphy settled back in the TV room's lounging couch. He was frail but he was as sharp as ever. "So, what's new with you?"

"Nothing much. I went to the gym today and everything seems to be working." That morning Grover spent two hours at his New York Sports Club completing three sets of twelve curls with a 60-pound barbell and he felt really good about it.

"They got a gym here, too, but by the time I get down there walking from my room I'm so sweaty and out of breath, I have to sit down before I make the long walk back upstairs," Murphy joked.

"You gotta pace yourself buddy. You don't wanna wear it all out at once ya know."

"And how's Ellen, and your boys?"

"Everybody's good. I'm goin' out to dinner with all of them tonight."

"Oh yeah? What's the occasion?"

"Today's number eighty-three. They wanted to celebrate with me."

"Hey, happy birthday partner! Y'know pretty soon you'll be old enough to be my roomie. In any case, I'm honored that you came up to see me, especially today."

"Who else would I visit at such an important time in my life?" Yes, he was into his ninth decade, but Grover was still vital, sharp of mind and incredibly fit for a man his age.

"You honor me Boy-o. But ya know, no jokin' here, you don't look your age at all. Believe me, spending the last few years in this place I do know what age looks like. I see a lot of guys here your age who look like the faces on Mt. Rushmore. You look more than ten years younger than you are. No kiddin!"

"Must be something in my genes." Most people who met Grover these days assumed that he was ten to fifteen years younger than he was. There was no hesitation in his step, nor was there a bend in his back. Only, on occasion, when the weather changed he would feel a pain in his old broken leg, but that was all he would allow the aging process to take away from him. With his hair colored by a professional colorist who gave him a natural looking mix of gray and brown, the only thing left in his presentation of self that seemed to give away a notion of personal entropy, was the wrinkling of the skin around his eyes and those "goddamn brown spots" on his hands. He still had the energy of a man decades younger. Grover reached into a brown paper bag. "Hey, I brought you something."

"What's that? Oh yeah, thanks. The New York Times Sunday Crossword Puzzles." Murphy drew the cover of the book close to his face. He'd left his reading glasses in his room but the type on the cover was big enough to see. "This is great. I'm pretty sure these are reprints of the puzzles I already did. The good thing is that since my memory is so off these days, they'll all seem new to me! Anyway, these will keep me busy. Thanks." Murphy was also reasonably healthy in his dotage but he had suffered a small stroke six years earlier that left his left arm unusable for anything other than a shirt-sleeve filler, and left his entire left side weakened. With that event he lost the ability to take care of himself. Murphy's wife Kate did that for him for a while after the stroke, but three years ago she succumbed to her own health issues. A bout with the flu quickly led to an untreatable case of pneumonia and that was that. Since Kate's death, Murphy's four kids, now beginning their own experiences with Social Security and Medicare, settled their dad into the Hebrew Home because of its sparkling reputation and proximity to their own families. Murphy had seven grandkids and one great-grandkid. They visited him often.

"So, whatcha doin' for your birthday?" Murphy asked.

"Ellen and the boys are takin' me out to dinner."

"Where?"

"Where do you think?" Earlier, Grover made it clear to Ellen and his boys that while he would not tolerate any kind of a birthday party he was always up for a good dinner somewhere special. All in the family knew that when Dad spoke of a "good dinner somewhere special" it could only be one place.

"Let me guess… they're taking you to Sparks?" Murphy knew the answer before he asked the question. Sparks Steak House on East 46th street was Grover's favorite place to eat. Sure, the steaks at Sparks were always perfect, but he loved going there even more because he got to repeat the story of how the Mafia boss Paul Castellano was "whacked" by John Gotti at the restaurant entrance in 1985. The investigation into that shooting was one of Grover's last major cases before finally leaving the NYPD.

"I guess you know my M.O. pretty well by now. Yeah, Spark's it is," Grover smiled.

"I remember how we used to go to that place all the time. They had the best sirloin I ever ate." Murphy sighed.

"I really love their creamed spinach."

"Yeah, the spinach was great, but I can't eat that stuff anymore." Murphy's digestive system was aging faster than he was. " 'Not good food for me, I'm into 'Ensure' these days. Ha! Anyway, so who's coming to dinner?"

"It's just Ellen and the boys, no grandkids. They can't sit still long enough yet to really enjoy the place." Grover's two sons had progressed well beyond their parents' humble beginnings. Both had gone to law school. David became chief house counsel at a very large international bank and Robert followed his family's genetically inspired career path into law enforcement. Robert was the head of the FBI's New York City office.

"You and Ellen did a great job with them."

"Thanks. I really am a proud poppa. Ellen did most of the heavy lifting though. She quit teaching to be a full-time mom. I just kept pushing my way through the job. But, we both did that. Your kids didn't turn out to shabby either." Tim and Kate Murphy had raised two doctors, a lawyer and a professional violinist.

"Yeah, we did push, didn't we? And I gotta say that I am proud that my ex-partner became a chief." Murphy, though already retired from the job, was an honored guest at Grover's promotion ceremony to Chief of Detectives. Then, later on when Grover became head of security for a mega financial firm in lower Manhattan, he brought Murphy back to work out of retirement.

There was a moment of silence as they both drifted to past recollections of their working lives together. This was how Grover's visits to the Hebrew Home would go until one of them seized on a memory. "Murph, d' you remember that business maybe twenty years ago, maybe twenty-five, with the guy who went looney in the office?" Grover looked into his partner's eyes and Murphy knew exactly what he was talking about.

"Sure do! It was Billy something. That was some scary stuff. Billy... what was his last name?"

"Uh, Schultz... Billy? Yeah, Billy Schultz. Ah, that poor schmuck."

Murphy remembered that afternoon of terror in an office full of young women and men that might have ended in total catastrophe. "Boy-o, you really pulled that one out of a hat!"

"I don't exactly remember his deal, do you, hmm?"

Murphy's eyes lit up a bit. "I remember it pretty well. Schultz was a broker who got his butt fired a week earlier. He came back to square things up."

"Oh yeah, now it's coming back to me. Not only was he pissed-off about losing his job, but there was a romantic thing, too."

"Not a good combo," Murphy smiled."

"Yeah, now I remember, he had a loaded Glock and four full clips in his pocket. He had a thing for one of the lady brokers in the place. Schultz held her hostage for almost four hours with the gun to her head.

"But my partner saved the day," Murphy remembered. "The hostage negotiation guys showed up, but it was you who took Billy's gun away."

"Yeah, right, and then the poor joker started crying. Pretty sad case."

"But no one died."

"True that."

"After that thing they listened to you about security, didn't they?" Murphy complimented his friend. "What did you call it after that thing ended?"

"I called it a "friendly fortress." It cost that company a lot of cash to do, but they listened to me and did it."

"Yeah, they loved you after that one!" Murphy beamed at Grover. "Then what about that business in 1993 with that truck bomb in the World Trade Center basement"

"Yeah, what about it?"

"That was something new to me. The bosses called you back onto the job! I never heard anything like that happening before."

Grover was called back by the NYPD as a consultant. Hands-on with the forensics team, he helped to locate nearly destroyed truck parts bearing the serial numbers of the vehicle that the perpetrators had rented to house their bomb. From that, the Feds were able to find out who rented it and from where. Unbelievably, the terrorist truck renter went back to the rental company to retrieve his security deposit and the FBI was there to grab him when he did. Everyone thanked Grover for his work in helping to break the case.

"Yeah, it was new to me too." Grover's wild days had been over for a long time before that explosion, and by the time it happened, even after he retired from the Force, there was huge respect for his abilities. In his day job at the brokerage house, Grover was also a giant. He saved his firm many millions of dollars and some extremely bad press as he came upon and then shut down an internal illegal scheme that could have wrecked the company's reputation forever. Grover personally delivered six junior brokers into the hands of the FBI after his team discovered criminal money laundering using client funds. The arrests and the ultimate prosecution of the five men and one woman was kept quiet and never got into the newspapers. Grover made sure of that.

"Boy-o, what year did you finally get off the job?"

"I retired in '86. I was C.O.D. (Chief of Detectives) for sixteen years."

"I hung it all up in '77. At the time I think I was the longest-lasting hairbag in the place. I never felt like retiring though."

"Nah, me neither. I still miss it all." While most cops looked forward to settling down to a quiet retirement with a full pension and a life of leisure, Grover didn't agree with any of it. His conception of what retirement might look like was grim. Screw retirement! "I just kinda wish I could still work. Maybe one more case."

"If you get one, take me along." Murphy squinted his wrinkly face into a smile.

"You're on!" Mandatory retirement was the only thing that finally did what Eugen Haupt attempted to do nearly sixty years earlier, it ended Grover's career. He was on an NYPD pension now, and that created in him a feeling that he was still on the job. As his logic would follow, he remained a peace officer and always carried a firearm. It was no longer that bulky Smith and Wesson .38 police special, though. Grover had updated his personal arsenal to the beat cop's new weapon of choice, the Glock 19. With that gun he went to the NYPD range in Rodman's Neck in the Bronx and regularly practiced squeezing off thirty rounds at targets from two clips against the

5.5 pound pull trigger. He was a great shot and everyone at the range knew the former Chief of Detectives. Grover was still a bigger than life character and no one at the range had the guts to question him about why he was there. His relationship with the new crop of NYPD brass was different. He was old and it was only out of respect that his colleagues at the NYPD might still call him one of their own, they just never called him anymore at all. On paper, at least, he remained an advisor to the Force and through some loophole in department secrecy and security rules, it allowed him to remain on its email lists receiving intelligence reports on a daily basis. Rules or no rules, it was clear to everyone at One Police Plaza that after a lifetime in law enforcement the elder Grover was done, but Doug Grover didn't agree and was not about to stop.

The two men sat around and recollected their glory days for another half hour and then Grover bade farewell. "Okay, I've gotta go now. There's a cab waiting for me downstairs and it's costing me money while he waits."

"It's always about money with you people isn't it?" Murphy winked at his friend.

"I'll be back soon so you don't have to deal with the widows in this place."

"Yeah, Boy-o, you gotta save me from Ida."

"Only you can do that Murph, that's up to you."

Murphy let out a sigh, "I hope I can control myself. Okay buddy, see you soon."

"Great." Grover stood and turned and began walking toward the elevator. "Hey Murph, by the way…"

"Yeah what?"

"Good Shabbos to you."

June 14, 2001

11:00 a.m., Koblenz, Germany

"You have the same name as my older brother Josef, so I will let you in." She winked at the visitor as she said it. The uniformed security officer smiled and flirted with the handsome, dark-haired, dark-eyed young man on the other side of the conveyor belt. There wasn't much need for this kind of security here, but since this was a federal building it was required, if not by law, at least by prudence. "May I see your invitation?"

He pulled a paper out of his coat pocket and handed it to her. His I.D. said that he was a graduate student at Goethe University in Frankfurt. The other paper was an invitation authorized by the office of the Minister of Education himself (obtained through his faculty adviser, Professor Eisenberg). Josef read her name tag, "Danke, Fraulein Hoff." Josef laid on the charm. *She is interesting, and good looking enough, he thought to himself. Ah, but I cannot be distracted.* As usual, he was having difficulty keeping his mind off sex.

She liked the sound of his voice and something about his credentialed importance excited her as well. After reading the introductory letter from the Minister she became even more flirtatious. Leaning forward over the table that separated them, she pretended to scrutinize his papers while allowing a tuft of her blonde hair to fall sexily over her forehead. The gesture was most surely a pretense to allow him a glimpse inside the open collar of her crisp, white blouse. Josef estimated that she couldn't possibly be older than 22 or 23. She finished reading the paperwork, stood up and handed it back to him with a wistful smile.

"Danke." The young man smiled in return, and offered up his laptop computer and backpack to be fed into the machine. She bent forward again but this time he didn't pretend to be oblivious to the sight of her ample and perfectly round breasts gently parked inside her blouse. *Another time perhaps.* He sighed. "Would you please direct me to the war archives section?"

"Take the lift up to the fourth floor and then turn to your left. It's the third door on your right. The room is locked, but if you knock there's someone there who will let you in. Remember, there is no photography and no mobile phone use in the building." She smiled at him again, suggesting that rules be damned, he could take all the pictures he wanted.

"Danke." Josef was a graduate student working toward his doctorate in history. He was humbled to know that from now on his work would bring him to rich repositories like this, The Federal German Bundesarchiv in Koblenz. Josef was here on a hunch, and it was a hunch that, if true, might lead to dramatic improvements in his career. What he didn't know yet were the consequences that his work would set into motion.

The elevator door opened on the fourth floor and he followed the security officer's directions. Passing a number of closed, windowed doors he saw tops of heads staring down at open books and documents. *"Ah, scholars in search of the truth, just like me, studying events that shaped the world of the past to lay the foundation to understand what was happening today. Remember Santayana,"* he often reminded himself, *"Those who do not learn from history are doomed to repeat it."* That was the familiar quote that everyone associated with the Spanish-born American thinker. Josef was also aware of a lesser-known bit of Santayana wisdom, *"History is a pack of lies about events that never happened told by people who weren't there."* He swore to himself that he would spend his career trying to disprove that concept.

The door to the wartime documents archive was solid steel with only a small window revealing an obscured view into the room behind. A try at the doorknob was fruitless as the room was solidly locked. He knocked with a rapid tap for about five seconds and some moments later a gnomish man in white shirtsleeves and an ill-knotted black tie unlocked the door and pulled it open. The librarian looked up above his black eyeglass rims to the face of his taller visitor. "Come in, please. You are Josef Dur-maz?"

"Yes."

"I've been expecting you Herr Dur-maz, please come in," the man seemed to relish the syllabification of Josef's surname. "I received a letter of introduction from your dissertation advisor, Eisenberg. He was very complimentary about you and your thesis. I've known Doktor Eisenberg for some time. Please have a seat, Herr Dur-maz." The little man sat down behind a desk that faced stacks of bound volumes and boxes. To the outside world he was a cipher, but in this library he was king. He talked fast and seemed to be very chatty, even a bit friendly. "My name is Mendelsohn, Herbert Mendelsohn. How long have you been working on your thesis Herr Dur-maz?"

Mendelsohn's odd pronunciation of Josef's family name made the graduate student somewhat uneasy. "I've been planning it for about a year now. I'm here because I believe there is information here that might be crucial to my research."

"I see, I see. And tell me please, what is the focus of your thesis" Mendelsohn paused, "so I might steer you in the correct direction?" Mendelsohn already knew the answer. He had read it in the letter from Eisenberg.

Joseph took a breath and spoke forcefully. He hoped that his response to this expected question would grant him access to the archive.

"I'm trying to locate documents to prove that Hitler's top espionage team did much more damage in the war than anyone imagined, perhaps as much or more to Germans than the enemy. There is current thinking that some at the highest levels of the German espionage services were not fond of Hitler, and attempted to sabotage his plans whenever they could — that they were decent men thrust into the lair of madness. My theory is that while what these men did to the allies was the workings of war, they also needlessly killed unwitting German operatives who believed that they had backup and cover to do their missions for the fatherland. I believe they knowingly sent lambs to be slaughtered."

"I see. Is there anything in particular, any incidents that you had in mind that might prove any of this?"

"Yes, the one called Operation Pastorius. In 1942 two teams of German agents were sent to America in U-boats and within days they were betrayed for some unexplainable reason by one of their number. They were all executed except for the man who turned them in."

"Yes. I am aware of that story."

"I want to discover the reason for that betrayal. It has not yet been properly explained." Josef closed his mouth and stared ahead.

Mendelsohn smiled. "Ah yes. I know of documents here that could help you to prove your point. Why does this interest you so?"

"I'm an historian, and this is a piece of unpublished history."

Mendelsohn removed his glasses and rubbed the bridge of his nose with the thumb and forefinger of his right hand. Josef noted that the man's hands were delicate and pale. They looked as if they had never seen sunlight. As Josef stared at his interlocutor, Mendelsohn's mood seemed to change in a tick. The benign smile disappeared and the little man became unexpectedly serious. Mendelsohn stared intently at the young graduate student across from him, searching for any indication of a lie. "You know there are revisionists out there, Herr Durmaz?" It seemed as if their meeting had become an interrogation.

"Yes. I do know that."

"My feeling, as a simple citizen of this country, is that the revisionists want to ease the blame on our nation for what happened. The world already knows what degenerates ruled Germany in the 1930's and '40's. The accurate presentation of history is very important to the world. I suppose that heroics for the fatherland by these, what did you call them…lambs?… might be looked at by some today as heroic. They were, after all, Nazis."

"Yes, of course." Josef knew where this conversation was going. He needed to immediately derail Mendelsohn's train of thought. "I have no aspirations to alter the inherent well-established truths about the war."

"Yet, in the course of a war one man's hero is another man's monster. Are you attempting to create heroes in today's world, making heroes of men who were intent on creating mayhem, the monsters?"

"I'm not here to make a hero out of anyone." Josef's eyes widened as he suddenly realized if he said the wrong thing to Mendelsohn he could be denied access. *Shit... he thinks I am a skinhead.* "I am not a revisionist. I am looking for facts and truth."

Mendelsohn's face contorted into a frightening sternness. "In my work here at this library I have met researchers who were not content with the current analysis of history. They were not content with the idea that things happened because of the moral corruption of a nation by its leaders. They were looking for facts that they could use to change the accepted interpretation of reality into their own."

"I'm just here to research my dissertation."

"Let me ask you Herr Dur-maz... by the way, Dur-maz? This is not a German name is it?"

"My parents are from Turkey."

"I see. Herr Dur-maz, a name says a great deal to me. My name is Mendelsohn. I was born here in Koblenz. My parents survived the war but they died very young in the years after. I was raised in the East when the Soviets took over from the Nazis. It was one group of tyrants picking up where the other left off. I dare say that in the Soviet view of the war, history might be somewhat different than yours. In any case, there are maybe but a handful of individuals in the world who can competently monitor your academic output, if you know what I mean. So, while I am here as a simple librarian I am also very concerned about the interpretation of these papers in my library. Let me put it out there to you more bluntly. I've had other so-called historians visit here, looking through these archives for proof to their theories that the Nazis weren't all bad. Do you understand? You're not one of those, are you Herr Dur-maz?"

"Of course."

"You may have complete access to my library. I am here only to be of service. That is my job. I know where things are but whether I can remember where they are filed, is always an issue for me."

"I assure you, sir, that I am not a revisionist. I know already what happened here during the war, these are the obvious broad strokes. It goes on today as well. Even recently, I personally have experienced similar attitudes. I am the son of immigrants." Josef stopped himself there lest he say too much. His thesis had nothing to do with him or his own ancestry. The actual truth was that he wasn't in the library to revise history or make any kind of a political statement. Rather, he wanted a path to a comfortable job somewhere, teaching history to college students. His road to that modest goal was a doctorate.

"No. I promise you that I am not one of those."

Mendelsohn put his black-rimmed glasses back on, "I am just being careful. This is a federal German library. I am supposed to treat all requests for information without influence, yet I am also the keeper of certain truths that need to remain as truths. You understand?"

"Yes, I do." Josef leaned forward in his chair. "Sir, I am a student of history. I come here with no axe to grind. I am looking for paper records to see if stories I have read and heard about Himmler, Canaris and the Abwehr are correct. There are yet untold stories about what these men did, not only to the world at large but to Germans as well."

"Good. Well then, Herr Durmaz let's begin your research." Mendelsohn was convinced. *Yes, there is something about this one that seems sincere.* "I will show you some things that no one has seen at all in probably more than fifty years, no one other than myself, of course." Mendelsohn rose up from his chair and motioned to Josef to follow him into the stacks.

Turning a corner, Mendelsohn tugged open a heavy windowed steel door and the two men entered a large, high-ceilinged chamber. The sight in front of him made Josef's jaw drop. There were rows and rows of metal shelves, more than four meters tall. In a room that maintained constant temperature and humidity, the floor-to-ceiling shelves were filled with boxes of papers, ledgers, journals, published books and binders full of communiqués and handwritten notes. He was overwhelmed. The volume of documents stored here was phenomenal.

"One thing we Germans like to do, Herr Durmaz, is to keep precise records of everything." Mendelsohn was proud of this room. He was its organizer and master. The librarian smiled with pride as he showed the collection to Josef. "I supposed at some time someone will decide that we must digitize all of this material, but for me, I prefer the old way. There is something that is always better communicated by the touch of paper and the musty smell of slowly decaying ink."

"I agree!" Josef answered excitedly. His eyes continued to survey the huge amount of archival material now available to him. "Are these all of the Abwehr records? I could be here for years."

"Yes, but the collection is incomplete. This is only what we have left. After the war the Americans and the Russians confiscated all of the German documents they could. The Americans took their documents to Washington and the Soviets took theirs to Moscow. There was a great effort on both sides to learn who were the internal spies and collaborators.

Funny, one side's spy was the other side's collaborator, no?" Mendelsohn snickered at his own attempt at profundity. "I would guess that those collaborators had a rougher time in Moscow than those in Washington."

"And I supposed it would have also been necessary to protect those who spied for the allies."

"Of course, that's true as well. There were deeply planted spies that both sides rescued at the end."

"The Americans microfilmed everything and later on returned all the originals to this archive. We never again saw the documents taken by the Russians."

"Yet," Josef's voice stammered as he was overwhelmed by the collection facing him, "this is a huge amount of material!"

"Yes it is, but I will help you find what you need." With that Mendelsohn selected a small stack of relevant volumes and then almost casually reached for one other small leather-bound book that was tucked into the corner of a nearby shelf. He motioned Durmaz toward a small table near the room's only window and placed the stack in front of his new guest. "This should be sufficient to get you started. Herr Dur-maz, I will go back to my desk now and do some paperwork. Please let me know when you're done with these and would like more."

"Thank you, Herr Mendelsohn. This is an amazing moment for me. I've known about this library for some time, but I had no idea how much was here. I am in awe."

"Please call me Herbert," the man smiled at his new charge. *You want to write about history, he thought? I'll show you history!*

Mendelsohn turned away from his guest leaving him alone in the room. As the steel door to the vault closed behind him he had a sense of confidence that this one would get it right. The librarian understood that history needed someone to tell it's stories accurately. He was an archivist, not a storyteller. Without the telling of the story, there is no history. His only requirement was that the history be told truthfully, to the facts. There had been other students who visited his library before, but Herr Doktor Eisenberg had alerted him to this one as special. Josef Durmaz would be the one to tell the story of the Abwehr and the Nazi excesses. This was the young man who would do it right.

Left alone with his first pile of documents, the student removed his jacket, hung it on the back of the metal chair and sat. Lifting a dusty ledger off the top of the pile, its musty odor of aged ink, paper and mold wafted up directly into his nostrils. It was the smell of history.

June 18, 2001

12:00 Noon, New York City

"Sir, just a reminder, you've got a lunch with your father on the schedule. He's in the reception area waiting for you."

"Yes, thanks Lori. I know all about it. Would you please bring him back here?" It was supposed to be an easy day today and a chance to have lunch with his dad, but for Robert Grover, FBI Special Agent in Charge of the New York office of the Bureau, those easy days were rare. He put down the report he'd been reading and stood up to greet his father.

"How's my boy?" Doug Grover strolled into the office and hugged his son. If there had been any misgivings about a relationship between him and the FBI in the past, those misgivings were obviously history.

"Hey, Dad! Glad you're here. Just finishing reading this report and then we can go out."

"Oh? Okay, I'm in no big rush." He sat down in the big armchair in the corner of the office. "Anything you can share?" Douglas Grover had retired from the NYPD more than a decade earlier, but he was always hungry for information about what was happening.

From Robert's perspective his father was the perfect consultant. He already had a high security clearance, he was well respected in law enforcement circles and most of all his instincts about things were generally spot-on. "Yeah, actually I can share this with you. You know about that disco bombing in Tel Aviv?"

"Of course. What about it?"

"I just got the Bureau's final report on the event. It was on my desk this morning when I came in. It's pretty short. There's not much in it and really much the same thing we heard right afterward. There's no mention of any real actors who were involved. I've tried to get more stuff from the Israelis, but they've been a bit tight with the info."

"Can I see it?"

"Sure." The documents attached to the report included FBI field interview transcripts and photographs of the area where the bombing happened. Robert brought the cover page of the report to his seated father.

The elder Grover began reading and a grimace came on his face.

SUMMARY OF INVESTIGATION:
Dolphinarium Discotheque Attack.
Date: June 1, 2001.
Location: Dolphinarium Discotheque, Tel Aviv, Israel

Bureau agents on the scene indicate probable terrorist suicide bombing.

Suicide bomber identified as one Saeed Hotari, a terrorist linked to the Palestinian group Hamas. Hotari blew himself up outside the beachfront location of the above mentioned discotheque in Tel Aviv, Israel. Explosion immediately killed the bomber and 21 Israeli teenagers awaiting entry to the disco. Currently 132 bystanders are recovering from blast effects.

Eyewitness reports say that the suicide bomber was waiting in line on a Friday night in front of the discotheque. The club was very busy and crammed with teenagers queued up to gain access to the club, a crowd predominantly made up of Russian immigrants to Israel.

Survivors of the attack interviewed later described how the young Palestinian bomber appeared to taunt his victims before the explosion, acting bizarrely among them dressed in clothes that led some to mistake him for an orthodox Jew from Asia, and banging a drum packed with explosives and ball bearings, while repeating the words in Hebrew: "Something's going to happen." At 23:27 local time, he detonated his explosive device.

While Palestinian Hezbolah claimed responsibility for the attack there is no evidentiary indication at this time of their organizational responsibility and Mossad conjectures that the bomber was a deranged lone wolf.

This report will be updated as additional information is learned.

Additional documents attached to this cover.

"This is pretty awful stuff, Robert." Doug handed the paper back to his son.

"Yeah, it is. I keep worrying that something like it will happen here." Robert Grover lifted his desk phone and pushed a speed dial number. The answer was almost instantaneous. "Would you please come in to see me right away." Almost before the phone was back in its cradle, FBI Agent George Allen was entering the office.

Allen glanced across the room and recognized the elder Grover seated in the armchair. He nodded toward Doug and turned quickly to answer his boss. "Yessir?"

"Did you read this report about the Tel Aviv disco?"

Allen assumed that it was okay to speak in front of this visitor. "Yes, I just did. Horrible."

"Agreed. And…?"

"We're all over these people."

"Which people?"

Allen knew exactly where his boss was going with the questions. "We have trusted informants in every one of these… er… communities. Unless we're talking about another lone wolf trying to pull something off here, chances are that something like this would be very hard to even start without us knowing about it well ahead of time. Even if there was a lone wolf, there's a good chance we already have him on our radar."

"Good. Have you been reading all the other reports about the chatter recently?"

"Yes sir. I'm on that, too. We've got eyes and ears open wide."

"You already know about that intel we've been hearing in the last few days... the stuff about something big happening in New York later this year?"

"We're primary-active on that, sir, along with all the other stuff we know as well."

"What don't I know about yet?"

"In a few intercepted emails there's been a couple mentions of the U.N. and in specific, the General Assembly."

"What about them?"

"No details yet, but we think that because they were mentioned at all, there may be some indication that the U.N. may be a target for something. We've shared that intel already with U.N. security and, of course, NYPD."

Grover thought for a moment, "and CIA and NSA?"

"As usual sir, we get that "need-to-know only business.""

"I would say that WE do need to know, but I guess that won't happen," Grover shrugged. "Okay, keep it up. No one knows anything before me. I don't want anyone learning about anything before I do."

"You got it, sir." Allen pivoted and left the room.

Doug Grover smiled proudly at his son. The boy has really learned how to do his job!

"Boy, have things changed and also stayed the same. I remember something like this when I was partnered with Murphy. Only then, the Bureau wasn't so chummy with us cops and wouldn't share anything about anything."

Robert smiled at his father, "Yeah, but now we're one big happy family."

"So, we can talk about all this all over lunch. Let's go, I'm hungry."

"Right, let's go." As they walked toward the elevator Robert complained, "These loose ends are driving me crazy. Loose ends... loose ends! 'Can't pin anything down." The head of the FBI's New York City office felt as if he was sailing through treacherous waters. One small mistake and his entire ship could go under in a matter of seconds. Maybe his father's counsel could make it all better, as it always had in the past.

June 21, 2001

1:30 p.m., Koblenz, Germany

"Josef, I have some more documents for you." Josef was back in Mendelsohn's library and the librarian had become personally involved with Josef's research.

"Thank you, Herr Mendelsohn. There is so much here to go through. I'm a little bit overwhelmed." Josef looked at the tabletop in front of him piled high with Nazi paper records.

"If anyone can do it, I have faith that it is you!"

The librarian in the past week had taken a real liking to the young man, and the same could be said of Josef about Mendelsohn and his research room.

"After you found the book last week, I had to go back to my thesis advisor, your friend Professor Eisenberg, to tell him that I needed to change the thrust of my doctoral thesis. It changed everything about what I thought."

"What did Eisenberg say?"

"Oh, at first he was his usual overly cautious self. He warned me that this could set back my plans for completing my work on time, and it could cost me more money for tuition and living expenses. He warned me about all of the academic chaos I would cause." Josef exhaled and paused, wondering if he should say what he was really thinking lest it get back to his professor. He decided that his relationship with Mendelsohn was reasonably solid, so he let go anyway, "You know, there are times when Professor Eisenberg can be a bit of a windbag and a pain in the ass. I think he's just gotten too comfortable in his job."

Mendelsohn chuckled to himself. "Ha! Yes, I've known that about him for some time. He means well, though."

"Well, I did win him over. The importance of what you discovered here overwhelmed even Eisenberg's stubbornness to accept changes."

"Yes, the book was really an amazing find, and I would venture a guess that it is a complete game-changer. I don't understand how it just sat here for all those years without anyone coming across it before."

It was Mendelsohn who discovered what would become the greatest find of all amid the paper debris left over from that Allied seizure of the Abwehr files in the final days of the war. In one of the odd, unimportant-looking cartons of office ephemera, Mendelsohn had come upon a stained and deteriorating leather-covered notebook. When he opened it and read what was handwritten on the pages between the fragile cover, he immediately shared it with his guest student.

"Since you gave me this book my research has taken an entirely new focus." Josef reached across the table and touched the piece of wartime history that was once the personal diary of Kriegsmarine Admiral, and Abwehr head Wilhelm Canaris. "Having this diary really forced me to change my thesis topic."

"And Eisenberg is now on board with this?"

"Yes, I think so, but very reluctantly."

"Then let us move forward!"

"Yes, let's, but I still haven't found any specific corroborating documents for this stuff," Josef complained as he gently opened the notebook to a random page. "Canaris' entries are detailed only to a point. There is ample discussion about the progress of Operation Pastorius but there is little detail, only some cryptic comments about the expected outcome of the missions."

"We will have to keep looking in some of the other ledgers and files on the shelves, but I am afraid that much of that other material went into the hands of the Soviets, and who knows where that might be today."

"Oh yes, the Soviets," Josef let out a long sigh. The research on any of this would be daunting. There was nothing on paper that had turned up yet explaining the specifics of Operation Pastorius beyond the submarine landings and the destruction of railroads that transported war materials from the manufacturing centers to the ports where they would be shipped to the British. The name "Wolfgang" appeared in numerous places that described someone who was close to Canaris, but there were no details about his mission or his identity. Or maybe Wolfgang was the name of a cell, more than a single person? No details in the diary except that he, or they, was codenamed Wolfgang. Yet, Wolfgang's mission, whatever it was, was apparently of great importance to the head of the Abwehr. But without corroboration, the diary and additional details, even if genuine, could just be the ravings of a man so deeply immersed in his own image as a spy master that he could write whatever he wanted, true or not. Josef didn't subscribe to that theory, so he was compelled to keep looking.

"My friend, you look apprehensive. What's on your mind?"

"I'm stuck. Canaris' diary makes references to things that are not in any of the other documents at all," Josef explained. "I thought the Nazis documented everything."

"It seems as if our man Canaris didn't personally document the things for which he was not sure of the outcome." Mendelsohn sat down in the metal chair next to the student. "We do know that this plot involved high explosives, no?"

"Yes… er, well, maybe. He wrote entries about a new explosive he had seen, but it was not cross-referenced in any of his other entries. But, according to the diary, yes, there were explosives discussed around that time. That is something we know." Josef looked questioningly at Mendelsohn.

"So, if there were explosives that means they were manufactured by Germans, shipped somewhere by Germans, and were delivered to other Germans for use. That means there is little doubt that a significant amount of paperwork must have been generated at the time. We need to find its trail."

"Yes, I've already come to that conclusion."

Mendelsohn smiled broadly, "And, I would bet that unless they happen to be in Moscow, the documents are all in this room somewhere. If it involved the German military you can be certain that someone wrote it down somewhere in at least triplicate, even if they didn't know what those explosives would be used for."

A smile also broke out on Josef's troubled face. "So, I suppose that I will continue my search!"

"Yes, but *we* will continue your search and *you* will likely find an answer here. Either his diary is a bunch of lies, or he was in the process of masterminding one of the most ambitious and heinous acts of terror in history."

"Thank you." Josef had grown to really like this man.

"You know what is the purpose of a diary?" Mendelsohn looked Josef in the eye.

"Yes… uh…sort of?"

"A diary is the one secret place you can tell your truths, a place where no one else is allowed."

"Well, yes, I suppose so."

"Imagine, if you will, that you are Canaris. You are a very powerful man with an enormous reputation for getting things done. You are also hiding things from your higher-ups, and history tells us that Canaris was a man who hid many things from many people. You know that some of your peers are also looking for any reason to take you down a notch or two. Now, you go out on a limb and purposely jeopardize some and kill others who execute your scheme. In the end there are no results, only a trail of blood leading to an indecisive outcome. The average diarist might not even write any of this in a diary, but Canaris did. At the least, he wrote some of it. I have no doubt that the diary is real, and what he wrote in it is real as well. What is missing, and for you to find out, are the details of what he wanted to do."

"Ah, yes." Josef was surprised by this librarian's insight.

"The reason, I think, that it is not to be found anywhere else is that this Canaris endeavor, unlike almost all of the others in the German military, was all done without paperwork. If whatever he was attempting to achieve, all worked as planned, the Admiral would have claimed credit with Hitler and been a hero. If it didn't work, no one would ever be the wiser to the failure. His reputation would remain intact."

"You may be right."

"And then there is the other part of Canaris that we know from already published history. While he was a patriotic German, he wasn't a believer in the Reich. He never even became a member of the party. Did you know that he helped Jews escape the SS? But, did you also know that he secretly spoke directly with Allied intelligence leaders looking for ways to shorten the war? Canaris seemed to be a conflicted individual. There must have been a point during the war where he turned against Hitler. I'm sure you already know that he was involved in both plots to kill Hitler, and for that, he was executed by the Nazis just before the war ended. But, before that happened, he managed to accomplish some spectacular espionage against the enemies of Germany.

I think Canaris was genuinely trying to help his country win the war that they started, not Hitler. You are researching an enigma. If he was indeed trying to pull off a catastrophe in America in 1942, why was he doing it if he was actively working to depose Hitler?"

"All good questions to be sure," Josef nodded.

"You are searching for traces of a ghost."

"Hmmm, a ghost with a cryptic diary. I'm looking for papers that don't exist, by a man who kept no records. This is a laugh, isn't it?" Josef chuckled to himself. "That saves me a lot of effort, but it also makes anything about my theory almost totally un-provable."

"Difficult to prove, but not un-provable," Mendelson chided. "You begin here and look for facts in this room that are part of your search but are obscured by time. Then you go beyond places like this and the piles of dead facts. Human beings speak to other humans. In order for things to get done, more often than not, it takes more than a single person to get them done. With so much human interaction occurring there is always a trail of some kind. Others who were involved may have also had diaries. There might be documents from secondary sources, like travel manifests, receipts, or requests from family members for information about their sons missing in the war. There are descendants who may have heard family stories about what happened to their ancestors. There may even be people still living who were directly or indirectly involved. Paper isn't as good for research as are people. You need to look for people who had links to others who had links to Canaris as this was all going on. You need to find someone else who was a part of the plot."

"All of his cohorts are dead. So that road is impossible."

"Well, what if it wasn't a peer of his, what if the eyewitness to this was someone who was involved in it at a lower level?"

Josef's brain started to tick again. "Yes, maybe. He did have people working with him. People who might have been part of the operation, at least verbally."

"In your reading through all the papers, were there any names that came up in his meetings?"

"No, the diary just lists operatives by their code names. In an apparent connection with this whole Pastorius thing, there was a naval officer named Garbers, someone in New York he called K. Haupt, and this Wolfgang, for example. I'm guessing that none of them were real names."

Mendelsohn rubbed his chin in thought, "Interesting."

"Also, one of the saboteurs who arrived in the U.S. by submarine was also named Haupt, but I don't think there was any relation."

"I am no detective, but I do surmise that those men mentioned in the diary are probably long dead, either by age or killed by the Americans who caught them, one way or the other."

"I've thought of that too." Josef stared at the floor. He was tired and feeling defeated by it all.

"The operative called Haupt was in New York? Maybe Wolfgang as well? Maybe they were trying to inflict what was going to happen in New York?"

"That's very possible, but probably only Canaris himself would have known that."

"Hmmm, and what if this Wolfgang wasn't a single person? What if Wolfgang was just a code name for a group of saboteurs?"

"That's a road I am afraid to take. It might lead in too many directions to follow. It would greatly complicate this game."

"No, think of it like a game of chess. The men on the board know nothing of the master plan." Mendelsohn stood up to his full, yet minimal, 160-centimeter height. With that, he was only at eye level with the seated graduate student, but his growing excitement suddenly made him seem much taller.

"I think that the people we are … I mean, you are searching for are the people who directly aided Canaris in his bunker. There may have been others junior to him still living today, a secretary perhaps, or a steward who might have overheard something while he was serving food, or an aide-de-camp. We're not, I mean, you're not looking for an operative. They're certainly all dead. You're looking for someone who most likely survived the war and its aftermath, someone who was there safe in the bunker with the spymaster himself."

"Maybe." Josef didn't feel much relief from this peptalk.

"Is there a list of his personal staff that you've come across?" Mendelsohn began pacing around and talking rapidly. His normally dull library routine was broken and he was excited.

"Canaris had a number of different secretaries. I've noticed a number of women's names on official correspondence, but no name seems to appear regularly on any document."

"What about stewards and the like?"

"No, nothing like that. There's only one other name that I've seen anywhere more than once." Josef opened his spiral bound notebook and searched through a few pages. "Uh, here it is. There is someone named Wenzl, Horst Wenzl. His name appears as a signature on a number of receipts for everything from Wehrmacht messages to laundry items. He also occasionally signed receipts for messages directly from Hitler sent to Canaris. I don't see any references to him other than that." Josef rummaged through a ledger that was on top of a pile of ledgers. "Wait, I think I just saw his name again in this book. Here it is, look, his signature is on a uniform request for Canaris."

"Let me see that," Mendelsohn leaned forward and examined the document with the eye of someone used to cataloging details. After a pause of about a minute he looked at Josef, "I don't think this uniform is for Canaris, take a look at this." Mendelsohn pointed out a minor fact that Josef had overlooked. The request was for a Kapitänleutnant's uniform.

"Why would he be requesting a Kapitänleutnant's uniform for an Admiral? Was Canaris going to a costume ball?"

"Because he was requesting it for himself? Horst Wenzl was getting himself a new uniform, not a uniform for Canaris. Wenzl was a Kapitänleutnant!"

"Yes! And since he was ordering it through the aegis of Canaris' office, the older man must have agreed to that. Wenzl might have been Canaris' assistant, his adjutant!"

"Well? Then this is a man you should be looking for, no?"

"I'm assuming he died years ago."

"You know what they say about assuming things?" Mendelsohn smiled.

"Okay, I'll try to see what became of him."

"A good first step, and if he is dead, he may have had children who heard his wartime stories."

"Sir, may I ask you a personal question?"

"Certainly."

"You are around all this information every day. You've read a lot of it and digested the implications of everything. Why am I the one who is writing about it?"

Mendelsohn smiled at the student. "My sense of the world is that only a few of us are placed here as storytellers, the rest of us are here to listen," he sighed. "I am a listener. You, I believe, are one of those destined to tell the story."

"Oh, I...I...thank you." Josef was tongue-tied and humbly understood Mendelsohn's remark to be a huge compliment. He was grateful and so embarrassed by it that he couldn't think of a thing more to say.

June 26, 2001

10:00 a.m., New York City

Doug Grover packed his gym bag, zipped it up and left the locker room at the New York Sports Club. It was one of his mornings when he worked with Iris, a 25-year-old totally fit trainer, who flirted with him incessantly to make him perform. It worked. Grover was tired but he was feeling great. His endorphins were flowing as he exited onto West 62nd Street.

"Hey mister," a voice called to him from behind. "Can you help me out? I need $5.00 to get a bus back to Jersey. I have no money and I gotta get home."

Grover turned and looked at the man. He had uncombed blond hair and was maybe 35 years old, but looked wrung out and tired. Grover was not in the habit of giving money to beggars. "Sorry pal, I have no change with me."

"Please, ya gotta help me. I need to get home."

"Listen, I told you that I have no cash with me." *And I wouldn't give you a cent even if I did.* Grover turned to walk away.

The man got physical and grabbed Grover's arm that was holding the gym bag, "C'mon old man, I know you got money, or maybe you could give me that nice watch you got on."

Grover wrenched his arm free from the man's grip and eyed him more carefully. This was no longer a simple panhandler on the street and decades of cop instinct immediately kicked in. *This guy wants to mug me!*

"Listen pal, I have no money with me and I don't want any trouble with you. If you know what's good for you why don't you just let this go and move on. I'll forget I saw you at all."

The man looked around and saw that the sidewalk was empty except for the two of them outside the gym door. "No old man, you won't forget me." He reached into his pocket and a switchblade knife clicked open. "Give me that watch... now!"

Perhaps it was just the poor fellow's bad luck, or maybe it was bad karma from some other misdeed committed against another citizen on another day, but this time he made a big mistake in choosing a victim. Grover, with all his years on the force and fresh from an invigorating session in the gym with Iris, his trainer, lashed out with lightning speed. Despite Grover's advanced age, within a fraction of a second he took control of the situation and had the man disarmed and lying face down on the sidewalk. Grover's powerful left-hand grip was holding the man's two arms behind his back and the full weight of his body behind his left knee was firmly pushing the assailant to the concrete. The knife was now in Grover's pocket and a Glock pistol was pointed at the man's head. He was screaming in pain. Grover sighed, "I told you to let this go, now we have a problem, don't we?"

"Oh come on… lemme go, lemme go!"

"Not today, my friend." Calmly, Grover put his gun back into its ankle holster, took out his cell phone and dialed 911. Then he just held the man down and waited. It took four minutes after the call was made for a sector car from the 20th Precinct to show up.

Two young cops got out of the car and were surprised to see an old man holding a much younger perp at bay. It was more than surprise, they were amazed. The taller one spoke first. "What happened here?"

"This man attempted to rob me with this knife. I took it away from him."

The other cop was amused and smirked as he said, "You took it away from him? This guy is bigger and a lot younger than you. How'd you manage to do that old man?"

The cop's old man remark lit a short fuse that if it burned all the way down, Grover would surely explode. He was not used to, nor did he like hearing beat cops question his abilities, especially based on his age. The cop's reaction set him off.

"Listen to me, officer, I was on the job for forty years. I left as a Chief, and I don't like it when smart-ass cops question me about what my capabilities are. Got that?"

Both cops were stunned by the old man's reaction, and immediately became more deferential. He was talking like a boss and that meant he must be a boss.

"Sorry sir. No disrespect meant," said the tall cop.

"Yeah, uh, yes sir…" the other cop stammered, "I'm sorry about that. It was just a surprising sight to see a private citizen take down a perp like that."

With that Grover calmed down. "Okay, no insult taken. Now would one of you want to please relieve me of this dirt bag?"

They replied almost in unison, "Yes, sir!"

It took another twenty minutes of Grover's morning to answer the cops' questions. By then three other sector cars had arrived and a crowd of onlookers gathered to watch the handcuffed perp leaning against a wall with a burly cop on either side of him. The first two on the scene gathered information for their arrest report, and then they took the man away to be booked.

Once the dust-up had settled, Grover continued on the short walk back to his apartment. Ellen was out shopping somewhere with a girlfriend and

Grover was ready to enjoy his time alone to read the Times. An hour passed and the phone rang. "Hello?"

"Dad, what happened?" It was Robert.

"What do you mean what happened?"

"I just got a call from the precinct commander in the 20th and he said you got mugged."

"No, that's not exactly what went down." Grover smiled to himself. "There was a guy who was trying to mug me, but he didn't succeed."

"Are you okay?"

"Yeah, no problem for me, but big problems for the perp." Grover then explained in detail what had happened.

Robert was smiling to himself. No doubt that mugger had no idea who he was mugging.

"Well, Dad, you really did it this time. You're gonna be getting a call from the Daily News any minute now. They called me about you. They want to do a story about what they're calling a Senior Citizen's Arrest."

Doug Grover always liked the publicity he got when he was Chief of Detectives, but this, for an odd reason, rubbed him the wrong way.

"Robert, I don't want to talk to the Daily News. I can already tell you what the guy is gonna write."

"It's not a guy, it's a woman." Robert interjected.

"I don't care. They want to write an article about a cute old guy cop who could have been killed while getting the upper hand on some low-life. I am not a cute old cop, and I took this guy down the same way I would have done it forty years ago, and I'm still in pretty damn good shape to do it." He was genuinely annoyed.

"Dad, get a grip, this is all good. No one is ever gonna call you cute. You're not cute. You never were cute. Be nice if she calls you. Think about it this way, the NYPD never really retires. Once a cop always a cop. Cops protect people. That's the story, the only story."

Grover had to agree with that. He paused for a moment and reconsidered. "Okay, I'll take her call and listen to what she has to say. But if I think she's going to screw me, I won't tell her crap."

" 'Sounds like a plan, Dad."

Grover changed the subject. "So, by the way, how's all that anti-terrorist stuff going?"

"Nowhere and everywhere. There's all this chatter going around on the internet. There's big talk about something happening in September. We think we have it centered on the General Assembly meeting at the U.N. but we don't know too much more than that. We're chasing something that we don't know what it is, or where it is, or who's involved."

Grover sank back into his chair.

"Robert, this all reminds me of the war. One time me and Murphy were chasing something or someone but we had no idea who, what, where or when something was gonna happen. All we knew was why. There was a war going on."

"Did you find anything?"

"Nope, and nothing came of any of it. This chatter you're seeing or hearing or whatever from this internet stuff is also probably nothing. Don't worry about it until you know there is a direct threat of some kind. Otherwise, you'll make yourself and the rest of the people in this town totally crazy."

"Yeah." Big sigh.

"Only thing is, in your job you gotta keep lookin' for that threat 'cause if you miss it, everyone will blame you," Grover joked.

"Thanks, Dad. I needed to hear that. I appreciate your experience."

"Okay then. Oh, my other line is beeping. It must be the Daily News."

"Could be! Okay, goodbye Dad. I'll call you tomorrow."

"Goodbye kiddo…" Grover clicked the receiver of his phone and there was a woman's voice.

"Hi, is this Chief Grover?" She introduced herself as Laura White from the NY Daily News.

"Yes, it is," Grover liked her tone. "Chief Grover, Retired," he corrected her.

"Well sir, I heard you had an interesting morning today?"

Grover eased into his chair and told her the whole tale.

12:00 Noon, Frankfurt, Germany

Dr. Eisenberg, long-time tenured professor of history and expert in medieval German social orders, was not a student of psychology. Lengthy years working his way up the ladder of Germany's structured university system gave him an understanding about how it all worked, but not much about how the people whose lives were tied to the system worked. His abrupt conversation last week with his mentee, Josef Durmaz, had left him taken aback, and as he thought about it over the weekend he was actually sympathetic to Josef's request, yet confused about the why of it all. Wasn't the entire goal of this kid's struggle to get out, to quickly get a teaching job, get married and live the good life? Wasn't his initial thesis subject enough to put him on track toward tenure of his own? Why change your ideas now, you foolish boy? It will only mean more work and a prolonged chase for that golden-ticket of a degree. What, after all, was this clueless boy trying to do? Ah, youthful excess! Durmaz's extra effort at responsible research had somewhat shaken the professor. It made him look deeply into his own institutional morality. Would he, way-back-when, have been as responsible as his student? Would he have ignored his discovery just to shave a year off his academic chase? Eisenberg was so rattled about it all that his brain couldn't deal with his inner voices and he began mumbling to himself. As there was no one sitting with him in the cafeteria at the moment to see him do anything untoward, he felt at-ease in exhibiting his frustration by simply shaking his head from side to side in disbelief just as a reflex to his own perplexed state. He was sure that if he did any more than that, someone would think he was crazy.

"Eisenberg!" A voice called to him from behind. "May we join you?" It was Rolf Penn, a considerably younger but equally tenured professor in the same history department, with an expertise in North African studies. Professor Penn carried a tray with a plate of today's special, a sausage and potatoes entrée. The man standing next to Penn, with a face unfamiliar to Eisenberg, but apparently a colleague of Penn's, stood beside him carrying a duplicate turquoise lunch tray. The man smiled at Eisenberg and shifted his eyes to his tray with a plate full of steamed vegetables and rice.

Eisenberg never really liked Penn and had always thought that the man was conceited and self-important, but he remained outwardly friendly and polite. "Rolf! Of course, sit down please."

"Thank you Professor Eisenberg, let me introduce you to my associate and friend from Tripoli."

Eisenberg, ever the stickler for formality, stood up and extended his right hand to Penn's guest. "Jacob Eisenberg. Pleased to meet you."

"Hassan, Hassan Al Jabar. I also teach, but not history, I teach chemistry and physics at the University of Tripoli," he smiled. "'Pleased to meet you, too." Hassan was Penn's guest. They met years ago in North Africa. For most of his adult life, Penn had spent his summers in Khaddaffi's Libya at a family villa that Penn inherited from his parents. Penn's property was on a private stretch of Mediterranean beach and he had many friends in Libya.

Penn's time spent in North Africa gave him a special expertise in that continent's history. While it may have appeared an odd field of study for a blue-blooded, blue-eyed, blond-haired modern Aryan, Penn had learned all about Africa at the knee of his grandfather, who had been an aide to Field Marshall Erwin Rommel. His Papa's stories of the Desert Fox enchanted-him and he developed a love for the continent, its people, and especially its history. In the mid 1950's, his grandfather bought a beach house right on the Mediterranean, and that was the where the Penns spent almost all of their vacation time. At the university, Professor Penn was often tapped as a reliable contrarian in campus debates about official German policy toward the Arab world. He would say that he was not so much pro-Arab, but that he was pro-Africa. Eisenberg and the rest of his colleagues often thought Penn was a closeted militant as well as an undeclared anti-Semite. Eisenberg always thought of him as a willing gadfly to anything that would set him apart from conventional thinking, and an enigma with a dark side. Yet, at this moment it was just lunch.

Eisenberg sat back down in unison with his two guests. The three educators began eating and made small talk. Eisenberg decided to mention his thesis student whose problems he was blowing up way out of proportion. "I am having a strange day in the wake of a decision from one of my doctoral students."

"Oh?" Penn responded, "Young students always have issues." All three men smiled and continued working on their meals.

"What is this student's issue, Professor?" Al Jabar asked.

"Well, he had a solidly academic original thesis topic, and then after months of research he decided to change it. It will set him back significantly toward completing his work in time.

"Children shouldn't be allowed to go to school!" Penn chuckled.

"Yes… ha!" Eisenberg nodded as he shoveled a piece of potato into his mouth.

"What was the subject of his research and what did he change it to?" Hassan inquired.

"His original idea was all about the Abwehr."

"What is the Abwehr?" Hassan asked.

"It was Germany's wartime intelligence office. Like the American CIA today," Penn interjected.

Eisenberg went on. "Until today my student was working on one idea for a thesis and then he abruptly announced to me that he was going to change it."

"I've had similar experience with my own students," Al Jabar added.

"What was his original idea, or hers, perhaps?" asked Penn?

"It's a young man. He was going to write about how the Abwehr boss, Admiral Canaris, used spies and saboteurs. Canaris was rumored to often send men on undoable missions, but those missions almost won the war for Germany."

"If you ask my opinion as an historian, it sounds somewhat hum-drum, no?" Penn took a bit of sausage.

"Yes, I suppose it was, and his new idea is decidedly more interesting. He has discovered information of a specific incident of Canaris' expense of

German soldiers in what was supposed to be a major sabotage event. These soldiers were knowingly sent to their doom in the quest for results that at best, historically, remain obscure."

"This sounds very interesting, something I would love to read when he publishes." Al Jabar smiled.

"The new thesis idea involves research into a particular duplicity toward its own field operatives. Agents were told that they were going to be spear points for the Fatherland, but Canaris' intent was, by design, that they would never achieve their missions and would probably die in their attempt. My student has information that the Abwehr, specifically Canaris, knowingly threw some of its people into the line of fire for absolutely no other reason than to keep the Allies off guard."

"Sending lambs to be sacrificed," Hassan asked, "for no reason?"

"Exactly! Yes, no reason. Perhaps that describes war in general. This story, of course, would taint the reputation and memory of Wilhelm Canaris. You know that Canaris came away from the entire sordid brief history of the Master Race with fewer scars than the rest of the thugs who ran this country at the time. He was reported to be a foe of Hitler, even while working for him."

"This sounds much stronger than the original thesis idea. I would think you should be happier about it, no?" Penn asked.

"You're right, though nothing was wrong with his first idea, other than its lack of excitement."

"I think you should take some pride in this," Penn opined. "How did he find this information?"

"I sent my student to do research at the Federal archives in Koblenz. Going through the stacks of official documents he made a genuine discovery, a small leather-bound notebook stuffed in a file folder along with small paper notes that had somehow escaped scrutiny even after its being impounded by the Americans and then later returned to Germany. It was a single book and no one, I guess, thought to open it when there was so much else there to read."

"That proves the value of first-hand archival research." Penn looked up from his lunch, "No one does proper research any more. They just read the scholarly papers about documents researched by others."

"Hmm, yes, no one does," Eisenberg smiled.

"And... so? Whose notebook was it?"

"The notebook was hand written by Canaris himself. It was his personal diary and is full of provocative new information about the Third Reich, his opinions of Hitler and his associates and also veiled details of the Abwehr's espionage activities." Eisenberg stopped himself for a second as he didn't want to upstage his student's scholarly work, but then, the audience was so enthralled at the moment he decided to tell what he knew, though only up to a point.

"Is it genuine?" Penn asked with a sliver of potato hanging on his lip.

"I believe so."

"This is an amazing find, no?" Hassan asked.

"Yes it is." In a quick turn of emotion Eisenberg's stress over the extra work that faced him suddenly turned into excitement over the impending professional jealousy that awaited his connection to this piece of historical treasure. He became protective.

"Of course you gentlemen will keep this all to yourselves. This is a piece of scholarly research that is still ongoing."

"Absolutely!" the two men said in unison.

"A number of things caught my student's attention in his initial research, the research about lambs to the slaughter." Eisenberg drew a deep breath, "In the spring and summer of 1942, the Abwehr launched a sabotage plan, something that they called Operation Pastorius. The stated goal of this activity was the destruction of railroads and wartime shipping to the East Coast ports. The efforts of eight trained saboteurs placed on U.S. beaches by a U-boat would cripple the shipping of goods to England to be used against the Wehrmacht. The first part of the plan was to land German saboteurs in the United States by submarine."

"Did this happen?" Penn asked.

"Yes, it did, exactly the way it was planned. Two submarines dropped off two teams of saboteurs, explosives and the lot along the Eastern American coast, one team in New York and the other in Florida. They quickly dispersed from the beaches and blended into the population. Yet, something happened and within about eight days after their arrival all the men had been arrested. Within a month they were tried as spies and all were executed shortly after that, all except for the man who turned them in."

"Who was the man who turned them in," Hassan asked?

"One of their group. What was interesting in this operation is that all of the saboteurs had lived in the States and came home to Germany to help the fatherland before the start of the war. They were dedicated to Germany's success. Most of them could speak English without noticeable German accents. They were chosen for the mission because they could blend into an American crowd without raising suspicion."

"Obviously, the man who turned them in had dual loyalties." Penn opined before stuffing a piece of sausage into his mouth.

"One would think so… and that's what my student thought as well at first." Eisenberg's voice remained flat, not trying to embellish any of the facts with any expression of interest or excitement.

"This doesn't sound like much of a plan," Hassan teased.

"It didn't until my student discovered the diary. Then we learned about the more devious part of the plan, a part that no one other than Canaris, and perhaps only Hitler himself had known about."

"What was in the diary?" Penn stared at him.

"The first thing was that the Judas in the group was under orders to do exactly what he did to gain American trust. He turned in his comrades under orders from Canaris himself. Perhaps the Admiral actually believed that the Americans wouldn't harm these fellows once they were caught, that they would spend the remainder of the war in prison, or that was what he told the operative to make sure that he didn't get cold feet about doing it."

"But for what purpose?" Hassan seemed to be enthralled by the story.

"We think Canaris planned, that once the supposed traitor made his case to the Americans, they would believe what he had to say about other infiltrations. For this short time after the capture, the FBI would believe everything else the traitor had to say. He could direct them to the wrong places while other teams could arrive in the U.S. and do major damage, the real goal of Operation Pastorius. The American Navy and Coast Guard, for the moment, would be on the lookout for more submarines with teams of saboteurs. If the Americans were looking for more U-boats, then they would be distracted from other ways of landing operatives." Eisenberg conveniently omitted the story of Wolfgang and his yet undiscovered mission. That, after all, was the central point of Durmaz's research and not yet a subject to share with competing academic entities.

"Yes, but..." Hassan interrupted, " with Americans now actively on the lookout for spies, how would anyone else get into the country without getting caught?"

"Ah, but apparently they did. Canaris' plan had worked well up to that point. The *how* of how they got in and what they did while there, that is what my student needs to find out."

Rolf Penn's eyelids narrowed ever so slightly. "I never heard of this before. This would be amazing, if it were real," he commented suspiciously.

Eisenberg smiled to himself and interpreted Penn's look as professional jealousy.

"Their target?" Hassan asked.

"Their target will be revealed in my student's final thesis. I cannot tell you that now." Eisenberg himself had no idea who or what the target was, but he pretended that he did. He was now sitting opposite his professional rival, feeling very smug. He had no idea how Josef Durmaz would prove any of it, but had a blind faith that he would.

"What I will tell you is that if they had achieved their goal, Germany probably would have won the war. America would have likely withdrawn from aiding Britain after whatever catastrophe was intended."

"So, the suggestion that the operatives were landed in America for purposes of sabotage was really a diversion for something else? But, I would imagine that any such plan would have been thwarted by the Americans who were no doubt watching absolutely everything during the war," Rolf Penn put down his fork. "What makes this one so special? There must have been many such plans."

What an annoying son of a bitch! With this opportunity to gloat over Penn, although knowing only the minutest detail of his student's research so far, Eisenberg vamped and embellished. "I will tell you that it was a much grander plan than anything ever before. No single saboteur disrupting factory production." Eisenberg caught himself. *Don't talk so much, you know none of this for sure!* He needed to soften the information, "er… this was bigger than that, much bigger.

"What happened?"

Eisenberg couldn't help himself and bragged, "In the weeks before the intended action the saboteurs reported back by radio directly to Canaris that they were there and safe. They sent almost daily progress reports indicating that they had achieved the preliminary parts of the plan. All was set to go in a major city. When the time was right they would trigger the plan and the war would be over. The radio messages were, of course, cryptic in nature, and Canaris' notes in his diary are only mildly paraphrased in content. He obviously did not want anyone to get information from the entries. This was a very secret operation. Yet, we can easily guess by reading the diary entries that the effort had progressed to near completion. In fact, all of the actual decoded telegram paper documents are folded in between the pages of Canaris' leather-bound notes. Yet, there is no other record of any of this in any of the other Pastorius related documents, only in Canaris' diary."

"Oh, God!" Penn gasped, "… quite diabolical!"

"And your student is sure that this diary is authentic?" Hassan asked

"Yes. My student spent a lot of time comparing handwriting samples with the diary, and also was able to trace the provenance of the diary itself. It is indeed that of Admiral Wilhelm Canaris."

"Yet, if my memory of wartime history is correct, no great disaster occurred anywhere in America itself during the war. The nation itself lost little or nothing in their homeland," Hassan said.

"Yes, save for Pearl Harbor a few months before, that fact remains to be explained. I'm sure that my student will track it all down. All I know is that the last thing Canaris wrote in his book was that the 'goods' were in place and the operative was waiting for orders, but it was the last message the Admiral received." Eisenberg suddenly stopped talking and he regretted what he just said.

"The goods? I would bet that means explosives, hmm?" Penn immediately grabbed onto Eisenberg's slip of tongue. "You didn't say anything about explosives before." Penn's interest was definitely piqued. It was now a game to see how much he could get his colleague to reveal.

"I did not say anything about explosives, did I? Canaris said that the 'goods' were in place. We can only guess what he meant by that. By conjecture, you think that he meant explosives? I will have to tell my student of that theory. In any case, the 'goods,' whatever they were, were in place. Maybe he meant guns, poison or a bow and arrow," Eisenberg teased in a mischievous way.

"And nothing blew up anywhere," Penn said.

"I really don't know. It is really up to my student to look into all of this before we can definitely write the history of this mission."

Penn didn't let up on his needling, "That would be an interesting find for your student! His thesis could actually read like a cheap detective novel." Penn said with a syrupy sweetness. "It could even be made into a major motion picture!"

Eisenberg forced a smile. *What a horse's ass. He's so jealous!*

Al Jabar's interest picked up. "What if there were explosives, long forgotten? This could have interesting ramifications. You know, it is often the case with forgotten explosives that they gain in potency over time."

"Really?" Eisenberg was grateful that Al Jabar had shifted the conversation toward chemistry and away from Penn. "They gain potency?"

"Yes, chemically speaking, the explosive mixtures often tend to become more volatile in heat or over time."

"Fascinating, I did not know that," Eisenberg raised an eyebrow. "I really don't know the details of what was supposed to happen. The idea of explosives adds an interesting sidebar conversation to my student's research, and I will review that with him, but we are talking about something that happened decades ago." Eisenberg was cordial, but cursing himself for starting this discussion at all.

Penn wore a sly grin, "Since the crucifixion of Christ, nothing has changed history more than well placed explosives. Rest assured, in any major plot, I would bet money that explosives were involved."

Eisenberg corrected him, "Caesar was slain by knives, Archduke Francis Ferdinand and Abraham Lincoln were felled by bullets, and the King of France lost his head to the guillotine."

"True enough," Penn acknowledged.

Hassan Al Jabar continued his train of thought, "In Libya we still find live World War 2 munitions and mines buried in the desert. They are just as deadly as ever, perhaps even more so because they are hidden and can be accidentally detonated. A shepherd boy or a sheep in his flock might come upon an exposed, long dormant mortar shell or a land mine in the wild. Desert winds reshape a dune and suddenly a long buried device sits millimeters below a light cover of sand. If the triggering mechanism is still live and potent, neither the boy nor his sheep would ever know what hit them until others found bits of shepherd and tufts of wool in the sand," Hassan smiled at his own macabre vision.

"Yes," Penn became more serious, "but, most likely the American authorities would have removed any threat, or perhaps, we have the ultimate time bomb!"

Hassan took it all in and became silent. He slowly lifted a forkful of rice to his mouth as he digested the thought.

Penn, trying to bait Eisenberg, became annoying again and kept pressing the mass media possibilities for Josef's thesis, "This student of yours has more than a doctoral dissertation on his hands. He really does have a potential film script! I mean, what if the explosives are still somewhere… ?"

"Rolf, this is a pointless train of thought. If there were explosives somewhere in 1942 in a heavily populated area, they would have long ago been discovered. And this dissertation is not about explosives, it's about the basic disregard for human life among military elites."

"Still, what if? 'What if' is the question asked by every historian. Ha! We should all go and look. Where did you say they were?"

"I didn't say because I don't know. It's smart not to speculate on things you don't know." Eisenberg replied patronizingly. "I am pretty sure that the powers-that-be caught Canaris' saboteur or saboteurs and that was that. Any capture of working spies would have been a wartime secret. No one here would be any the wiser over what became of the plot."

"Yes," Penn said, "but, there would be fascinating implications if they didn't foil it."

Hassan agreed with Eisenberg, "We don't know any of this yet. Someone has to do research. In America there must be paper records somewhere if they stopped a plot. Law enforcement agencies write everything down. The truth exists somewhere in a file cabinet."

"Ah! So we have the interest of professional academics! I'm pleased. Be assured that with my supervision, my student will find everything he can to get to the truth, and all of it will be there in my student's published research. I hope that you read it when he finishes." As if by magic Penn's jealousy fueled in Eisenberg a new enthusiasm for Josef Durmaz's work. Rather than his earlier lamentation about Josef's youthful, bad judgment as a doctoral candidate, the elder educator now vigorously defended it to his colleagues. If Josef did indeed find something astounding in his research it would reflect well on Eisenberg, as well as on his department. "I will make sure that my student is totally focused on his amazing discovery."

Penn spoke slowly as he chewed on the last morsel of his lunch, "Your student has some important work in front of him."

"Yes, I suppose he does. That's why I have encouraged him to go forward with his research." With that lie Eisenberg looked at his watch to avoid eye contact and quickly lifted his bulging briefcase from beside his chair. "Ach! I have a seminar in seven minutes! I have to go. 'See you later Rolf, and very nice to meet you Hassan. I hope I didn't bore you with all of this."

"Nice to meet you too. I was definitely not bored!"

Eisenberg trotted toward the cafeteria door and was out of sight a moment later.

"This is a very interesting story, Rolf. I think it borders on the amazing."

"Yes. I agree."

"Well, I too, must go now. I have classes on Monday, a flight home to Tripoli in four hours, and I haven't yet begun to pack my things." Hassan gave Rolf a bear-hug and headed toward the door in Eisenberg's wake. "I will see you soon, my friend."

Rolf waved slightly at the blur of a man rushing out of the cafeteria, "See you soon my friend."

June 29, 2001

7:00 p.m., New York City

Robert Grover's eyes focused on the West Side skyline outside of the 26th-floor kitchen window. His parents had done well and their Lincoln Center high-rise apartment afforded a spectacular view. From this concrete crow's nest on West 62nd Street, the younger Grover was taking in a grand cityscape that included the entire Lincoln Center complex and Fordham University as well a long look down Ninth Avenue. As a view, it was as spectacular as the lull in the conversation was irritating. The current FBI New York City Special Agent in Charge sat directly across the kitchen table from the retired NYPD Chief of Detectives Douglas Grover waiting for a response to a question he had asked moments earlier. At work, subordinates fell over themselves to all of his questions immediately. The answer from his father wasn't coming as quickly.

"Ever since that mugging, Mom's been worried about you."

"It's really not a big deal, Robert."

"It is a big deal. Mom is really upset."

"She worries about everything. Nothing happened to me."

"That's this time. Mom is worried that if it happens again you might not be as lucky to walk away from it. She knows you, Dad. She knows that you're stubborn and you never think to back down in anything."

"The two of you are really amazing." Doug expressed his irritation with the line of questioning. "I took down a mugger and that was that. You should be proud of your old man, not a critic."

"Dad, you know that guy could have really hurt you, or worse."

"I don't think so."

"You're not on the job any more dad, you know that don't you?"

"What do you think? Of course I know that. I'm not some helpless old schmuck who decided to be a hero. What do you think? Did I ask that jerk to come after me?"

It had been a few days and Robert Grover had time to think about the other possible outcome of the attempted mugging of his 83-year-old father. It had shaken him and caused him to worry. "Dad... if something had gone wrong Mom would have been left all alone. It would have been the end for her."

"So what did you think that I should have done in that situation? Should I have given the son-of-a-bitch my Rolex? Then what? Should I have let him take my money? Then what? Should I have stood there if he decided to cut me with that knife?"

"I'm just sayin'…."

"Just sayin' does not put you in my place." Doug spoke in a direct tone that Robert remembered from one of the numerous fatherly lectures delivered at random moments of childhood misbehavior.

"I did what I needed to do at the time and I knew exactly what I was doing, and I would do the exact same thing if it happened again. You might be too young to remember this, but I was actually a street cop for a few years and I dealt with a lot worse than this lame-ass putz with a knife."

"I don't mean any insult. It's just that this guy was bigger and younger than you, and…"

"And… I disarmed him just the way I would have if I was still on the job. That's it, no more of this stuff!" While Grover, for a brief moment, enjoyed his celebrity as the octogenarian hero who had taken down a violent mugger, this conversation with his FBI-agent son put an end to that enjoyment. He was officially done with it all. "I don't want to hear one more word from you about this. I'm okay and it's okay. Okay?"

Robert turned his eyes back to the window view and away from his father's intense glare. Shit, the old man can still put on the bull. "Yeah, okay, Dad. Just please be careful out there."

"When I need help, I'll ask you for it," the aging cop bristled.

"Jesus, Dad, c'mon…" The younger Grover knew this was a conversation that he couldn't win and knew he had to drop it, at least for the present. Then, repeating that standard segue moment from his catalog of childhood-subject-changers, he rose from the table and opened his parents' refrigerator. Funny, he thought to himself, some things never change. Peering inside the big Sub-Zero, the head of the NYC FBI office took out a container of grapefruit juice, grabbed a glass out of the nearby cabinet and filled it, much the same way he did when he was a boy, right up to the brim of the glass. He lifted it to his mouth and took a big sip, taking the juice down to a less precarious level. The time it took to do that was enough for a proper shift in topics.

"So, what's new on the job?" The elder Grover knew he had diffused the mugging issue, at least for a while. Yet, the question wasn't just a turn of phrase. Doug always enjoyed learning what was going on at his son's work at the FBI, even though it had taken him a while to get past the idea that not all the agents at the FBI were jerks. After all, his son was, as he often bragged to friends, in charge of the whole damn place.

"So yeah, there's some more stuff going around on the internet and from some phone intercepts in the past week. We've been following some odd chatter out there." Robert sipped his juice.

"Chatter?"

"Yeah, you know, things… emails, monitoring user-groups, chat rooms, postings on the internet, listening in on phone calls to people in the Middle-East and some snitch information." The information about the chatter was classified, but Robert really didn't care. Even though Douglas Grover no longer had any kind of official security clearance, his son felt comfortable sharing this with him, and trusted that it would go no further.

"Pretty creepy that you guys are reading email and listening to peoples' phone calls, huh?" Detective Douglas Grover had always tried to keep his investigations legal. The FBI's tactics, in Doug's opinion, always bordered on the illegal, yet the old man wasn't judgmental about any of it. He was savvy enough to understand that his son was just caught up in the sway of the intelligence community.

"In my day if you wanted a wiretap you went to a judge to get it. None of this secret listening-in crap."

"So do we, Dad. No one is breaking any laws. There's a legal check to everything we do. We do get the warrants from the FISA court. Anyway, this isn't domestic stuff, it's international espionage and terrorism we're tracking."

"Isn't that the realm of the CIA?"

"We're working closely with the CIA, and the NSA."

"That's not what I heard," the elder Grover's historical knee-jerk reaction to the FBI revealed itself. "You might be working with them, but are they working with you?"

Robert parried the parental scolding, "In any case, as bits of information, none of it really seems all that important, but when you look at it all together," he drew a deep-weighted breath for emphasis, "something is in the works, some kind of a terrorist thing. 'Could be as big as the attack on the Cole." Robert referred to the attack on the USS Cole in Yemen.

"What kind of stuff have you heard?"

"The big takeaway from the chatter is they seem to want to take something down, maybe in New York later this year."

"They?" The older Grover always liked to hear about cases in progress. He had an opinion about everything he ever heard. "What's the analysis?"

"We're pretty sure that some group of Mid-East actors is planning something big to happen in New York, but we don't know anything more than that yet. I personally think because they seem to be talking about it happening in September, that it has something to do with the U.N. The Bureau analysts in D.C. think there's a threat to the U.N. during General Assembly time."

"What kind of threat?"

"We dunno yet. 'Still working on it. Some of the Bureau forensic guys believe that there's a group somewhere in Pakistan or Afghanistan, some religious zealots who want to attack the U.N., probably the General Assembly meeting in September. Maybe it's guys in a Toyota pickup with AK-47's or maybe it's worse than that."

Doug Grover's attention was rapt. "Well, what do you know for sure?"

"Uh... some cryptic stuff about teams and Jihad... and all that Allah akbar stuff. That's pretty much all we have at the moment. Agents are checking up on the usual suspects for some talking, but I don't hold much faith that we're going anywhere with that."

Robert stood up from the table and walked over to the kitchen window that faced Downtown. Traffic jammed the avenue as far as he could see inching its way toward the Lincoln Tunnel entrances down in the low forties. In the haze he could make out the twin towers in the financial district all the way at the lower end of Manhattan. With the sunlight reflecting off the car roofs, the mass of slow moving vehicles resembled a gargantuan, undulating snake slithering down the avenue in the early summer glare.

The hardened cop eyed his son with paternal worry. *He's doing some heavy lifting.* The NYPD Chief of Detectives part of him didn't care a whit over any other lawman's emotional state, but the dad in him was concerned and felt the need to moderate his kid's worry, even if that child was a grown man in his fifties and the head of the FBI's New York office.

"This chatter thing that you're talking about... s'got you pretty tense, doesn't it?"

"A little," Robert attempted to show a modicum of nonchalance to his dad, but that wasn't possible and Doug saw right through it. He was definitely carrying a heavy burden and deep down inside he wanted his dad to step in and make it okay, just like he had always done when he was young.

"You know it may turn out to be total crap," the older Grover opined. The scenario was familiar. Some bad thing was thought to be in the works, but there was no solid evidence of it anywhere. He had been there before.

"It's probably nothing, just analysts getting chills from stuff they hear about."

"Probably true, Dad, but there's way too much intel coming in from too many places not to follow up."

"You're absolutely right about that. No matter what it is, how stupid sounding or impossible sounding, ya gotta follow up."

"Yeah. That disco bombing, we knew something like that was brewing from intel from the same sources we're listening in on now. Then a guy blows himself up in a crowd and kills a bunch of people. We knew a few days beforehand that something was going to happen! We passed that along to the Israelis, and it still happened. All this is stuff about September is coming from the same sources… so, while nothing is real yet, my gut says that they're gonna try something in New York and I think it will have to do with the U.N."

"That's a genetic family trait, ya' know, the instinct," Doug smiled.

"Yeah, well that's all we really have to go on, instinct. There's been nothing specific. My big problem is that Washington is on my back to make sure whatever it is won't go down. I feel pretty much the same way, especially as this is all on my watch."

"So, then you tell me what you need to be doing right now." Doug reached deep into his early parental training. "What's the way to solving a problem of any kind?"

Robert smiled at his dad and both of them mouthed silently the words that had been spoken aloud many, many times in the Grover household, "You need to do more police work!"

July 2, 2001

10:00 a.m., Frankfurt, Germany

Josef steeled himself before knocking on Eisenberg's office door. He had spent the past week and weekend preparing for this meeting. *This is the hard labor I have to do. He wants me to discuss my thesis with him every week like this. He's just a windbag, but unfortunately he's my windbag.* He took a deep breath and knocked.

"Come in, Josef."

Josef opened the door and sat down. Eisenberg's small office was cluttered with books, papers and knick-knacks that had some importance to him but were meaningless to everyone else.

"I have made some progress in my search for corroboration."

"Really! That is good," Eisenberg said with a smile. Unbeknown to Josef, as a result of the lunchroom encounter with Professor Penn, Eisenberg was now fully on-board the Josef Durmaz bandwagon. It took the interest from that martinet Penn to get him to this point, but now he was genuinely excited.

"What have you uncovered since last time we talked?"

Josef immediately sensed the change in his mentor yet proceeded slowly in case he misread the situation. "My research at the archives library has turned up the name of a man I believe might have been Canaris' adjutant and office aide-de-camp. I think he was at least four decades younger than his boss and was there when his boss was writing his diary. I'm going to try to find what became of him or his descendants. If he survived the war and he is among the living today, he would be in his eighties right now."

"Fantastic! Who is he?

Josef hesitated in his response. *Yes, there's something different here with Eisenberg.* "His name was or is Horst Wenzl, he had the rank of a naval Kapitänleutnant. I need to find out what became of him. Wenzl must have been in the room, so to speak, and if he is still living, he might know a lot about this Operation Pastorius."

Josef felt good as he filled Eisenberg in on the details of the search and its current goals. "If Wenzl is already gone he may have had children to whom he told stories. Otherwise, I will need to turn my research in another direction, but this could be a big first step, if I am lucky."

In previous work, this son of Turkish immigrants had been lucky indeed. Josef Durmaz started his chase of history during his final undergraduate year.

A paper about the war led him to an interview with a former Wehrmacht infantry sergeant. The man had been in the army before the Nazis came to power and surrendered to the Allies when it was all over. Now, as an old man, he was very open about his life and experience. He began the interview boasting proudly about his service to Germany. He claimed that while he was not at all a believer in the Nazi cause, he was always a soldier. "Orders were orders" and in obeying them to the letter, he defended the dignity of his fatherland. Josef, a gentle but pointed interviewer, slowly drew confession after confession out of his subject. Some of the stories were horrible, and in the middle of their conversation, the man began to express his regret for the things he had done. The young interviewer had cleverly led the old soldier through his military memories of battlefield horrors to the darker things he had done while following orders. He admitted that he needlessly beat Jews with his rifle butt, and drove Jewish families young and old into the streets, and into the waiting hands of the Gestapo. He admitted to knowing that his action doomed innocent people to the death camps. By the time the meeting was over, the interviewee was in tears. For his efforts Josef received the highest grade possible for his paper and it set him on the path to the study of history.

Eisenberg sat quietly as he listened to his student explain his plans in detail and his agenda for actually finishing his dissertation in time for his originally sought graduation date. Eisenberg, the old pedant himself, now sounded very impressed with this brilliant young man, the same student he had berated for changing a thesis topic a few days earlier.

"This all sounds very good to me. There is little more I can say to you at this point other than go and, if he is still among us, get to Herr Wenzl before time takes its toll on the memories of history."

For the first time in their relationship, Eisenberg was acting like a proud father rather than the pedantic obstacle he usually was. "I must ask you, how do you plan to find this Wenzl fellow?"

"I'm going to start at the office where they keep the military archives. I am told that every soldier who has ever served in the German military in the past 100 years is listed there. If Wenzl is still with us, then I will find him there. If he is dead, I will read his service records for other ideas, and look for any descendants elswhere."

"Good, good! Now, a more personal question… if I might ask, how are you paying for things as you do your research?"

Josef was taken aback by the question about his personal finances. "I have a few marks in a bank account that was left to me by my uncle, my father's oldest brother, and I also have a collector who might be interested in purchasing my car."

"You would sell your car to pursue this study?" Eisenberg was impressed.

Josef's still-functioning East German made Trabant now had value as a relic. "Even without selling my car, I should have enough in my pocket to feed myself and pursue this for a while."

"Well, you can always buy a new car." Eisenberg paused and thought for a second, "Perhaps I have a bit of cash that I've stuck in my desk drawer here for such an occasion and I can add that to your funds."

Eisenberg reached into his middle desk drawer and pulled out an old leather billfold. It was full of big bills, what looked like a great deal of money. "Here. You'll need this."

Josef was stunned. He had totally misread this man. "Thank you sir, but I cannot take this."

"Why not? I keep putting money in here with the hope of someday chasing some big piece of yet un-documented history. In all the years I have been teaching, I think that your theory is the closest that I've come to that. I want you to have it for your work. You can give me back what's left when you finish your thesis, and thank me when you get a prize for your historical research someday."

Eisenberg forced the wallet on his student and Josef clutched it to his chest with a heartfelt look of thanks on his face. "I want you to have it."

"Sir, I so greatly appreciate your support." Josef stood motionless in Eisenberg's office, simply stunned by the old man's personality shift.

"Good. Now go ahead and make history yourself!"

July 8, 2001

10:30 a.m., New York City

"Amazing, just amazing!" Grover folded the Sunday Times onto his lap and looked at his wife. "This kid in Mississippi had his arm bitten off by a shark. They found the shark, killed it, retrieved the kid's arm and sewed it back on!"

"Are you commenting on the progress of medical science?" Ellen smiled at her husband, "Or are you just reading out loud?"

"No… uh … just sharing that story with you."

"Thanks for sharing." Ellen was used to Doug's random readings from the newspaper and most of the time she humored him about her lack of interest in any of it, but this time she was mildly annoyed. Ellen was seated across their living room involved in a novel. Doug's interruption made her lose her place.

"Oh, you're reading, sorry. 'Just thought you'd be interested."

"Normally I would be, but I'm reading."

"Yeah, oh, sorry again." Doug made a faint smile, but continued anyway. "What amazed me was that they caught the shark and got the kid's arm back. You may think this is a stretch, but that is some amazing police work."

Ellen closed the cover on her book and stared at her husband. Doug's mention of the words police work triggered the next response.

"I'm very impressed that you can find a link to police work in every aspect of your life. The thing is, honey, you are retired and you are no longer doing that for a living. I no longer have to worry about you the way I did years ago when you left for work each day or night."

"I know that. You don't have to worry about me anymore. I'm retired, but I'm not dead."

That sent Ellen over the top. She had not brought it up earlier, but the topic was simmering in her head for the past week.

"You could have been dead a few days ago with that mugger. Robert says that the guy had a police record for nearly beating someone to death for no reason. He could have built on that record with you!"

Her voice level rose in rapid increments, "You had no business fighting with that guy. You are not a cop anymore!"

"What was I supposed to do? He was trying to rob me! I was not going to stand there and allow him to take anything that was mine."

"And if he tried to stab you with that knife he had? Then what? I would have been an instant widow."

"That is not going to happen. When I go it'll be because you poisoned me or something." Doug made a joke and immediately regretted it.

"Honey… I want you to promise me that you will no longer take cop-style risks." Ellen was as angry as he had ever seen her. "You're not a kid anymore and I like having you around too much for you to get killed doing a job that you're no longer getting paid for. Do you understand me?"

Doug knew she had him backed into a corner. He stared at her for a long moment and quietly responded, "I get you. I understand. I will be more careful."

She didn't stop. "Careful is not what I'm going for here! If you're at the corner deli buying a candy bar while some jerk comes in to rob the place, what are you going to do?"

Doug sighed, "I'm going to step back and raise my hands in the air and tell the guy which pocket my wallet is in."

Ellen recognized the passive-aggressive sarcasm in Doug's response but took the statement as a pledge. "Good. That's it. Now I want to read my book."

Doug stared at her for a moment and understood that she was frightened about the thought of a future without him. Both had aged together in a nice way. No disease, no trauma and Doug had no idea how long either one of them would be here. He would have to be careful and keep his nose clean at the risk of upsetting her.

"I got ya. No more heroics, I promise." Using Tim Murphy's longevity as a yardstick, he figured they could both be around for a considerable length of time and she wanted to make sure he was there for all of it. But, he also knew that there was too much going on in the world for him to totally withdraw his attention.

She didn't raise her glance from the open book on her lap, "Thank you."

He went back to the Sunday Times and pretended to read, but what was now in his mind was the conversation he had with Robert a few days earlier. There was chatter in the air and Robert's sources at the CIA had warned the FBI that as of the first of the month, something was in the works. The U.N. General Assembly would bring the world's diplomats together in a concentrated area of Midtown Manhattan in September, and Robert's concern was that a few bad actors could turn the event into total chaos. Yes, he had just promised his wife to keep safe, but as a cop he wanted to make sure none of that bad stuff would be allowed to happen, and as a parent he wanted to spare his son the angst something like that would cause to his boy.

July 9, 2001

11:13 a.m., Koblenz, Germany

"Fraulein," Josef shifted his eyes from the young woman's bosom and pretended that he was attempting to read her nametag, "Uh, Fraulein Schneider, would you be able to help me a bit?" *Ah, another siren with keys to my treasure!* Josef put on the most appealing smile he knew how to make. The result was as he expected. The attractive young blonde clerical functionary turned her eyes on his and locked in. *How come all the women in these places look like this?*

"Yes," she beamed back, "what can I do for you?"

"I'm a graduate student at the Goethe University in Frankfurt and I'm doing some research for my dissertation. I could use your help."

The words research and dissertation seemed to ring undefined in her brain, but then she nodded, "Um hmm, yes?"

This treasure was different from the archival library that sent him on his present journey. Josef had entered another whole new world, the repository of all German military personnel records dating back to the Franco-Prussian war of 1870. It was an amazingly rich store of data that told the backstories of long dead soldiers and their struggles in whatever wars they were involved, and there had been quite a few. The attractive young girl with whom he was speaking sat alone in a four walled cubicle, there to help whomever came in to find lost relatives, pension records or, as in Josef's case, links to history. He was alone with yet another gatekeeper to his research goals. This one, he thought, was a lot prettier than his new friend Mendelsohn.

"I am told that this is the repository for all of the German navy's enlistment records from the Second World War?" Josef smiled wider.

"Actually sir, this archive has access to all German military records, army, navy and otherwise," she corrected him.

The sound of her voice did something odd to him and made the hairs on the back of his neck tingle slightly. The sound complemented the visual. Josef noted that Fraulein Schneider's slim torso was neatly packed into a tight white blouse that was crisply tucked into a just-above-the-knees, dark blue skirt. While trying to maintain a professional distance he was suddenly struck by her perfect features. In previous similar encounters he had always been able to turn off his primal uges during the pursuit of the academic, but now it mystified him as to why his scholarly self was suddenly aching for this total stranger, a mere clerical worker, but so it was. What was unusual this time, was that his desire was getting worse at a pace far quicker than it ever did. He was beginning to sweat.

Josef's thinking rapidly deteriorated into heat and he lost track of what he was saying. He also lost control of his eyes as they drifted their focus down over her breasts and then to her smooth legs. His imagination took over after that. *Stop it! I am not a sex fiend! Damn, what is wrong with me?*

She noticed that he was looking at her legs and seemed to take the cue by momentarily uncrossing and re-crossing her thighs giving him a fleeting glimpse up her skirt and the darkness beyond. "Yes sir, this is the place," she smiled provocatively.

"Uh, yes." His train of thought was totally gone and he turned his eyes to his written notes to get himself back to business. "Uh, yes, for my dissertation, I'm looking for the enlistment records of a German naval officer, a Kapitänleutnant named Horst Wenzl who served as an adjutant for Admiral Wilhelm Canaris from roughly 1939 to 1943. I would like to know what became of him following his enlistment in the Kriegsmarine... uh, at the end of the Second World War." Josef said the words and then forced his eyes to leave her body to evaluate his surroundings.

"Canaris," she asked?

"No, no, Wenzl, he worked for Canaris." *Too bad, all that sexuality with absolutely no knowledge of history.* "His name is Wenzl."

"Very good. Let me search." She turned her back to him and faced her computer terminal.

Now he had a view of her back and smooth neck. Her white blouse was sheer enough that he could clearly see the ghostly lines of her bra straps and an essence of her pink skin tone underneath. *Control yourself, you moron!* After just a few minutes in the presence of Fraulein Elsie Schneider, Josef was totally lost. The worldly doctoral candidate was turned into a quivering mass of desire. He could analyze it all he wanted to, but the truth was that because of his all-consuming research, he hadn't been with a woman for over a year. The sexual depravation had finally taken its toll, unfortunately for him, at this very moment. *I really need to get focused here. Stop it!* "Shall I spell the name for you?"

"No sir, I know how to spell it. I have cousins who are Wenzl's." Her fingers raced over the keyboard abetted by her complete knowledge of the archival catalog on which she was working. In short order she had pulled up twenty-six records of Wenzls who had done service in the Kriegsmarine from 1925 until 1945. "What did you say was this officer's first name?"

"He is Horst, Horst Wenzl."

She typed some more, and then some more after that. "Hmm... odd... unusual."

"What is?"

She beckoned him to come closer to her side of the desk so that he could view the monitor screen better. Worried about his self-control, he paused a second, but then went closer anyway. "Yes? What's the problem?" *Damn, she smells good too!*

"There are thirty-two Wenzl's who served in the navy during that wartime period. Funny, I think I actually may be related to them in some distant way, ha ha!" Her laugh slightly relieved his unease in her presence. "There are actually three Horsts listed here. One served as a cook on the heavy cruiser *Prinz Eugen*. The other one was a naval tugboat captain in Bremen in 1918 but the third one at a Kapitänleutnant's rank has nothing listed at all on his service record. Just his name, nothing else?" She pouted slightly. "There has to be more. This is unacceptable."

Ah, that German desire for complete documentation of everything. Josef drew closer to her and his knee accidently touched hers. He actually thought he had experienced an electrical shock from the contact as they stared together at the Wenzl record. Even to a layman the screen page was unusual. There was nothing more than the man's rank, Kapitänleutnant, his name, a place and date of birth, 5 April 1917 - Dresden. There was nothing more. "Hmm? He would be 84 now."

"Yes, that is true, but there is something wrong with all of this. Look at this." She became less interested in flirting with him and more interested in the implications of this imperfect record in the database. "Without all the details, this name should not be in this database. Before making an entry all the information needs to be complete before it can be input." It was turning out that Fraulein Schneider, whatever one might assume about her intellect, was a professional and was now confronting a dilemma unusual in her experience.

"What does this mean?"

"It means that starting in 1990, a year after the wall came down and paper records from both East and West became one, all of the old paper records from the Kriegsmarine were entered to the computerized archival system. It is apparent that someone either neglected to include, or erased Herr Wenzl's details."

"You mean on purpose?" Josef asked.

"I can only guess at that. One thing I am able to see is that his file has been visited a number of times since the input date. On paper it was viewed in 1961, then in 1974, and after the data was entered in the computer in 1991 and most recently about six years ago in 1995."

"That's odd, who would be looking for him so long after the war?"

"Maybe relatives searching for pension money. If he died in the war they would be receiving money, and of course if he was living he would be on a pension."

"Does this list any relatives?"

"No, the rest of the file is blank." She let out a sigh and the erotic sound of it blew oxygen on his smoldering lust. "As I scroll down all of these names you will notice that every one of them is complete. There are records of births, deaths, marriages, postings, battles and whatever there is to know about all of these men who fought for Germany for over a century. Yet, this one man is just listed by name, place and date of birth." She leaned back in her chair and stared into his eyes. "This is odd, isn't it?"

"Yes, truly very odd."

"The only time I have seen this before is with some of the rocket scientists."

"Huh? What about them?"

"After the war the Soviets and the United States scrambled to gather up as many of the German rocket scientists as they could. The scientists had the information about how the V-2 was built. Both sides were gearing up for the cold war."

"Yes?" Josef was surprised that this object of his repressed desire actually seemed to know something about history.

"When I first came to work here I did an exercise for myself to better understand the computer system. I searched for Werner Von Braun, Fritz Mueller and Krafft Ehricke, the names of the men I head learned about in school." She sighed for a moment, "…and each one that I searched in the system came up like this man."

"No other records? Just their names?"

"Exactly. I then searched the names of men who were being sought by Interpol and the Israelis as war criminals. It was the same result."

"Someone went through all these records and removed details?"

"They didn't just remove details, they removed everything."

"Why do you think this happened?"

"I think that a number of these men went into hiding after the war and may have assumed new identities."

"But who did the editing on the records? Who had access to all of this?"

Elsie Schneider turned to him with her palms firmly placed on her knees as if she was telling a story to a young child, "I would guess that it was the same people who gave them all new identities. These files have been accessible to many people over the years. Any alteration could have been made by some old Nazi cronies who got away after the war and were working for the new German government, or it could be foreigners. No one will ever really know. It is done. That's it."

"So… does this mean we'll never know what became of Herr Wenzl?"

"Yes, and no." She smiled at him with a kind of confidence that hinted of a solution to his problem. "There are still paper records on all of these men. We could go and look through them. But, it would take some time."

We could go? He was suddenly overwhelmed by her use of the word "we." "Yes!" He was unable to think of anything more to say. This woman, who had so besieged his senses, was also clever. What was even more exciting to Josef is that she appeared to be interested in him as well. *What to do? He would need to ask for her phone number so that he could suggest that they could work together. Oh, but if he got involved with any woman now what would happen to his doctorate?* His mind began to race. *What would happen to my plan for teaching and living the comfortable life of an academic? There is so much I have to do. I cannot get involved now, but I need her for any and all of this.* He looked at her for a long moment pretending to be thinking about Wenzl, but in actuality regretting the inability to immediately get her into bed. He shrugged. "So, what do WE do next?"

She was two steps ahead of him, and equally attracted to the young man before her. He was unlike most other government functionaries who offer only the minimum of contact. She thought quickly about a way to stay involved with him. "If you like, sir, I could help you in your search for this officer." She quickly came up with a clear and logical reason for moving their relationship forward on a professional level. "You know, it isn't good that there is an unfinished record in our computer file."

"Well, thank you Fraulein Schneider. I really appreciate that."

"You can call me Elsie."

"Thank you, Elsie. And, please don't call me sir. My name is Josef." Josef had no idea how fortunate he was that she had offered to help him. It would go way beyond their physical attraction to one another, and it would change both of their lives from that moment on.

"Josef… good. I know just the places we can look."

July 10, 2001

11:00 a.m., Riverdale, The Bronx, New York

"Boyo! Glad you came!" Murphy was in the TV room standing by the window.

"Hey, Murph!" Grover eyed his elder partner and friend. A month earlier Murphy appeared weak and frail. Now he was on his feet and Grover immediately noticed that there was no walker in sight. "Livin' on the wild side are we?"

"Whatcha mean?"

"Where's your walker? You wanna end up with a broken hip around this place?"

"What if I tell you that I haven't used that walker in two weeks? Just a cane now."

"Really? How come?"

"Well, this lady I met here, I think I mentioned her to you last time…"

"Oh yeah… the one who invited you to her room?"

"Mmm yeah. That one…. Her name's Ida. Ida Goldstein."

"So, what did she do to you, steal your walker and your wallet?"

Murphy smiled broadly. "I'm not gonna dignify any of that with a response, but just let's say that Ida has changed what's left of my life."

"Oh?"

"First of all she's younger than you… not by much, but she's still, ya know…."

"I don't know, but I can guess."

"Anyway, she convinced me to go to physical therapy with her in the gym here. It's hard to believe, but since I started going a few weeks ago, and I go every day now, I'm able to get around with just a cane. I actually feel much stronger."

"That's terrific!"

"Yeah, and it also makes it easier for me to get to her room when I want." Murphy laughed out loud, despite his age he still had a randy twinkle in his eye.

Grover let out a loud ha ha! "Great to hear that you're going to the gym. It really helps me too."

"Oh yeah!" Murphy lifted his right arm and pointed his index finger at his guest. "The gym! I read that article about you in the News this weekend. You goddamn took down a perp on the sidewalk outside the gym!"

" 'Wasn't that big a deal." Grover played down the incident.

"Yeah, you're a hero again! And I can tell everyone in this place that I know you. What is it, you're 83 years old and you took down a 25-year-old scumbag with a knife?"

"He had the knife, not me."

"Yeah, you know what I mean," Murphy chuckled.

"Like I said, it was not a big deal and no one would have ever known about it or cared."

"So afterward did you call the *News* and tell them?"

"Of course not. After it was over and I went home, minding my own business. The Captain in the two-oh called Robert and told him. Then I got the call from the reporter, and then I got the flak from Ellen, Robert and the grandkids."

"Flak? Why?"

"They all worry that I could have been killed. That the guy could have taken me down."

"Boy-o, the only guy I ever saw take you down was that guy who threw you off a fire escape, and look what happened to him!"

"Yeah, that's what I said, but I've been getting a lot of grief and worry from all of them. Robert wants me to give up my piece. No more trips to the range. He wants me to lay off all my cop thinking."

"That'll never happen." Murphy's look turned serious. "Listen to me Boy-O, I only wish I was in your shoes when I was your age. Maybe I could have kept my strength and health better than I did so I didn't have to end up in a place like this. You tell your boy that he should be happy his dad is healthy enough to still do the cop stuff."

Doug let out a deep sigh, "Yeah, you're right, but so is Robert. What if that bastard had stabbed me and I either died or became incapacitated? Ellen would be all alone. Not good at all."

"I get it, but as I've learned sitting here in God's little waiting room, you never know when it's your time. You gotta be who you gotta be."

"I agree, but I am going to think about dealing with stuff differently. I worry about Ellen if I'm not here."

"Ha, if you're dead and if she comes to a place like this one, she'll find some other guy and do just fine." Murphy smiled a mischievous grin.

"Thanks partner. You always know how to make me feel better."

"Hey, you're welcome," Murphy smiled and quickly changed the subject. "So did you bring me any more crossword books? I finished the last one yesterday."

"You finished it? When do you have time to do all those damn crosswords? There were 250 of them in that book."

"I sit on a couch with the widow Goldstein and we do them together. She likes doing crosswords. Remember, they are not a test of knowledge they are....

"...I know, they are puzzles. Puzzles are not a test of knowledge, they need to be solved not answered. When you get five across, you have the first letter of five down. I know, I know."

"Yes and no. Yes, you're right about the puzzle aspect of doing them, glad you were paying attention all those years. And, no, they are not a test of knowledge at this moment, they are a magnet for cozying up to Ida. She loves to sit with me while I do them. She says they get her into a mood."

"Mood?" Doug raised a puritanical eyebrow. "You should stop taking that Viagra stuff. If you keep going like this it's gonna kill ya."

"We all gotta go some time." Murphy smiled. "I'll tell you what. You keep chasing bad guys and I'll keep chasing Mrs. Goldstein. 'Fair deal?"

"I'm not sure that is a fair deal."

"So tell me, how's Robert doing?"

Now the conversation turned serious. "Well, I'm worried about him."

"What kind of a family do you have? Everyone is worried about everyone else?"

"I worry because the FBI director is a really tough boss and at times he asks Robert for too much. The kid is really stressed out at work."

"Doug, he's what, in his fifties? He's not a kid. He's the boss of the friggin' FBI office. Stress is part of the job."

"Yeah, I suppose, but I can't help it. He's my kid."

"Gotcha. I understand completely." Murphy slowly lowered himself into the armchair across from the TV. Doug sat down in the chair next to him. "Ya know, all you can do is to be there for him. He didn't get to where he is all by himself. Your advice along the way got him to where he is. It's like in *The Godfather*, you're his consigliore."

"Aside from my wife who wants me to join the rubber gun squad, I don't think he needs an old guy telling him how to do his job."

"You're looking at it the wrong way, Boy-o. There've been bad guys forever, and there have been good guys on the other side. You've handled all different kinds of bad guys. You know how to do that much better than most. Your experience could be something helpful to him. You don't gotta take a bullet, but you gotta be there for him. Don't pull back."

Grover sat quietly and mulled over what his partner just said. Doug the husband didn't want to worry his wife, but Doug the father had other issues. He had always been there during Robert's rise in the Bureau and he knew first-hand that his son had as good instincts as any cop he ever met, yet there were those moments lately that it seemed like Robert was emotionally awash in an incoming tide of doubt. It was only recently that he noticed that Robert was sharing even more than he ever had before. Maybe he was no longer on the job, but Douglas Grover still had many decades of experience that could be of use.

"Whatcha thinkin' about, Boy-o?" Murphy broke the silence.

"I think you could be right for the first time in your life."

"I appreciate the compliment. Coming from you it's a miracle." Murphy smiled. "What am I right about for the first time in my life?"

"Truth is that I can't give it up. Ever."

"Yeah, so what?"

"So if some schmuck comes at me with a knife again I'm gonna try to take it away from him."

" 'Sounds like you got a new plan for your life now. End it with a bang, huh?" Murphy joked.

"I'm going to help Robert do his work and if I get killed in the process Ellen will meet another nice Jewish guy right here at the Hebrew Home."

"Sometimes you amaze me, Boy-o."

"Sometimes I amaze myself."

10:07 a.m., Frankfurt, Germany

Rolf Penn sat alone at a cafeteria table nursing his cup of coffee and reading the newspaper. It was roughly a month after the disco bombing in Tel-Aviv and the Israeli official investigative report of the incident had hit the world press. Wednesday's edition of *Frankfurter Allgemeine* included an investigative article about the event. The story took almost a full page and told the background tale of a lone suicide bomber along with a chronological account of his whereabouts until he detonated his lethal explosives. There were interview snippets from eyewitnesses to the carnage. *Ah, the struggle that humanity experiences to upend the ruling order*, he thought to himself. *Too bad that a body count is the only way to make change.*

Professor Eisenberg emerged from the cafeteria line and entered the main dining area. His eyes searched the room for a place to sit. Eisenberg's two hands firmly balanced a tray carrying a large white ceramic mug filled with coffee, a glass of orange juice and a piece of flaky pastry. Bulging out from under his left arm was a small stack of manila file folders. One wrong step and everything would be all over the floor. When he noticed a table near the exit door where Rolf Penn was sipping a cup of coffee and reading a newspaper, he smiled. Eisenberg was always looking for an opportunity to gloat to Penn about his work. Perfect, he thought. He approached the seated man, "Rolf, may I join you?"

"Of course," Penn smiled invitingly although in reality he would have preferred to be left alone. "Taking a break?"

"Yes, just a quick break." Eisenberg was feeling good. What better way was there to abet a good mood than spending a moment or two bragging to one's rival? He gently placed the tray on the table without spilling a drop of the steaming liquid and he laid the folders on the empty chair next to him and sat down. With a deep exhale he reached for a sugar packet and lamented with some glee in his voice, "Well, I've been very busy since we last spoke a few weeks ago."

"Oh?"

"Yes, guiding my student on his thesis research is taking a lot of my time." This was of course a lie, but Eisenberg enjoyed the posturing. "I am reasonably sure that if the details of the Canaris plot in the States will be found and, as you said, my student will not only have a doctoral thesis, but a best-selling book as well." Eisenberg smiled with a look of ownership of the entire project.

Penn did not want another sparring match. "Good for him, I wish him well in his research." He then pretended to forget what the entire story was all about. "What was that research again?"

"You remember, the possibility that a Wehrmacht sabotage effort made it to the U.S. and got very close to doing something very bad," Eisenberg seemed to delight with his sparsest explanation of the details.

"Ah, of course, yes I do remember." As much as Eisenberg seemed to dislike Penn, Penn liked Eisenberg even less. Still, a veneer of professional cordiality hid all that. "Have you learned any more about what was the Canaris diary?"

"Hmmm, no, nothing new. It is written in a cryptic way. The man wrote in euphemisms and images. It's almost a code that needs to be deciphered." Eisenberg lied. He knew exactly what was written in the diary and the absolute goal of the Wolfgang mission, but he could only guess at the details of its implementation. Understanding the plan was one thing, but everything else about it remained a mystery and would still need to be gleaned from other sources or by cross referencing the hand-written diary with other documents.

"One thing that occurred to me at the time you first told me the story, is the question of how this qualifies as research for a doctoral dissertation? Where is the academic research that leads to an original conclusion? Without research all of this will end up reading more like a cheap detective novel, not original academic research?"

So this is what he's thinking! Yes, yes, yes he's still jealous! "Oh I think all of that will be covered in detail when my student and I work out the form of his final document." Eisenberg was sensing something about Penn that seemed more disingenuous than before. Yet, they sat together sipping coffee in a collegial way. Their feelings toward each other wouldn't have been obvious to anyone watching because both of them behaved outwardly with great self-control that hid their mutual level of cordial contempt.

Penn changed the subject, "Did you read this account of the bombing in Tel Aviv last month?"

"Yes. Awful business. Crazy."

"Not so crazy, I think, more a clash of societies. One brave man fighting and giving his life against an enemy culture."

"Are you calling a suicide bomber who indiscriminately kills a bunch of civilians a brave man?"

"Yes, perhaps I think his was a brave gesture to show his love of his people. He surrendered his own life for the good of his beliefs. For all of humankind's progress in science, philosophy and ethics we remain a tribal world. We fight when our tribe is threatened. I suppose that I could agree with the idea that one man's bravery is another's treason, but the actor in any dramatic gesture made for the protection of his people is brave to my mind." Penn's blue eyes stared directly at Eisenberg's as if in a challenge. "There are times when things that may have been unthinkable eventually became the deciding moments for the great watersheds of history."

"Bravery? You call that bravery? At this point in human development we should be beyond this craziness. This one man's insanity led to the carnage of innocents."

"They are not innocent if they are complicit in the actions of a brutal culture."

"So we've learned nothing since the Code of Hammurabi? An eye for an eye? So you think that killing innocent people is the road to progress?"

"It is *a* road. Maybe not the only road, but terrorism could be a quicker road that ends years of suffering for millions. What was it that Robespierre said more than two centuries ago about terror? "Terror is nothing other than justice, prompt, severe, inflexible; it is therefore an emanation of virtue.""

Eisenberg didn't know how to respond other than blurting out, "Robespierre was insane."

"That insanity was what overthrew the tyrannical French monarchy and allowed a democracy to emerge," Penn shot back.

As historians, both men were theoretically pledged to honest analysis without taking sides, yet this was something deeper. The genteel luster of an ivory tower post of observation was supposed to temper the emotional passions of those involved in chronicling history, yet neither of these men was a neutral observer. Eisenberg knew that Penn spent a lot of time in North Africa and perhaps developed some ego-involvement with that continent's ethos, but Penn's political views had never before come up in any conversations and now the older academic was both surprised and appalled by his fellow educator's remarks. Out of discomfort with where this conversation was headed, he tried to end this subject. After a lengthy pause Eisenberg sighed, "Sadly it seems that bombs are always the method in conflict."

Penn also became uncomfortable discussing his political views with this adversarial colleague, and changed the subject back to a less controversial one, their earlier sparring. "So, speaking of bombs, how is the search for those Abwehr documents going?"

"Ah yes, it's going well. My student continues his research for corroboration of his original theory."

"You still haven't mentioned what he is looking for?" Penn was smiling, though his smile had a chill to it. "Is it still such a big secret? Are you afraid I will write a book about it first?"

Eisenberg, ever the realist, sighed. "I am less concerned about that and more concerned that there will be nothing there to find."

"You know, my mind has been working since you mentioned this last time."

"Really? How so?"

Penn leaned back with exaggerated nonchalance centering his coffee cup on his chest between his two hands. "I actually did some research myself out of curiosity."

Eisenberg tried not to react lest he give anything away, he simply followed with a question, "Operation Pastorius... yes, and...?"

"Well, from my casual research and what we talked about last time, I think if this is more than just conjecture, I think that it all wasn't just about some saboteurs placed ashore in the U.S. to create arbitrary damage to wartime factories and railroads. I have a sense that their mission would have been much bigger. My sense is that the goal of this Operation Pastorius was something on a grander scale, an effort by the Wehrmacht to bring the Americans quickly to their knees. Hmmm?"

Penn's armchair analysis and reasoning was getting very close to the Josef Durmaz theory and the professor feared that Penn had somehow developed an insight into the student's research. He was afraid that Penn might use that insight to short-circuit the academic impact of the final thesis. The older historian hedged his reaction and tried not to reveal his anxiety, "I don't know the details yet, but I suppose this is something we will find out in time."

Eisenberg felt the urge to get up and leave the table. *Penn was digging, but why? Surely he would not attempt to hijack the thesis project. Or would he? That would be total academic suicide for him. Is he trying to one-up me? What is going on? What does he know for fact?* There was a look on Penn's face that Eisenberg could only describe as sinister. Eisenberg averted his eyes and stared at a calming Matisse print on the cafeteria wall.

"What's your student's name again? I want to make sure I keep up with his research. It's of huge interest to me," Penn teased in a feigned professional manner.

"I don't believe I did mention his name, but it is Durmaz, Josef Durmaz," Eisenberg reluctantly offered.

"Durmaz. Hmm. Not a German name? I will remember it. I'm hoping to see great work from Herr Durmaz, or probably Doktor Durmaz." Penn smiled, took a sip of his coffee and placed the cup back on the table never once losing eye contact with Eisenberg.

The remainder of the cafeteria break was spent in silence. When Eisenberg finished his last bite of pastry and sip of coffee he stood up to leave, "Well,

I must go. Nice to chat with you Rolf." Of course, that wasn't at all true. Eisenberg headed for the doors.

Pausing for only a moment, Penn noticed that Eisenberg had forgotten his stack of file folders. He reached over to pick them up and was about to make an effort to hail his coffee partner to come back for the papers. Then he noticed the thickest folder on top was labeled "Durmaz." Penn decided to return the files to Eisenberg a little bit later, after he had time to read through everything first.

10:15 a.m., Koblenz, Germany

Josef Durmaz and his new girlfriend, Elsie Schneider, pulled up in the parking lot of the non-descript Federal German Storage Warehouse located a few kilometers due south of the Koblenz wartime archives building. To say that the warehouse was non-descript was not an exaggeration. The plain concrete walled structure sat unmarked and unknown amid much larger and sprawling commercial structures all around it. Elsie and Josef had been on the trail of the missing Horst Wenzl files for several days when Elsie tracked down the last officially known site of the original material stored on paper. This warehouse was the end of that trail.

Josef had not yet sold his car. Eisenberg's cash infusion to the cause, combined with his spare savings, allowed him to put that off for a while. They parked the aging 1971 Trabant 601 under a weed-like tree in the otherwise vacant parking lot alongside the building. Josef got out and slammed his door hard, the only way it would stay shut. "It doesn't look like there's anyone here."

The car's 1960's-era zeitgeist fit the surroundings and invoked memories of his youth. The Trabant was a treasure handed down from father to son as less of an heirloom than the handing off of an albatross. This vestige of the Communist-era manufacture of automobiles in East Germany was still, somehow, running. The Trabant was the East German idea of a family car, but for what kind of a family? It was built with very little power under the hood, a two-cycle engine that on a good day could generate a staggering 26 horsepower. It's gas and oil fuel mixture burned freely with no pollution controls of any kind. It carried four passengers with the added threat of a gasoline tank mounted directly over the hot engine block. One small leak could lead to disaster and it often did. But the good thing about the Trabant was that it was affordable for some of those who lived on the wrong side of the Iron Curtain and wanted things that people in the West took for granted. With the reunification of Germany more than a decade old, the

Trabant assumed a new role. It was a car that was cheap to maintain on a student's budget. But nothing could hide the fact that while the Trabant had doors and four wheels, it was built more like a riding lawn mower.

Josef watched Elsie get out of the car. Taking her cue from Josef, she slammed her door with the same force. The sound it made jolted her and she looked across the car at him and smiled sheepishly, worrying she had damaged his ride. He smiled back with a no-harm-done kind of look. While they had talked on the phone in preparation for this excursion, this was the first time they had seen each other since the day they met in her office cubicle. Josef was again feeling that uneasy stirring in his loins, and she was feeling something similar, yet neither said a word about it. She was wearing a tight pair of jeans and a loose short sleeved blue blouse that was gathered into her slim waist. As she turned and started walking toward the door, he followed behind her, the perfect vantage point for him to stare at her body without her noticing.

At the door an older security guard met them. The man was unkempt, noticeably flabby, and wore a uniform shirt with a large area of color just below the name tag pinned to his pocket. From a distance, the color looked like an official badge, but up-close it revealed itself to be detritus from a recent encounter with a sausage, mustard and sauerkraut. All in all, he was not much of a guard, but sufficient to protect this backwater of forgotten bureaucracy.

The guard asked for identification. Elsie pulled out her government ID card and without a second glance he waved them into the building. *So much for security*, Josef thought. All that appeared before them was a long and empty corridor. "Do you have any idea where we have to go?"

"Yes, I've actually been here before, once." She looked from left to right to get her bearings and then quickly began walking down the corridor with an air of certainty. All Josef could do was follow along and enjoy staring at her ass.

Some eighty feet down the hallway they arrived at a double door. An open padlock hung on the hasp and Elsie effortlessly pushed one side open. The portal revealed an enormous cavern full of boxes. Everywhere they could see, from floor to ceiling, were metal shelves filled with file boxes of different shapes and sizes, boxes loaded with tons of paper information now on the way to a state of obsolescence, due to digital archiving.

"I'm told that in a year or so all of this is going to be turned into recycled shopping bags and shipping cartons."

"Turning history into pulp," Josef sighed. If he had the time he would have liked to explore all these records of peoples' lives. There's so much history to be told by simply reading between the lines.

While Elsie was excited to have met Josef, she was also excited to work on this project with him, and was earnest in her quest for results. "We can start here. These storage boxes are in alphabetical order. This area here is the "W's." Elsie pointed to a sign on the wall above the highest shelf it showed a big letter "W". There were many, many cartons in the section, cartons that held a paper file on every single soldier and sailor whose last name began with a "W" and had served in the German army and navy from the First World War until 1945.

Josef looked at the boxes and then shifted his glance to Elsie. He had already decided for himself that at the end of this day he would be spending the night with her. That was that, but for now he valiantly tried to put his ardor on hold as he approached the stack directly in front of him. "Thank God for the alphabetization."

Perhaps as a tease, or maybe simply blind luck, the box immediately facing him was labeled "Kriegsmarine: Wenstrom – Welz". It seemed too good to be true. Wenzl would have to be in this box, the very first one he looked at! The carton was securely placed under four other cartons of equal size. Carefully, they worked together to remove it from its stack and Josef lugged it over to a table in the center of the room. For a moment he stared at it. "Look at this… this is odd, isn't it? An English label alongside the German one, 'Navy: Wenstrom to Welz'. Why is that?"

"That is odd," she said. "Do any of the other boxes over there have the same labeling?"

Josef walked back to the stacks and a gave them a once-over. "No, none of the others that I can see have any English on them."

"Odd, hmmm." She stopped him as he started to open the sealing tape. "I think that I am the only one of us legally allowed to do that." She found a scissor in the metal table drawer and used one blade to slice open the tape. "You know, you never told me why you were searching for this man Wenzl."

"He was a witness to history. He may have shared stories with his family or friends that I can learn. In a perfect world if he is still alive I could get his eye-witness account in person to confirm the authenticity of the diary left behind by his boss, Admiral Canaris. I really need to talk with him if he is living."

"Well, maybe you'll get lucky today." She winked at him as she removed the lid. There, neatly suspended on a hanging file rack inside were perhaps fifty yellowed manila folders in alphabetical order all with the tabs up and easily readable. In clear sight were a dozen or more folders all labeled "Wenzl."

"Well, there they are. Why do you think this man is still living?"

"I'm not so sure he is alive, but if he's still here he would be in his eight-ies now. I imagine that if he was lucky and survived up until now and I am lucky too, I might get a chance to interview him.

Elsie's hands went directly through the rack of folders. Five files down in the pile she found two that bore the name Horst Wenzl. "Oh god," she squealed, "this is so amazing. I can't believe we found him so quickly!" She tugged the files out of the hanging rack and her excitement became short lived. "It's not him. He isn't here!"

One folder was a First World War tugboat captain in Bremen and the other was a cook on the *Prinz Eugen*, but no file at all for the adjutant to Canaris. Elsie let out a deep sigh and then looked at all the remaining boxes on the metal shelves. All of a sudden the bright prospects of easily finding the correct Horst Wenzl became challenging. "Your man's file seems to be missing from this box."

Josef was still feeling positive. "Where could it be?"

"I don't know, but it is more than odd." Elsie turned her face toward him. Her mind was working out the details of a suspected scenario. "As his computer file exists, albeit without any details other than his birthplace and age, that inputted file would have come directly from this file box, but there is no file in this box."

"Someone removed his paper file either before or after it was placed here for storage?"

"Yes, it appears so," Elsie became pensive. She loved mysteries. She was a reader of Agatha Christie and now she channeled Miss Marple. "I think the same person who removed the file also was the person who put the English language label on the box."

"Someone who spoke English, not German," Josef's instinct led him to the same conclusion. "I would bet you're right."

"Yes, someone removed the file. Maybe even before these boxes were stored here." The rush of unexplained details momentarily stymied Elsie's organized mind.

Josef sat on the edge of the table and rubbed his chin. "There is something to this. When I began my research at the Bundesarchiv, the librarian there told me that right after the war, the allies grabbed all of the German wartime documents they could find. The Russians never returned the papers they took, but the Americans did. Maybe this was in the hands of the Americans and that's why there's an English label on the box."

"But, why this box out of all these boxes?"

"Because the Americans were interested in Wenzl. What if there was something about Horst Wenzl that singled him out to the Americans?"

"Yes!" You said that he was an adjutant to Canaris?"

"Hmm, yes?"

"What did this Canaris do?"

"He was the spymaster for the Wehrmacht. He ran the Abwehr."

Elsie became excited. "Then Horst must have known things that the British or the Americans needed to know after the war. Maybe they didn't want anyone else to find him and learn what he knew."

Josef was impressed with Elsie's detailed reasoning. While she may not have had the same formal education that he experienced, she was clearly as smart as a whip. "Good thinking! But what do we look for now? There's a missing file and no trail to find said file."

"Let's keep looking through this box and some others. It could be that the file was misplaced." Elsie was trying to be encouraging, but in her gut she knew that this was probably a futile exercise. Her hands sifted through the hanging files. She isolated all the Wenzls and laid them out on the table. There were twenty-six folders in all. The missing Horst was not among them.

They both stood there quietly trying to think of their next move. Finally Josef spoke, "I have an idea. We know that Horst was from Dresden. Maybe there is some other Wenzl who is from Dresden as well. It's a small chance, but maybe there is a living, distant family member who can lead us to Horst."

She beamed at him, impressed with his detective skills. Together, one by one, they opened twenty-five of the twenty-six folders. Some were from the Second World War and some were from other time periods. In all the cases not one Wenzl hailed from Dresden. Maybe one of these other Wenzls was a relative, but it would take years to track them all down. With a sense of disappointment looming, Elsie reached for the single remaining folder. She opened it and in a flash her eyes lit up. "Look, this one is also from Dresden!"

Josef leaned over her shoulder to examine the file. The motion brought him very close to her hair, so close that he unexpectedly inhaled a whiff of her perfume. It rattled him deeply. One more moment like that and he thought he would lose control of himself. As it was, he wanted to tear off her clothes right then, but he knew that he needed to focus on the matter in front of him. Her clothes can be removed later. The sober doctoral student took control of the human male body and forced its eyes onto the open folder. It contained some of the most detailed paperwork he had ever seen, the service record documents of one Hermann Wenzl from Dresden. Unlike Horst's missing files, these were complete with a level of detail that included lists of his inoculations, allergies, shoe size, dental records, postings and names of family members. When Hermann Wenzl joined the Kriegsmarine in 1943, he had just turned sixteen. Josef's eyes scanned the written facts before him, "Oh, my god!," he yelled.

"Amazing! This is amazing!" she agreed.

The documents clearly showed that Hermann Wenzl was a gunner's mate who saw action on a coastal patrol boat just before the end of the war. Listed among his relatives was an older brother who was also in the navy, whose name was Horst, a brother who worked in naval intelligence at a Kapitänleutnant's rank.

"Looks like Hermann is Horst's younger brother and he obviously survived the war! Look here, he has been receiving a pension up to the point when all the wartime papers were digitized, around ten years ago. He could be alive! He would just be in his seventies now. He could tell us what became of his big brother!"

"Wow!" His eyes shifted to stare directly into hers, "Will you help me find him?"

She gazed up at his face and immediately felt an overwhelming surge of warmth for him. Alone together in this abandoned dusty wastebasket of history, they were now on the trail of a mystery man. "Yes," she said, "I'll help you," and then threw her arms around his neck and kissed him hard, "… find whatever you're looking for." The rest of her words were unintelligible, mumbled in his ear as her hands groped to open his belt. "Yes, whatever you're looking for…."

July 21, 2001

7:40 a.m., Dresden, Germany

For Josef the nearly five-hour drive from Koblenz to Dresden seemed to fly by. Just having someone along for the ride eased the isolation he normally felt in his studies. *History is so much more enjoyable with a beautiful woman along for the ride!* Since Wednesday, when they got the scent of Hermann Wenzl, they found each other and then wasted no time in attempting to find him. Elsie scoured his naval records and discovered that up until four years ago Hermann was still living with his wife in an apartment on St. Petersburg Strasse in Dresden, his city of birth. The rest was simple detective work, really simple. She found his telephone number and with Josef listening alongside the earpiece, she called him. She told him that she was calling in her role as an employee of the German naval archives and asked if he would be willing to talk to an historian about his service in the navy. She embellished the story a bit and, without being specific, made it sound as if the interview would be a part of an official historical study that she was doing for the German government. On the telephone she told Herman that they were unable to meet him in Dresden until the weekend. "We have a number of others we are interviewing in places along the way to our visit with you."

Hermann seemed friendly and agreed. He told her that he was busy all day Saturday, but he would be home later in the evening and said that he was happy to speak with the historian whenever they arrived after that. So, on Friday night after work she and Josef hopped into the trusty, rusty Trabant and, at the car's top speed of 100 KPH, made the drive. They planned to spend the night somewhere along the way, see the sights in Dresden during the day on Saturday, and arrive at the Wenzl home after dinner, around eight.

The Second World War had taken a huge toll on Dresden. For centuries the city had been a hub of art, culture and learning, an academic and artistic bastion, but the war put an end to all that. Over a three-day period in February of 1945, American and British commanders sent more than 1,200 planes over Dresden, dumping more than 2,400 tons of high-explosive bombs and another 1,500 tons of incendiary bombs. The result was a gargantuan fire-storm that destroyed over ninety-five percent of the historic central part of the city and left 25,000 casualties. Following Germany's surrender to the allies, the city didn't fare much better. The Russians occupied Dresden and in post-war geopolitics it became part of the new DDR, and little was done to restore the city under Russian regime.

"How long do you think it will take to get to their apartment from here?" Josef asked his Elsie while at dinner.

"If you finish your dinner quickly we could be there in about twenty minutes, a bit after eight o'clock," Elsie smiled at him. The adventure with this new boyfriend had energized her to a point where any remnant of her bureaucratic self was suppressed. She was almost bubbly.

He smiled back at her, gulped down the last drop of his café au-lait and stood up. "Let's go!"

The drive from the restaurant took them to a six-story DDR socialist-era apartment complex not far from the shoreline of the Elbe. Though it looked institutional and drab, the dusky past-sunset skylight reflecting from the building's windows made the entire development look jewel-like in the gathering darkness, even beautiful. Josef found a visitor parking spot and slid into it. While the other cars in the lot were not Mercedes or BMW's, they were at least a few decades newer than his heap. This was the new East Germany. People had more money and there wasn't another, once ubiquitous, Trabant anywhere to be seen.

In the vestibule they rang the buzzer labeled "Wenzl – 6F." As with other communist era buildings, that meant it was on the ground level. Apartment 1F would have been on the top floor. Flicking on the hallway timed light switch, they made their way down the dingy corridor reading the alphabetically ascending door numbers. At the end of the hallway they found themselves in front of door "F." Josef looked somewhat nervous, but Elsie wasn't at all fretful. She reached up and rang the doorbell. Inside, the sound of a person walking slowly to the door got louder. A click of a few locks and the door opened. Josef almost couldn't conceal his surprise when he looked at the man.

"Hello, you are Fraulein Schneider? Please come in. I am delighted to be a part of your research." The elderly man was genuinely friendly.

Then, his wife appeared out of the kitchen and added to the greeting. "Yes, please come in. I've made some pastries and coffee. I hope you're not too full from dinner."

Josef Smiled for a long moment while Elsie put on the charm. "Thank you so much for seeing us tonight. We are truly sorry if we are imposing, but this is a very important historical study and we have a number of people with whom we are speaking."

Josef could not stop staring at Wenzl. He was trying to make sense of what he was seeing. For whatever reason, the younger brother of Wilhelm Canaris' adjutant, a wartime Nazi officer, assistant to the head of the Abwehr, Hermann Wenzl was wearing a kipah, the traditional cap worn by

Jewish males. Josef was so confused by the sight that he could not speak to ask a question.

Elsie could, "How was your day today, Herr Wenzl?"

"Quite nice, thank you. We just returned from shul at the end of Shabbos. Anyway, please come in and sit down. No need to do this by the door," Hermann joked.

Words finally started to come to Josef. "Very nice to meet you sir. I am Josef Durmaz. I am an historian and this is Fraulein Elsie Schneider from the military records office." They continued a line of stilted small talk as they entered a living room.

"Nice to meet you both. Please sit down. Klara, my wife, insists that you sample her pastry while we speak. Do both of you drink coffee?"

"Why, yes, thank you," Elsie spoke for them.

"Klara," Hermann yelled to the kitchen, "would you please make some coffee for these nice young people."

"I already did," came the reply.

They followed Hermann into his modest living room. It was painted a pale yellow, replete with overstuffed comfortable seating and decorated with photos, paintings and the memorabilia of a lifetime. Josef immediately noticed small items of Judaica on the *étagère* next to the window. He had to ask. "Sir, if I may ask without seeming rude, I am immediately struck that you served in Hitler's Kriegsmarine during the war and, please pardon my bluntness about this, but if I am not mistaken, you are a Jew?"

Wenzl smiled, "Yes, that's true. As a matter of fact I am the head rabbi in the new Dresden Synagogue a few blocks from here. It just opened this spring. That's why I was unable to meet with you until after the sunset on Shabbos."

Elsie sat back listening, but her public school education didn't allow her to grasp the full ironic nature of Josef's discovery. Josef was mildly flummoxed for a moment but then continued his questioning. "How is it that you, as a Jew, served in Hitler's navy?"

"The war was a difficult time for us all." Hermann lowered his body into a comfortable easy chair and he let out a deep exhale. "You see, I am the child of a Christian father and a Jewish mother. According to Jewish tradition… no, Jewish law, I am a Jew. My father was a military man who fought for Germany with the Kaiser. In a world of institutional anti-Semitism he was different, yet he was also a professional soldier and a loyal military man. He was fond of Hindenburg. As an historian you may know that the army supported Hitler when he threw out the leaders of the S.A, the brown shirts. The army leadership then threw its weight behind Hitler. My father was a soldier in that army and with his job we were always moving, billeted around the country. No one got to know us that well to know that we were Jews. Neither of my parents were at all religious and yet my father always respected my mother's religious beliefs. As he had no real religion of his own he encouraged her to raise my brother and I as Jews. When things started to get ugly in the late 1930's my father wisely told us to tell no one about our family's background. We simply were the Wenzl family from Dresden. No one knew otherwise. My older brother Horst even attended the naval academy and achieved some rank. He was schooled alongside some of Germany's most important naval figures of the time. Later he got a job at the side of a high ranking Nazi official and I followed in his footsteps a few years later."

A high ranking Nazi official indeed! I know exactly of whom you are speaking! "That is fascinating!" Josef was thrilled to meet this man. Not only was Hermann open about his history, a fascinating story, but he also acknowledged the existence of the mysterious Horst Wenzl. "What did you do in the navy?"

"Not much. I received some training as a gunner's mate, but I never got to sea. They sent me into a bunker in Berlin to work in a communications office for the general staff. I think I got that job because it was my brother's doing. He was in a position that made him able to move me away from the battles and to keep me safe from combat." Wenzl smiled and for a moment seemed to be lost in his memories. "My big brother probably saved my life." Hermann reached over to the shelf next to him and reached for a small framed black and white photo. "This is a picture of Horst just after his graduation from the naval academy."

Josef took the photo and stared at it. It was the photo of a fearsome looking young man in uniform. The thing that made him fearsome was a long scar on his cheek. "Handsome fellow!"

"Well, he was handsome, but that scar made him look like a monster. It was the result of a playful duel with another cadet that turned angry. Our mother nearly fainted when she saw him with it."

"You said that your brother worked for a high ranking somebody. Do you know for whom?"

"Yes, I do. He worked for Wilhelm Canaris, the head of the Abwher, the navy's espionage operation. Have you heard of him?"

Yes, yes, yes! Josef was almost unable to conceal a laugh so he coughed instead. "Yes, of course I have heard of him."

"That man was a merciless conniver and was responsible for many innocent deaths. My brother worked for him and with that job was also stuck in a bunker during the war." The old man then smiled broadly, "Incidentally, it turned out that Herr Canaris was a much more complicated figure as I later learned. In any case, I think it was our father who pulled strings to get

Horst in there."

"Fascinating! What became of your family after the war?"

"While Horst, that's my brother, and I were safe in Berlin, deep underground, and we simply surrendered to the Russians when they reached the city. My parents remained here in Dresden. In 1945 the Allies all but erased this city with bombs. The fires that resulted from the three-days-long attack turned it into a farrier's furnace, a firestorm." Wenzl drew another deep sad breath before he finished the thought, "I believe that my parents were incinerated in the flames."

Listening intently, Elsie seemed to tear up. "Oh my god, that is awful!"

"It was an awful time for the world as well."

Josef waited for Wenzl to offer up more information about Horst, but the old man had no more to say. Josef pried. He leaned forward from his position on the couch, "Is your brother still living? If so, do you think he also would speak with me about his experiences in the war?"

· Wenzl's face looked pained as he answered, "Yes, he is living, at least I think he is. We haven't spoken in many, many years. I only know that he is still alive because his pension comes to a bank account here in Dresden that I administer for him. I've been doing that for some years now."

"Pension?" Elsie's eyebrow flickered ever so slightly. The records in her computer showed no link to any pension payment to Horst Wenzl, and, in fact, it showed nothing at all about Horst Wenzl. *This man was being paid a pension with no link to his computer file. How odd!*

"Yes, I get one too. It's not much in my case, but it's a help. Horst's pension is a bit bigger than mine because he was at a higher rank. Each month I authenticate payment of funds to an American bank account somewhere. He has access to the money, but I don't know how. Really, the only indication I have that he is alive is that the balance on the account always shows a monthly withdrawal. Otherwise, that's the only contact we have any more."

"You had a falling out?"

"Yes, it was very bad. After the war, he was very secretive about what he was doing for this Canaris fellow. But as time went on he told me more and more. As I listened I was shocked that Horst appeared to have become a Nazi in spirit, you know, describing his work to me as 'we did this' and 'we did that'. Some of the things he described to me were horrible. I was also a part of the war machine, but I am comfortable in the thought that my actions probably didn't get anyone killed, at least not directly from my actions. I don't think I can say the same thing for Horst."

"You did what you needed to do to survive, I guess."

"Yes, I attempted to hide in plain sight; he did not. I worked as an office boy delivering memoranda and documents between departments. I know that also helped Hitler, but it was what I could rationalize as minimal involvement while preserving my own skin. While he, as a Jew, assisted Hitler in the attempted domination of the world."

"Surely he was also just trying to survive, like you?"

"No, I didn't know that. All I knew was that members of my mother's family were arrested by the Gestapo and never seen again. After the war, Horst told me that he probably could have saved our aunts, uncles and cousins, but it would have drawn attention to himself. Neither of us was selfless, but I think he was selfish. He didn't even try. He seemed to be bragging about that. I called him a coward and sometime later, his arrogance flipped a switch in my soul, and I couldn't stand being with him anymore. We had a big fight about it and it ended up with us no longer speaking to one another."

"Since...?"

"Since 1955."

"That's a shame, two brothers who no longer speak," Josef offered.

"Yes, we said very hurtful things to each other. Sometime later, a friend of his tried to bring us together again, but it didn't work. The man told me a story about what Horst had claimed had really been going on. Unfortunately, by that time Horst had moved away somewhere, I don't know where, and after the things I said to him, there was no going back. He would never accept my apologies, nor, probably, would I accept his. The last thing we ever spoke about was him asking me to administer his bank account. I only keep the account open in his name, but I really don't look at it."

"You have no idea where he is? You said he was somewhere in America?"

"I do have an idea."

"What did that friend tell you about what was 'really going on' with Horst?"

"I have cake!" Klara Wenzl entered the room with a loud interruptive flourish, a silver tray full with pastries and a small pot of coffee. "Please take. I am sorry, but I could not go shopping today. It's all that I had in the house." It was all she may have had, but it was enough for a crowd. Over the years the omnipresence of cake in the house had taken its toll on the formerly svelte Klara. Josef's eyes drifted from a framed black and white photo of a younger, bathing-suited Klara on the shores of a lake, to the now ample woman who had seemingly grown wider than her height over the years. He guessed it was the effect of tasting too many samples of her own baking. "Please take!"

"Thank you." Elsie leaned over the tray and dished out a thin slab of Sacher Torte to Josef and then herself. "Ooh! This is delicious. Where did you buy this?" She pretended to squeal a bit.

"Oh, no. I Didn't buy it, I baked it." Klara said with some pride.

"Yes, she did!" Hermann cleared his throat and continued his story.

"Horst was always much smarter than me. In truth, we were both Nazis. How odd! Two Jewish brothers as Nazis."

Josef's attention went back to the old man. "It was a strange time for you," Josef opined.

"Horst survived and somehow, perhaps a decade after the war, and after our horrible fight, he disappeared from my life."

Josef continued to subtly pry. "You said you had an idea where he went?"

"It was really just a story told to me by an acquaintance, a poor fellow who just died recently, who knew us both. He told me that Horst had moved to America, but, considering his position during the war, I didn't think they would let him into their country. I was sure that they didn't want war criminals in America."

"Would he have been considered a Nazi war criminal?"

"Perhaps. I do think that his association with this Admiral Canaris would have put him on someone's bad-man list."

"Yes, probably so."

"But," Hermann leaned forward in his chair and dropped his voice to a lower range, "this same man told me that in fact it was the Americans who took him from Germany and settled him in the U.S."

"Why would they do that?"

"Well, after the war, like me, Horst ended up in the Russian occupied zone, the DDR. The acquaintance told me that the Americans rescued Horst from the East as a payback for his service during the war."

"Payback?"

"Yes. I didn't believe this, and was sure this man was lying only trying to reunite us brothers. He said that Horst had been a spy inside the Abwher for the Americans."

"And you do not believe he was?"

"I do not. He let our mother's family die in some foul extermination camp when he might have saved their lives. That smells like a Nazi to me."

"Yet, you must admit that he could have been working for the allies?"

"Perhaps. But hard to believe."

Josef was overwhelmed by the implications of Hermann' s tale, and what a tale it was! Two Jewish brothers in the Kriegsmarine during the war and one of them may have been a spy for the allies in the office of the head of the Abwehr, to say the least! The information made his mind race in ten directions. "Your family's story is really unusual. I would like to include it in my paper."

"Please do. What do they say, 'those who don't learn about the past are condemned to relive it'?" Hermann smiled. "Maybe we can all learn how to avoid the next madman's attempt at killing off an entire group of human beings."

"Is there anything else you can tell me about your brother? Anything that might help me to locate him?"

"Don't you have the same files that brought you to me? He was also in the Navy, he would be in there as well no doubt."

Without thinking Josef blurted out, "The only thing in the Horst Wenzl file is his name, rank and service affiliation. We found you totally by coincidence."

"What do you mean? Were you searching for Horst and THEN you found me?"

Oh shit, I don't want to come off as deceitful. For whatever reason, Josef decided that Elsie's ruse to get them to meet Hermann would somehow backfire if he knew that they were looking first for Horst. "No... no...! I misspoke. What I mean is that when we found your file we also came across a nearly blank file for someone named Horst with the same family name. Now that I know that your brother is Horst, it all became somewhat of a jumble in my head. Pardon my confusion." Josef hoped that explanation was enough to diffuse his slip.

"Ah, I see. Well, what is in a name? My mother's family was Weinstein before she married my father. I doubt that either of us would have been in the naval records if our name was Weinstein. Ha!"

"No, I guess not. Ha!"

"But really, the only thing that I know about my brother, at least I think I know about him, I now suppose could be true. I never tried to find out. That friend had said that they got Horst out of the DDR and gave him a new identity in America. For a while I thought that the American bank account was simply a ruse and that Horst had gone to Argentina with some of the other old Nazis, but then how would I know? My friend also told me that the Americans made him a citizen, too. I'm also not sure how he knew all this, it sounded so far-fetched!" Hermann's expression was rueful as he said this. "How does a Nazi become a U.S. citizen?"

"That's a very good question."

"Would anyone like some more coffee and cake," Klara asked?

July 24, 2001

8:13 a.m., New York City

In his job as the head of the New York FBI office Robert Grover had cultivated many close friendships in law enforcement and intelligence circles. This
often led to unpublished information that helped him do his job. Today's
breakfast meeting with a former FBI colleague and good friend, a man now
working in some unspecified corner of clandestine government work, would
not help to allay Special Agent in Charge Grover's current anxieties. Grover
was already seated at their usual breakfast spot. "Joe, so good to see you!"
Robert patted his friend on the back as they sat.

"Did you order yet?" Joe Harris sat down.

"Not yet."

Harris attempted a brief smile but it quickly turned into a blank expression that was impossible to read. "I can't stay too long today. Some big stuff
is going down and I'm on the team writing the report for private eyes only."

Grover didn't have to guess what that meant. Private eyes meant that the
report was more than just important.

"Understood." Robert decided not to ask his friend for any details unless
they were forthcoming on their own. Whatever Joe knew was somewhere
above Robert's security clearance.

The waiter approached. "Good morning, are you ready to order?" Both
men ordered eggs and the waiter left them.

Harris immediately cut off the pleasantries and got to the point of
today's breakfast. "I'm going to tell you something that has to be kept very
quiet. You can't talk about this with anyone. I shouldn't be telling you, but
it involves you, and because of the way things seem to be going in DC this
stuff may not get to you. I won't go any farther than that."

Robert knew from past conversations such as this one, that Joe trusted
his confidence. "Go ahead. I never heard any of this from anyone."

"We've intercepted some chatter with a specific threat and we don't think
that the White House wants to hear it at all. My friends are working on an
appraisal of it to present to the President, probably next week."

"What can you share?" Robert knew the drill. There were times when the
political fallout from scary intelligence, if acted upon too hastily, might be a
threat to the politician's career.

"We've intercepted a communication from a very reliable source that
indicates one group is determined to strike in New York some time soon."

The usually unflappable Joseph Harris actually looked worried, and that look caused Robert to worry as well.

"Nothing specific?"

"Nothing that we can determine at this point."

"We've been poking around as well." Robert shared what his office was able to learn, and for Robert those latest intelligence reports were not heartening to read. "We've got a couple of well-placed snitches on the street here and they're telling us the same thing."

"My pals at the NSA are reporting more 'chatter' too. There's too much being talked about out there for this to be random. I can tell you some inside dirt that some of the President's closest advisers think it's nothing to worry about. They're trying to shield him from it. It's crazy."

"It is crazy. Why would you even think to make any of this up?" To some the chatter was just online bravado, idle threats hurled by malcontents and lesser forms of life. To Grover, however, a threat was a threat, idle or otherwise. His problem was how to keep any of it from doing damage anywhere. "I don't know if this has shown up in your research, but my guys think there's going to be some kind of a crisis surrounding the U.N. General Assembly meeting in September."

"What makes you think that?"

"One of our more reliable sources told us about it. This source is embedded in a group we've been watching for a while. They're getting instructions from a home office somewhere. We don't know who they are, but they're very vocal. They've been talking about the General Assembly for a few weeks now." The United Nations General Assembly gathering in September, an annual conference of all the member nations in the U.N., was always a particular security headache for both the NYPD and the FBI. During the General Assembly, all of the world's leaders come to New York along with huge diplomatic and security teams, and they all need coordinated protection. Now, with some unknown group repeatedly, specifically and confidently threatening the UN, as if the plans were already in place, such protection would need to be that much more serious. Some kind of a sinister plot was being discussed, not as a hypothetical conversation such as, what if we attacked the Statue of Liberty? There was no "what-if" to this one. It spoke in more definite terms using the word *when* rather than the more uncertain speculative *if.* The FBI man was very concerned. He would need to get his agents working harder on this one.

"That's pretty interesting. It's not exactly what we've been hearing, but it could be *what* they're threatening to attack. Is it okay if I share that intel with my people?"

"Of course. Share it... yell it out loud on the mountaintop!" Robert was fed up by the intra-agency secrecy. "Joe, there's no such thing as 'need to know' in this business. We all need to know."

"I hear you bro. I hear you."

The waiter arrived at their table with their breakfasts. Neither man had much more to say.

July 25, 2001

9:45 a.m., Frankfurt, Germany

"All I can tell you is that this has been a remarkable journey so far." Josef laid out all the details of his search for Horst Wenzl to his mentor, omitting, of course, his romantic session with Elsie in the archival paper storage room. Eisenberg had been silent with eyes wide as he listened to Josef's report about the empty file in the military records computer database, and then the empty folder with the English labeling in the storage archive. The professor's biggest reaction to the account had been a horizontal back and forth head motion in complete disbelief that the Wenzl brothers were Jewish.

He finally spoke. "History hides some amazing stories. You have certainly uncovered one of them. That there were Jews working among their potential annihilators is an astonishing tale for a war novel, but has little bearing on Operation Pastorius and the duplicity of those in charge of its management."

"That's not entirely true sir." Josef gently pushed back, "I think that if Horst Wenzl was working for the Americans as a mole in Canaris' office, then it's plausible to think that he could have given the Americans the whereabouts of the saboteurs, and other information about what their plans had been."

"That account would negate your theory about Canaris knowingly sending lambs to their slaughter, no? If the Americans learned about the saboteurs through a spy in the Admiral's office?"

"I suppose, but the diary says otherwise. That man's desertion and the revelation of the whereabouts of all of them was part of the plan. It is possible that Wenzl sent that information on to the Americans as well."

"Yes, that could be true, but only true if Wenzl knew what was going on. Remember, none of this is documented anywhere else other than Canaris' personal diary. It is entirely possible that as a low ranking young officer he knew nothing at all about what Canaris had going on. My guess is that Wenzl was there but knew very little about the bigger plan, or at least he may not have known about it until after it happened."

"Yes sir, but what if he did know? And, I have another possible theory. What if Canaris knew that Wenzl was an American mole in his office and went along with it? Wenzl would have been a perfect tool with which Canaris could manipulate and feed his enemy all kinds of misleading information."

"Ooooh, you have so many theories. There's an awful lot more work that needs to be done before you publish anything, and the truth is that there may be only one person in the world who knows the truth behind any of this."

"I totally agree with you and I thought of that already. This leads me to my next step. Sir, I need to go to America to find Horst Wenzl."

Eisenberg was excited by Josef's enthusiasm, yet he remained somewhat skeptical about his ability to find Wenzl. The professor smiled in a fatherly way that might have been taken as condescending. "And how do you know that he's there? Didn't the brother tell you that he thought Horst was in South America?"

Josef wasn't deterred, "I have an educated hunch, that's all."

"Ah, the educated hunch! That's not much to go on. And, just how do you plan to find someone who has been in hiding, most likely under an assumed name for the past half-century?"

"I have already begun to do some of that research here." Josef cleared his throat. "I have been working with a person from the archives office who was able to do a request from the Navy pension department. It appears that Horst Wenzl has been drawing a military pension for quite some time now."

"Really?"

Josef had been doing his homework, or at least Elsie was doing it for him. "Each year a military pensioner must do a proof of life filing with the office. The document is an affidavit form onto which the receiver of a pension must indicate that he or she is alive. A fingerprint is also required on the paper. And, while the money is automatically posted to a bank account in Dresden that is managed by his brother, the Rabbi, Horst appears to be drawing from that account on a monthly basis. Oddly, though, the funds are going into a German bank when they could just as easily be deposited into an account in a U.S. bank. I don't understand why that is happening."

"Maybe he's doing it to remain as hidden as possible. The German bank adds a level of anonymity to him and his whereabouts. He wants to be lost in society."

"Possibly you are correct. In any case, since this money is being transferred by his brother to a U.S. bank, I am reasonably certain that Horst is living in the U.S."

"That is amazing!"

"Have you got any idea where in the U.S.? It is a large country," Eisenberg smiled.

"The monthly payments all go to a bank in New York. I would assume he is living under an assumed name, but I also assume that he is living in that area."

Eisenberg was now beaming at his pupil. "This is fantastic detective work, Josef! I am truly impressed. If he is living under a false name, how do you think you can find him, as he apparently doesn't want to be found?"

"I have been working on that, too. The Americans have a law called the Freedom of Information Act. It basically allows any citizen to obtain unclassified government documents upon request. I have filed two such requests with the American Federal Bureau of Investigation for such information."

"But you're not an American citizen?"

"It doesn't matter, the law says they have to honor all the requests to the best of their ability."

"Eh, you said you filed two requests, why two?"

"I've asked for information on anyone named Horst Wenzl, and I have also asked for information about a man frequently mentioned in Canaris' diary who was instrumental in Operation Pastorius in New York. He is mentioned as K. Haupt."

"What does he have to do with it?"

"He may have been Canaris' man in New York. Interestingly, he is not mentioned at all in any of the other paperwork I've seen so far. He was part of Canaris' personal network of spies that had infiltrated the U.S. and the rest of Europe. Most of those men are not listed in any other documents either. The diary has it all. In any case, after Pastorius failed, there were no more mentions in the diary of either man, Wolfgang the saboteur or K. Haupt."

"Interesting!"

"Yes. What if the U.S. FBI caught this Haupt fellow along with the saboteur Wolfgang to end the plot? Another case of lambs being led to the slaughter by the spymaster."

"And what about those explosives and the Wolfgang mission?"

"I still need to learn more about that. If he planted those explosives somewhere, they were most likely found when the man was arrested. Because it was wartime, no one heard about any of it."

"You might find information about the explosives in the FBI freedom file?"

"Maybe. Who knows what I will find at this point."

"Fascinating!" Eisenberg was looking forward to rubbing it all into Rolf Penn's face when they next met. "And, what is your next step?"

"I am going to New York, maybe as soon as next week, and with the documents I get from my request, I'm going to find my man. I have to sell my car. I have a collector interested in it right now, and I'll use that money for the trip. That should be enough for the plane fare and some small living expenses." Josef was enthusiastic.

"I fear it will not be enough." Eisenberg knew that what was unfolding here in his office would become fodder for newspapers and the other media. His name would be associated with the successful telling of this tale. The story about an incomplete attempt to kill Roosevelt would put this student, and his history department on the map. "I think you will need more cash than you will get for your antique set of wheels. Sell your car, but allow me to pay for your plane fare."

"Oh no, professor, you already have helped me so much! I couldn't accept any...."

"Be quiet. This is an important piece of history. I am well off enough not to worry about the price of an airplane ticket. I will buy you that ticket and I expect that you will come back with Horst Wenzl's personal account of wartime life with Wilhelm." Eisenberg smiled broadly.

August 2, 2001

4:00 a.m.

For Rolf Penn, the word ego would have likely made a great nickname. Penn fed on the adulation by others. It was the personality trait that colleagues, and especially Eisenberg, found to be most offensive about the man, and it was the inciting factor affecting much of his behavior. Along with Penn's high-maintenance ego came a corollary lack of a sense of right and wrong, and an aura of dishonesty. The mechanics of promoting his own self-image separated his formidable intellect from all essence of fairness, morality and consequence. Feeding the ego meant making sure he was the object of awe among his friends and peers, no matter what. Today he would stretch this personality trait to its limits.

Penn's politics were also shaped to feed his ego. His sincerity for any political cause was simply an adjunct to his vision of himself. So this late afternoon, as the sun blazed through his office window, he drew the blinds almost totally shut to keep out summer heat, walked over and locked the door so as not to be interrupted by anyone walking in, and then sat down behind his big, messy desk in his latest effort to aggrandize himself in front of someone whose respect he was craving. Shoving some papers aside he picked up his mobile phone and dialed a number. A moment later the recipient picked up on the other end. "Hassan?"

"Hello, how are you my friend?" Came the voice from the other end.

"I am well, and you?"

"Quite well, though very warm. The sirocco is already building, very early this year. I think the winds won't wait until the fall as they normally do. Europe will be in for a dusty spell sooner than normal."

"It is hot here as well." Penn paused, enough of the pleasantries, now it was time to feed the ego. "I'm calling to tell you more about a story you heard when you were here a while ago. I know that you were interested in it at lunch that day." He could feel the excitement bubbling as he was about to tell it.

"Yes?" Al Jabar listened intently.

"Do you remember that colleague of mine with whom we ate?"

"Yes I do. He was a professor... his name was... give me a moment... Eisenberg? That's right isn't it?"

"Yes indeed, you've got a good memory. Well, I know how interested you were in Eisenberg's student's research."

"Ah, yes, I was fascinated by it. The idea of finding old wartime undeto-nated explosives somewhere?"

"Um hmm, that's it. In any case, it fascinated me as well. So, I started doing what any good historian would do, I began my own research into the incidents. After looking at all the documents, I've discovered some others. I have more information on that story to tell you." Penn neglected to men-tion that his research consisted of stealing and reading a mislaid file folder in the cafeteria. The ego continued to speak through the mouth of the man, "And I've made some discoveries myself that will prove that theory." *Take credit as much as you can. Hassan will be impressed,* the ego prodded him.

"Okay...?"

"If you remember the story, there was a saboteur who made his way to the U.S. in the summer of 1942. He was supposed to create a catastrophe."

"Yes, I remember, and there was a question about where he was, and if his act was going to involve explosives."

"Correct. Since we first talked about this, I've had an unexpected oppor-tunity to study parts of the diary myself. It does confirm a few of my theories from that first conversation with Eisenberg, and things that only a genuine historian can glean from the readings. *Keep taking credit!* These are things that both Eisenberg and his student have missed. I've been going over all of this for the past few weeks trying to corroborate my own theory and I think I can confidently say that, yes, there were explosives involved in the Canaris operation. While I understand that I am reading between the lines, in my professional opinion, I believe the saboteur's mission was a plot to assassinate the American President, Roosevelt." *Hassan will be very impressed by all this.*

"This is written down in the diary?"

"No, not exactly written, it is just based on my reading of the diary and my knowledge of everything that was happening in Germany at the time. Humbly, I say I'm an historian. A real historian must be able to read between the lines."

Of course there were many lines missing from that reading. Penn had not seen the entire diary, only photocopies of the parts of it that were inside Eisenberg's folder. His subtle sneer at Eisenberg's credibility as an historian was supposed to sound self-deprecating but it didn't come out that way. His delivery revealed the ego's latent smugness, and that's the way Al Jabar heard it.

Hassan did not laugh. "Really!" *A bit pompous aren't we?* "This should be very exciting for the student doing the research, hmm?" And why are you calling me about this?

"Yes, but since you were there to hear Eisenberg's version, and what I think was your interest in the story, I wanted to share my thoughts about it with you. Though I still have no specific information about where this was supposed to happen, I now have a reasonably good idea. I am confident that it was to happen in New York. In the direct transcripts of the Canaris diary, he talks about bringing down the house, though, I don't know what house he is talking about. At first I thought that it might be The White House, but now I think the statement is more figurative than accurate."

"Interesting." Aside from Al Jabar's reaction to Penn's self-aggrandizement, he was, in fact, interested in the story. "But, what makes you think this was a plot to kill Roosevelt?"

"This Pastorius mission was a big endeavor for Canaris. While we do know that he was part of the various plots against Hitler, he was also a patriotic German who felt that the Nazis had drawn the fatherland into the wrong war. When he learned about the existence of the concentration camps, he was appalled, and he began a secret crusade against Hitler himself. He was anxious to end the war quickly, win or lose. Anything to end that war, either deposing Hitler or winning it outright, would be something he wished to happen."

"And killing Roosevelt would shorten the war?"

"The Pastorius scheme was devised just about four months after the Japanese attacked Pearl Harbor in Hawaii. America was already shell-shocked by that attack. America was providing material support for England, but there were loud voices in the U.S. opposition party who didn't want Roosevelt to join in the war against Germany. The aviation hero, Charles Lindbergh, was a crusader in that effort. In any case, Canaris believed that if Germany was successful in removing the President of the U.S., perhaps America would have been demoralized out of fear, and might abandon their war effort. Canaris reasoned that one more catastrophic event would cower the nation. He would achieve his purpose. The fighting would end."

"That's an interesting theory, but what evidence is there that it happened?"

"No specific evidence other than what I have read in Canaris' diary, but everything points in that direction. This is my world, and I understand it clearly." Rolf chuckled as he embellished his resumé over the phone.

"Ha! Yes my friend, you are a big expert in the study of history, and the human motives behind the history as well."

Though Penn was unable to see the man's face, he assumed that Hassan Al Jabar was smiling at the other end of the phone. "And, I do know for a fact that Canaris had placed an operative in the States who was sending back almost daily radio messages indicating that the plan was on schedule and he, or they, would be ready to bring down the house... I think onto Roosevelt."

"I see, but didn't we also learn that nothing of the sort happened in

1942? History says that Roosevelt didn't die."

"Well, I know this is based on nothing but my own analysis of what I have read, but it stands to reason, I think, that the operative did indeed place his explosives somewhere to bring down "the house" on Roosevelt."

"... but he never achieved his mission."

"I have some thoughts on that as well. If you stay with me in my line of thinking for a moment more, I think that you will be satisfied. It seems as if this event, whatever it was, was supposed to happen at the end of August or the first few days of September in that year."

"And?"

"Looking at the calendar we know that Americans celebrate a post summertime holiday at the beginning of September. Roosevelt would always celebrate this holiday with his family away from Washington. They would gather at either his spa at Warm Springs in Georgia, or at his family's ancestral estate in Hyde Park, New York. So we can pretty much rule out The White House as the house in question for the location of an assassination attempt. First of all, the place is impenetrable and Roosevelt would not have been there during that time frame. Canaris had spies in the U.S. government and he knew that. I also think that Canaris would not have chosen Warm Springs as a place to make his symbolic catastrophe happen. It is too out-of-the-way for this kind of spectacular plot. I think the spymaster knew that Roosevelt would travel to Hyde Park, but that place, also, was too off-message for an assassination full of symbolism. No, Canaris was looking for maximum impact."

"So they were planning to kill him on his way to his family home?"

"Yes."

"An attack on his motorcade?"

"No, I don't think so. He would likely have traveled by rail, far safer for security's sake. Roosevelt had his own private railroad car, much like the corporate jet crowd these days. Canaris would also know that in nearly every trip by train from the capital to the estate in Hyde Park, the President would stop over in New York City. As it is today, New York was at the center of all of the places that were funding America's military buildup. That would be my guess for the site of the proposed catastrophe. I think that the saboteur planted his bombs somewhere in New York City where Roosevelt would have been at the end of that summer."

"Brilliant analysis, Rolf," Al Jabar, who had often experienced Penn's ego, pretended amazement at the logic of his friend. "But how do you know this is more than a theory?"

"I don't. It's really all just based on what I read and my experience as an historian, and in life. What drives people to do certain things? I think it is a combination of access and drive. If you understand the motives of the thinker, you can extrapolate the information you need to know. If you are able to get into the head of the thinker, you will be able to figure out what he was thinking at the time."

"Yes, I see," Al Jabar reflexively nodded his head in assent. *And your motives are all tied into your overwhelming ego.* He found the story to be as interesting as the teller was making it sound, even though the storyteller was a buffoon.

"I think that it would have easily been possible to obtain advance knowledge of Roosevelt's itinerary. Canaris had people everywhere. With that information the saboteur would simply have to set his explosives in a spot where he knew Roosevelt was going to be at a specific time, maybe in a building or maybe in his car or railroad train."

"Then, why do you think the mission failed?"

"I think that something happened to the man who placed the explosives. He may have been caught in the act, but I do not think that happened. It would have been in the newspapers. I looked into the incident of the submarine landings that were part of this operation, and once their FBI caught the eight Germans who landed on the beach, it became a huge news story, a great bit of publicity for the FBI's publicity-conscious Hoover. I think that if the Americans caught someone planting bombs somewhere in New York City, that also would have been heavily touted in the press. I searched through the microfiche of The New York Times for the rest of that year in our university library, but did not find any stories about bombs having been discovered. As I read the Canaris diary over again, I believe the saboteur had finished his job of preparing to kill the President, and was simply waiting for his prey to step into the trap. Then he stopped corresponding. He was gone."

"So, you believe that he placed explosives somewhere?"

"Yes, I do."

"Where?"

"Somewhere Roosevelt might have visited on that late summer weekend."

"Where his train car might have been?"

"Yes, exactly. Some place where his train car may have passed or briefly stopped."

"Fascinating! And…" Al Jabar hesitated before he formed his next question, "am I understanding that you think those explosives are still in place somewhere in New York City?"

"Yes. That's why I called you. I knew that you were very interested in the story you heard from Eisenberg that day." *It really wasn't me who called you, it was my ego. I'm looking for adulation.*

"I was interested, definitely. I love stories like this." If Penn could see Al Jabar's face on the other end of this phone call, he would have been confused. It was not an expression that might indicate adulation for this man. Hassan Al Jabar's expression now took on a look of revelation. He asked, "I wonder if there's a way to prove what you've postulated here?"

"If I had the time and the funding, I would go and look by myself, but alas, I am a poorly paid professor of history at a small German university. I will leave those expeditions to those with time and money to pursue them. Eisenberg's student is on that trail already."

Hassan's brain began grinding the information it had just acquired. There was definitely something here that might be of use to him. "Where do you think would be a good place to look for these things?"

"Good question!" The ego had been challenged and it needed to come up with an answer. "Hmmm. I would suggest looking at places where Roosevelt's railcar might have traveled. That was his route, and that's where I think the saboteur most expected to run into him."

"Mmmm! That is undeniably very interesting." Al Jabar understood that listening to Penn's theories was one part of the required quid-pro-quo. "Rolf, you have always impressed me with your thinking. Thank you for sharing this with me. Ha, maybe you will be able to write your own analysis of the Canaris diary before Eisenberg's student does it," Al Jabar laid it on thickly. He had an idea forming inside his head and if there was more information to this story that was forthcoming, he wanted to make sure that this showoff shared it with him.

Penn smiled to himself, "Always glad to be of help to you."

August 3, 2001

11:25 a.m., New York City

"Sir, can I bother you for a second? Something interesting just popped up on my desk." FBI agent Jim Grant looked into his bosses open office doorway. "I thought this might interest you."

"Sure. Whatcha got?" Robert Grover was happy to shift from his usually dark train of thought for a moment.

"I kind of remember a while ago, when you were talking about your dad's career in the NYPD during the war, that you told me a story about how a suspect threw him off a fire escape and he broke his leg."

"Yeah. That was a big story in my family while I was growing up," Grover half-smiled when he thought about it. It wasn't a smile about the awful incident itself, but rather about his memory as a small boy sitting on his father's shorter leg listening to it all being told. By the time he was ten, Robert had heard the story so many times that he would often correct his father on inconsistent details, and no matter how many times he had heard it, the idea of a burly thug tossing dad off the second floor of a building always grabbed his total attention. "So, what about it?"

"Well, I'm this month's filter on FOIA[1] requests. I get to see all of them before they get assigned to the archivists for fulfillment."

"Sorry to hear about that," Grover had real sympathy for this Special Agent because there was nothing at all special about looking through the FOIA requests. Being the "filter" was tedious work that needed full attention to detail. One missed document or inadvertent delivery of un-publishable information could result in anything from a lawsuit against the FBI to someone being killed. Agent Grant knew he had to be very careful in handling the requests.

"Anyway, I'm looking through the list of FOIA stuff coming specifically into the New York office and there's this one from a German history professor in Frankfurt who wants to get two FBI files from World War II in New York."

"Oh? 'Doesn't sound like anything special."

"Nope, 'didn't sound that special to me either until I read the names he was looking for. One is for someone named Horst Wenzl, I don't know that name, but the other is a name I think I do know. Someone named K. Haupt?" Grant raised a questioning eyebrow and stared at his boss.

[1] Freedom of Information Act

"K. Haupt?" Grover immediately sat up straight in his chair and waited for the next words to come out of Grant's mouth.

"Yeah. Wasn't Haupt the guy you said threw your dad off the fire escape?"

"Haupt? Yes, the guy was Haupt. It was definitely Haupt!" Grover sat up and became genuinely interested, "And, this history professor is looking for information on Haupt?"

"Yup, seems like that's the case. Just thought you might want to know."

"There's no other part of that request regarding *why* he wants the information?"

"Not much, just that he's writing a graduate thesis about the Nazi spy boss, Wilhelm Canaris. I know who he was, but the request was about Haupt. That's all. It's pretty much just a routine request under FOIA."

"Really? Haupt? The way my dad used to describe him was like a character out of a 1940's detective movie. The guy was an old-school petty thief. He used to steal from people in Yorkville when Dad was in the 19th. They called him the Katzenjammer Burglar."

"That's funny."

"The other thing I remember that my dad learned was that the Bureau was using him as a snitch. Maybe that has something to do with this German guy?"

"I don't know. These things rarely say why someone is looking for information. Some people say why, but in the majority of cases, it's just a send me the information kind of thing."

"Thanks for bringing that to me. I have to tell my dad. He'll be amazed, I'll bet."

"The only additional thing that's in this request is that the professor says he's coming to New York sometime in the next few weeks to do some of his research. He asked if we could speed up the FOIA process for him. He'd like to come and get it from us in person when he arrives. We normally don't push these FOIA's, but if you want me to, because of the connection here, I could put a rush on this one."

"He's coming to New York?" Grover leaned back in his chair and stared at Grant. "By all means, do put a rush on it, and also, when this guy comes to pick up the files, call me. I want to meet him and find out more. This is too interesting. I bet Dad'd like to meet him too."

"Sure thing. Will do." With that, agent Grant rose to his feet and left Special Agent in Charge Robert Grover alone with his worries about internet chatter.

August 5, 2001

4:39 p.m.

It was Sunday and most of Manhattan's apartment-bound denizens were in their caves, protected from the eighty-seven degree heat and high humidity by laboring window air conditioners. Those without air conditioners took walks in Central Park. The lucky ones were at the beach, and the luckiest ones were elsewhere, places where the oppressive heat and humidity were held in check by natural filters such as the seashore, or trees and mountains. The least lucky ones were at work. Such was the lot of NYPD officer Agnes Rodriguez and her partner Officer Brian Lynch. They were doing a four to twelve shift in a sector car out of the Midtown East Precinct. Agnes was driving and Brian was scanning the sidewalks as they turned Southbound onto Park Avenue at East 64th Street.

It was oppressively hot, and by mid-afternoon on this weekend day the sidewalks around town were almost empty, save for the odd doorman or sweaty entrepreneur re-selling cold bottled water to motorists stopped at red lights. "Aggie, I'm getting hungry. I missed lunch before I got to the house. Ya wanna go 10-63 and get something to eat?"

Agnes thought about it for a moment, "Nah, not yet. It's a little early for me right now."

"Okay, but if we see some guy selling tube steaks on a corner somewhere I'm gonna grab one."

"Sure thing." Agnes turned onto 50th Street and drove the car past the entrance to the Waldorf Towers apartments. At Lexington she turned right and went around the block on 49th headed back to Park Avenue.

It was just about mid-block when Brian noticed something odd. The polished brass door at street level, just before the Waldorf's through-the-block porte cochère, was ajar, and there was a man's head sticking out searching both ways on the empty block. When the man noticed the police car approaching he quickly pulled his head back and closed the door behind him. Brian immediately sensed something wrong. "Aggie, stop the car... did you see that?"

"You mean the guy at that door?"

"Yeah. He saw me lookin' at him and he ducked. Something's not good."

Officer Rodriguez pulled the car to the curb and the partners got out and walked to the door. It was locked. "Brian, whatcha wanna do here?"

"Maybe the doorman has a key. I think we should check this out."

Officers Lynch and Rodriguez entered the through-the-building automobile drop off area and found a doorman with a key. Together they all returned to the brass doorway. Brian asked the doorman, "where does this go?"

"It goes down a flight of stairs to a railway platform under the hotel," the helpful doorman replied.

"Trains stop here?" Agnes asked.

"Nah, used to, but not anymore. It goes back to the time the hotel was built and guests sometimes arrived by private railway car."

"I guess that time is over," Brian said.

"Is it open to Grand Central?" Agnes asked.

"No, only from the hotel here, or if you approach it underground from the tracks. No other way to get down there."

"I just saw a guy pop his head out of the door, and when he saw me lookin' at him he slammed it and locked it behind him." Lynch stared at the door as the doorman unlocked it with a key.

"Um, it coulda been a railroad guy. From what I know about this door, it's only to be used by MTA workers to access the platform down there. There shouldn't be anyone down there who doesn't work for the railroad."

"Somehow I got a feeling that this guy I saw was not working for the MTA." Brian's cop-sense analyzed the incident.

Agnes raised her walkie-talkie to her lips. "One-Seven Boy to Central... kay." A momentary pause.

"Go 'head One-Seven Boy." The radio cackled.

"We're on a ten-ten, at the Waldorf Astoria on 49th street. Looking for suspicious individual. No additional assistance needed at the moment."

"One-Seven Boy, that's a copy."

The doorman unlocked the entry door. Agnes clipped the radio back onto her belt and she and Lynch descended the metal stairway down one flight to the platform below street level. It was very hot in the tunnel, and much to their surprise, it was exceptionally well lit. The doorman followed them down.

"So, where did that guy disappear to?" Lynch turned and stared in all directions into the darkness of the surrounding cavern. Whoever it was that ran down the stairs, he or she was long gone.

"This place is really off-limits to everyone except the railroad guys. I don't know how anyone could even get in here without a key," the doorman wondered.

"You said it yourself, whoever it was, got here along the tracks from the main terminal. What is it, just five blocks underground?" Lynch opined.

Agnes walked about fifteen feet down the platform and was surprised at what she saw. "Holy cow! What is this?" Before her stood a vintage, early twentieth century style railroad car left derelict on a siding. "What is this?"

"I don't know this for sure, but I've been told that this is Franklin D. Roosevelt's armored railcar. It's been here since he died. He used to always stay here at the Waldorf. They would bring him down here inside his personal car and drive it right off that elevator and onto that train car with him in it. I suppose no one ever saw him as a cripple because he never had to walk in public."

"Geez, how about that!" Lynch was impressed. He stared at the car looking at what appeared to be openings in the sides for gun barrels. "Look at that, this thing was an armed fort!"

"Yeah, it is armored and has bulletproof glass. I think the secret service would send sharpshooters along to protect him in case they ever got stopped on the tracks," the doorman added.

Meanwhile Officer Rodriguez made her way to the opposite end of the platform. "Hey Brian, c'mere and take a look at this."

"Whatcha got?" Lynch joined his partner who had a flashlight shining at a long stretch of unused platform. It was thick with a gray dust that had settled there over a long period of time, many years. In the dusty carpet they could clearly make out what looked like fresh footprints headed off into the darkness of the tunnel.

"Somebody's been walking here recently. I think our guy got away here." Agnes shined her light into the rail tunnel where the beam seemed to be eaten up by the darkness. "Probably just a homeless guy."

"Well, not much more to do down here." Brian turned back toward the stairway and the others followed. "I can't believe there's a hotter place than this in all of New York."

At street level the doorman shut the door and made sure it was locked. "I guess that's it, huh?"

"We'll let Metro-North know that there's a possible pedestrian in their tunnels," Agnes said. "I'll call it in."

"Okay." Brian then took the doorman aside, "If you see anyone sticking their head out of that doorway again, give the precinct a call. There really shouldn't be anyone going down there. Someone could get seriously killed on those tracks, or worse," Brian smiled. "But anyway, thanks for taking us down there."

"No prob officer."

Agnes added, "Yeah, thanks. Seeing that railroad car was really amazing."

"Glad I could be of help." The doorman turned and walked back toward the hotel entrance while the two cops got back into the sector car.

"So, Central is notifying the railroad cops to look out for him. Whatcha think that guy was doing on the tracks, whoever he is?" Agnes asked.

"I'm pretty sure he wasn't a railroad guy. When he saw me eyeballin' him he ducked down there real fast. Probably just some poor schmuck looking for a safe place to sleep. Too many like him out there. There's really no other reason for anyone to be hanging out there in that overheated hell-hole."

Agnes picked up her radio, but before she pushed the transmit button she looked at Brian... "Ya still hungry?"

Brian nodded. "Yeah, I'm always still hungry."

"One-Seven Boy to Central, kay," Agnes called.

"Go ahead One-Seven Boy."

"That ten-ten was negative. No suspicious person found. Notified Metro North police. We're going ten-sixty-three."

"Roger that One-Seven Boy, have a good lunch."

A few blocks south a thin tall man emerged from the shadows at the northern end of platform 14 in Grand Central Terminal. He was careful to make sure he was not noticed as he casually re-entered the populated world around him. He was dusty and hot, but he was also smiling.

August 6, 2001

3:15 a.m.

The charge d'affaires at the at the Libyan consulate in Manhattan readied the diplomatic pouch that was scheduled to go back home. Most of
the documents were not what anyone might consider secret. There were
medical reports on the health of various diplomats, accounting files burned
onto CD-ROM discs, and a few reports from the African nation's clandestine workers in New York. None of it was of any great value to anyone, but
would help analysts back in Tripoli figure out what the rest of the world was
saying about Libya and it's leader, Khadafy.

The real value of the diplomatic pouch was that it was totally secure
from airport or customs inspection by any government other than the one
that sealed it. No one could open it for scrutiny anywhere. Any government
official doing that would create a major breach of international diplomatic
understanding and precedent. Such action was never even considered by
any intelligence agency. That level of security also allowed the absolute
most secret of communications to travel without any chance of having their
confidentiality compromised. The pouch was more secure than encrypted
email or telephone conversations, and even private meetings which could be
bugged or overheard. A handwritten or machine-typed message on a piece
of paper left no footprint anywhere. Materials in the pouch included the
mundane as well as the biggest secrets. Physically, the pouch wasn't really a
pouch. Rather it was a secure lead lined, (to prevent it being x-rayed) fiberglass, fire-resistant attaché case with a built-in thumb wheel combination
lock and a formidable-looking padlock, all of it there to maintain the secrecy
and security of the information within. This pouch was being packed for
its trip to Tripoli and in less than two hours it would be handcuffed to its
diplomatic courier for the trip home. The box was set to travel at 5:00 p.m.
Since it was only 3:15, it remained open on the charge d'affaires desk.

"Sir?" A young man appeared at the door of the office."

"Yes?" The diplomat recognized the young man. He had seen him in the
building from time to time, but didn't know his name or what he did at the
consulate. "Can I help you?"

"Sir, I have this small package that I would like to include in your pouch
back to Tripoli?"

"Certainly," the diplomat was gracious. "I don't think we've actually
met."

"Oh, excuse me," the young man was very polite, "I am François. I work for the Mukhabarat el-Jamahiriya. I am here in New York on intelligence matters."

"Nice to meet you." The diplomat rose to shake hands with the young spy, then without a question, took the package and stuck it into the fiberglass case. François left the office immediately. The package, wrapped in brown paper and addressed to Colonel Hassan Al Jabar of the Mukhabarat el-Jamahiriya, would be in Colonel Al Jabar's hands in Tripoli in less than fourteen hours.

August 16, 2001

9:00 a.m.

Doug Grover took a sip of his coffee and reached for the ringing kitchen telephone. "Hello?"

"Good morning, Dad. How are you?"

"Pretty good. Pretty good. 'Just havin my coffee."

"How's Mom?"

"She's good. We went to the movies last night and saw the remake of *Planet of the Apes.*"

"Any good?"

"Not bad. I kinda liked the Charlton Heston one better, but this one had better special effects. Mom likes the sci-fi stuff more than I do, but I go along anyway." Robert couldn't see his father's smile. "So anyway, my boy, to what do I owe the honor of this call?"

"So, remember how you used to tell me the stories of your days in the 19th?"

"Sure. You used to love 'em."

"So, when I came to work this morning there was a folder on my desk. A history professor from Germany filed a Freedom of Information request about an old case that the Bureau was involved in during World War II."

"And?"

"This professor was asking for a couple of names, one of them I think you will remember. Does the name Haupt ring a bell?"

"Haupt? That is a name I will never forget as long as I try to walk in a straight line. The SOB tried to kill me back in '42. What a night that was! I remember…"

Robert interrupted the onrushing story. "Dad, you told me this one fifty times. I know what happened."

"Oh yeah, I suppose I did tell it few times. So this guy is asking questions about Haupt?"

"Yeah, he's asking about Karl Haupt. I read the file. This guy was a real baddie."

"The guy is asking about Karl?"

"Yeah, Karl."

"Not Eugen?"

"No he's asking about Karl. That's the guy you had the tumble with, right?"

"Nope, Karl was the father of the asshole who threw me off the fire escape."

"Oh, would that be Eugen?"

"That's the lug."

"I see here that you were on the scene when the Bureau arrested Karl."

"Yeah, I was there. Crazy time back then."

"The German guy is looking for stuff about Karl, but there's a lot in here about Eugen, too. Looks like the kid was working for the Bureau at the time."

"I knew that too." Doug's memories were whetted. "Yeah, he was workin' for the Bureau okay, but the Bureau was also workin' for him. Your predecessors were protecting him for some screwball reason."

"There's stuff in here about that, too."

"Yeah, me and Murphy tagged along when they brought the old man in. I don't remember all the details, but Karl looked more like some guy on his death bed than a bad guy."

"Well, anyway, this professor wants to know about Karl, not Eugen. The file, once stamped "Top Secret" back during the war, but not a secret now. You wanna come and look at it sometime?"

"Yeah, I would enjoy that."

"I've got another idea. This professor is coming to New York to follow up on his research. You might be able to help him do whatever he's doing."

"Wow. I really have to think about all this. There was a lot going on back then, but I don't really remember the details too well. But, yeah I would love to meet this German guy."

"He's coming here in a week or two and I'll figure out a way that you can meet him."

"Sounds good."

"I'll keep you posted."

August 22, 2001

10:36 a.m., Frankfurt, Germany

"When you start the car you need to pull on the choke knob until it is running smoothly. Once it's running you can slowly push the choke back to the dashboard," Josef instructed the heavy man sitting in the Trabant's narrow driver seat. "This is an amazing little car and it will give you good service if you treat it well."

"Thank you, but I am very familiar with these cars. I know all about chokes, but I won't be using it as a regular mode of transportation. I'm a collector, not much of a driver."

"Of course, I understand. It's just that I have owned this car for so long, I am very connected to its idiosyncrasies." Josef laughed to himself, *I feel its pain.*

"Well, rest assured that I will take good care of it. It really is in great shape, and I'm going to keep it in a heated garage." The heavy man reached into his wallet and pulled out a signed check. He handed it to Josef. "I believe this is the amount we agreed on?"

Josef examined the check. "Yes it is. Thank you." He sighed, "I'm sad to see it go."

"May I ask why you are selling this car?"

"I am leaving for a trip to New York and I need the cash for my work there."

"Ah! Well, have a great trip. I believe all the paperwork is done here, so I thank you now and say goodbye."

"Yes…" After one long hesitant moment, Josef opened the Trabant's passenger front door and got out for the last time. The man behind the wheel gave him a friendly wave goodbye and drove off. Josef stood motionless as the Trabant rounded a corner two blocks away and disappeared forever. Then he looked at the check. *So much money for that wreck! I can't believe he paid so much for this car!*

August 23, 2001

4:00 p.m., Tripoli, Libya

The front doors to the Penn family's Mediterranean seaside villa were open wide to embrace the late afternoon sea breeze. Rolf was half-napping on a lounge chair in a shady spot on his Italian white marble veranda, enjoying the cooling zephyr that pushed back against the intense desert sirocco. The temperature was peaking and any wisp of wind was welcome. Penn was at the beginning of a three-week summer holiday before his fall classes were set to start back in Germany. His wife and boys were going to join him in a few hours. He was in his favorite place on earth and totally relaxed. A voice roused him by surprise.

"Rolf, I hope I am not interrupting you," a man was standing by the open doorway.

Penn blinked a few times and recognized his surprise visitor, "Oh, Hassan, good to see you!" Penn rose from his rattan chair and stepped toward the man, embracing him with a bear hug. *Why is he here?* While his arrival in Tripoli just hours earlier went unnoticed by any of his neighbors, it was immediately known to the Libyan intelligence office.

"Likewise my friend. Good to see you, too." The two held onto each other for a brief moment and then sat down across a white painted coffee table.

"I just arrived last night and I was going to give you a call today about perhaps having dinner soon. You beat me to it!" Penn smiled.

"Yes, I was following your arrival." Al Jabar made it clear that his eyes and ears were everywhere. Hassan, while once a genuine academic with a doctorate in chemistry, had, over the years, become one of the most powerful members of Libya's intelligence apparatus. Rolf suspected this, but had no real knowledge that it was true. He was unaware of Al Jabar's connections, and Hassan had the perfect cover necessary for espionage work. His academic credentials allowed him to easily pass muster as a professor of chemistry, and that allowed him to travel frequently back and forth to Europe and other places, always under the guise of attending conferences.

"To what do I owe the honor of this visit?"

"I must speak with you about that story that you called me about a few weeks ago, the one about the old Nazi plot in New York City. It is something that I thought best discussed face-to-face, rather than over the telephone."

"Yes? What about it?" Penn began to feel the hair on the back of his neck tingle. There was something in his old friend's demeanor that felt menacing, something he had never noticed.

"Yes. I must tell you that you were uncannily correct in every one of your theories."

Penn felt flattered. "How so?"

"The information you gave me about the possible existence of explosives somewhere in New York that were possibly meant to kill Roosevelt. Do you remember that?"

"Certainly, I do."

"I have a man in New York City who went to look for them."

Rolf's shiver now traveled down his spine. "Really? I don't understand… you have a man in New York City, and…?"

"Yes, I don't think we've ever discussed it, but in addition to my work in chemical engineering I also have an advisory interest in my government's global view." Al Jabar didn't need to explain any more about his role in the Libyan dictatorship. His eyes told the suddenly frightened Penn everything he needed to know.

"Oh, and your man in New York? What was he doing?"

"Why, he was following up on your brilliant historical research."

Penn's stomach began to churn and he sat there waiting for more information.

Al Jabar kept talking. "He had success."

Penn's jaw dropped. He was stunned. "Really?"

"Um hmm. My man in New York is quite reliable. I told him the whole story as you told it to me. His first directive was to discover if Roosevelt was indeed in New York sometime at the end of August, 1942. It is a fact that was simple to find, as the newspapers did report that he spent the Labor Day holiday at his Hyde Park home on that weekend you spoke of."

"Ah, so I was correct?" Penn's ego was now stoked beyond his initial reaction to the news. His initial sense of dread began to ebb.

"Yes, you were, but it gets better. My man learned that Roosevelt would stop for meetings at the Waldorf Astoria Hotel in New York City on any trip to Hyde Park from Washington. He would do so to refresh himself after a cramped three-hour train trip. The Waldorf Astoria has a train car platform directly beneath the building. Roosevelt's car would stop there. All very simple."

"Yes, it seems so." Penn's usual over-inflated sense of self was now in the stratosphere. While his conjectures were built on what he read from the Canaris diary, he was still just guessing when he spoke to Hassan on the phone. Still, he remained cool at the news.

"In any case, my man went down into the rail tunnel under the hotel to see for himself what it looked like. Do you remember that you told me that Canaris wrote about 'bringing down the house'?"

"Yes, that was a striking phrase. Very direct. I assume that it figuratively meant bringing down the American Government."

"Maybe not. What if it was a physical description of the sabotage plot. Maybe the house that he was talking about wasn't the government, but an actual structure. And, maybe that structure was the Waldorf Astoria Hotel. Though nothing actually happened, Canaris may have been attempting to bring down the Waldorf Astoria Hotel onto Roosevelt when he stopped there on his train trip to Hyde Park."

"Really? And how are you so sure of this?"

"Because, as you suggested, the explosives that the saboteur planted are still in place."

Penn was now truly stunned. He just sat and stared at Al Jabar with a blank gaze. All manner of thoughts raced through his brain. This had to be the most amazing piece of deduction of his entire career. But, why had Eisenberg's student not discovered this as well? The answer to that, he deduced, was simple. Eisenberg's student doesn't have the same intellectual grasp of the master plan as I have. A real historian knows exactly what to look for. If there were explosives anywhere to be discovered, that would be just another piece of relevant information for the larger academic dissertation. What his friend Hassan had discovered was something else, something even more amazing, and it all came from Penn's self-proclaimed brilliant mind.

"Yes, my friend, your theory about the explosives yielded this. Your deductions are nothing short of genius." Al Jabar reached into his bag and pulled out a dusty box-shaped thing about the size of a bar of soap.

"What is that?"

"If you remember when we first heard this story at our luncheon with your colleague, you used the term 'diabolical'? This is indeed a small part of a diabolical plot. I cannot explain what became of the man who did this work, but he did it extremely well. For whatever reason, no one in the last nearly sixty years had come near finding this. But, my operative, armed with the information about the possible existence of explosives, and the idea of bringing down the house, went to look. Putting together all the details, he finally came upon the least obvious place to hide a bomb. Voilà, this is a brick of plastic explosive!"

"Explosive? Is it still…explosive?" Penn instinctively leaned away from the brick.

"Yes, it is, but without the proper detonator it remains totally inert. No danger here. My man found this piece of plastic explosive and one other like it, in place atop pillar supports that are holding up one side of the hotel over the railraod tracks. Without those supports the entire huge building would come crashing down onto the tracks and the streets above.

"I was right!" he almost shouted out, but his actual reaction was total amazement. *How the hell did I figure this out?*

"You were, as it is said, spot-on." Al Jabar smiled. "These pieces of plastic by themselves are completely harmless, but touched off by an electrical or concussion-trigger they will make a very powerful explosion. Both of the pieces that my man found were still in place with trigger mechanisms like this one. We removed it from this piece of plastique so that we wouldn't have an unfortunate incident here." Hassan held up a small detonating cap about the size of a .45 caliber bullet. "This is a concussion cap. The force of any nearby explosion would trigger it and all the other similar caps nearby. All of this is still very powerful. We imagine that there are more of them, but my man had to leave the tunnel before he could check out all the pillars."

"I am pleased!" So, he thought, an educated yet wild guess after reading parts of the Canaris diary had proven to be true. While he was both stunned and amazed at the accuracy of his theories, they were just theories. He pretended that his analysis of the details was the norm. "Hassan, there was simply no other way to explain all the details that I read, but in any case thank you for confirming what I expected to be true. But what now? What's your interest in this?" Penn was smiling, but inwardly he dreaded to hear the expected answer.

"Ah, my friend, that is why I have come to you today. This is something that cannot be discussed in front of others, or especially over the telephone. I need to take this discovery further."

"Further?"

"My colleagues and I have been discussing the planning of an event that would happen in New York sometime next month. Something that would immediately get the world's attention and let everyone know that the tyranny of the world's superpowers is still no match for us."

"Which colleagues? At the university?"

"No, not at the university. Other colleagues with whom I deal for the work that I do for my country," Al Jabar responded.

Penn was sweating heavily. He had the feeling that he and his overwhelming ego had unleashed something terrible. "And you have plans for this discovery of mine?"

"Oh yes, we've had something in the works for some time, but this discovery will make things considerably easier to implement. There are already brothers in arms placed in strategic spots ready to carry out our plan. We've been in touch discussing details. All of it around the United Nations gathering in New York in September."

"And?"

"Our plans are, how can I put this delicately, also somewhat diabolical. I am going to share them with you because I believe that we are brothers in arms."

Penn was now frightened. Normally, if anyone fed his ego, they would have triggered Penn's loyalty. Now he wanted no part of it. He lied, "Yes, of course, we have always been brothers-in-arms."

"Good. I can tell you that there is a grandness to our scheme, and genuine simplicity in carrying it all out."

"Please explain?"

"We plan to use those explosives as they were intended. My colleagues and I are planning an incident that will happen in New York."

"An incident?"

"Well, you might also call it an attack. We've had thoughts about small-scale attacks in America for some time, but we've not carried them out. A small-scale attack smells more of criminality than political force. A small-scale attack can be played down in the press. What you have given us is the idea for a large-scale attack, something that will make them, that is the Americans and their allies at the U.N., tremble in their shoes."

"I see." Penn had always been an armchair radical. He had marched in anti-government and anti-Western protest events. He spoke in a radical way in his lectures and encouraged like-minded students to pick up their symbolic weapons to challenge the powers-that-be. This, however, was different. This was actual warfare being discussed by someone whose job it was to make war. It was an outcome that Penn had not considered when he had phoned his friend in Tripoli to boast. His ego had opened Pandora's box.

"I will share this with you, but you must speak of it to no one."

"Of course," answered Penn, now afraid. He would now be blamed for anything that might happen as a result of his sharing Eisenberg's information as his own. This had gone beyond radical academia, real lives were now threatened by his information. He asked, "So, what is the plan?"

"We know for a fact that American presidents all stay at the Waldorf Astoria when they are in New York."

"I didn't know that. Why?"

"It's an interesting story. There are rail tracks directly below the hotel. In the event of a crisis in the streets above, the leader of the nation can be whisked out of town without danger, and without anyone seeing him leave."

"Ah!"

"Because of that high level of security, many of the delegations that attend the U.N. also stay at the Waldorf Astoria. It is the safest place in the city. There is so much security in that building at this time of year, that it is like a fortified medieval castle."

"I suppose it is." Penn thought for a moment. "So, if you have all this in hand now, what do you need from me?"

"The diary. Do you still have it?"

"Um, well not all of it, just some photocopied parts."

"I would like to have it."

"I will gladly give it to you. But, like I said, I don't have all of it. I only got to see a few of the pages that referred to this operation."

"Oh," Hassan paused, "but, it is important that we see the entire document."

"Why do you need it?"

"My man was only able to locate those two plastic bricks. But, there must have been more to generate enough force to topple a building of that size. I think the diary may have information about where other bricks are planted. It is important to know in advance how complete the saboteur's work was before he disappeared. Like I said, a small disaster smells of petty criminal behavior. A catastrophe has the perfume of strength."

"Ah, but the authorities probably found whatever else was there already." Penn yearned for a way to back-pedal all that he had started. "We already know that the saboteur didn't finish the job. Nothing ever blew up," Penn reminded his friend.

"Yes," Al Jabar agreed, but continued to push. "And you also told me that he, or they, radioed to Canaris that the job was finished and they were awaiting their prey. It stands to reason that if he was prepared to carry out the plan, then there were more of these bricks in place, am I wrong?" Al Jabar saw the fear in his friend's eyes. His smile dropped away along with any pretense of accommodation of their past friendship. Hassan Al Jabar became at once threatening, demanding and ruthless.

"I really don't remember that detail." Penn smiled, but inside he was morose.

"Perhaps, but before we move forward we need to make sure. I cannot risk my man going down there again and getting caught. It would ruin everything. I need to see that diary." Though he spoke calmly, Al Jabar's voice now had an edge that Penn had never before experienced, "Your family has been coming here to Libya for years and it is felt among my colleagues that you are sympathetic to our country. Ha, you are almost a Libyan!"

"Thank you, Hassan. I think all of us have always felt comfortable here." Penn now understood that he was in real trouble.

"Good, then you will go back to Germany and get a copy of the complete diary?" It was not a question.

"Ohhh… what? Wait a moment. I actually have no access to that book. It is either with Eisenberg, his student, or locked in an archive somewhere. I do not have that diary myself."

"Yes, but surely you have a way to get it, no?" There was no more friendship between them. Penn was a mouse trapped in a glass tank with a hungry snake.

"Uh, I guess I could try," Penn attempted to stall any action. "I suppose that when I get back to Germany, I can see if I can copy it."

"Good! Then I will make arrangements for your trip home tonight."

"Now? Tonight? Hassan, my family is already in the air on the way here to meet me. They are supposed to arrive in a few hours. I cannot leave now, I have no way to let them know that I will be leaving, to tell them that they have to go back home."

"I was aware of their travel plans. There's no reason for them to go home. I'm sure they will enjoy their holiday in Tripoli without you until you return. The sooner that you get back here with the diary, the sooner you can start your holiday with your family. Don't worry. My colleagues and I will meet them at the airport when they land and bring them here. We will take care of them while you get the book."

The threat was now clear. There was nothing more to protest or discuss. "Oh, I see. Then I will go and pack my bag." Penn understood. His wife and sons were to be hostages. There was no way to warn them to return home. "Can you tell me what your goal is, if I am able to find the diary and bring it to you?"

"Simply, that while all of the diplomats and the President of the United States are in their beds at the Waldorf Astoria during the U.N. General Assembly, we plan to 'bring down the house.'" Hasan smiled.

August 26, 2001

7:15 p.m., New York City

As it was his bi-weekly ritual, the FBI Special Agent in Charge of the New York Bureau, Robert Grover, visited his parents' Lincoln Center apartment for dinner. With his younger brother living in Denver, Robert had become the nearest caretaker of his aging parents. For Robert, dinner with Mom and Dad was never an onerous responsibility, rather it was a totally pleasant escape from the pressure of his job and a reminder of his roots. Robert enjoyed the company of his parents and, though the kitchen was newer, his mother's cooking had that same old comfort factor that he loved. Ellen Grover, by the time she turned 80, had refined her menu repertoire into a small list of memories that her older son was unable to resist. Tonight's meal was no exception. She cooked his absolute favorite meal. First came the home made mushroom barley soup, followed by a large stack of tender pieces of chicken breast, fried golden brown in a crust of egg, breadcrumbs, garlic powder, salt and black pepper. The fried chicken was paired with roasted potatoes, seasoned with parsley and butter, with sides of her special garlicky creamed spinach, and a cucumber salad. Ellen never let down her son Robert's expectations. By the end of the meal, including cake and coffee, it took some time for him to get over the effects of overeating. As usual, the recovery area was in the Grover's living room. Father and son left the table to sit there and talk while Ellen happily cleaned up in the kitchen.

"Boy, that was great." Robert sipped a glass of Pellegrino water.

"Yup, it was," Doug sighed, "I really can't eat like that anymore, but I do it out of love!"

Robert smiled at his dad. There was a momentary silence, a segue was coming.

Doug broke it. "So, what's become of that chatter?"

" 'Still there. We keep hearing stuff and our sources on the street keep telling us that someone, somewhere has something in the works before the end of summer. Our analysts figure that all fingers are pointing at the U.N. General Assembly meeting around the middle or end of September. Of course, it's all just chatter, no solid corroboration on any of it."

"What's the chatter saying?"

"Nothing specific. The geniuses at the CIA say that they keep hearing words like Jihad and martyrdom and that it will be very big."

"I've heard that stuff before so many times... it usually is just talk.

Nothing ever seems to happen from intel."

"I hope you're right." Robert didn't have much more information than that to give his dad. "I do know that the President is being briefed on the intel, but no one in D.C. seems to be taking it all that seriously."

"There are always rumors."

"Yeah, but with all this internet babble coming from different places we gotta take it seriously."

"You know, I've heard that Roosevelt was told a few days before Pearl Harbor that the attack was going to happen. They were just rumors, but no one acted on them and look what happened. We also had some advance intel when I was still at NYPD headquarters about those lunatics who drove that bomb truck into the World Trade Center basement. We should have acted on that before it happened, but we didn't, and you see the result."

"Well, I gotta make sure that nothing like this happens on my watch." Robert sank back in the big easy chair. "We've seen reports that some religious fanatics in Saudi Arabia are threatening to do something but the Pres is playing it down saying we shouldn't be "swatting flies." It's one thing for Washington to downplay this stuff, but it's another thing if something blows up here, and I don't want that on *my* head."

"Well, I suppose that you're all on top of it. There's always some guy out there trying to make his mark here in New York. Hey, if you can make it here, you can make it anywhere, huh?"

"Yeah, I suppose," Robert smiled, "New York is *the* place." There was a moment of silence and then he shifted gears. "Oh... by the way, I brought you something."

"A present?"

"Not really, but you'll be interested I'm sure." Robert reached over to his leather brief case and pulled out a manila file folder. "This isn't all of it, there's a lot in the file, but I copied the stuff I thought would interest you."

"Oh?" Doug reached over and took the file folder and opened it on his lap. "Oh! This is the Haupt file you were talking about."

"Yeah. There's also another name in there that he's looking for, but I didn't copy those pages."

"Who was that?"

"Someone named Horst Wenzl."

"Nope, never heard of that one. Was he a pal of Haupt's?"

"I don't think so. Anyway, I wanted to tell you that the German guy is gonna be in New York in a few days and I'm going to arrange for him to come up to the office to pick up all these docs. Wanna be there to meet him?"

"Oh yeah! That would be terrific. Funny, ya know, that Eugen Haupt actually changed my life for the better."

"How do you figure that?"

My ruined leg kept me out of the army and let me marry your mother," Doug smiled.

"Yeah, true that!" Robert grinned back at his father.

"Well, I...I...don't know this Wenzl guy, but I do remember both of the Haupts. Karl was a gangster, like from the old school... a knee-cracker who worked for Dutch Schultz. He had a rap sheet that read like a crime novel."

"Dutch Schultz? That Dutch Schultz?"

"Yeah, that one. Tim Murphy and me worked on that case. Me and Murph found out all this stuff about the old man like, when he was young he was Shultz's right hand man. He did everything from collections to enforcement. Schultz really trusted the guy, but that was his big mistake. Karl was also a Nazi. I mean, a real one. I think, even before he became a Nazi, he had a thing about Jews, and guess what, Dutch Schultz was one of us. I'm pretty sure that Karl finally set up his boss to be hit. Anyway, all that happened way before I ran into him. When I met him he was a hollow lookin' old guy with emphysema."

"You were working gangland stuff when you were in your twenties?"

"No, we were on burglary. We just happened in on that one. Eugen was a burglar, and that led us to his old man."

"New York was a rough place when you started out, huh."

"Yeah, Murphy, me, and a bunch of guys from the FBI New York office finally busted old Karl. It was kinda sad though. By the time we got cuffs on him he couldn't have enforced a delivery from a florist. He looked like crap. He was in his bathrobe, and he was coughing and spitting up. There was something big going on in the city, I don't really remember it that well, but there was some kind of a bomb threat. But, I really don't remember all the details..."

"But you do remember this guy Karl Haupt?"

"Oh yeah, I do. But, we were after his kid, not him. The kid, you know, the guy who..."

"...threw you off the fire escape. Yeah I know," Robert smiled broadly.

"Yeah, in any case, I was, I think, 23."

"For whatever reason, this FOIA request is about the father, not his kid."

"I wonder why this guy wants to know about the father," Doug asked? "The old man was nothing more than a wheezing old gasbag when we took him in."

"Seems like he might have also been a Nazi spy who was reporting back to the biggest operators in Berlin, to Admiral Wilhem Canaris himself."

Doug sank back in his chair and pondered this information. "So Karl was the real deal! Do ya think that Eugen was also a Nazi? I always thought he was just a dumb-ass burglar, and your guys would never tell me what he was doing for them."

"I haven't read through the whole thing, but I bet all your answers are in this folder."

Doug's memory was now thoroughly whetted and details began falling into place in his brain, "We thought the son knew where some bombs were hidden, or something like that, and we knew the old man probably knew where his kid was. Karl wouldn't give it up so we locked him up just so we could question him. No lawyers, just us and Karl, for the sake of national security, 'ya know."

"You'd never get away with that today."

"But the son? We never could nab him for anything that would stick, and in the middle of all of this he died. Actually, he died a hero."

"How?"

"In a crazy and unbelievable way. He stopped an armed robbery going down in a cigar store on Wall Street and got himself killed in the process. We'd been looking for him all over the city, and he calls his FBI handler to say that he wants to come in and tell everything. Then he gets himself shot right after that phone call."

"Geez!"

"Yeah, Eugen was a huge guy, lean and musclebound, and he was really fast. That's how the SOB got the better of me on the fire escape. In that cigar store, he must have been pretty sure that he could take the perp out, so he decked him and killed the guy with one punch. But, as bad luck would have it, the perp's gun goes off as he's going down. The bullet hits Eugen in the gut and it's all over, just like that. Kinda poetic justice, if you get what I mean."

"You always used to tell me that 'you can't make this stuff up.' "

"Wait… now it's coming back to me… the bombs! Eugen had a rented basement hole where we found some kind of a short wave radio and some evidence of possible explosives… your guys never told me if they really were explosives, by the way. So we took, or your FBI guys took, Eugen's old man into custody because …hmmm…. we were looking for bombs that he or his kid might have set up somewhere in the city."

"Yeah, there's stuff in here about the search for explosives in important buildings."

" 'Big waste of time though. We never found anything. I remember that between the Department and the Bureau we looked everywhere in the city, but nothin'. Me and Murphy were on the team that searched the tracks out of Grand Central. We didn't find crap, just garbage and some huge rats, really huge rats."

"So, no bombs?"

"Maybe there were, but we couldn't find them. If they were for real, there was no way to figure out where they were. Anyway, since we didn't find anything anywhere, and with Eugen dead, we all forgot about the threat. Bottom line is that nothing ever happened."

"Great story."

"It wasn't that great if you lived through it."

"And, what happened to the father, Karl?"

"The old man died a few days later in custody. We never did pin anything specific on him. Kind of a pathetic thing all around. I heard he had a coughing fit in his cell, but I think he fell apart when the Bureau guys told him that his kid was dead. No great loss, either one of them, in my opinion. I do remember that Karl's wife had to bury both of them at the same time. That was kinda sad."

"And, now what's amazing is that here's a grad student writing about something that you were involved in almost sixty years ago."

"Yeah, you live long enough and you become historical," the elder lawman smiled. "You know what else is coming back to me? That name, Canaris? That's the name that Eugen used on the lease to rent an apartment on the upper East Side. He told the landlord that he was ...Canaris... Willy Canaris!"

"And you didn't think anything about it at the time? Wilhelm Canaris was the big German spy boss."

"Nope. At the time, no one on the NYPD had ever heard of Canaris. Maybe the FBI guys knew who he was, but they didn't tell me and Murph. I suppose if we did know his name it might have changed the way we looked at our boy Eugen."

"So, Eugen rented the place under the name Willy Canaris? Pretty dumb for a real spy."

"Not really surprising for that mutt. Oh yeah, that apartment... that's where the pressure started that there might be explosives somewhere. There was an unusual and distinct smell of almond in that apartment. And, we found some wax paper that might have been wrapped around either some kind of explosives, or maybe just marzipan, at least, that's what some genius from the Bureau suspected."

"Did they take the wax paper to the FBI lab?"

"Yeah, and I seem to remember that they did test it, but I don't remember if there was any positive result that came back. Or maybe it did come back, but our pals at Hoover Town decided not to share that with us. Who knows? Ya' know, sometimes the smell of almonds actually comes from almond cookies. That wax paper could have been wrapped around pastry."

Robert smiled. Despite his present job, he had often listened to his father's rants berating the Bureau. It was a source of regular conversation among the Grovers. "Is that all that you found?"

"Well, truth be told, the thing that made us think it really was explosives and not baked goods, was that shortwave radio set in the room, but that coulda' also been a ham radio operator's rig, too. Your Bureau guys really didn't let me look at it too long."

"My guys? Oh yeah, Dad, oh yeah. Ha, that would be a giveaway clue huh?" Robert smiled.

"Ya know, that summer of 1942 was also comin' right after Pearl Harbor. Everyone was looking for Nazis and Japs. In June, I remember that your boys arrested eight saboteurs that came here by submarine."

"I do know about that one."

"Yeah, but from the NYPD perspective, me and Murphy were trying to protect citizens from this Katzenjammer burglar guy. We were fighting our own war on the streets of New York."

"Looking back, d'ya think Eugen was working for Canaris?"

"From what you just told me, it's lookin' a lot like that might be true." Doug Grover sat in his easy chair mildly stunned by the conversation. For decades, the ache in his leg reminded him of the Katzenjammer-dumb-ass who tossed him to the street in a moment of violence. He never gave Eugen Haupt credit for having any brains at all, but suddenly the implication was that Haupt was much smarter than he ever thought. "'S funny, if Karl and Eugen were terrorists and we never knew that. It was just dumb luck that they stopped themselves in their tracks!"

"...and you never found any explosives?"

"Nope, nada, not a thing. Hey, maybe Eugen got cold feet about all of it and threw the stuff in the river? Maybe that's why he contacted his FBI handler and tried to come in off the street. Who knows what he had, if he had it, or what he did with it, if he had it? All I know is that nothing blew up anywhere in the city at that time."

"So, anyway, this guy is gonna be here next week and I definitely think you should meet him and tell him what you remember. It's really an amazing coincidence that you actually know the guy he needs info about."

"You bet! I would love to talk to him. Set it up!"

9:30 p.m., Frankfurt, Germany

It took a couple of days back in Frankfurt and a clandestine foray into Eisenberg's office in the middle of a Friday night, but a very frightened Rolf Penn made a photocopy of Eisenberg's copy of the entire Canaris diary. Once done, he carefully replaced the original in the file box where he found it, hoping that no one would be the wiser that its secrets had been compromised. When that was done, he called Hassan to tell him that all was well, and then he telephoned his wife to tell her that his business back at work in Germany was finished, and that he would join his family early the next morning.

"What in the world made you go back to Germany even before we arrived here? Gunter and Artur were very upset, and so was I, that you were not in the house when we got here," Berta Penn scolded.

"My dear, there are times when business needs attention at the very moment it happens. This was such a case." He would never be able to tell her the real reason for his trip.

"What could it be that would make you rush back even before we get here?"

He decided to vamp. "I had a disaster with my book. The file I sent to the publisher was corrupt and they were set to send it to the printer. I had to go back to get them the file that was only on my office computer."

"Couldn't you get someone to do it for you without having to fly back? I could have done it for you."

"Dear, you were already in the air on your way here when I got the news. Frankly, I don't trust anyone at the school to go into my computer files." *Ah… the perfect excuse. I just hope that Bertha would never meet Jules, my publisher, in person. She would surely discuss the matter with him.*

"Well, it was a disappointment for all of us. Thank goodness your friend Hassan met us at the airport to drive us here. He is so nice for covering for you. He told us that you called him with an emergency and that you had to get back to Germany right away."

"Hassan is a good friend," Rolf said with a scowl that she was unable to see.

"He's been checking in on us every day to make sure we are okay and have everything we need."

Penn winced, "He's very nice that way," he spoke without the sarcasm that he really wanted to include. "Hassan will meet me at the airport. No need for you to leave the house to come to get me." Not only was there no reason for them to travel and pick him up, but he also knew that Hassan wouldn't let them go anywhere near the airport if there was a chance at all that they could escape. "I will be with you in the afternoon."

"Well, that's good. We miss you, Rolf."

"I miss you, too."

"I'm going to take the boys across to the beach right now. See you tomorrow. Have a safe trip."

"Goodbye, dear." Penn hung up the phone and contemplated what he and his ego had gotten himself into. It was one thing to be a vocal radical. It was another thing to actually threaten human lives. In the past he had defended the rights of, what he called, oppressed nations such as Khaddaffi's Libya, to rise up against their oppressors. This was the first time that his rhetoric put him on the front line of that fight. He was terrified with the thought that he alone would be instrumental in whatever plot that his childhood friend, Hassan Al Jabar, now Colonel Al Jabar, was hatching. But, what could he do about it? If he told anyone about it, his friend in Tripoli might even harm him or his family. There was nothing he could do.

Penn walked across his living room and opened his liquor cabinet. He poured himself a glass of whiskey, sat down and stared at the wall, considering his options. He had knowledge about specific details to what could turn into a major catastrophe. If he called anyone to tell them of the issue, he was sure that his family would suffer a grim fate in Libya. If he didn't tell anyone at all, he would be complicit in a potential mass murder. He was also sure that no matter what happened, once the plans were in place to set off the explosives under the hotel, both he and his family would be in great danger. Any attempt to foil the plot that could be traced back to him specifically, would also mean certain death. It took him a while, but he had an idea, something that he hoped would not backfire.

August 29, 2001

4:30 p.m., New York City

From her window seat vantage point, Elsie gazed at the landscape around the Lufthansa 747. As the big plane taxied across the JFK Airport tarmac toward the arrival terminal, Elsie was transfixed as she stared at the distant skyline of Manhattan, a sight she had only before seen in photographs. Josef, sitting on the aisle seat, was transfixed staring at Elsie. After a short, but normal, ritual delay in getting a gate assignment, the plane finally came to a stop, and the soft chime signaled that it was time for everyone to stand and deplane.

Neither of them spoke as they rose from their seats and removed their carry-on bags from the overhead compartment. Eight hours seated left them achy. They both were tired from an early departure from Munich and the foretaste of the all-invasive wave of jet lag that would no doubt make itself felt shortly.

"I told them I was taking my vacation early." Elsie said.

"Huh?" A weary Josef stared at her blankly.

"I told my supervisor at the archives I was going to take some holiday time now."

"Oh… yes, of course." Josef smiled weakly. "I think that once we arrive at the hotel we should take a nap."

"I think you have a good idea there." Elsie winked at him and put her hand on his as they waited for the crowd to get moving. The implications of the wink were that the hotel was a sure thing, but the nap might be more speculative.

Within the hour they progressed through customs and immigration checkpoints and were standing at the curb with their suitcases. It was a warm midafternoon but not overwhelmingly hot, with the temperature at eighty-one degrees. A slight breeze off Jamaica Bay cooled them.

"I know this may seem extravagant," Josef smiled, "but we could be waiting here for an hour to get a bus. I think we should get a taxi."

"Do we have enough money to do that?"

"I think so. For what that fool paid me for the Trabant, I don't think we will easily run out of money on this trip." He laughed, they marched over to the taxi line and very quickly found themselves getting out of their cab in front of their hotel on Lexington Avenue and 50th.

The man at the front desk greeted them in English and then pardoned himself before switching to German.

"No, that is okay," Josef said. "I am fluent in English. Please speak to me in English."

Elsie was not as fluent in English but was able to understand some of the conversation, and as Josef was filling out his guest form the man said, "Oh, Mr. Durmaz, I think there's an envelope here for you. Let me check in the mailroom." She understood that.

He returned in a moment, handing Josef his room key and a white envelope addressed to him. "Do you need help with your luggage, sir?"

"Uh, no, thank you. We can carry it ourselves." Josef replied, not wanting to have to tip the man, nervously staring at the envelope in his hand. He was puzzled. The printed return address indicated that it was U.S. Government issued.

"What is it?," Elsie asked in German?

"I don't know. No one knows that I am staying here. This is odd."

"Who is it from?"

"It appears to be from the FBI." The couple, dragging their bags, moved away from the registration desk toward the center of the lobby and sat down on a couch. Josef gently opened the envelope. He scanned it for a minute and translated to her as he read it out loud.

> *Dear Mr. Durmaz,*
>
> *Welcome to New York. I am the FBI's head of the New York office and it has come to my attention that your Freedom of Information file request is being processed. When you come to our office to pick up your documents, please ask to see me in person. I have additional information for you that might help you in your historical quest.*
>
> *Sincerely,*
> *Robert Grover,*
> *Special Agent in Charge, FBI New York Southern District*

"But how did he know we were staying here?" Elsie was perplexed.

Josef exhaled a deep breath in a knowing way and said, "The man is the Special Agent in Charge of the FBI in New York. I imagine that for him, we were not too difficult to find."

"Ha!" Elsie became a bit giddy. "I think this is going to be a wonderful trip."

"Yes, I agree."

"So, let's go upstairs and take that nap."

August 30, 2001

3:30 p.m.

Douglas Grover awoke in his favorite chair after dozing off for a bit. *How long have I been out? Oh, 3:30, only a half hour. Not too bad.*

In his short sleep he had been dreaming about the fire escape on a hot April night, the train tunnel, and the large rats. The recent conversation about Eugen and Karl Haupt brought it all back, and the memories wouldn't leave him alone. *What the hell were we looking for down there? Explosives... bombs... but we never found anything anywhere and nothing happened at all.*

He rubbed his eyes, stood and approached the big picture window facing south. Out there was his city. For a big part of Douglas Grover's life there was no crime too big or small in that city that didn't come under scrutiny from his team. The detectives of the NYPD solved their cases because they were the best, yet in all honesty, that wild goose chase of a hunt for German explosives with the FBI back in 1942 never yielded anything. As time passed, though they had physical evidence that might have indicated the existence of almond smelling explosives in that basement, the case fell away without resolve. *Didn't Haupt once offer me some almond cake or something like that?* Through the years, he wondered to himself what it all had been about. *Were there really any explosives? If there were explosives, what happened to them? Did Eugen throw them in the river? What was Haupt about to tell his FBI handler before he got himself shot? What was the significance of that piece of paper with all those numbers?* There was a truth there, but what the hell was it?

"Oh, you're up. Good." Ellen saw that he was awake. "Robert called. He said that those people from Germany were here in town and they want to meet you. You have to call him back and tell him when you are free and they'll come here if you like, or you can meet them in Robert's office."

"Oh, I think that the office would be a better place. I don't want strangers up here in my house." Actually, Doug didn't care about strangers coming to his home, but he knew that they might make Ellen a bit uncomfortable. "Yeah, it's more professional to meet them in his office anyway."

Ellen smiled and turned to walk back to her kitchen, "Well, he said you should call him back as soon as you can."

"Okay, I will." Doug picked up the phone on the end table and dialed. It was a private line to Robert's electronically secure desk phone. Only two people in the country had that number in their phone book, the FBI director in D.C. and Doug. It rang only once.

"This is Grover," came a voice.

"And this is Grover," responded his father.

"Hey, Dad."

"So, the German kids are in town and they want to talk, huh?"

"Yeah. When can I set it up?"

"How about tomorrow morning after I hit the gym? Then I'll have a little color in my cheeks and I won't scare them so much."

"'Sounds good. How about 10:00? I'll have a pass waiting for you in the lobby."

August 31, 2001

9:52 a.m.

The time zone shift had left Josef Durmaz and Elsie Schneider a bit wide-eyed. They both woke up at 4:30 in the morning and neither was able to fall back to sleep. Now they sat in the waiting room of the New York City FBI office awaiting whatever. For some unknown reason, they had been invited by the head of the office for a personal visit, each of them issued a "VISITOR" plastic badge. Despite the uncertainty of the situation, both Josef and Elsie were excited, yet a bit perplexed as to why the Special Agent in Charge of the New York office himself had invited them to talk about Josef's research document requests. The mystery would soon be over, as a young woman wearing a similar ID tag walked into the waiting area and smiled at Josef.

"Are you Mr. Durmaz?"

"Uh, yes, and this is my associate, Fraulein Schneider."

"Nice to meet you both. Special Agent Grover is ready to see you now. Please come with me."

Another institutional enclave. I really need to change my life. Josef humored himself as he and Elsie followed the assistant down a gray-green corridor lined with file cabinets on one side and work cubicles on the other. In truth he was a bit nervous in the presence of the bureaucratic details of the place, but also so excited he would not have changed a single second of any of it. On the way, he glanced over at Elsie who was beaming and seemed to be more at ease than he in the government office complex. They turned one last corner leading to a single office door. The woman knocked on the door, opened it and announced their arrival.

"Sir, this is Mr. Durmaz and his associate Ms. Schneider." She waved them in and then exited the room, shutting the door behind her.

Josef extended his right hand and Robert Grover took it. In good, but halting English, Josef said, "Sir, thank you so much for inviting us here."

"So good to meet you, Mr. Durmaz, and you too, Ms. Schneider. Please have a seat."

"Thank you." He and Elsie sat down in a small conference area to the right of Grover's big desk. In an armchair adjacent to the table they noticed a nattily-dressed older man smiling at them. Robert continued his greeting. "And over here is someone who I think you will enjoy meeting. This is my father, Douglas Grover. My father's career was ... er... is also in law enforcement."

"Oh, your father?" A bit confused, Josef smiled anyway and shook the older man's hand as they too exchanged greetings. Elsie did the same. He turned toward Robert, "Thank you so much for inviting us to meet you. Although, I must ask, do you extend this same courtesy to everyone who's asked for information under your Freedom of Information Act?" Josef smiled broadly at his lighthearted inquiry. "I imagine that if you did that you would be meeting people like me all day long."

"No, not really," Robert replied, "in fact not at all. The reason you are getting this treatment is that one of the people you've asked about is someone my father actually met and had dealings with about sixty years ago."

"Really? That is amazing!"

"Yes, its true," Doug chimed in.

"You knew Horst Wenzl? That is truly amazing!"

"Yes, that's amazing," Elsie agreed in a small voice. "Were you in Germany?"

"Actually, no. I didn't know anyone named Wenzl, but I did know Karl Haupt."

"Oh, I see, Haupt. Ah! His name was Karl?" Josef repeated with a look of confused revelation. "And how did you come to know him?"

"I was a young police detective in New York and in 1942 and I had some interaction with Karl and his son Eugen. They were very … uh… memorable for me." Doug leaned back into his armchair and his leg throbbed with the mention of the names.

Robert interjected, "My father arrested the older Mr. Haupt as part of a major wartime investigation. When I saw the name Haupt on your FOIA request I was reminded of stories that I heard from my Dad when I was a boy. That's why I asked you here, and I asked him to join us this morning."

"Oh, I see." Josef began to feel heightened excitement. He was getting closer and closer all the time. He launched into a detail of why he was there. "Well, I am looking for information about Herr Haupt because I am writing my doctoral thesis in history on a specific event in 1942 that might have changed the course of the war. It is all based on the personal diary of Admiral Wilhelm Canaris, the Nazi spymaster. Herr Haupt is mentioned by name in the diary as being the Admiral's personal representative, his personal spy here in New York. Haupt is a regular figure in the diary from about 1939 until 1942. I've been able to corroborate the entries in the diary with official payments to Herr Haupt through a number of banks. I have paper proof that Herr Haupt was running a major Nazi spy organization working for Hitler in America."

"Hmm, we did know about his mob ties, but there's no mention of any spying activity in these files, only some German-American Bund activity in the late 1930's. The Bureau was watching him then," Robert said while leafing through the papers in front of him, "but, that's all we have until the incident of his arrest in August of '42."

"Ah, that explains that," Josef continued. "Herr Haupt's name disappears from the pages of the Canaris diary by the end of that summer, as does any record of payments to him beyond August, 1942. He was mentioned many times by name up to that point, but he disappears from records in the middle of a major Canaris sabotage effort with the code name Operation Pastorius. As part of my research, I hope to discover what Herr Haupt's link was to Canaris, and what may have happened to him."

"Ha! Haupt was a Nazi. Operation Pistorious, huh?" Doug Grover leaned forward with a big smile on his face.

"That Pastorius sir," Josef smiled.

"Well, whatever you call it, sure thing, I can fill in the blanks for you on exactly what happened to that sonofabitch, and maybe you can answer some longstanding questions that I've never been able to figure out."

"Absolutely!" Josef grabbed Elsie's hand and squeezed it realizing that his dreams of academic security were every minute getting closer to reality. "What would you like to know?"

"Tell me about Karl Haupt?"

"From the information in the diary, Herr Haupt was recruited by an un-named Canaris operative in 1939. At that time Haupt was a leader of one of the German-American bunds and also had ties to the underworld. His résumé was useful to Canaris who was looking for politically reliable, and somewhat fearless, recruits to do clandestine work in the United States."

"What was Haupt doing? He never left his apartment when I met him, he was sickly."

"He may have been sickly by that time, but he was a major Nazi operative. He was the Admiral's man in New York. His job was to run a spy network and get information to Canaris. He was also a point of contact to spies and fifth-columnists. He ran a network that allowed them to come and go into and out of America with ease. There was a major attack in the works in 1942 involving some sort of catastrophic event in New York. Haupt appears to be the man who helped a master spy code-named Wolfgang to get a footing in this city, and attempt to do whatever he was up to. Sick or not, Herr Haupt was reporting back to Canaris regularly."

"And what about the son, Eugen? Was he also on the Admiral's "A" list?" Robert asked.

"No, not that I've read in any documents. There's no mention of anyone other than Karl. Karl was the resource person. Perhaps he got his son involved, but not officially, or at least not in any paperwork that I have read."

"So I was right, Eugen wasn't the smart guy at all. He was just a dumb burglar," Doug mused.

"The son was a burglar?" Elsie asked in her own broken English. "And you caught him?"

"Not really. I never was able to catch him doing a burglary of a home. Just one time, we did catch him burglarizing a bakery, but it turns out that he was doing that for the benefit of the FBI. He was working for them as, what we call, a snitch."

"It may be a fact that he was also working for his father and the FBI at the same time," Josef speculated.

Robert interjected, "So, according to this admiral's diary, what was the big thing going on in New York? What was supposed to happen here?"

"This is something that is not clearly described in the diary, but it was supposed to be very big, something that Canaris would personally bring to Hitler as a devastating blow to the Americans." Josef sat up straight in his chair and began to tell what he knew so far about Operation Pastorius. He recounted the entries into Canaris' diary that revealed that a new high powered explosive was developed by German chemists, that two submarines had landed in Amagansett and Jacksonville as a subterfuge to keep the U.S. on a lookout for submarines, and finally he told about Wolfgang and his trip to America by pleasure craft.

"This fellow Wolfgang, obviously a code name, did land in New York and got very close to achieving his mission. While I cannot yet prove this theory, I believe that it involved these new high explosives. But, nothing of note happened in New York that summer, and Wolfgang, even after reporting that his mission was right on schedule, suddenly disappeared. I assume that he was stopped and arrested by the authorities. But, since I don't know his real name, I had no way of trying to do a Freedom of Information request about him. After the last diary entry at the end of August, 1942, he was not mentioned again at all, sort of like Karl Haupt. It remains a mystery."

"From my recollection from reading the history of this place, the Bureau arrested a lot of Nazi collaborators that year, but all of them were basically acting as spies, not saboteurs. It seems as if we missed the elder Mr. Haupt in that because there's nothing at all about it in this file," Robert said. "I would have to ask for more files to see if we arrested anyone planting explosives then. That's a more detailed research project and could take a while to get."

"I would love to see a report like that, but it doesn't bear directly on my personal line of research. I am looking into the efforts of this one man named Wolfgang."

Doug let out a lengthy breath. "So there really were explosives! Holy…

Damn!"

"Dad, you knew about this?"

"Yeah. Murphy and me were working with the Bureau right at that time. We got involved in the whole thing because of our connection with Eugen. We were actually on a major hunt for explosives and we never found anything anywhere. We were just following the wrong bomber. So, Eugen wasn't the guy?"

"No sir. The bomber was a German infiltrator. Canaris sent him personally. Wolfgang was the code name of the saboteur."

"Oh, my God! After all these years." The usually unflappable Douglas Grover, former Chief of Detectives of the NYPD was speechless. "Wait till I tell Murphy about this one!"

"Hey, Dad, I just had a thought. Eugen was killed just about the same time that this Wolfgang character fell off the map. Do you think that Eugen might have been Wolfgang?"

"Nah, that would have required brains, something that Eugen clearly lacked. He really wasn't smart enough, and also, he was already here. He didn't come into the country in 1942. By that time, we'd already been stuck with him for years."

"Yes," Josef added. "Actually, we do know for certain that Wolfgang was an operative who entered the country at some time during August of 1942. If this Eugen Haupt was already living here at the time he could not have been that man."

"What happened to the son?" Elsie asked.

"He was shot and killed while stopping a robbery in a cigar store. He was a hood who died hero. Go figure."

"Oh, my goodness!" Elsie leaned back in her chair.

Doug mused, "But, let me ask you something else, what about those explosives? Why do you think that Wolfgang's mission involved explosives?"

"Well, for one thing, the diary talks about the explosives. I think that in reading the diary chronologically, the mention of the newly developed explosives is interwoven very deeply with the Wolfgang mission to New York. I think that Wolfgang, whoever he might have been, brought those explosives with him here to do serious damage to something or other. I just don't know the details of what he was trying to blow up, or, for that matter, why he didn't do it and what got in his way to stop him." Josef let out a breath. "It would be a fine thing if these documents shed some light on what happened to Wolfgang."

"My partner and I were involved with the Haupts and also the FBI search for mysterious explosives hidden somewhere in the city. I remember that for a few days, the whole NYPD was going nuts about it, but we never found anything. We never heard anything about anybody named Wolfgang and, better still, nothing blew up."

Robert let out a sympathetic breath, "Well, no help on this end. I read through this stuff and there is no answer to that question."

"And who is this other person you're looking into? This Wenzl person? What's his story?" Doug asked.

"Ah, this could be more productive than the Haupt story as I believe that the man is still living and is somewhere in the U.S."

"A Nazi living here?" Doug asked.

"This is another odd story. Wenzl was Canaris' personal aide, fresh out of the German naval academy. He was with the Admiral from 1941 all the way to the end of Canaris' life."

"What happened to Canaris?" Robert asked.

"He was hanged by the Nazis just as the war was ending, after they learned of his complicity in a plot to kill Hitler. Canaris was not a happy Nazi."

"This story gets better and better all the time!" Doug smiled."

"Yes, it does. In any case, after the war ended Wenzl was stuck in East Berlin until somehow, for some undisclosed reason, he was whisked away by the American government," Josef explained. "There are many missing documents related to his status, but with Fraulein Schneider's help I have been able to determine that he was brought here to the U.S. right after the war."

"Who brought him here?" Doug asked.

"I think I have the answer to that one," Robert leaned across the small coffee table in the conference area and paraphrased a document in the Wenzl folder, "He was working for the British MI5 and the OSS as a mole in the German high command. He was sending information directly to Washington to Wild Bill Donovan. Wenzl wasn't on the Bureau's books, he was working for the spooks at the OSS. They got him out of East Germany to pay him back for his wartime services."

Josef was stunned, "This explains everything!"

"Yes, everything!" Elsie couldn't contain herself. "When we searched for Horst Wenzl's records in the German military personnel archives, the only documents that existed were of his name. There was nothing else at all about him. Josef and, I mean, Herr Durmaz and I did locate a relative of his, a brother who told us that Wenzl was still alive and was living in the United States. Here is an even more strange part of this story: Wenzl's brother is a rabbi in Dresden."

"A Jewish Nazi?" Doug was becoming more and more amused by the whole story. "How the hell does that work?"

"It is a long story that we heard from the brother in Dresden, but it's enough to say that they were not known to be Jews during the war, and basically hid right in the middle of the Nazi rat's nest. Wenzl and his brother were children of a mixed marriage. Their father, a Christian, but their mother was Jewish. She was Weinstein."

"Well then," Robert rifled through the pages of the FOI print-out, "I definitely think that this is your man. When he came here he dropped the name Horst Wenzl and became Harry Weinstein."

Josef was gleeful, "Now that I know he was an American spy in the German high command, it explains the missing documents and the reason he was brought to this country."

Robert handed the two FOIA folders to Josef. "Well, this stuff is all here for you to study. I'm sure you'll want to spend a lot of time going over all the reports and details in there. I think you will be pleased, as the folder on Wenzl does have some direct information regarding his recent whereabouts. In fact, if he hasn't moved in the past seven years, that's when his file was last updated, he's living not far from here."

Josef and Elsie were stunned and stared at each other. "You mean you know where he is living? An address?"

Robert smiled, "His address and telephone number are in that folder."

Elsie, the more demonstrative of the duo, couldn't contain herself and leaned over to hug the FBI man. "Thank you so much for all of this. This information is just astonishing!"

"Not so fast!" Doug interjected. "We're not done. I'd like to know more about all of this. I'd like to know what was Wolfgang's mission? Did he really have explosives with him and, if so, what became of them? This is something I have not thought about in fifty years."

"Of course, of course. I will share with you whatever I discover."

The elder Grover sat up straight in the chair, "Here's something for you to think about. In the summer of 1942 we were chasing Eugen because we thought he might be a spy, and he might have planted explosives somewhere in New York. I never really believed that he was bright enough to be handling explosives, let alone actually have the stuff to be a spy. So despite evidence that there might really have been explosives present in the city at that time, I discounted the idea because I really couldn't believe that Eugen was capable of doing any of that."

"I see." Josef nodded.

"So, now, I hear about this fellow Wolfgang and suddenly I'm thinking that if he was close to completing his mission, whatever it was, he must have indeed had explosives and he did something with them. Combine all that with the fact that he had contact with Karl, and obviously Karl's son. I really was right about not worrying about Eugen as a saboteur, but now, hearing that there actually was a real saboteur, wow!"

"Yes, wow indeed." Robert seconded his father's amazement. "And you say that Wolfgang was on a mission here in New York to blow something up, and according to this diary he nearly completed his mission?"

"Yeah," Doug picked up the train of thought, "If Wolfgang was keeping his boss up on his plans and all was going okay until he disappeared, he must have planted those explosives somewhere, waiting to set them off. If he did plant them somewhere, we never found them. We don't know what happened to Wolfgang and we don't know what happened to the explosives."

"So, you are saying," Josef drew back a bit, "that you think Wofgang's explosives could still be in position somewhere? That they are still here?"

"I gotta say, that as the head of the FBI office here in New York, I'm going to get more information on this whole operation. That may take a bit of time, but my gut says a pretty strong maybe."

The old detective nodded his head. "Things like that don't just disappear without human help. If he planted bombs, either he left them there, or he or someone else took them out." Years of police work had given him the ability to cut through the informational clutter and to see things with total clarity. In his heart Doug knew that his theory was correct, but un-provable. "Or, there never were any explosives and this Wolfgang guy was sending back bogus reports to please his boss. Not likely. But, here's a modern day worry, let's say there are explosives planted somewhere. Let's say, in an old building that's scheduled to be torn down. Ya' see where I'm going with this?"

Robert anticipated what he was sure his father would ask next. "No Dad, no can do. You couldn't find explosives then, and you won't find any now. They are not there. Whatever this Wolfgang guy did, never panned out. I wish I had the manpower to go looking for something that maybe existed somewhere, fifty-nine years ago, something you didn't know where it was then (if it was there at all) and something you think might be there now. You know that I don't have anyone I can put on this. You know that we have other fish to fry right now."

Doug just frowned, but there was nothing more that he could say.

Josef, sensing he was about to be in the middle of a family disagreement, quickly changed the subject. He opened the Wenzl file and read the top page, "Ah, so it appears that Fraulein Schneider and I are off to a place called Livingston Manor, New York, looking for a man named Harry Weinstein."

"Harry Weinstein," Doug said aloud while looking directly at his son, "now that is a story to tell!"

"Yeah, Dad. Harry Weinstein. How about that!"

Josef asked, "Is this someplace we can reach by the subway?"

September 1, 2001

1:15 p.m., Livingston Manor, NY

Elsie had not spoken for at least a half-hour. Her eyes were fixed staring out the rental car window as she took in the late summer countryside along Route 17. It was Labor Day Weekend and by this time of day, all those retreating to the mountains from their urban coops were already there. There was no traffic to speak of. The rush of air that enveloped the fast-moving car created an interior cloud of vehicular white noise that made conversation only an option if one wanted to make an effort at it. Neither of them really did. Josef was also silent, and he, too, was lost in his thoughts. Finally, she turned and looked at him. "Do you suppose Horst will be happy to see us?"

"Hmm? I think not. He's been hiding for decades. I think we did the smart thing by not calling ahead to tell him we were coming."

"Why wouldn't he want to meet us?"

"I get a sense, after meeting with his brother, that the whole wartime era is something this man would like to forget."

"Ummm, maybe so. He's been living a very different life in this country."

It had been a non-stop, three-day-long journey and by this point they were both weary. Two hours of driving on foreign roads, combined with jet lag and the excitement of anticipation numbed them, rendering both silent. It wasn't hard for the ebbing tide of road noise to flood back into the car and submerge them once again, each in their own thoughts. Each remained silent for about twenty minutes until a road sign appeared, indicating they were approaching the exit for Livingston Manor.

"I think this is the exit coming up." Elsie's attention left the scenery on the outside of the car and turned to the manila folder on her lap. "Horst is in his eighties. I would guess that he is no longer working anywhere and we will probably find him at home."

"Yes, that sounds right." Josef flicked the right turn signal and the car moved onto the exit ramp. At the end of the ramp he pulled over to the side of the road and stopped the car. "You have the map, tell me where to go."

Elsie opened the map and searched for the road listed in the FBI documents. "I think…" she paused as her finger traced the thick black line on the paper, "that you should make a right turn at that next street over there and follow it for about two miles."

Josef checked his rearview mirror and when the coast was clear he pulled back onto the road, drove one block and turned right.

"This whole thing is becoming more and more amazing as it happens." They were on a semi-rural street with only an occasional house near the road and fewer other landmarks of any kind.

Elsie was upbeat, "I know. I'm really excited. You will have your dissertation done and I'll be able to fill in the blank lines on that incomplete Wenzl file on my office computer," she laughed.

"Yes," he smiled at her, "I suppose that's an added benefit to all of this." Then, he became serious for a moment. "You know, there is a good possibility that Herr Wenzl will not want to speak with us at all about his past. How should we approach him?"

"What do you mean?"

"Should we address him as Herr Wenzl or Mister Weinstein?"

"I think we should call him Mister Weinstein. That's the name he's been using since he came here. After all, we did visit with his brother, and we know who he is."

"Should we tell him what we are doing?"

"We can start by telling him the truth. You are a graduate student at Goethe University in Frankfurt doing academic research for your dissertation, and this is a footnote to history."

"And?"

"And…? And his participation will allow those in times-to-come to have a better understanding of a horrible period in human history that he experienced first-hand, and maybe be able to avoid a similar chain of events in the future. His memories will help others to understand it all."

Josef was momentarily stunned by Elsie's articulate reasoning and insight. He stared at her face for a second and then forced his eyes back to the road ahead of him. For someone who was not an academic, her analysis of Josef's mission was as good as that of any professor he'd studied with. "You amaze me every time you speak."

"Turn right, here!" Her finger abruptly pointed at a small dirt road between two fence posts. He slowed the car and turned. The road, lined with thick underbrush and scrub trees, featured only dirt tire tracks with a row of brown weeds between them. Joseph moved the car along the rutted lane slowly so as not to jar them out of their seats. About a quarter of a mile off the paved highway, they arrived at a small, well-cared-for two-story house with a clean, late 1980's Oldsmobile parked in front. The wood framed building featured a covered porch that spanned the entire front of the building and wrapped around its western side. The porch was neat, with two white painted wooden rocking chairs on either side of a swinging bench hanging from rafters in the unfinished ceiling. There were flowers in two window boxes, and the whole place looked well-maintained and friendly, puting the two of them at ease.

Josef parked next to the Olds. He and Elsie paused for a moment to hug before getting out and walking to the front door. Josef nervously pushed a doorbell button and then waited. After a long moment, the sound of approaching footsteps from inside raised their level of excitement even more. When the door opened it revealed a tall, elderly man, neatly dressed in tan chinos and a blue work shirt with a button-down collar.

"Yes? Can I help you?" The old man warily eyed his visitors.

"I'm looking for a Harry Weinstein, are you Mister Weinstein?" Josef spoke in his clearest English, but even those brief words revealed his native German accent.

Josef's inflection was enough to make Harry shake slightly as he immediately knew that he was speaking with Germans. Suspiciously he measured the young couple at his door. *Salesmen? Religious fanatics looking for converts? Misguided Nazi hunters?* There was something about the encounter that instantly set off in him feelings of dread, that a long-held secret was about to be blown-up in his face. Harry had anticipated a moment like this many times before, but this was the first time that anticipation bore material heft. His eyes narrowed and he seemed to wince in the expectation of great pain, a prescience that was a part of his soul, part of the psyche of a man who had been hiding in the shadows for the past half-century. He'd been, for some unexplainable reason, on edge for weeks since that diner breakfast debate with his cronies on Nazism. Was this the event he knew would come? Was this irrationally anticipated moment the beginning of the end of the past fifty years of his life? Was Harry Weinstein about to die to give new life to Horst Wenzl? Reluctantly he admitted to his name. "Yes, I am Harry Weinstein."

Elsie sensed the apprehension in the old man's voice and spoke first. She spoke to him in German. "Herr Weinstein. I am Elsie Schneider and this is Josef Durmaz. Josef is an historian doing research for his doctoral dissertation. We've been searching for you for a while because we believe you can tell us firsthand stories about a period in your life, specifically, about historical events to which you may have been a witness."

Somehow the combination of hearing his native language spoken for the first time in some time, and the softness of her voice, relaxed Harry and he let down his guard. "Uh, come in Fraulein, and...uh you, too, Herr... Durmaz?"

"Yes, Durmaz, Josef Durmaz. I am very pleased to meet you. Very pleased!"

Josef and Elsie followed the man into his living room. Much like the house's exterior, this room was neat and comfortably decorated. The walls were painted a cheery yellow and there were prints of flowers and landscapes framed and hanging on every wall. The room had no sense of clutter, not an extraneous piece of paper anywhere. Harry was a man who appeared to like order in his life.

Elsie was again the first to speak, "I'm sorry that we didn't reach you by telephone before we came here, but we just arrived two days ago from Germany to do research for Josef's dissertation and we decided to drive here from New York City right away."

"Really, from Germany?" Harry sat down in his favorite armchair and motioned for Elsie and Josef to take seats on the couch opposite him. "What could I possibly help you with? I'm a retired truck driver whose stories have long been ignored by even my closest friends," Harry smiled a cordial but nervous smile.

"Actually," Josef cleared his throat a bit before he said his next words, "I believe that you are the same person as one named Horst Wenzl? Herr Wenzl, who was adjutant to Admiral Wilhelm Canaris during the war?"

There was a long pause. *I knew this day would come.* For a long moment Harry just stared at Josef across the room and the sound of his breathing became obvious and rapid. "I am just an old man. What do you really want?"

"This is the truth. I am doing research for my doctoral thesis. I have no other motive than that."

"I see," Harry remained skeptical. While he had paid his dues spying for the Allies during the war, he worried that perhaps the news of his status had not trickled down to the relentless Nazi hunters that were everywhere.

"Herr Weinstein. I am sincere. I already know a great deal about you and what you did to help the Americans in the war. Fraulein Schneider and I have gone to great effort to find you. You were an eyewitness to an awful period of German history.

Harry's throat was dry and he just rasped, "Perhaps."

"We visited with your brother in Dresden just recently." Elsie added her soft voice to calm the frightened old man. "He told us about you, but could not tell us where you actually were."

"You spoke to Hermann?" Harry stared into her eyes in disbelief.

"Yes we did. He said you and he had fallen out from each other."

After another long pause Harry spoke softly. "Yes, that is true. We have not communicated with each other in a very long time. I have no contact with him at all, other than his efforts to make sure I receive my navy pension." Harry looked directly into Elsie's eyes for some kind of reassurance or comfort, "How... how is my brother doing?"

Elsie smiled, "He's doing very well. He has a nice, comfortable home and he just became the Rabbi of a new Dresden Jewish congregation. He told us all about what happened to your family during the war."

Harry paused and then opened up, "He blames me for things over which I had no control at all, doesn't he? Hah! Hermann is a rabbi! I guess this has all come full circle."

Elsie could see that the old man was softening.

Then, suddenly he simply said, "Yes, I am Horst Wenzl. I was adjutant to Wilhelm Canaris." Another long pause, then, "Yes, I was, but I had nothing to do with the camps."

"You need not worry about any of that. We know that. I only want to speak with you about Admiral Canaris. We know you were not a part of any of the atrocities that occurred."

"Hermann thinks I could have saved our relatives from their doom. Maybe I could have done something for my own kin, but that would have surely drawn attention to me and my other job. I was on a tight-wire. I was a spy. I had been sending reports directly to the head of the OSS. They needed me to do that. I regret many things in my life, but not that."

Josef tried to be consoling, "I understand, I really do. Sadly for your relationship, your brother sees things differently, I suppose."

"He has no idea how painful it was to simply keep quiet and watch as relatives disappeared to their doom."

"Well, maybe I can share this story with him once my work is done. Maybe he will see you in an entirely different light if you can help us."

Harry just stared. This was too much to absorb quickly. Another long pause, "Yes, perhaps I could tell you things."

Josef stared for a moment at the old face that stared back at him. There was a huge scar on the old man's left cheek. The cruel looking scar seemed oddly fixed on a kindly face. "I have so much to ask you. I think that you have experienced things that will help explain a number of big questions about the subject of my thesis."

"What can be the harm, eh? Everyone who I will tell you about is already dead. No one will be prosecuted based on anything I might say. Ha ha."

"Yes, sir, I guess you're right."

Suddenly Harry's mood changed. The sense of threat had left him and he became anxious to finally unload his long-buried burden as history's witness. These people look honest and sincere "What do you want to ask me?"

Josef's interlocutory with Harry began with a bunch of standard questions about age, place of birth and how he had joined the Kriegsmarine. The old man answered all the questions freely and even boastfully. He was forthright and frank with every response. He spoke about his time at the Naval Academy, his fiery youth in Berlin's 1930's bar scene, and his love for the German Navy. He talked about the cadet sword fight that left him scarred. He also relived his terror about possibly being discovered as a Jew.

"What happened to you when the Allies reached Berlin? Were you arrested?"

"The Russians came into the city where I was and there was chaos. I quickly got out of my uniform and put on civilian clothes. There was no one who knew me at all in Berlin, so I wasn't too concerned about someone handing me over to the Soviets, but I knew that I had to get out of the city. If I was found out I would certainly be arrested and who knows what else. During the day I pretended to be a laborer carting away rubble from bombed out buildings, and at night I slept on the streets. I needed to reach an American person so I could turn myself in. The OSS had promised me that once the war was over I would be taken care of. One night I was asleep in an alleyway and three men surrounded me. They didn't speak at all, they just threw me into the back seat of a car and when I got out, I was in the American sector of the city. I had been rescued. The rest of how I came to live here is, frankly, quite boring."

"That's quite an amazing story. Now, I wonder if you could tell me about your position in the Abwehr?"

"Yes, the Abwehr. I was adjutant to a brilliant man. He was a German, not a Nazi, a highborn, well-educated and actually somewhat human person. Of course, you need to balance that with his association with the vermin that were in power. Canaris was playing a chess game with real men's lives and at times, those lives were treated as if they were mere pawns in an intellectual game. Lives could be lost, but it had nothing to do with his aristocratic sense of duty to the Fatherland."

"How so?"

"I suppose the most wrenching for me was an operation he had called "Pastorius.""

Oh, my god! I haven't even had to ask about it. Josef pretended to listen without enthusiasm, but it was very difficult to do so. "Yes, please tell me about it."

"Canaris told me at the time that it was named after the first German settler in America, the first German to gain a foothold, if you will. The operation involved sending two teams of saboteurs to America with the supposed mission of blowing up railroads and factories. They traveled by U-boat and they actually made it to the American shores, along with large quantities of explosives and detonators. They successfully disappeared into the population. Yet, they were all captured within a bit more than a week after they arrived. All were executed except for, I believe, one of them who turned in all the others."

"I know about some of this already. We know that the mission failed horribly. To be honest with you, Pastorius is the subject of my thesis. What I am trying to prove is that Canaris actually sent the men in the submarines on a false mission, and that he knew they would be captured and executed."

Harry smiled at Josef, "A very astute conclusion! You will be a great historian, and perhaps a detective as well, no? Ha! Well, what you say is partly true. I'm not sure my Admiral was aware of the punishment for, or cared much about, what would happen to the men if they were caught. That wasn't anything he concerned himself about. He looked at the overall bigger picture, just trying to make the Americans worry about U-boats when the main focus of the Pastorius plan was to send a lone saboteur to create the worst kind of havoc imaginable. It was very important to get this man to America so he could do his worst."

"Which was?"

"Let me tell you right now that Herr Admiral did not share everything with me. He told me only some things, and others I learned through measuring the people who came to see him in his office, reading decoded telegrams and such. I was not aware of the reasoning behind all his decisions, but I was aware of almost all of the details. I read every decoded signal from the field. I overheard almost every conversation he held in his office and, when he wasn't there, I went into his office and read the entries he made into his personal leather-bound diary. The diary contained his deepest thoughts and especially the details of this Operation Pastorius. Whenever I could, I would send that information to my contact with the OSS."

Josef and Elsie glanced at each other and Josef decided to tell Harry more of their truth. "I actually have that diary in my possession, at least, it is in my apartment back in Germany."

"You have the actual diary? Where did you find it?"

"It was in the Federal German Bundesarchiv in Koblenz. It was mixed into a box with loose papers and office supply requisition forms. The requisition forms are how we found you. All of it, all of it is an historical treasure."

"Yes, it is a treasure." Harry's eyes seemed to glaze over a bit as the tension of the moment left him. "Herr Durmaz, I must tell you that despite the fact that Canaris was a high-ranking military leader during the war, I have a sense that he knew of my secret life as well. I think he protected me." A long pause, "And, my master had a secret life as well."

"What do you mean?"

"Canaris hated the Nazis. He was involved in a number of plots to try to assassinate Hitler and his boys. He often worked to subvert Hitler's plans and directives. Canaris personally went to and convinced General Franco in Spain not to allow German troops to enter the country to attack Gibraltar, and he made sure that the Abwehr had nothing to do with the persecution of Jews. I would not say that he was not an anti-Semite, but he even helped a noted orthodox rabbi to leave the threat zone safely."

"I was aware of some of that through my readings," Joseph interjected. "I also know that he was arrested and eventually hanged in 1945 for the act of high treason for trying to kill Hitler. He is a very interesting historical character."

Harry leaned back in his chair and sighed. "My boss was unique. He was first a German, and don't misunderstand me, he was a part of it all – the mastermind behind many deadly military operations, but, he was not a Nazi. Can you understand the distinction I make? His country was at war and for whatever reason, he felt a patriotic duty to protect it."

"He came from the upper classes and wealth?" Josef already knew the answer but asked it anyway.

"Yes, he did. He, how you say, suffered no fools. So, he was not at all fooled by Hitler. In rapid time after he took over the Abwehr, it became obvious to him that Hitler was doing abhorrent things. He was one man, but he actively worked for the overthrow of the Führer and the entire evil lot of them. When they finally marched him to the gallows in the Flossenburg death camp they stripped him of his clothing to hang him naked… to humiliate him for his efforts. Even after all that he did in wartime he was not a war criminal, he was, just as my father was, a soldier. While all the high command was responsible for the war and the atrocities, I think that Canaris was one of the very few who regretted what they had gotten themselves into." Harry paused for a long breath, "I also think, though I have no evidence, that he knew I was born a Jew and he was protecting me by keeping me in his employ at Abwehr headquarters."

Elsie was rapt. "There's been much argument over the years about mass guilt and complicity. The Admiral seems to go beyond that."

"He rewarded your loyalty." Josef added.

"Amazing," Elsie blurted out. "A human being among monsters."

"Well enough of my opinions that have been brewing in my head for the past sixty years. This is not what you came all this way to ask me."

Josef layed out his hand. "To be honest Herr Weinstein, even though my main area of interest is operation Pastorius, all of your story is very important to me."

"Well, what do you want to know? What about it?"

"The diary talks about much of it, but it lacks details."

"What details do you need to know?"

"I know that the two U-boat teams that landed here were all rounded up within a few days after they came ashore. My theory is that this was part of the Canaris plan."

"That's a very accurate theory."

"The story in the newspapers made it simple at the time. I read the accounts from the New York Times back in 1942."

Harry leaned back on his sofa, "I too read those newspaper accounts. We received copies of western newspapers in the bunker. Canaris, who was fluent in four languages, read the allied press accounts of the war every day. I remember that he and I discussed that the men had been captured. He asked me if I was a chess player. I told him I was not. He called their capture a pawn sacrifice. At the time I didn't understand the meaning of that, but now I do."

Josef nodded, "Yes, the papers told of how one or two of the men turned the others in. One of the saboteurs got cold feet and decided to be a hero. That seems to be very bad spycraft, no?"

"Yes, ha, awful spycraft but brilliant as well. I believe that after the capture, Americans upgraded their search for U-boats while easing their scrutiny of other ways that spies might enter the country." Harry stopped and stared at Josef, "But you know this already, don't you? You have his diary."

"Yes, I do know a lot, but I need corroboration before I can write about this as fact. I need to know the truth from someone who was there."

There was another long pause as Harry stared at the floor before speaking. "This presents a problem for me. If you write about any of this, you will have to tell the world of my existence. I have attempted to leave this horror all behind. In my world, everyone knows me as Harry Weinstein. I would prefer that situation to remain in place. I don't wish to be famous or infamous. I am an old man who just wants to live out his days without tension."

Josef didn't know what to say. He and Elsie had come a long way to meet the one person who could substantiate the information needed for his thesis. Neither of them had considered that the subject of their search would want no part of it. "Yes, I understand."

Once again Elsie came to the rescue. "Herr Weinstein, maybe I have a solution. You can corroborate Josef's ...eh, Herr Durmaz's research, and also remain anonymous."

Josef stared at her, "Yes?"

"The man who can attest to the things that occurred in Canaris' office is named Horst Wenzl. You are clearly no longer Horst Wenzl, you are Harry Weinstein. But, for the purposes of Herr Durmaz's research, we can honestly say that Horst Wenzl participated with no mention of a Harry Weinstein."

"Yes, Fraulein, I think if we can make that distinction, I can then be of service to you."

Josef smiled broadly. "Yes, we can make that distinction. Harry Weinstein has nothing to do with my thesis."

The conversation then continued for hours, revealing startling details.

September 2, 2001

9:22 a.m., New York City

"Sir, can we speak for a moment?" Special Agent Jim Grant knocked on Robert Grover's door.

"Sure, come in." Grover put down a file he was reading and looked up.

"Some new chatter out there... kind of specific."

"Oh? How?"

Grant handed his boss a piece of paper and Grover read it, and then he read it again a few times. It was short and to the point. "Imperialist nations in New York, feel our sting. We will bring down the house. All is in place for victory. Allah akbar!"

"Where is this from?"

"It suddenly popped up on the internet in one of those holy war chat rooms," Grant explained.

"It is specific to New York. What 'imperialist' nations are there in New York?"

"Sir, it seems pretty clear to the analysts that this is talking about the U.N. Seems like they're threatening to do something at the U.N." Grant shifted nervously from foot to foot as he awaited his boss's reaction to the printout.

"It's an expected target, but not an easy one. There's huge security at the U.N." Grover leaned back in his chair and rubbed his chin in a way that implied he was seeking insight from unseen forces. "And what's this line about bringing down the house? Are they going to try to blow up the U.N.?"

"We think that either this is talking about a physical attack at the U.N. or something associated with the U.N., or a U.N.-related location where 'imperialist' nations are located."

Grover couldn't contain his smirk at that line. It was a frustrated smile that accentuated the needle-in-a-haystack quality of the search his office had ahead of them. The U.N. General Assembly would be meeting in this city in just a few weeks and there was now a direct threat on the table to the security of that event. Grover decided that this was too big for his office alone to manage.

"Okay, let me check with the Director on how Washington wants to handle this. Meanwhile keep looking."

"Yes sir." Grant closed the door behind him as he left.

September 3, 2001

9:40 a.m.

Josef leaned forward in the desk chair in his hotel room and, with his elbows on the table, dialed an outside line. The phone on the other end rang three times and then an official sounding voice said, "This is Doug Grover."

"Mr. Grover, this is Josef Durmaz calling. We met a few days ago in your son's office at the FBI."

Doug Grover had given Josef and Elsie his phone number after their meeting, with an offer to help with anything else they might need to know about Eugen and Karl Haupt. "Yes, Josef, good to talk to you again. How is your research going? Did you have any luck finding that Weinstein guy?"

"Yes. Great luck! He was a little bit afraid of us when we first got there, but after we explained why we were there, he felt comfortable to talk with us and he was most helpful. His memories are very sharp and full of information. We spent a full afternoon with him on Saturday and much of the next day as well."

"That's really great. I'm happy if I was able to be of any help, too." Grover said with a smile.

"Yes, sir. You have been very helpful, and I thank you for that." Josef paused for a moment, not sure of what to say next. He had more to ask but wasn't sure how to bring it up.

Grover sensed that there was more to this phone call than a simple offer of thanks. "Well, I appreciate your calling me. Let me know if I can be of any more help to you."

"Uh, there is something else that you could do. Maybe you can ask your son if he could arrange something for us? Elsie would like to see the railroad tracks under Park Avenue."

A nerve in the back of Grover's neck sparked the beginning of an icy chill that eventually trickled down to the base of his spine. "Why do you want to go down there?"

"It comes out of our conversation with Herr Weinstein and his recollection of Operation Pastorius."

"Yes?"

"Herr Weinstein, who was indeed a mole for the United States in Admiral Canaris' office, remembers that a saboteur had been sending back dispatches from New York about his intended mission in 1942. From his memories and our interview, I am now reasonably certain about the details of that mission."

"What was his mission?"

"The saboteur was planning to blow up the Waldorf Astoria Hotel. This was not to be simply a small explosion. He had enough high-capacity explosives with him to topple the entire hotel to the street. Herr Weinstein says that the saboteur named Wolfgang radioed back to Berlin that he had successfully completed the preparations for his mission."

"How would he have done that?"

"He had placed plastic explosives on every subterranean pillar holding up the Waldorf Astoria above the railroad tracks below."

"Why the Waldorf?"

"It is the place where President Roosevelt's private railcar would be. He was going to blow up the hotel from underneath and bring down the building when Roosevelt's train pulled into its private rail platform. His job was to kill Roosevelt in a most spectacular way."

Grover sat there silent and shaken. For the first time in over five decades he remembered the fruitless details of the mad scramble to find explosives somewhere in the city back in 1942. The faces of the FBI agents, the Haupts, and Murphy raced through his mind. Now it suddenly dawned on him that there were indeed explosives planted somewhere that no one ever found. Haupt was not the saboteur, but he probably knew the man who was, and also knew what the target was. Haupt was going to tell it all to his FBI handler when he got himself killed. Whatever became of the saboteur himself was a lost footnote, but he obviously never got the chance to detonate his explosives.

"Herr, I mean, Mr. Grover, are you still there?" Josef's voice broke through Doug Grover's reverie.

"Uh, Yes, I'm here. I was just remembering some things that were sparked by what you just told me."

"So, I was wondering, for the sake of my dissertation, if there would be any way you could help Fraulein Schneider and I go under the hotel to examine where the President's railcar came in? I would like to see the places that he supposedly put his bombs. Maybe your son would call someone for permission to search and take some photos of the underground area? It would be a big help to my research."

Grover's brain raced on about all the details. Finally closure to a nearly sixty-year-old case. Amazing!

"Of course, I can help you. And I would be happy to go along with you as well. What do you hope to find once we're down there?"

"I would like to see how this plan would have worked if the saboteur had achieved his mission. I would love to get a physical sense of where he might have placed his bombs." Josef paused, "And, I suppose, in a perfect world, I would love to see if those planted explosives are still there."

Thrilled at the idea of solving this lifelong mystery, Grover was emphatic, *Of course I'll help you, and I'll accompany you as well, I just won't tell Ellen or Robert that I'm doing that.* Doug Grover was instantly back on the job. He still had friends in high places and he would reach out to them right away. "I'll make a few calls and see if we can get down there."

"Thank you so much."

10:00 a.m.

The thin, tall man re-entered the tunnel, this time from inside the Waldorf. He had located building plans in the City's municipal files and drew no attention to himself. After descending two flights of brightly lit stairs, he was blinded by the sudden darkness. It took a few moments for his eyes to adjust to the tunnel light. All was quiet as railroad maintenance workers were done for the day. He was able to see what he needed to look for by flashlight. The extension ladder he had used last time was still there and he quickly climbed to a spot from which he could see the tops of a several of the pillars. From his vantage point he could see atop every pillar, the small cakes, encrusted with dust, sitting neatly, untouched for decades. Nearly sixty years after their placement, amazingly, they were still there. From what he had learned from his colleagues in Tripoli one of the cakes that he sent back in the diplomatic pouch had been successfully detonated and was hugely powerful. He reckoned that what he was able to see around him, and what was likely out of his viewing range, could still do immense damage if triggered. All indications pointed to the fact that this new plan would be successful. The tall man's work would indeed "bring down the house."

From his backpack, he removed a small black box. In it was a cell phone that was attached to a very small explosive charge. He placed the box on the cake atop the nearest pillar and duct-taped it in place so it wouldn't move. All he would need to do to set off the bombs was make a phone call. *This will do the trick,* he thought. He was finished, but as he reached for his flashlight it fell and smashed itself into small pieces on the concrete at the pillar's base. Now it was very dark, and as he got halfway down the extension ladder, his foot missed a rung. He fell hard for the remaining six feet of his trip down. Stunned, but unhurt, he brushed himself off and rubbed his left arm to ease the pain of what was certain to become a large bruise. In the dark he collapsed the ladder and was able to place it where he found it. There was no way to recover his flashlight, but it was no longer necessary. The broken pieces would join the other pieces of scrap newspaper, candy wrappers and soda cans that littered the dark and filthy tunnel. No one would ever see it. It was camouflage by garbage.

He made his way along the track to the doorway that he used for entry and was gone without anyone having noticed he was there in the first place. He was a ghost, a spook, he didn't really exist at all. His job was done.

1:20 p.m.

Murphy was sitting on a lawn chair on the grass in the expansive, park-like lawn outside the Hebrew Home's central building. The afternoon sun was on his face and he was enjoying the Labor Day quiet. It took the familiar voice of a visitor to rouse him.

"Murph, you awake?" Grover looked down at his friend and noticed that there was no cane or walker anywhere in sight.

"Hey, Boy-o I was just takin' some rays. I've learned that a good tan hides the wrinkles. How come you're not out at the beach for the holiday?"

"Nah, we never left town. New York is really a nice quiet place in the summer when the other residents all leave together for the hills." Grover sat across from his friend. "So where's your cane?"

"I actually don't really need it. I've got strength in my legs and my balance is really good now. I'm even developing some muscle tone."

"Aha!" Grover knew what this was all about. "So, how *are* things with your girlfriend?"

"Doug, in all seriousness, I think I'm in love." Tim Murphy flashed an unusual smile. " 'Not so sure what I can do about it at this point, but she's really a doll. She's taken years off my oldness."

"Well, you still look like crap," Grover joked. "But it's nice to see she's taken the bad with the good."

"Thanks for the compliment. I'll remind you to respect your elders."

Grover was delighted to hear that Murphy was happy. "Well that is terrific! I am so glad to hear you're doing good. And when am I gonna meet this lady?"

"You kinda just missed her. Her daughter came by about an hour ago and took her out for the day."

"Sorry to hear that. Maybe next time."

"Yeah, maybe next time."

"Yeah, and next time I come I'll call ahead and make sure I can catch you lovebirds together in one place."

"So what's new with you Boy-o?"

"I have an interesting story to tell you. It's gonna take you back a few years, but it is really an amazing one." Doug related the entire tale of the FOIA request about Karl Haupt which revealed the existence of Horst Wenzl, aka Harry Weinstein, and finally about the explosives under the Waldorf.

"Holy crap! I remember that day very well. I remember the tunnel, and the rats. So, what can you do for this German guy?"

"He wants me to arrange a tour of the tunnel for him."

"Did you?"

"Yeah, I called a few of my old cronies at Metro North and we're going to look around tomorrow."

"We? Didn't you promise Ellen and Robert that you were done with the cop stuff?"

"This is not cop stuff. I'm helping a scholar write a doctoral dissertation. How is *that* cop stuff?"

"Doug, as long as I have known you, somehow everything turns into cop stuff. You are going to get severely yelled at, for sure."

"Oh, c'mon. Nothing bad is going to happen."

"No? Remember the stories that track guy told us about the third rail, getting hit by a train, or those rats? Just be careful. You're not 23 anymore."

"Murph, you can't be serious! All the guy wants to do is tour the spot where this saboteur was supposed to do his work, take some pictures, and go quietly back to Germany. That's all."

"I'm just sayin', Ellen will not be happy with you when you get home, and," he made a lengthy pause for effect, "neither will Robert."

"Stop being my conscience. Everything will be fine. I'm acting as a tour guide, not a cop."

"But, that *is* amazing stuff you just told me. I mean, what if that Wolfgang guy did plant something. We were walking around it and had no idea. We could have been killed way back then!"

"Yeah, but there's still a lot of questions. What happened to the guy? What happened to the explosives? The Waldorf is still standing. How come he never did it? And for me, the biggest question is, how did Eugen Haupt figure into all of this? Not to speak ill of the dead, but Eugen was never what I would call bright enough to make this all work."

"I hate to bring it up, but Eugen was much smarter than you or me. We were the cops who were never really able to pin anything on him. So who's the smarter one?"

"Maybe so. I guess I'll find out tomorrow."

"You got five down, now get five across."

"How's that?" Grover stared at his old partner.

"You have the answer to one part of the puzzle that you didn't have before. Knowing it, is gonna help you solve the rest."

"You and your crossword puzzles."

"My crossword puzzles never got anyone killed." Murphy grinned. "I'm hot from sitting out here in the sun. Let's go inside and I'll let you buy me an iced coffee."

Grover stood up, as did Murphy. Grover noticed that the man was no longer feeble looking or wobbly. "I must congratulate the widow Goldstein on the amazing work she's done here."

"She'll like that." Murphy smiled and the former 19th Precinct burglary squad went inside to share a cool beverage.

September 4, 2001

2:00 p.m.

It wasn't hard for Doug Grover to call in a favor. He didn't need to ask for Robert's help on this one. He still knew pretty much everyone involved in the city's infrastructure. A quick phone call to the head of the Metro North Railroad Police and a next-day grand tour was arranged, complete with a contingent of railroad managers who themselves were happy to get out of the office to do something fun. It was a bit after 2:00 p.m. that Elsie and Josef met Grover and a Metro North entourage at the entrance door to the easternmost platform on the Grand Central Terminal upper level. The group included the Grand Central Terminal general manager, his assistant, the Metro North senior manager of track maintenance operations, and a maintenance man. Grover was happy they were there, but he also thought the crowd was overkill for the mission at hand.

"Will we be in any danger from being hit by a train?" Elsie asked the head of operations.

"No, ma'am, we're clear to walk on these tracks. Our central controller has us on his radar. There are no trains that are going to be anywhere near us. As a matter of fact, this stretch of tracks is rarely used any more, so let me warn you in advance its really pretty dirty down there. The dust settles and there are no trains that go by to stir it up." He then handed everyone a hard hat while he and his man each carried a powerful flashlight. With that, the group's journey began.

They descended from the north end of the platform into the darkness, one man with a light in front and the other at the end of their line. While they walked they received the standard admonitions about staying together, being careful about where they walked and keeping away from the third rail.

Grover gingerly moved over the railroad ties, looking down at them with every step. *No need for a trip and fall here,* he thought. He could see that the Metro North man was right. The railroad ties and the steel tracks themselves were covered in a half-inch of gray dust in which every footprint was visible. Grover was enjoying this outing, but only up to a point. The entire walk underground to the Waldorf brought back memories of that day that he and his cronies were searching for something sinister somewhere, somehow. He remembered the smells, the heat and the rest of it, and his leg ached in sympathy with his 1942 memories. Thankfully, the uptown trip over the tracks was short.

"Well, this is it folks. This is the Waldorf platform and the hotel is right above us at this spot." The head of track maintenance operations waved his arm as if he were the doorman at a private club.

Josef examined the tall pillars around them. From their track level position nothing extraordinary was evident. "Sir, may I borrow your torch?"

"Torch?" replied the befuddled track worker.

"He means your flashlight. The Brits call it a torch." Doug acted as a translator.

"Oh, yeah, sure thing." Bernie, the track worker, handed over his powerful light to the graduate student.

Josef tilted the light up to see the top of the nearest pillar. It looked like nothing more than a pillar. "My research tells me that the man in 1942 claims that he placed something on top of each of these pillars. I want to see if that ever really happened."

"Huh? Is that why we're here?" The MTA head-man was stunned. "Some guy put something up there in 1942 and you think it's still there? Ha, a time capsule thing, huh?"

"Yes, sir," Josef smiled, "very much like a time capsule. I just want to look and see if that is true."

The head track-man was non-plussed, "And you think we wouldn't have found anything wrong here in sixty years of doing stuff on these tracks?" There was a note of indignation in his voice at the suggestion that there was a lapse in his team's professional workmanship. Despite all the obvious detritus and garbage surrounding them in the darkness, the indignant boss said, "There's nothing on top of any of these posts, especially if it had been put there sixty years ago. We are serious about track maintenance here."

With age and experience, the formerly brash Doug Grover had become much more of a diplomat, "Hey, no offense meant here. This is just part of this fellow's graduate research. He's a friend of mine and I'm just trying to help him with his paper, okay?"

The track-man muffled his skepticism and said, "Yeah, I understand. What do you need to do here?"

"Is there a way we can get up to the top of one of these pillars to check it out?" Doug Grover pressed his tour hosts.

"Yeah, sure." The head of track maintenance said. "Bernie, get a ladder and we can go up and look."

Within a minute Bernie returned with a sixteen-foot extension ladder and leaned it up against the nearest pillar. "Who wants to go up?" Bernie asked.

"You go up Bernie, you work here," replied his boss.

"And what am I lookin' for when I get up there?"

"Jesus," the manager said in an exasperated tone in front of the crowd of

VIP's. "Anything that shouldn't be there."

Unfazed by the sarcasm, Bernie scaled the ladder and at the top reached his hand to feel around the darkened top of the pillar. "Hey, what's this? This shouldn't be here."

"Bring it down. Let's look at it," ordered the boss.

Bernie came back down the ladder and handed a small rectangular thing the shape of a cake of soap to his boss. The boss handed it to Josef who looked at it in the flashlight beam. Josef blanched white when he saw it and he handed it to Doug Grover. Doug stared at it and both of their faces showed total amazement. In a flash, Josef knew for certain that the dreams of his doctorate degree, his future teaching career and the good life were solidified. In this moment also, Doug Grover understood that perhaps the most perplexing case in his entire career as a cop had finally been solved and the head of Metro North maintenance knew that they would have to add an entirely new chore to their standard maintenance bible.

Also in that moment, Doug Grover once again took on the persona of the NYPD Chief-of-Detectives, "Gentlemen, I think we need to notify the bomb squad and clear this entire area immediately, and maybe the hotel as well. What we have here is a very old piece of plastic explosive and there's probably a lot more of it up there."

Grover took out his cell phone and made a call. All hell was about to break loose and the next hours would be full of challenges. This tunnel was now a crime scene. As he looked down to take a step, it was then that he noticed other footprints in the thick dust, a short distance away from the group.

3:30 p.m.

The tall man had been keeping an occasional eye on the hotel since his first venture underground nearly one month before. His watchman-like routine took him on an afternoon stroll from his small desk at the Permanent Mission of Libya on East 48th Street, two blocks west to Park Avenue to stare at the building, and then back after the sojourn. All had been quiet around the massive hotel, and his frequent trips to look at it from across Park Avenue over the past few days and hours since he planted the trigger box, were basically to take in the magnitude of what his foray underground would achieve in just a few weeks. His imagination allowed him to watch the entire façade of the hotel crumble to the street below. It gave him chills as well as excitement. So, it was of almost equal amazement that this afternoon, all of a sudden, in a furor of approaching lights and sirens a small army of police cars, fire trucks and black SUV's began arriving and surrounding the hotel. The arrival was immediately followed by an invasion of, what appeared to be, at least a hundred uniformed cops, firemen and camo-uniformed men and women. This all followed a steady stream of hotel employees and guests exiting the luxury hotel en-masse and being ushered more than a block away. Finally, when two large trucks marked Emergency Service and Bomb Squad arrived, he took a wild guess that what was happening at the Waldorf somehow involved his handiwork. He scoured his memory. *Did he leave something behind that was found? What could have happened to lead them all here? Does anyone else know about the cakes? Did someone see me leave the tracks and did they call the police? Or, could there be another operation going on that I wasn't told about?* He thought quickly to himself, *I need more details.* There was no way to be sure what was going on. He decided to ask a cop just as any other nosy New Yorker might.

"Excuse me officer, can you tell me what's happening here?"

"It's a fire drill. We do these things all the time to make sure that we can evacuate big hotels in case of fire. Nothing serious, nothing to see here." The cop's deadpan response and lack of enthusiasm suggested that what he was saying might actually be the truth.

"Ah, ok, thanks officer." The tall man withdrew himself from the conversation knowing that the cop would have no memory of it later on, and more importantly, no memory of him.

He continued watching intently for a while from across Park Avenue, a face in a growing crowd of curious people that had begun to form. All of them believed the fire drill story, but the tall man had doubts about exactly what was going on. He returned to his office at the embassy to call his superiors in Tripoli to tell them of this possible cause for concern.

4:30 p.m.

Robert Grover and an FBI team arrived on the scene about two hours later. Robert had received a phone call from his father alerting him to the discovery below Park Avenue. They met each other at the Roosevelt train entrance to the tunnels and together, father and son cops descended the metal stairs to the tracks below.

By now the flashlights and ladders were replaced by large powerful work lights and the entire tunnel was as bright as day. The FBI team, the NYPD Bomb Squad team, and Bernie from Metro North railroad maintenance were quietly working together. The Grovers approached the FBI Bomb team leader and Robert asked his man, "So, what have we got here?"

"Well, sir, so far we've found twenty-six cakes of what appear to be some kind of a plastic explosive, each one sitting tucked into the darkness on top of twenty-six different support pillars to the hotel. My guess it that they've been here a long, long time. I'm sure there are more of them and we are still looking."

"Amazing!" Robert Grover was stunned. "What do they look like?"

"Well, sir, they look like bars of soap, but they're also kind of diabolically set. Whatever the bomber had planned, this was supposed to be really a big boom." The bomb team leader motioned for his boss and his father to follow him. There, a few feet away was a large table set up in the bright light and on the table were twenty six cakes of plastic explosive. "Take a look at this, sir," the bomb chief indicated a small metallic tab on the side of each cake. "Our bomber set these things to go off all at once without any hard wiring between them." The bomb man took a pen from his pocket and indicated a silver colored button on one of the cakes, "You see this? There's one of them in each cake. My guess is that these are trigger mechanisms that go off when there's a nearby blast. They're not wired together, but the explosion of any single one of these cakes would create a concussion that would compress this trigger and release enough of an electric charge to set off any other of these caps around it. Someone wanted to bring this building down."

"When do you estimate that these were placed here?" Robert asked. "Are we in danger of being this close to it?"

"Boy, that's a tough one, but we're not in any danger at the moment. We have to see what this stuff is in the lab. I would bet these things have been here for decades. This is very old stuff. It's very stable, but very old. It doesn't explode that easily."

"Do we need to evacuate the hotel?"

"No sir, I think nothing is going to happen here today. We'll find all of them. We hopefully have nipped it in the bud. We've got the NYPD bomb disposal truck coming to take the cakes to Rodman's Neck." Rodman's Neck was the NYPD's pistol range and bomb disposal facility in Pelham Park in the Bronx.

"Good. Nipped it in the bud," Robert repeated.

"But, we did also find something else that's a bit more unnerving."

"What's that?"

"Well, like I said, these cakes have been here for god-knows how long. But, one of them was touched recently, maybe even just a day or two ago. It was brushed clean of the dust and dirt and it had this device duct taped onto it."

The bomb expert pointed his pen at a small black plastic box about six inches long and four inches wide. "That, sir, I believe, is a remote control trigger. I've got it a fair distance away from the cakes over here. We opened it and deactivated it. There was a small explosive charge inside and I will bet you there's a cell phone attached to that. Someone calls the number and the whole world comes to a stop."

"You think that was set there recently?" The elder Grover's eyes were fixed on the black box.

"Yes, sir. That one has been here for no longer than a day or two."

"Just a day or two?

"Yes, sir." The man motioned for Robert and Doug to follow him to a post roughly mid-block under the hotel. "We found it on top of this post here. Also, when we turned on all the lights we could see that there was recent activity around this one post. It looks like a lot of the dust was messd up here, almost like someone fell on the ground. We also found a smashed flashlight with no dust on it." The three men stared up to the top.

The disturbance in the dust beside the pillar had been cordoned off with yellow "crime scene" tape.

"Yeah, someone was definitely here recently," added the former NYPD Chief-of-Detectives Grover. "Now, here's the big question: all of these cakes have been sitting here for a long time. All of a sudden our grad student learns about them by reading a sixty year old diary and, what do ya' know, someone else comes down here to set them all off. What does that say?"

Robert looked at his dad with admiration. His old man still knew how to ask the right questions. It was obvious that Josef Durmaz and Elsie Schneider did not know for certain that there were explosives in the tunnel, but someone else did know. "Who else knew about Josef Durmaz's research? By the way, where are those two?"

"I sent them upstairs to wait in the hotel lobby. No need to have civilians at a crime scene." Doug Grover smiled.

The Grovers climbed the stairs to the hotel lobby where, amid a sea of uniformed police officers and firemen, sat Josef and Elsie on a sofa, waiting for their hosts to come up from the tracks below. Josef saw them approaching and he stood. Elsie stood up next to him. "Mr. Grover," he extended a hand to Robert, "so good to see you again."

"Hello Mr. Durmaz, and Ms. Schneider, good to see you too." Robert indicated that they should all sit down to talk about what was happening below ground. When they were all comfortably seated Robert paused for a moment to collect his thoughts before he spoke. "Josef, may I call you Josef?"

"Yes, of course."

"You've led us to an amazing discovery and you've stopped a possible catastrophe. We all owe you a big thank you."

"You're very welcome," Josef beamed back at him.

"But this discovery of yours raises some questions."

"Oh?"

"Who else knows of your research?" Robert stared directly into Josef's eyes awaiting his response.

"My research?"

"Who else knew that you were coming to New York?"

"Do you mean who else could have known about the cakes? Even I was not sure of their actual existence until now."

"That is the question." Robert didn't mention the black box and its dangerous suggestion of what might have happened if they hadn't discovered it. "Who else knows about the details of your research?"

Josef scoured his brain for a moment, "Well, aside from Fraulein Schneider and myself, my thesis advisor in Germany knows about it, and you all know about it. Also, Mr. Harry Weinstein knows about it, but he's the one who told me where to look."

"So, this thesis adviser of yours, who is he?"

"Professor Eisenberg? He is the head of the Department of History Studies, a man in his sixties and has been a tenured professor at my university for quite some time. He actually gave me his own money for me to make this trip."

"Can you give me any contact information for Professor Eisenberg? I would like to talk to him." Robert's question was phrased less like a request and more like a demand.

Josef sensed that there was something more pressing than simple questions about his research. He immediately complied with Robert's request.

"Of course I have all his information right here." Josef opened his pocket notebook, turned to the page for Eisenberg and handed the book to the FBI man. "Is there some kind of a problem?"

"No, there's no problem at all. We just have to investigate this in a very official way, you understand?" Robert smiled in a very nebulous response.

Elsie gripped Josef's arm and stared at Grover. "Josef," she said in almost a whisper, "there must be something else going on." She looked over at the FBI boss and said, "Josef and I will help you in any way we can."

Robert stared into her eyes and said, "Thank you, ma'am."

Epilogue

The NYPD's retired Chief-of-Detectives now understood the details of his most perplexing case. Eugen Haupt, the burly thug who had broken his leg six decades earlier was not all bad. The man had been about to spill the beans about an attempt on President Roosevelt's life, but was killed stopping a robbery in a cigar store before he had the chance to do anything about it. There were indeed explosives in New York and they had been set in place by a Nazi spy. Grover mused to himself that Haupt had actually done him a favor by breaking his leg. Doug had stayed out of the Army and was able to marry his sweetheart Ellen, raise a family and have a stellar career in the NYPD. Without that family there would have been no Robert Grover at the head of the NY FBI office, and no one to follow up on the Haupt story that led the authorities to the planted explosives.

Josef Durmaz's doctoral thesis was written and accepted by the university. He was granted a Doctor of History degree six months after completing his work. He and Elsie Schneider were married shortly after he delivered his dissertation. While the dissertation was never sold to a publisher, its amazing details are available for anyone to read in the university library.

Professor Eisenberg, when later interviewed by the FBI, remembered that he discussed the Canaris diary in front of two colleagues in the university cafeteria one day. One of the men was fellow professor Rolf Penn and a colleague and friend of Penn's from Libya, a chemistry professor named Hasan Al Jabar. The FBI was able to learn that Al Jabar was a high-ranking Libyan intelligence officer and from that, the Bureau was able to piece together the details of the plot. Though nothing was ever proven for certain, three Libyan diplomats to the U.N. were told to pack their bags and leave.

Rolf Penn and his family remained in Libya and were not heard from in Germany again. The FBI concluded that Penn had some complicity in the plot but were unsure what that might have been. His abrupt departure from the history department in Koblenz opened the department doors for the hiring of a new history professor, Dr. Josef Durmaz.

Robert Grover's successful, yet totally accidental, solution to a dangerous situation put him in the FBI spotlight for immediate advancement. His team had located and neutralized sixty-two cakes of high-grade plastic explosives that the FBI lab was able to determine were made in Nazi Germany and dated to the early 1940's.

A catastrophe with a fascinating story had been averted. The internet chatter had put all of the New York office of the FBI on alert that something bad was going to occur in the city. That awareness allowed them to jump on the case in an instant, and solve it. The FBI would classify this event so that no one would ever hear this story in public, but inside the Bureau, Robert Grover's team got credit for stopping mass carnage in a quiet way. The D.C. office wanted to applaud the investigative effort and Robert was invited to brief the Director in person. It would be a big day for him in Washington. First, he was to meet the Director in his office at 11:00 a.m., and then be taken to a private lunch with the Vice President at the White House. Before boarding the U.S.Airways shuttle 8:00 a.m. flight to D.C., Robert's spirits were higher than they had been in months. The beauty and clarity of the blue sky in New York that morning was spectacular, and as the plane took off and crossed the northern tip of Manhattan Island, Robert looked down from his window seat and took it all in with some sense of awe. It was a brilliantly clear morning and he could see well past the lower end of the island, all the way to the Atlantic Highlands of New Jersey. This Tuesday, September 11, 2001 would always be a memorable day.

Afterword

The inspiration for this story originated with a unique journey under the beautiful, beaux-arts style Grand Central Terminal in New York City.

I'm a lifelong New Yorker, and by trade a television producer-writer. A few years ago, while working at The Discovery Channel as an Executive Producer, a project took me and our camera crew on a tour of the inner workings of Grand Central where I learned how the Terminal is intricately entwined with the urban infrastructure around it. The subterranean tracks not only link the city to the rest of the country, but also weave a large web under the streets and buildings above. Manhattan's posh Park Avenue is entirely built above railroad tracks. All the cross streets above are bridges, and many of the buildings on Park Avenue have underground connections to the tracks. Travelers would come and go on one of the Terminal's forty-four train platforms and sixty-seven tracks, but in the age of the private railcar, well-heeled industry titans could enter the city without going above ground. They would park their wheels directly beneath some luxury hotel, most notably the Waldorf Astoria. The Waldorf became a central part of this story.

Since the moment it opened in 1931, the Waldorf Astoria has attracted American chief-executives. Following his term in the White House, former president Herbert Hoover actually lived in a Waldorf suite from 1933 until his death in 1964. I learned that President Franklin D. Roosevelt took advantage of the hotel's underground railroad platform to allow him to enter New York City without having to travel in public through the streets. During wartime, this was invaluable security. I was amazed to be shown FDR's armored private railcar, marooned at that time on a detached section of track under the hotel. Because of its location and the proximity to the United Nations, the Waldorf has been a Presidential and international diplomatic destination.

On that day of filming, I was shown many other historical, hidden places in Grand Central that are never seen by the public. That fascinating tour was the inspiration for this story.

While this is a work of fiction, it is based in reality. This is a story about real places, and real events. Indeed, two German submarines in June of 1942 deposited teams of saboteurs on Long Island and in Florida. The Long Island U-boat captain was, in reality, Kapitanleutnant Hans-Heinz Linder.

Coastguardsman John Cullen did confront those Germans on the beach. There were indeed German-American Bunds in New York that supported the rise of Adolf Hitler. Kapitan Heinrich Garbers was a genuine German operative who ferried spies and saboteurs to Africa and South America via false-flagged pleasure sailing yachts. Admiral Wilhelm Canaris was a real and enigmatic character who was executed near the end of the war for participating in plots to kill Hitler. Operation Pastorius actually happened, and its saboteurs were quickly apprehended.

But why so quickly, for a sophisticated plan? That's where the speculation begins and the story starts. Did something like this really happen? Could it have happened? Maybe no, but, maybe yes.

Stephen H. Schwartz
New York, 2022

Acknowledgements

First, and most of all, I thank my wife Melanie Roher for her support since the beginning of this idea, and for her amazing talents as the graphic designer who created this volume, in collaboration with the excellent book designer, Barbara Balch. Melanie also patiently read and edited the last draft. My sincerest gratitude to Fawn Allen for a final read and very professional copyedit.

My thanks, also, to the real Doug Grover, dear friend and fellow sailor, for the use of his name, and to his colleague Ed McDonald for his kind words of support.

I owe a large debt of thanks to my friends and colleagues who had the patience to read this manuscript at various stages, and who gave me the courage to publish. To my friend and talented author, Dallas Murphy, your editorial insights and guidance were invaluable. Joe Harris, Neal Goff, and Richard Factor also provided notes and observations that were incredibly helpful. Others who encouraged me to move the ball forward are author friends Jeanne Mackin, Larry Mollin and Laurie Gelman. And, a big thanks to Neal Goff for his marketing acumen in publishing, and to Peter Burford whose guidance all along this journey, and whose professional talents as a publisher made this all real.

About the Author

Stephen H. Schwartz is an Emmy Award-winning creator, writer and producer of reality and documentary television programming. He has been a senior executive at the Discovery Channel and Senior Vice President of Programming for The Style Network. Steve served as Executive Producer at TLC where he was the moving force behind, and the Executive Producer of, TLC's hit series "Trading Spaces," a program that created a new genre in the industry. Steve also created and was Executive Producer of "Trading Spaces'" sister series, "While You Were Out." As a respected consultant, Steve was an Executive Producer and advisor for the Lifetime Network. He is currently a consultant for the REELZ Channel.

Earlier in his career, Steve worked as a long-form documentary producer, writer, and director for some of the television industry's top organizations, including CBS, ABC, and Lifetime. Other career highlights include serving as Senior Producer for Michael Moore's "The Awful Truth," and Executive Producer of programming for FX Networks, including the groundbreaking show "Breakfast Time." He also was an Executive Producer for the syndicated "PM Magazine," and was a creative consultant for the original David Letterman Show on NBC. His first book, "Police Emergency Squad No. 1," chronicled the daily lives of two members of this elite unit of New York City's finest.

Steve is an avid sailor, and lives in New York with his wife Melanie and various golden retrievers.

CPSIA information can be obtained
at www.ICGtesting.com
Printed in the USA
LVHW021811140423
744361LV00007B/442